HEIR

Map

N / W / S / E (compass rose)

- Tiborum
- JADUNA LANDS
- KARKAUS
- Firan Wastes
- FIRAN
- PANIWAL
- IMAANA
- BRIJNA
- ODISTA
- ARMAANA
- MEHBAHN
- DIYANE
- STRURI
- WALIBAR
- KEGAR
- Kegar
- THE SOUTHERN OCEAN
- to OLD KEGAR

THE EMPIRE

MARINN

Nur

TRIBAL LANDS

Navium

Sadh

Isle South

THE EASTERN SEA

Jibaut

DEVAN

THE SOUTHERN SEA

Loli Temba's house

THAFWA

Kegari war camp

Burku

BULA

ANKANA

SUNN

IRAJ

Current Imperial Chart of the Known Lands of

THE EMPIRE

and the

SOUTHERN LANDS

PRAISE FOR THE
AN EMBER IN THE ASHES QUARTET

An instant *New York Times* bestseller
A *USA Today* bestseller
A *Wall Street Journal* bestseller
One of *TIME*'s 100 Best Fantasy Books of All Time
One of *TIME*'s 100 Best YA Books of All Time

NAMED ONE OF THE BEST BOOKS OF THE YEAR BY
Amazon * Barnes & Noble * *The Wall Street Journal* * BuzzFeed
LA Weekly * Bustle * *Paste Magazine* * Indigo * *Suspense Magazine*
The New York Public Library * PopSugar * Hypable

"This novel is a harrowing, haunting reminder of what it means to be human—and how hope might be kindled in the midst of oppression and fear."
—*THE WASHINGTON POST*

"A worthy novel—and one as brave as its characters."
—*THE NEW YORK TIMES BOOK REVIEW*

"A captivating, heart-pounding fantasy."—*US WEEKLY*

"*An Ember in the Ashes* mixes *The Hunger Games* with *Game of Thrones* . . . and adds a dash of *Romeo and Juliet*."—*THE HOLLYWOOD REPORTER*

"Fast-paced, well-structured, and **full of twists and turns.**"—*NPR*

"**Blew me away** . . . This book is dark, complex, vivid, and romantic—**expect to be completely transported.**"—*MTV.COM*

"This is a page-turner. There comes a moment when it's impossible to put it down. Sabaa Tahir is a strong writer, but most of all, she's a great storyteller. *An Ember in the Ashes* glows, burns, and smolders—as beautiful and radiant as it is searing."—*THE HUFFINGTON POST*

"It's addictive, and **there's no way you can put it down** before you figure out what happens to the characters you have fallen for over the course of the 400 some-odd pages. So I didn't."—*BUSTLE*

"Spectacular."—*ENTERTAINMENT WEEKLY*

"**Fresh and exciting** . . . Tahir has shown a remarkable talent for penning complex villains."—**A.V. CLUB**

"One of the best YA series of the last decade."—**BUZZFEED**

"Let me tell you, it does not disappoint."—**BOOK RIOT**

"An unabashed page-turner that scarcely ever pauses for breath."
—*THE CHRISTIAN SCIENCE MONITOR*

"Fast-paced, exciting, and full of adrenaline."
—*BUCKS COUNTY COURIER TIMES*

"Thrilling . . . Tahir meticulously plots these novels, ramping up the suspense and including plenty of surprises."—*THE BUFFALO NEWS*

"Delivers in every way . . . The stakes have never been higher, and the tension is acutely felt as Elias and Laia run for their lives."
—*USA TODAY'S HAPPY EVER AFTER BLOG*

★ "Tahir proves to be a master of suspense and a canny practitioner of the cliffhanger, riveting readers' attention throughout . . . [An] action-packed, breathlessly paced story."—*BOOKLIST*, **STARRED REVIEW**

"Excellent."—*KIRKUS REVIEWS*

"The rare sequel that improves on the original . . . unputdownable."
—**COMMON SENSE MEDIA (FIVE STARS)**

"This series is an epic hero's journey, with love, adventure, and magic woven throughout. Recommended for every young adult collection."—*SLJ*

"Be prepared to be blown away by this fantasy-thriller-adventure."—*GIRLS' LIFE*

"I was so engrossed with this book that I missed a connecting flight. If that doesn't convince you to read *An Ember in the Ashes*, I don't know what will. An explosive, heartbreaking, epic debut that will keep you glued to the pages. I hope the world's ready for Sabaa Tahir."
—**MARIE LU,** *NEW YORK TIMES* **BESTSELLING AUTHOR OF** *LEGEND*

"With *An Ember in the Ashes*, Sabaa Tahir shows us light in the darkness, hope in a world of despair, and the human spirit reaching for greatness in difficult times."
—**#1** *NEW YORK TIMES* **BESTSELLING AUTHOR BRANDON SANDERSON**

PRAISE FOR
ALL MY RAGE

AN INSTANT *NEW YORK TIMES* BESTSELLER
AN INSTANT INDIE BESTSELLER
WINNER OF THE NATIONAL BOOK AWARD
WINNER OF THE MICHAEL L. PRINTZ AWARD
WINNER OF THE *BOSTON GLOBE–HORN BOOK* FICTION AND POETRY AWARD
A WALTER AWARD HONOR BOOK
AN NPR BEST BOOK OF THE YEAR
A *BOOKPAGE* BEST BOOK OF THE YEAR
A *KIRKUS REVIEWS* BEST BOOK OF THE YEAR
A *BOOKLIST* 2022 EDITORS' CHOICE TOP OF THE LIST WINNER FOR YOUTH FICTION
A *SCHOOL LIBRARY JOURNAL* BEST BOOK OF THE YEAR
A *SHELF AWARENESS* BEST YA BOOK OF THE YEAR
A BUZZFEED BEST YA BOOK OF THE YEAR
A *BOSTON GLOBE* BEST BOOK OF THE YEAR
A CHICAGO PUBLIC LIBRARY BEST BOOK OF THE YEAR
A NEW YORK PUBLIC LIBRARY BEST BOOK OF THE YEAR

◆◆◆

"*All My Rage* is a love story, a tragedy, and an infectious teenage fever dream about what home means when you feel you don't fit in."
—**THE NEW YORK TIMES BOOK REVIEW**

"An incredibly profound story of devastating loss, friendship, family, identity, and personal struggles."—**NPR**

"This is the kind of book that positively climbs into your bones and steals your breath in the very best way."—**BUZZFEED**

★ "Put this book at the top of your list."
—**SCHOOL LIBRARY JOURNAL**, starred review

★ "An unyieldingly earnest generational story for contemporary audiences, *All My Rage* is a knife-sharp narrative with an obliterating impact that will leave readers thinking of it long after turning the last page."—**BOOKLIST**, starred review

★ "A deeply moving, intergenerational story. An unforgettable emotional journey."
—**KIRKUS REVIEWS**, starred review

★ "A gift every step of the way."—**BOOKPAGE**, starred review

★ "Heartbreaking but ultimately hopeful, this memorable novel leaves the characters with what they deserve most: a future."—**BCCB**, starred review

★ "This standalone novel feels timely and important and should be on every library shelf for teens."—**SCHOOL LIBRARY CONNECTION**, starred review

★ "[A] powerful, viscerally told novel."—**PUBLISHERS WEEKLY**, starred review

★ "This unforgettable multigenerational contemporary YA novel delivers pain, heartache, and anger—but also love, hope, and redemption."
—**SHELF AWARENESS**, starred review

ALSO BY SABAA TAHIR

All My Rage

AN EMBER IN THE ASHES QUARTET

An Ember in the Ashes
A Torch Against the Night
A Reaper at the Gates
A Sky Beyond the Storm

HEIR

SABAA TAHIR

putnam

G. P. PUTNAM'S SONS

G. P. PUTNAM'S SONS
An imprint of Penguin Random House LLC
1745 Broadway, New York, New York 10019

First published in the United States of America by G. P. Putnam's Sons,
an imprint of Penguin Random House LLC, 2024

Copyright © 2024 by Sabaa Tahir
Map design by Sabaa Tahir / Map illustration © 2024 by Francesca Baerald
An Ember in the Ashes excerpt copyright © 2015 by Sabaa Tahir

Penguin Random House values and supports copyright. Copyright fuels creativity, encourages diverse voices, promotes free speech, and creates a vibrant culture. Thank you for buying an authorized edition of this book and for complying with copyright laws by not reproducing, scanning, or distributing any part of it in any form without permission. You are supporting writers and allowing Penguin Random House to continue to publish books for every reader. Please note that no part of this book may be used or reproduced in any manner for the purpose of training artificial intelligence technologies or systems.

G. P. Putnam's Sons is a registered trademark of Penguin Random House LLC.
The Penguin colophon is a registered trademark of Penguin Books Limited.

Visit us online at PenguinRandomHouse.com.

Library of Congress Cataloging-in-Publication Data
Names: Tahir, Sabaa, author.
Title: Heir / Sabaa Tahir.
Description: New York, New York : G.P. Putnam's Sons, 2024.
Audience: Ages 14 years and up. | Summary: Told in alternating voices, three teens, whose fates intertwine to stop the murder of innocent children, journey across two warring nations to ensure a better future for their people.
Identifiers: LCCN 2024022597 (print) | LCCN 2024022598 (ebook)
ISBN 9780593616949 (hardcover) | ISBN 9780593616956 (epub)
Subjects: CYAC: Magic—Fiction. | Murder—Fiction. | Fantasy.
LCGFT: Fantasy fiction. | Novels.
Classification: LCC PZ7.1.T33 He 2024 (print) | LCC PZ7.1.T33 (ebook)
DDC [Fic]—dc23
LC record available at https://lccn.loc.gov/2024022597
LC ebook record available at https://lccn.loc.gov/2024022598

ISBN 9780593859858

1st Printing

Printed in the United States of America

LSCC

Design by Rebecca Aidlin
Text set in Sabon LT Pro

This book is a work of fiction. Any references to historical events, real people, or real places are used fictitiously. Other names, characters, places, and events are products of the author's imagination, and any resemblance to actual events or places or persons, living or dead, is entirely coincidental.

The publisher does not have any control over and does not assume any responsibility for author or third-party websites or their content.

For Cathy Yardley, who has waded with me through the muck of my ideas for a decade. Your forbearance and love are a gift. Thank you for reminding me that I have things worth saying.

And for Sami, my very own furry Light of Eärendil.

HEIR

PART I
THE FALL

1
Aiz

Kegar, the Southern Continent

Aiz wished she didn't hate her enemies with such fervor, for it gave them power over her. But she was a gutter child, and the Kegari gutters bred tough, bitter creatures, ready to stab or scheme or slink into the shadows—depending on what the moment required.

What the gutters didn't offer was luck. Only a divine entity could bestow good fortune.

So, with dawn approaching, Aiz crept through the hushed, wood-beamed halls of the cloister and out to its stone courtyard. Her thin shoes and ragged skirt did little to protect her against the foot of snow that had fallen in the night. Still, she shoved forward, grimacing into the biting wind that whipped off the mountain spires and stole her breath. Perhaps it would steal her anger, too. Today, of all days, she needed a clear head.

For today, Aiz bet-Dafra would commit her first murder.

The orphans of the cloister and the clerics who cared for them still slept. Lessons began after sunrise. Kegar—a crowded city of a quarter million—was quiet beyond the cloister walls. Aiz was alone, accompanied only by her fury as she regarded the blackened timbers on one side of the courtyard. The orphans' wing, still in ruins ten years after it burned to the ground.

Her chest tightened. She could hear the screams of the children who'd died there. She dug her nails into her thigh, into the ridge of skin beneath her patched skirt. Mostly, she ignored her scars. But some days, they still burned.

Your anger will be the death of you, Cero, her oldest friend, told her years ago. He'd seen her lose her temper too often to think any different. *You must control it. Get what you need. Forget the rest.*

She needed vengeance. Justice. She needed her plan to work.

Aiz stopped before the statue at the center of the yard: a woman wearing bell-sleeved robes and looking toward the mountains. Her stone face had hollow cheeks, thin lips, and a heavy brow; her hair was swept back from a high forehead. She wore a headdress carved with a beaming half-sun. Aiz liked to imagine that she and the woman in the statue had the same brown hair and light eyes.

The woman had many names. Vessel of the Fount. First Queen of the Crossing. But here in Dafra slum, where so many were orphaned by military drafts, illness, and starvation, she was Mother Div.

The statue's plaque was pocked and weathered. But Aiz had learned the words as a child: *Blessed is Div, Savior of Kegar, who led our people to refuge in these mountain spires after a great cataclysm engulfed our motherland across the sea.*

"Mother Div, hear me." Aiz clasped her hands in supplication. "Don't let me fail. I've waited too long. If I'm imprisoned or tortured, so be it. If I'm killed, it is your will. But I must succeed first."

Strange, Aiz knew, to ask the patron of light and kindness to bless a murder. But Mother Div loved orphans, too. She'd have wanted revenge for those killed in the fire. Aiz was sure of it.

A Sail passed overhead, its shadow like that of a giant bird, before winging off to the north. Tiral bet-Hiwa, the highborn commander of the air squadrons, sent patrols over the slums. A reminder that the Snipes who lived here were being watched. And a promise that, if they were lucky, they could join the watchers. Aiz observed the aircraft for a long time, and jumped when she heard a step behind her.

Sister Noa crunched through the snow, her frayed woolen skirt dragging. "Light of the Spires, little one," the old woman greeted Aiz.

"Long may it guide us," Aiz responded.

Sister Noa lifted a brown, wrinkled hand to Mother Div's stone forehead before wrapping her own scarf around Aiz's neck, waving off her protests.

"You'll be working at the airfield," Noa said. "While I laze."

"Drinking tea with biscuits," Aiz said, though the cloister was too poor for both. "Bossing your servants about."

Noa smiled at the lie, dark eyes sparkling beneath the paling snow clouds. As a cleric in Dafra slum's biggest cloister, she'd be on her feet all day, no better than a servant herself—overseeing lessons, running the kitchens, ensuring the care of any who came to the cloister for aid. And shivering all the while, no doubt.

She smoothed Aiz's hair back with the same hands that had smacked her when she stole barberries and held her when she screamed at the death of her mother. Noa seemed old even then. Now she was gnarled and wrinkled as a thorn-pine.

The cleric peered at Aiz. "You're troubled, little love. Tell me a dream."

"I dream of a Kegari spring." Aiz smiled at the familiar question. "And a belly full of siltfish curry."

"May Mother Div make it so," Sister Noa said. "The sun rises. Get to the airfield. If you ride with Cero, you'll arrive before the flightmasters give you a hiding."

Noa nodded to the cloister gate. Beyond, a horse stamped its hooves in the cold. The figure beside it paced in circles, equally impatient. Cero.

The calm that had entered Aiz's heart at Noa's touch evaporated, replaced by a memory: A night six months ago, before a new crop of pilots was announced. Waiting with Cero in his quarters to find out if they'd been chosen for the elite Sail squadron. Aiz had paced from cot to window, unable to sit still until Cero took her hand. His touch elicited a spark, a kiss, confusion followed by delight and laughter and hope.

And then the morning after, Cero became a pilot and Aiz became nothing.

"I don't see why he lives here," Aiz said. "Taking up a bed. Eating our food. He can quarter with the other pilots."

"The cloister is his home," Sister Noa said. "*You* are his home. Don't punish him because Mother Div saw fit to make him a pilot. Now, get moving, love."

Aiz tucked the scarf back around Noa's short white curls. She needed it more than Aiz did. "Go inside, Sister. Warm your bones for a bit longer."

When Sister Noa had shuffled away, Aiz regarded Cero, waiting beyond the cloister gate. He hadn't spotted her yet.

She turned away and snuck out the back.

By the time Aiz arrived, the airfield and its runways bustled with pilots, flightmasters, engineers, and signalers. Aiz's fellow drudges scurried amid the chaos, lowborn Snipes like her hauling buckets and poles and ice-encrusted flight leathers.

Beyond the airfield, the Sail-building yard was equally busy, crowded with scaffolds and skeins of twine, reams of canvas, and stacks of cured reeds. The Aerie stood beside it, casting a long, blue shadow. Like many of Kegar's buildings, it was slope-roofed, made of wood and stone and shaped like the slash of a quill. It housed hundreds of pilots and drudges.

"Snipe!" A flightmaster grabbed Aiz's elbow and dragged her to the stables. He was a Hawk, a highborn, like most of the Aerie's bosses. "Muck out the stalls. Then report to hangar one. A dozen Sails need waterproofing."

Aiz sighed and grabbed a pitchfork. Stable work was stenchsome, but at least the building was well constructed, with stone walls that kept away the wind and wide doorways that offered a clear view of the airfield.

Out on the launching pads, dozens of Sails awaited pilots. From here, the craft looked like piles of sticks and canvas, rustling in the wind. But Aiz knew better.

Every Kegari child, regardless of birth, was tested for windsmithing skill at age fourteen. When Aiz had shown a talent for it, the flightmasters put her in a Sail, and she was sent to the Aerie for training.

She'd never forget how it felt in the single-seater cockpit: The cool bowl of Loha, the metal that flowed into liquid at her touch, fusing with her hands before shooting out through the Sail's hollow frame; the sight of the curved, triangular wings lifting like the pinions of a coastal gull. The way her blood fizzed at the caress of the wind—before she inevitably spiraled to the earth, unable to control her magic.

She'd spent years trying to control it. She'd failed.

Now, face hot with envy, Aiz watched Sail after Sail spring to life, canvas stretching tight as the reed scaffolding filled with living metal. The Sail pilots would wing north across the mountains to drop bombs on distant foreign villages. The waiting Kegari army would pillage grain and goods to send home. And thus, Kegar would survive another season.

Aiz's people had long ago stopped producing enough food to feed their own. For the last century, the raids were ever present, ever essential. So were the pilots who led them.

Which meant that whether you were born a low Snipe, a middle-class Sparrow, or a highborn Hawk, becoming a pilot guaranteed food, shelter, clothing, training. It meant a life. A future.

Reins jangled and Aiz whirled to see Cero leading his mount, Tregan, into the stable. His dark hair was scraped back into a high bun. Purple smudges beneath his eyes made his green irises look black. In blue-scaled flight leathers, he managed beauty and gravity, even as he leveled a stare at Aiz.

"I waited for you."

Aiz shrugged and pitched a particularly large scoop of filthy hay over her shoulder—barely missing Cero. "Your problem, not mine."

"Spires, Aiz, but you're difficult." Cero, usually as emotionless as the mountains, sounded almost annoyed.

"And you're cranky." She glanced at him from the corner of her eye. "Don't see why."

"Right, because I'm a pilot." Cero walked Tregan to her stall and she snapped at him. Aiz smirked. The mare had always liked Aiz better than Cero.

"Having my basic needs met only costs subservience to the Triarchy," Cero went on, "and offering my life to a Spires-forsaken megalomaniac who shouldn't oversee a dog kennel, let alone an army."

"Shut your gob!" Aiz looked around frantically. The stables were empty, but that didn't mean no one had heard. Lord Tiral bet-Hiwa led the flight squadrons. He was also heir to one of the three Triarchs who ruled Kegar. His family had spies everywhere.

"What's he going to do if he hears me?" Cero said, leaning against the thick wall of the stables. "Throw me in the Tohr? The Sail squadron leaves tomorrow. Tiral needs me dropping bombs on innocent villagers, not moldering in prison."

Cero sounded bitter, not proud. His ability to windsmith—to bend the air currents to his will—was prodigious. That's why he'd been chosen to pilot a Sail.

He hadn't expected that Aiz would be left behind. But while Cero could tame the wind, Aiz enraged it. While Cero lifted a Sail into a precise spiral, Aiz tore the canvas wings to shreds. She could shift a scent and call a breeze, but any more than that and the wind defied her.

No point in grieving what could have been. Aiz had found another purpose.

"He deserves our respect." Aiz spat out the lie. What Tiral deserved was a knife to the jugular—which was exactly what Aiz planned on giving him in a few hours. But if Cero guessed Aiz's plot, he'd try to stop her. Tell her it was too dangerous.

"Tiral's our fleet commander." Aiz thought of the knife in her skirt, sharpened in the darkness of the cloister's forgotten tunnels. "Without him, we'd all starve."

"He doesn't care about us." Cero fixed his eyes on Aiz and she found it difficult to look away. "Be wary of him."

Aiz went still. Cero never spoke idly. He must have seen her entering Tiral's quarters. Or leaving. She thought of what Tiral had said months ago, when Aiz first allowed him to think he was seducing her. *Keep our secrets to yourself, little Snipe. Wouldn't want anything to happen to you.*

Cero's expression was severe enough that Aiz wondered if there was something between her friend and Tiral. She'd often been clueless about Cero's entanglements. He'd kept an affair with a seamstress so quiet that Aiz didn't learn of it until the woman showed up at the cloister, demanding to see him.

"I don't care who you dally with, Aiz." Cero's detachment stung. "But don't make assumptions about Tiral. The only person he cares about is himself."

As he spoke, he spun a ring on his finger. Aiz used to have one like it. An aaj. One of Cero's many creations. It let them communicate without speaking. She'd returned it to Cero after he'd become a pilot.

"Done lecturing?" She let her voice ice over and scooped more hay. "I have work to do."

A shutter went down behind Cero's eyes. He left the stable. Aiz knew she'd hurt him, which both upset and satisfied her. But she couldn't dwell on Cero. She only had time for one man today.

Waiting was torturous, the hours crawling by in a blur of mucking hay, waterproofing Sails, and dodging the flightmasters' blows. Eventually, the rose-gilded snow clouds bumped along south and the wind's screams quieted to whispers. Night fell. Aiz was helping to light the airfield's lamps when one of the signalers called out.

"Incoming!"

He pointed to the snow-drenched spires that encircled the capital, jutting into the sky like triumphant fists. The moon highlighted the approaching Sails, and Aiz's pulse quickened.

"Get those lamps lit, you Spires-forsaken rats!" the closest flightmaster roared, whip flashing. Within moments, dozens of signalers flooded the field, blue fire held high.

The Sails landed with well-practiced precision. All but Lord Tiral's, which was the largest; it turned on a wingtip not once but twice as he surveyed the squadron. He didn't spiral down until the rest of the fleet had landed.

Aiz hurried from pad to pad, collecting goggles and caps and empty bowls of Loha. All the while, she watched Tiral for a weakness. Tiredness or an injury. Something that would make it easier to stick a knife in him.

The only oddity she saw was familiar: his hand strayed to the thin book always tucked into his belt. When she'd first spotted it months ago, Aiz thought it was the Nine Sacred Tales, the parables Mother Div told to guide her people. Or if not that, a journal or a record book. But as best she could tell, it was a volume of children's stories, useless to her unless she wanted to beat him to death with it.

Unfortunately, it was a bit small for that.

As Tiral strode around his Sail, pointing out the damage it had taken to the flightmasters, Aiz paced in the shadows, consumed with hate.

She'd never understand why Mother Div gave Tiral windsmithing skill when he spat on everything she stood for. When he orphaned children by conscripting their parents and sneered at the clerics who carried out good works in Mother Div's name.

Tiral looked up, as if sensing Aiz's ire. He was twenty, broad-shouldered, of medium height, with pale hair and a crooked nose that made him memorable instead of ugly. His saurian gaze fixed on her. It took all Aiz's effort to keep her face placid. He nodded once.

She knew what he wanted. For once, she was happy to give it to him.

Aiz made her way to the Aerie, past the forges where metallurgists alloyed the Loha used for the Sails, wrinkling her nose at the stench. Rumor was that their supply of Loha—husbanded for a thousand years—was running out.

Without Loha there would be no Sails. Without Sails, the raids would fail. Then they'd all starve, Hawk and Snipe alike.

Aiz entered the Aerie from a side door and made for the bathing chambers. In the past six months, she'd learned to navigate the labyrinth of servants' passages with ease. On her way to Tiral's room, she saw others like her. Dead-eyed Snipes in revealing robes, doing what they needed to survive. They didn't acknowledge each other.

She wound through the innards of the keep to the secret door that led into Tiral's room. The stones of the tunnels were ancient, and she shifted one aside and hid her knife behind it. Then she knocked on the door thrice.

He made her wait. Unsurprising. He enjoyed the idea of Aiz shivering in the tunnel, not knowing if he'd allow her in or not. Aiz had worked hard to cultivate the image of a besotted Snipe. On the nights he left her outside, she sniveled and pleaded.

Pig. He thought he had so much power. Tonight, he'd learn different.

Soon, she heard movement. The door opened, and dim blue light spilled into the passage. Tiral's pale skin gleamed, like he was part specter.

"Aiz," he purred, and took her by the arm.

"My lord," she whispered. *Say it. Say it one last time.* "Thank you for allowing me in."

"I'm nothing if not generous, Snipe."

Lord Tiral drew her through his living quarters, the fur settees strewn with boots and fresh flight leathers. She caught a glimpse of herself in his mirror—small-boned and light-skinned, her dark hair spilling to her lower back, her blue irises seeming to glow. He nudged her onto his bed. Aiz's head sank into the goose-feather pillow that could fetch a week's worth of grain.

At least he was quick. Like many of Aiz's bed partners, he fell into an untroubled sleep after their coupling. Aiz observed him, her lip curling.

To their people, Tiral was a brave fleet commander. But to Aiz, he was the murderous child who, years ago, snuck into the cloister in the dead of night to set fire to the orphans' quarters. He'd listened to them scream as they burned, all because they'd made him look a fool in front of his father during an official visit.

The clerics, Sister Noa included, had gone before the Triarchy. Begged those three crooked monsters for justice. Even Dovan, the High Cleric of Kegar and leader of its many cloisters, made an impassioned plea.

The Triarchy did nothing. In time everyone forgot about the dead orphans—even Cero, who'd nearly died himself that night.

Aiz hadn't forgotten.

She rose from the bed, donned her shirt and skirt, and moved to the passageway for the knife. She was nearly there when Tiral stirred. Aiz swung toward his desk, feigning interest in his things. If he awoke, he'd only see her snooping. Amid the scrolls and quills and military orders, her gaze snagged on a book. *The* book.

She ran her fingers across the cover. The leather was slick, like the skin of a long-submerged sea creature. The imprint on the cover was triangular and reminded her of the tangled forests of the Spires. The hair on Aiz's neck rose, though she didn't know why. She opened the book.

THE FALCON AND THE THIEF

In the abiding evenfall of the northern climes, a lone falcon winged his way home after a long and—

Bah. Just a story. Aiz closed the book, listening for Tiral's snores before opening the passageway and retrieving her blade.

The bed dipped as she returned to it, and Tiral muttered in his sleep.

Aiz wrapped her fist tight around the knife. *Get what you need. Forget the rest.* The faster the better. Right in the throat. Cero had long ago taught her where to strike to kill a man. *No one can keep us safe all the time*, he'd said. *Not even the clerics.*

"In the name of Mother Div," she whispered, "I take my vengeance."

Aiz brought the blade down.

And gasped when Tiral's hand shot out, catching her wrist with breathtaking swiftness. His eyes opened, and he smiled.

"Oh, Aiz," he said. "You poor, stupid fool."

2
Quil

The Martial Empire, the Northern Continent

Zacharias Marcus Livius Aquillus Farrar, heir to the Martial throne and a prince of Gens Aquilla, did not need four fully armed Masks following him everywhere he went.

Quil—as he preferred to be called—had fought for his aunt, Empress Helene Aquilla, in the southern borderlands at the age of thirteen. Since he was fifteen, he'd bested at least two assassins a year with relative ease. He'd crisscrossed the dunes of the Tribal Desert and the forests of Marinn a hundred times with only his best friend, Sufiyan, for company. Here in the busy markets of the Empire's biggest port city, it was no different.

Especially since he'd long since realized he was being followed, and the Masks hadn't. Named for their silver face coverings, the Masks were the most elite soldiers in the Empire—and the most feared. But they still made mistakes.

"Stop glaring at the poor guards, Quil," Sufiyan said at the prince's scowl. "You'll scare them."

"They're Masks," Quil said. "They're not allowed to be scared."

Though perhaps they should be, Quil thought, considering how many had died ugly, unnatural deaths in the past few months. Usually, Masks were the ones holding the blades. But yesterday, two more had been found split open, according to the report Quil received from a western guard captain.

He couldn't stop thinking about it. But he also couldn't share any details with Sufiyan because Aunt Helene had told him to keep the Masks' deaths quiet.

The prince felt like a sailor fresh to land after a season at sea. Off-kilter. Uneasy. And now some cloaked miscreant was shadowing him.

Still, none of this was Sufiyan's problem, so Quil kept his brooding to a minimum as he walked with his friend through Navium's bustling evening market.

Quil didn't much like cities, but Navium's merry populace, azure coastline, and mouthwatering food made it hard to find fault. With dinnertime approaching, Quil's stomach rumbled at the smell of lime and chili shrimp, grilled minced chicken on mountains of snowy rice, and a specialty of Navium: triangle pastries filled with smoked winter vegetables.

In one corner of the square, multicolored Tribal lanterns glowed; a Kehanni—a Tribal storyteller—performed a tale. It was one of Quil's favorites: about heroes named Laia of Serra and Elias Veturius who, with Empress Helene, saved the world from a jinn driven mad by grief and betrayal. The audience cheered as the three proved victorious.

Beside him, Sufiyan smiled. Quil, meanwhile, scanned the crowd, the stalls that packed the square, the wagons behind the Kehanni.

There—a flash of movement from above. His shadow had taken to the rooftops.

The guards hadn't noticed; unlike Quil, their attention was fixed on the market, which was full to bursting with travelers from all over the Empire and beyond its borders: Tribespeople from the east in embroidered road leathers, selling weaponry and silks; Scholars, who'd ruled this land before the Martials, arguing about philosophy and politics. The Martial classes were here: Mercators hawking goods; wealthy Illustrians haggling with them; and Plebeians, many of whom wore colors that identified the Illustrian families they worked for.

In some way or another, all were Quil's people, though it didn't always feel like it. His father had been a Plebeian, but Quil hadn't experienced their struggles. His mother had been an Illustrian, but the upper-class families looked down on his Plebeian blood. He was raised by the Tribes for his safety, fostered with Sufiyan's family, Tribe Saif. But in the end, he was a Martial, a reminder of the Empire that had once ruled over the Tribes.

I belong nowhere, Quil had told Aunt Hel as a boy, back when he still shared his woes without fear of her judgment.

You belong to your people, she'd said. *The people of the Empire.*

Sufiyan stopped to buy a cone of pastries, flattering the pale-eyed chef with praise. A banner over her stall displayed a loaf of bread crossed with a stalk of wheat. She must have been from a bigger Mercator family—Gens Scriba perhaps, or Gens Vesta. Her gaze flicked over Quil once, then took in his guards. Her eyes widened and she curtsied.

"Your Highness," she said, cheeks pink. Quil cursed internally, because now heads were turning. "Glory to the Empress. My thanks for your custom."

Sufiyan rolled his eyes—he'd been the one who'd stopped, after all. But Quil smiled and moved on quickly, pulling up his hood and trying to shake off his disquiet. He missed anonymity.

"Drop back," he told his guard captain without explaining, using the flat affect his aunt insisted on. When he was a boy, he said *please*, but that made the Masks uncomfortable.

The guard captain hesitated, as if weighing the possible wrath of the Empress later against the guaranteed anger of the crown prince now. After a moment, he and his men disappeared into the crowds. Quil's entire body unclenched.

Sufiyan offered Quil a pastry. "Your leash is loose, and you're fed," he said. "Let's focus on why we're here."

"To satisfy the unending greed of a ne'er-do-well acquaintance I've been saddled with for eighteen years," Quil said, even as the shadow disappeared again, dropping from a rooftop into an alley.

Sufiyan shook his head. "You're here to generously purchase a token of appreciation for the closest thing to a brother you have, to mark the auspicious occasion of his eighteenth yearfall. You unthankful boor."

"You're forgetting Tas. I've known him since birth."

"I meant the literal closest. Since I am standing three feet from you, and Tas is skies-know-where."

Zacharias.

His name was a whisper carried on the wind. Quil looked up, surprised. No one used his given name except Aunt Helene, or Suf when he wanted to be irritating. The prince turned to Suf, but he was busy fondling a ruby-studded dagger that probably cost a month's pay for the entire Fifth Legion.

"A fine yearfall gift." Sufiyan flipped the dagger deftly between his fingers. His weapon of choice was a bow, but like Quil, Suf was trained to use anything to defend himself. Once, when some Illustrian twit had mocked Sufiyan's parentage, he knocked the man unconscious with biting nonchalance and a clay flute.

"My prince." The dagger merchant nodded to Quil. "I thank you. My family is Plebeian—" His weathered face filled with pride as he looked over his goods. "I received a Prince's Gift to start my business."

At this, Quil perked up. He'd established the grant last year, after seeing so few Plebeian traders in the markets.

The merchant offered the dagger. "Take it, with my compliments."

But Quil shook his head and dropped his voice. "There's a woman behind me—Mater Candela. Richer than the Empress. She collects shiny things. I expect you to charge her double and get away with it."

The merchant grinned and slapped Quil on the shoulder. "You're a canny Plebe at heart, my prince. Always knew I liked you."

Quil's chest warmed at the compliment. He wondered sometimes how his people saw him. As the quiet son of a monstrous man, perhaps. Or a shadow beside an incandescent empress. *Canny Plebe.* Quil preferred that to either of the others.

A silver mirror gleamed the next table over, and Quil glanced in it long enough to make sure he still had tabs on the shadow trailing him before offering it to Sufiyan. "More fitting, no? Since you're obsessed with your face."

"I got the looks; you got the royal title. It's only fair." Sufiyan examined his reflection. "Speaking of royalty. Have you talked to your aunt yet?"

The prince shook his head. Once, he'd told the Empress everything. Now he didn't know how to begin a conversation with her. They disagreed on too much—especially his future.

"The last time I said the word *abdicate*"—Quil moved on from the jewel merchant, Sufiyan following—"she didn't speak to me for a month."

"You're twenty, Quil," Sufiyan said. "Keep dillydallying and you'll have a crown on your brow, an empress who bores the hair off your head, a brood of bawling babies, and no desire to hear the word *abdicate* yourself."

An empress . . . A face flashed unbidden in Quil's mind. Short dark hair, wary eyes, and a rare smile. Ilar's quiet self-assurance had fascinated him from the moment he met her. She was never boring. She'd have been a great empress.

But she was dead. Had been for more than a year. Grief reared its unwelcome head, but Quil was no stranger to it. He pushed it down deep, where his other secrets lived.

From one of the many drum towers that speckled the city, a series of booms thundered out. Quil translated easily. *Fourth Legion, Second Infantry Patrol, report to South Cothon Barracks.* The prince frowned.

"Isn't the Fourth Legion supposed to be in Antium?"

"Maybe they're bored of freezing their backsides off and came here for some sun."

Zacharias. Get out of the square.

The prince jumped at the voice—as sharp as if someone had shouted in his ear. Sufiyan chattered on, oblivious.

Quil weighed the risk of answering this voice against his own curiosity. The latter won. When he stepped into the darkened building moments later, scim drawn, a hooded figure emerged from the shadows behind the apothecary's dusty counter.

"Put that big knife away, boy."

Quil recognized the woman instantly.

"Bani al-Mauth." The prince sheathed his scim and bowed. *Chosen of Death*. She'd been a runaway, a revolutionary, a slave, and a murderess.

Now she was a holy figure who guided restless spirits from this life to the next. She took the pain that anchored them to the human plane and cast it into another dimension—the Sea of Suffering—so the ghosts could move on in peace. It was a task that confined her mostly to a haunted wood on the edge of the Martial Empire. The Waiting Place, it was called, for the ghosts unwilling to move on from it.

Quil had met the Bani al-Mauth many times. Often when she visited Empress Helene. But mostly when she came to the Tribal Lands to see her family—including Sufiyan, her grandson, and his parents, Laia of Serra and Elias Veturius.

Of course, he'd seen her more recently, too. But almost as soon as he thought about it, the woman growled at him.

"Dash that thought from your head, boy." She must have read his expression. "You know better. You know the cost."

He knew. But sensations still crowded his mind—things he didn't want to remember from that night months ago. The mountains. A cavern. The iron tang of blood. So sharp, as if he'd walked into a slaughterhouse.

Which, he supposed, he had.

"You." He forced the thoughts away—he'd gotten better at it since he'd last seen her. "You were following me."

"Thought you'd catch on quicker. Been shadowing you since the palace."

Well, that was embarrassing. "Should I get Sufiyan?" Quil's face heated. "He'd want—"

"My grandson and his family want nothing to do with me," the Bani al-Mauth said. "I came to get your help."

"My help?" Quil shook his head. "You're the one who knew about the dead boy, not me. How?"

"Felt it coming," she said. "Tell me what you know about the others who died like him."

Quil met that dark blue stare. The Empress had told Quil to speak to no one of the Masks' deaths. *Especially not Sufiyan or his family.* She didn't have to tell Quil twice. Sufiyan's little sisters were only fifteen and thirteen. And Laia and Elias had been through enough.

But the Bani al-Mauth was different. When Quil was a child, she arrived in Antium and demanded to speak to the Empress. Quil was visiting from the Tribal Lands and expected his aunt to reject such an abrupt summons. Instead, she'd cleared her evening.

"Maybe we should go to Aunt Hel together," Quil offered, but the Bani al-Mauth waved away the suggestion.

"Your aunt's acting like everything is fine. She's doing nothing about the murders."

Quil's hackles rose. He might resent Aunt Hel, but he'd be damned before he would let anyone else say a word against her. "Those dead Masks were young and Illustrian and they were murdered in the Tribal Lands. She kept it quiet because she knew it would look like the Tribes had killed them. She didn't want Illustrian families out for blood."

"I'm not talking about the Masks," the Bani al-Mauth said. "I'm talking about the children. Ruh was the first—" Her voice caught, but she cleared her throat. "Then your girl—Ilar."

Quil's chest twisted at the sound of their names, which conjured their faces, their scents, their voices. *Stop. Don't think of them. Bury it.*

The Bani al-Mauth went on. "Two more children were found the next day in Nur. Street urchins with no families. A dozen more, after that, all over the Tribal Lands and the southern Empire. And then for months, nothing. Until now."

Fourteen children dead. Quil hadn't known about a single one. The store, already dusty and dim, felt much colder.

"Three died in Serra a few weeks ago," she said. "Two in Navium. Four as far north as Silas. All under age twenty, all with the same gaping wound, their hearts shriveled to gray ash. Those are the deaths I've heard about."

"There were six Masks, too." Quil's stomach churned as he remembered the report from the morning. "Two found yesterday in the borderlands. You speak to ghosts. Don't you know about them?"

The Bani al-Mauth considered him. "Not every ghost comes through the Waiting Place."

"That wasn't an answer."

"You remind me of your aunt. Pain in the arse, that girl. Sharp as a scim, though. Heard more than she let on. You do too, I'd bet."

"I didn't hear about these kids," Quil said. "She never said a word."

"You do something for me," the Bani al-Mauth said. "You ask her why, the next time you see her. And one more thing." Her tone lost its edge. "How are you, boy?"

A simple question. One that elicited a waterfall of thoughts.

Quil didn't often let himself think about Ruh and Ilar. But he did now: Ruh's hands when he told stories about shadowy ghuls and evil tale-spinners. Ilar's laugh, shy like she was out of practice. The way she saw past his reserve and drew him out with her questions, as if nothing he said could bore her. *Tell me about the palace in Antium. Tell me about getting lost in Navium's harbor. Are there truly whole streets of kite makers in Serra?*

"I've done as you asked," Quil said. "I try not to think about it."

"What of your magic? Will you get training from the Jaduna?"

Quil tensed at the mention of the Jaduna. "You told me to forget what I saw that night," Quil said. "In return, I don't want to talk about the magic. Ever."

The Bani al-Mauth shrugged and shook the dust from her cloak. "As you wish. I must return to the Waiting Place. Speak of this to no one. And, boy . . ."

She cocked her head. The shadows of the apothecary appeared to nibble at her edges.

"Watch your back. The air is wrong. The ghosts are restless. Something's coming."

No, Quil thought as she faded into the dark. *Something's already here.*

3
Sirsha

Sirsha knew she shouldn't have stayed in Raider's Roost as long as she had.

The settlement festered like a forgotten canker in the foothills of the Serran Mountains, a cesspool of liars, thieves, and worse.

Now Sirsha stood in one of the Roost's miserable, rain-soaked alleys in the dead of night, surrounded by a gang of miscreants. She was weaponless and—irritatingly—bootless, with nothing but her wits standing between herself and complete destitution.

Or possibly death. But she was, at this moment, primarily concerned with destitution.

She'd spent the last seven years saving up every penny from every job so she could leave the accursed Empire forever. She wanted warm weather, clear water, and a nice little inn to run in the Southern Isles. She wasn't about to lose her dream to a pack of poorly dressed halfwits.

"Give us the money, tracker," said the head thug, a pale weed of a girl called Migva. She packed a meaner punch than one would suspect, and she shook out her hand—sore from the beating she'd dealt Sirsha. "I'm tired and hungry and sick of hitting you."

Sirsha glanced behind her, to the shack she'd lived in for the past few months. It was an ugly, ramshackle sort of place, held together by spite and dirt, like most of the Roost. She'd rented a room in it from a hulking gem dealer too scary for even a Roost rat to cross. They'd worked out a trade: between her other jobs, she tracked down items or people he was interested in, and he ran off anyone who might want to rob her. In a lawless place like the Roost, it was a cushy trade.

Everything was dandy until the gem dealer's lover caught him cheating with the handsome tea merchant from up the lane. An hour later, the gem dealer was dead, his lover fled with his gems. Now the vultures circled.

"I told you, I don't have—*uff*—" Migva swung her fist low, and Sirsha landed on her knees, gasping. Her sopping, dark hair slapped across her forehead, and mud oozed between her socked toes. Skies, was there anything more disgusting than the feeling of wet sock?

"You've searched me a dozen times," Sirsha said. "I don't have anything."

"You must think I have dung for brains," Migva said. "You hid it. If you don't tell us where, I'll leave you in pieces all over the bleeding Roost. You're a filthy foreigner. No one will help you."

Sirsha glared at Migva through her non-swollen eye. The Roost rat came off as a petty thief, pecking at the crumbs left behind by bigger crooks. Clearly, Sirsha had underestimated the hag. Migva was smarter than anticipated. Nastier, too. Up close, she had that hungry glint that Sirsha knew well. The eyeshine of a predator, of someone who'd learned to hurt and kill out of necessity long ago, and found she enjoyed it.

Not for the first time, Sirsha wished her magic was useful for more than just tracking down jewel thieves.

A scrawny boy stood beside Migva. Last month, he'd tried to sell the gem dealer fake rubies. Sirsha convinced the big man not to kill him.

"You. Boy," Sirsha said. "I saved your miserable life when you were swindling the gem dealer."

The boy shifted from foot to foot, dagger shaky in his hand. "Migva, maybe we—"

Migva spun, drawing her blade across the boy's throat so fast that his blood was soaking into the mud before Sirsha understood what happened. She weighed her life against her savings. Would she enjoy spending years scraping together enough gold to leave the skies-forsaken Empire? No. But would it be better than getting thrown to the crows for their morning meal? Most certainly.

"The money's in the back bedroom," Sirsha said. "In a safe behind the painting of the ugly dog. Now that I think about it, the dog looks a bit like you, Migva. Did you ever sit for a painting—"

Sirsha doubled over when Migva leveled a kick at her belly. But even with her face in the muck and a broken rib or two, she smiled at the snickers from Migva's gang.

"What are you waiting for?" Migva roared at the thief closest to her. "Get in there!" The boy glanced at his dead companion and scurried inside. Half a minute later, he emerged.

Empty-handed.

Migva grabbed Sirsha's hair and dragged her to the outer wall of the shack, pinning her next to a barrel and a rusted rake. "What game are you playing?"

"No game!" Sirsha gasped. "The gem dealer's lover must have taken it. I swear that's where I put it!" Sirsha didn't bother controlling the shrill fear in her voice. If nothing else, it might keep Migva from decapitating her.

Migva released Sirsha, disgusted. "You're stupid *and* pathetic." She gestured to another of her gang. "Kill her."

"No—no, please—" Sirsha cowered—rather convincingly, she thought. Until one of Migva's minions grasped her neck.

At which point Sirsha latched a hand onto the rake and swung it up into the man's nether regions, relishing the bastard's howl of rage and pain before spinning the rake into the side of his head. Sirsha shoved him at Migva and darted into the shack, bolting the door behind her. It wouldn't hold back the gang for long. But it might delay them enough for her to get the hells out of here.

She swept up her boots, her blades, and her pack before diving into the bedroom. The ugly dog painting lay on the floor, and the hidden cabinet gaped open, empty. *Ah well.*

Sirsha threw herself into the closet, fumbling with a tiny latch on the floor as the front door splintered open. The latch gave and Sirsha was through, barely managing to close it before Migva's goons flooded the room. She padded down a narrow tunnel and through a secret door to a back alley. Once outside, Sirsha squelched through the mud, stopping at an alcove a few houses down to look back. Nothing.

She stripped off her socks and shoved the dark red leather boots on. She might get blisters, but skin would grow back. These boots fit like a glove and had carried her hundreds of miles. She wasn't about to dirty their insides.

As she eased out of the alcove, someone shouted ahead of her.

"There she is!"

Sirsha flung one of her poison-tipped needle blades at the scout and ran, a fading groan telling her she'd hit her mark.

Exits. Exits. Sirsha knew the Roost well—better than most who passed through here. Problem was, Migva lived here too. There were countless less-traveled paths out of the Roost—most of which were incredibly dangerous.

Sirsha knew of one that no sensible person would traverse. She headed for it, flitting from alley to alley, one eye behind her. She thought she saw movement and crouched low in the shadows beside a tavern. When no one emerged, she continued until she reached the eastern outskirts of the settlement.

The Roost was sprawled in a narrow space between two immense rock faces. From afar, the rocks shot straight upward, appearing impassable. Sirsha knew better. She picked past the outlying huts and tents, and made for a fissure in the stone. The opening was just wide enough for her. She pulled on a pair of gloves and began the dangerous climb up.

The rain made it treacherous, and soon she was sweating. As she picked up speed, she heard a scrape from below.

A face peered up at her. Even from a distance, Sirsha recognized Migva's lupine features, twisted into a snarl.

"Bleeding hells," Sirsha muttered. She'd like to think that Migva would slip and fall to an unceremonious death. But the girl was like a Jibautian spitting cockroach—mean and strong and impossible to kill. Sirsha looked to the thin slice of sky above, the rain-bloated clouds illuminated by a stroke of lightning. Everything hurt. Her bones felt like shards of glass. But it wasn't far to go.

Sirsha grimaced as she climbed. Every time she looked over her shoulder, that bony wretch was getting closer. When Sirsha emerged from the fissure onto the cap of the rock face, Migva was a mere twenty feet behind, and Sirsha panted with exhaustion. She clambered forward, squinting in the dark.

The rock ahead sloped down toward the Jutts—land formations that looked as if the earth had grown spikes. Beyond was the Serran Mountain Range. It would be spectacularly foolish to traverse the Jutts in this weather.

Which was why Sirsha staggered toward them. The way down to the Jutts was steep. But if she was careful, she could avoid tumbling head over feet into the wide chasm below, and reach one of the thin rock bridges she knew lay in that direction.

"Come back here!" Migva screamed, hands shredded from the climb.

"When has that order ever worked for you, dog-face?" Sirsha slipped and went skidding down the slope toward the chasm, her fall halted when she smashed into a ridge, jarring every bone in her body. Lightning flashed and she jumped at what looked like a figure ahead, huge and hulking, standing near a spot of flat land beside a boulder.

A moment later, it was dark once more and she wasn't sure what she'd seen. Her distraction cost her. Migva knocked into her, tearing the breath from her body.

Sirsha lurched forward, and Migva's gaze caught on the thin gold chain around Sirsha's neck. Her eyes shone with sudden greed, and she lunged for it, sending both of them rolling down the rocky slope. They were approaching the chasm too fast.

"Stop, you idiot!" Sirsha screamed as Migva tried to rip the chain off. "You're going to get us killed!"

But Migva was past caring, and all Sirsha could do was try to fend her off with one arm while scrabbling for a grip with the other. There were knobs of rocks here, vines, ridges. If she could grab one, she could arrest her fall.

Just before the slope dropped off into the gorge, her fingers caught on something rough. An old dead vine that she felt a sudden and abiding love for. She latched onto it, and though it stretched taut as gravity pulled her and Migva closer to the cliff's edge, it did not give. Sirsha shoved her thumb in Migva's eye and kicked out viciously. The Roost rat released her, startled at the sudden attack. She hurtled down into the darkness, her panicked scream echoing until it was suddenly cut off.

"I did warn you," Sirsha muttered. She didn't dare move. She was practically vertical, with no clear sense of what was anchoring the vine. Gingerly, she felt for a foothold.

As she did so, the vine slackened. Sirsha fell, dropping away into death. *Bleeding, burning hells. Sharing a grave with that pasty-faced bitch. What an end.*

Until quite suddenly, she was hovering. Not dead. Her beloved vine stretched taut and she held on to it for dear life, dangling over the Jutts' maw. Inexplicably, the vine began to inch upward.

No, Sirsha realized. Someone was *pulling* it upward. Quickly. After only a few minutes, she was out of the crevasse, and she tried to get a look at whoever had saved her. She saw a flash of a lamp and a huge figure before the rain blurred her vision. Seconds later, a hand pulled her to a flatter spot on the rocky slope that had nearly killed her.

"You can let go. You won't fall from here." The voice was a deep rumble that Sirsha didn't recognize. Lightning flashed and she caught a glimpse of an unfamiliar man. He was taller than her, with light eyes and dark hair. His face was grim—marked by sorrow. He appeared to be twice her age.

"Are you Sirsha Westering?" he asked. "The tracker?"

Before he could so much as think about drawing a scim, she had a knife to his throat, the blade cleverly concealed in a strap on her wrist. "It's pronounced *Seer-shah*. And who wants to know?"

She expected anger from him, or irritation. Men didn't like being bested by the likes of her. But he smiled and nodded downward. He held a blade to her stomach. As quickly as it appeared, he was flipping it back into his belt and holding up his hands.

"I'm a client," he said. "And I've got a job for you."

4
Aiz

Oh, Aiz. You poor, stupid fool.

Aiz couldn't move. Couldn't plunge the knife into Tiral's neck, couldn't shift it even an inch. Tiral grinned, squeezing her wrist until she cried out and dropped the weapon.

He swiped it up and backhanded her so hard that she flew off the bed. One word pounded through her brain. *No. No. No.*

"Did you really think you could kill me?" Tiral sounded almost delighted. Humiliation coursed through Aiz. He kicked her in the stomach, and she dropped to her knees. Tiral laughed.

"That's better. Beg for my forgiveness and I'll make sure your death is quick, and that none at your cloister suffers for your stupidity."

Aiz didn't care about a quick death. All she wanted was for Tiral to hurt. To know pain and suffering. Yet she knew he was offering a gift, final though it was. The cloister, the clerics, the orphans. She hadn't considered what he'd do to them if she failed.

"Or don't beg." Tiral smiled. "And I'll let the Questioners take you apart limb by limb in the Tohr with all your precious clerics."

Aiz stared down at her pale hands, scarred from a childhood in Dafra slum. A lock of hair fell in her face and she held herself still. The Tohr's vermin-infested cells were peopled with broken Snipes who'd defied the Triarchy. *Your anger will be the death of you.*

The death of you.

Then she felt the ridges of her scars and the lick of flame. She heard the orphans screaming, and all she could think was how much she hated this snake of a man. The air in the room stirred as Aiz gathered her will, praying to Mother Div that this one time, the wind would do her bidding.

For a glorious moment, the wind shot out like a whip, tight and brutal. Aiz nudged it tighter with her mind. Tiral grabbed at his throat, coughing.

A second later, Aiz flew back, slamming into the stone wall. The air around her transformed into flaming needles, stabbing at her skin. She screamed, clawing at her face so frantically she didn't hear Tiral until he was in front of her. He hauled Aiz up by her hair and leaned close, his breath hot against her ear.

"I never let my guard down, Snipe."

She cringed, let him think for one instant that she was afraid.

Then she spat in his face.

His hand loosened enough for her to tear free and knee him between the legs. He doubled over with a groan. Aiz reached for the wind again, but this time, she didn't try to control it. Instead, she fed her wrath into it, and it exploded out of her.

The wind howled, knocking Tiral flat, tearing his bed to splinters, ripping his desk in half, and shredding the hearth to rubble. The window that faced the mountains shattered. A spark jumped, erupting into flame on a settee. Aiz shrieked in joy. *Yes!* She *knew* she could control the power that lived within her. She had always known. Now, finally, it was at her fingertips.

In a moment, it was over. Aiz fell to her knees, so drained she thought her skin would shrivel away.

Get up. Already, she heard distant shouts of alarm. She dragged herself through the debris toward the secret passageway. She could still escape. Warn Sister Noa to empty the cloister so Tiral couldn't hurt anyone.

Her hands shook as she reached for the door's latch. It wouldn't budge. She tried again, screaming in frustration, even as someone banged on Tiral's door.

"Commander Tiral? Commander!"

A surge of heat. The fire had spread to the remnants of Tiral's bed and fed greedily upon the wood.

"Mother Div, help me." Aiz choked on the smoke. "Help me, please." Tears of dismay streamed down her face. There was no way out. She'd die here. And though Aiz had told herself that she was ready to leave this earth as long as she took Tiral with her, now she found herself thinking of Cero. Of everything unsaid between them—everything she didn't let him say. Of Sister Noa, who would mourn her as if her own daughter had died. Of the orphans, and the stories of Mother Div that Aiz would never tell them.

The flames closed in; the smoke thickened. Aiz dropped low and her hands touched something strange and soft in the rubble.

Tiral's book. The pattern on it reflected the spreading flames.

The beams of the room groaned and the stone under the shattered window crumbled away. Snowy air swirled around Aiz, blessedly cool.

"Thank you, Mother Div," Aiz sobbed. "Thank you." She crawled toward the opening, but as she did, Tiral heaved a breath. The bastard was still alive.

Which meant even if Aiz did get out of here, he'd hunt her down.

Aiz looked back at the book, the flames inches away from it. She didn't know why it was precious to him, but perhaps she could use it as leverage. She snatched it up, wrapping it in its oilcloth cover and stuffing it in her skirt. Then she skittered toward the opening in the wall and squeezed out.

Her belly lurched as she looked to the snow-covered ground far below, to the slick rock. But this was her only choice. She dug her fingers into a timber and began to descend.

The wind tore at her, too wild to control, an enemy determined to bring her down. It seemed to be mocking her. Laughing, screaming her name. *Aiiiiz.*

The rock beneath her left foot crumbled, and suddenly her leg was dangling in open air. She pawed at the wall, but it was smooth as glass, without so much as a crack in which she could wedge the edge of her shoe. *Mother Div, help me. Please.* Aiz's arms ached at the weight of holding herself up. Her fingers grew numb.

Then her foot slipped. *Better to die like this than to starve or rot in prison*, she thought wildly as the wind tore at her. *At least it will be fast.* Laughter bubbled up from her chest, shrill and brittle, transforming into a scream as she fell.

"Aiz. *Aiz*, damn you, wake up."

Dragging her eyes open was, possibly, the most difficult thing Aiz had done in her life. Cero's pale, handsome face appeared over hers, his expression angrier than she'd ever seen it.

"You are a Spires-forsaken fool," he hissed. "What were you thinking climbing that wall? Why is the Aerie on fire?"

Aiz's temples pounded, and she felt the back of her head. It was soaked with blood, though she didn't feel a wound.

"Don't touch!" Cero snapped, helping her sit up. She recognized the stark gray walls of the cloister. They were in one of the antechambers that bordered the courtyard. Through a window, Aiz spotted Sister Noa setting up the meager morning meal.

"How—how long since—"

"It's been hours. I was waiting for you to wake before getting Noa. Didn't want her heart to stop at the sight of you. You fell almost forty feet. It's a miracle you're not dead."

"No—no." Aiz tried to stand. "I can't be here. He's going to come for me—"

Cero bade her sit, his anger fading. "Aiz. You're injured. You're not making sense. Take a breath and tell me what happened."

"You became a pilot," Aiz whispered. "I didn't. It's—it's not fair—"

"You were born knowing the world isn't fair. You work around it like always."

"I can't!" Aiz said, wishing to the Spires that she could think more clearly. "I must go, Cero. I tried to kill Tiral. Then I took something from him."

Cero's face blanched. "Tell me he's dead."

Aiz shook her head. "He was alive when I escaped. He knew I'd planned to kill him, to get revenge for the orphans. All this time I've been sleeping with him, trying to gain his trust. And he *knew*."

"Spires, Aiz. I could have told you that he uses people." Cero looked away, his words bitter. "Pretends he cares so he can toy with them."

"You too?" Aiz whispered, feeling strangely relieved when Cero nodded.

"Once, after you weren't chosen for the flight squadron," he said. "I thought if I talked to him—got to know him—I could convince him to let you train more." Cero laughed bitterly. "I was naive. He used me, and when I brought you up, he—"

Cero went silent at the sudden thudding on the courtyard gate. A sneering voice rang out.

"Clerics," Tiral called from beyond the cloister's outer wall. "Do let me in. I'd like a word with one of your wards."

"You shouldn't have brought me here," Aiz said. "He'll punish the entire cloister if he finds me."

Cero hauled her to her feet, steadying her when her legs turned to rubber. "He won't find you," he said. "Come on."

As Sister Noa approached the gate, Cero pulled Aiz into the cloister's serpentine hallways. They made their way down a short flight of stairs and into the kitchen storeroom.

"You'll have to leave the city," Cero said.

"No. I stole this book from him," Aiz said. "I'll hide it, and then I'll beg for mercy for the cloister. The book is leverage. Tiral will kill me, but I'm dead anyway, Cero. Of starvation or in one of his wars."

Cero stiffened as he pulled her through a door and into a hallway of the cloister she hadn't seen. "Don't be pathetic," he snapped. "You're worse than the Hawks. The second things get a bit tough, you fall apart."

"*A bit tough?*" She glared at him. "What do you call our entire existence?"

"A gift," he said. "Walk faster."

The words snapped her out of her self-pity, so quintessentially Cero that she wanted to hug him. But he was already moving. Aiz ran to keep up with his long strides, following him through a narrow gap in the rubble and through a hallway carved with runes. This was part of the ancient structure erected after the migration—or so Sister Noa had told Aiz when she was a girl.

"Cero," she said. "Listen." They were deep in the bowels of the cloister, where torches were few.

"Do you hear them?" she whispered. "Voices. Tiral's soldiers are in the tunnels. We should split up. You can't be seen with me."

"Patience, Aiz," Cero said. "Almost there." He led them deeper below the cloister, where the ground grew slick with moisture. Water rushed distantly.

"How do you remember all of this?" Aiz asked. "I couldn't find my way back to the cloister if you put a blade to my throat."

"Didn't you ever wonder what I was doing while you were begging fairy tales off the clerics?"

"They're not fairy tales," Aiz snapped. "Your mockery is—"

"Not our biggest problem right now." Cero turned yet again, this time past a grate crusted with ice and rime and into a narrow passage. With every moment that passed, Aiz's mind grew clearer. These tunnels didn't go on forever. Eventually Tiral would find them. Corner them. When he did, he couldn't find Cero with her. Tiral might need pilots, but he'd never forgive Cero for helping the assassin who tried to kill him.

The sounds of pursuit grew louder and Aiz's palms, slick with sweat, slipped against the rock as she crawled through a space slightly wider than Cero's shoulders. Water thundered close by. Finally, they emerged onto a ledge. A river surged below, its rapids a milky white. Aiz stopped short.

"I can't swim."

"I'm going with you," Cero said. "Take off your shoes and cloak so they don't pull you under. The river will spit us out near the docks—"

"Come out, come out, little Snipe!" Tiral's voice echoed down the tunnel and Aiz jumped in surprise, nearly tumbling into the river.

"If he finds you with me," Aiz said, "he'll kill you. If I jump in and he finds you alone, he'll know you helped me and kill you."

"Get your shoes off, Aiz!"

But Aiz shook her head. She didn't know life without Cero. They'd been born within weeks of each other. They'd both had only one parent. When Cero's father and Aiz's mother were conscripted, their children turned to each other for comfort. He'd listened to Aiz telling the Sacred Tales, even if he'd never believed. And she'd always found his inventions brilliant, even when she hardly understood them.

Angry as Aiz had been these past few months, it hadn't been at Cero. It had been at herself and at the knowledge that her dreams—of being a pilot, of saving the cloister—they were dead.

Aiz pulled the oilcloth-wrapped book from her clothes and shoved it into Cero's shirt. "Keep the book. Hide it well. It's the only leverage I have."

"Stop talking nonsense. The current will be strong, but—"

Aiz twisted away and drop-kicked him right in the chest, hard enough to send him tumbling into the water. His arms arced, elegant even in the face of a surprise shove from his best friend, and he disappeared beneath the rapids. A few seconds and twenty feet later, his head broke the surface. He tried to find purchase along the sides of the tunnel, but there was nothing, and Aiz watched until he disappeared into the gloom.

Then she turned, rose to her knees, and bowed her head, arms at her sides. Which was exactly how Tiral found her when he stepped out of the tunnel a minute later.

He put his sword point to her heart.

"Where is my book?"

Aiz meant to treat with him. If she bargained, she could save the cloister from his punishment. But some stubborn part of her refused, a voice within telling her not to speak of the book. She'd never kill Tiral now. But at least she'd taken something he valued.

"What book?" She let dull confusion fill her expression. He thought so little of her that he believed it.

His soldiers beat, blindfolded, gagged, and dragged her out of the cloister and through the city. Her clothes were in tatters, her shoes gone. When her blindfold was removed, she found herself in the Aerie's long gathering hall. The building was simple and stark, with high, foggy windows and a vast wood-beamed ceiling.

The stone was cold beneath her feet, and she shivered. Three thrones sat before her, one for each of the Triarchs, embedded in the base of a staircase.

Aiz had just enough time to realize that two of the thrones were occupied when Tiral shoved her face to the floor.

"Bow to your betters, Snipe," he hissed.

As the stone dug into Aiz's nose, it occurred to her that she shouldn't be in front of the Triarchs of the Realm. She was naught but gutter trash. Punishment should have been death if Tiral wanted to make it quick, torture in a dungeon if he didn't.

"Commander Tiral, you're meant to be hauling back enough food stores to get us through the month," a woman's cold voice spoke. The raven-haired Triarch of Clan Oona—the bloodsmithers. They used to work as healers, but they'd lost the skill generations ago. "What is this?"

Tiral offered Triarch Oona a short bow. "This Snipe tried to assassinate me. She is a threat to us all."

"Your clan should deal with this directly," Triarch Ghaz said with a frown. He was a young man in practical flight leathers, his curly hair a brown halo around his head. "You pulled us from a meeting with the Ankanese ambassador."

"And the fine Ankanese wine he brought," Triarch Oona murmured.

Triarch Ghaz looked Aiz up and down. "You expect us to consider this girl a danger to the Triarchy?"

Clan Ghaz were once custodians of mindsmithing, but, like the bloodsmithers, they'd lost the ability. Still, Triarch Ghaz had taken his throne by outmaneuvering every member of his clan. Aiz looked down, worried that he would peer into her mind and read how much she hated the Triarchs—including him.

"She's a threat." Tiral paced behind Aiz like a hunting dog. "Because I don't believe she acted alone."

Tiral nodded to his guards, and a moment later, they dragged cleric after cleric into the gathering hall. All thirty were from Dafra cloister—the entire clergy. All were bound and gagged, Sister Noa among them, her eye bloodied. Aiz winced. The old woman had put up a fight.

Behind her limped Sister Olnas, her gray hair falling from its usually neat bun. Clerics did not marry, but Olnas and Noa were as good as. Olnas would be frantic at Noa's injury.

"No!" Aiz cried. "They had nothing to—"

Tiral slapped her, and blood from her already cut lip spattered the floor. "Silence, rat."

The Triarchs didn't so much as look at Aiz, their gazes fixed on a woman following the clerics in, escorted but not bound.

Her skin and hair gleamed as white as the Loha used to power the Sails. She wore a simple cream robe, embroidered with the half-sun symbol of Mother Div. Despite the soldiers on either side of her, she appeared serene. She bowed her head to the Triarchs.

"Light of the Spires, Triarchs."

"Long may it guide us," the Triarchs intoned. Aiz stared, mouth agape. The High Cleric was the holiest living person in Kegar. Aiz had only ever seen her from afar, leading the Summer Rites to bless the raids.

"Holy Triarchs," Tiral said. "I submit that the clerics of Dafra cloister planned the assassination to seize power. The girl was merely a tool. Tell me, High Cleric: Why did your clergy plot so cunningly against a son of Kegar?"

"My people did no such thing," High Cleric Dovan said. "Triarchs, I beg you to hear reason. Commander Tiral sees shadows and threats where there are none."

"My son commands the flight squadrons of Kegar," a voice growled from the door. It was Triarch Hiwa—Tiral's father—who'd entered the hall silently. "Seeing shadows and threats is his job—one that has kept our people fed."

Triarch Hiwa, blond like his son, offered Tiral a bare nod before striding to his throne, guards trailing. He had a heavy brow and a curled lip, as if forever displeased.

Aiz's heart thumped rapidly. Strange how in a moment, the nightmare images from years ago came rushing back. Triarch Hiwa's visit to the cloister. *Let us see what these children can do.* The clerics trotting out the orphans. One sang. Another showed off her weaving. Ros displayed his skill with a bow.

You'd make a fine soldier, Triarch Hiwa had said to Ros. Then he sneered at his own son. Tiral was a few years older than Ros at the time. *The Snipe is a better shot than you, boy,* Triarch Hiwa had said, cuffing Tiral across the cheek.

That night, Tiral crept into the cloister and burned the orphans' wing down. Only Aiz and Cero survived.

Within a year, Tiral's father had named him heir.

Triarch Hiwa sat upon his throne now. His name meant *wind*, and his clan was known for the one skill remaining to the Kegari: windsmithing. His gaze settled on Aiz with the weight of a fist. She kept her face down, her anger leashed. She'd done enough to harm the clerics.

"So, this is your assassin," Triarch Hiwa said. "She doesn't look like much. That said, an assassination attempt makes the Triarchy look weak. Do you not agree, High Cleric?"

As Aiz glanced between the highborns, she realized that she was witnessing some power struggle far above her station. One that had been going on for longer than she knew. It did not matter what she'd done. There was a greater storm here, and she and the clerics were caught in its currents.

Aiz followed Tiral's gaze to the ornately carved throne atop the staircase behind the Triarchs. It was the largest throne, for it belonged to Mother Div, who commanded three elements: blood, mind, and air.

In our hour of greatest need, the clerics told the children, *Mother Div will return in the body of the Tel Ilessi, the Holy Vessel. And the Tel Ilessi shall deliver us back to the homeland from whence we fled, so long ago.*

The throne had sat empty for a thousand years, since Mother Div left

Kegar to her three children—the progenitors of Clan Oona, Clan Ghaz, and Clan Hiwa.

Now Tiral stared at that throne like a Snipe gazed at fresh bread.

"Aiz bet-Dafra was under the clerics' care when she undertook this assassination," Triarch Oona noted, red robes rustling as she steepled her fingers. "They must have known something."

High Cleric Dovan now looked alarmed. She turned her full attention to Triarch Ghaz, who had not yet spoken against her.

"Triarch Ghaz, you and I have prayed to Mother Div together. You have seen the benefits of the cloisters and how we educate the orphans. You know us."

Hiwa spoke before Ghaz could. "Commander Tiral. As the attempt was made against you, what punishment would you have the assassin and her accomplices bear?"

"They should be sent to the Tohr for questioning," Tiral said without hesitation. "We will learn how deep the plot runs. If the clerics have nothing to hide, then they need not fear. As for the girl—" Tiral circled Aiz. "Death would be an easy path for her. If she survives her questioning, she can live out her days in the Tohr to think on her crimes."

Aiz began to tremble. Not for herself—she couldn't give two figs if she was alive or dead—but for what she knew the clerics would endure at the hands of the Tohr's Questioners.

"There is no need for this." The High Cleric's voice shook. "Lord Tiral, we can discuss—"

"Perhaps," Tiral said. "But not right now."

"What—what will happen to the children?" Sister Noa spoke up. "If we are to be imprisoned?"

"Better for the orphans to serve in the army than learn sedition at the knees of the clerics," Tiral said. "Don't look so shocked. I was younger than most of them the first time I fought at my father's side. Many nations train their children even earlier. The Jaduna begin battle magic lessons at age four. The Empress of the Martials went to a military academy at age six."

"The girl and the clerics will be questioned," Hiwa said. "The orphans will be conscripted. Witnessed and agreed?" He turned to his fellow Triarchs.

Triarch Oona nodded. "Witnessed and agreed."

Triarch Ghaz regarded the clerics, a wealth of protest behind his eyes. None of it reached his lips. "Witnessed and agreed," he said.

Triarch Hiwa nodded to the guards. "Take them to the Tohr."

5
Quil

Later in the evening, Quil bought Sufiyan a sketchbook and pencils for his yearfall—small enough that the gift wouldn't feel like a burden. Suf said nothing of what happened in the market. He thanked Quil for the gift and disappeared into the arched hallways of Navium's royal palace. To draw, Quil hoped. Or more likely to forget his sadness with whoever happened to be around.

For his part, Quil knew he should find his aunt and ask her about the deaths she'd kept from him. But he couldn't come right out and say it because she'd dodge his questions. He'd have to be clever.

He walked through the imperial gardens, breathing in the cool sea air. Quil spent so many nights under the stars that most Martial palaces felt like prisons to him. But Navium's was different.

Aunt Helene had insisted on extensive grounds with mosaic-tiled pools, flowers tumbling down high archways, and neat hedges that bloomed a fiery red in the autumn. She groused about the groundkeepers eating up the treasury. But when she passed through these manicured spaces, she always lingered—as Quil did now.

The prince slowed in the sculpture garden, where human warriors battled jinn—magical creatures carved to look like smokeless fire. In one corner, a Scholar man offered a Martial child a carved horse. In another, a falcon screamed in triumph, wings outstretched.

Someone had lit the lamps along a black stone path, and Quil followed it to three figures carved of pale gray marble. They stood with heads bowed and hands clasped, as if in supplication. His long dead maternal grandparents, and his Aunt Hannah. All had died at the hands of his father, Emperor Marcus Farrar.

The most hated man in Martial history.

His father had been cruel and murderous, as well as an inept ruler. He'd nearly lost the Empire when Karkaun barbarians invaded twenty years ago. Sometimes, Quil was certain that Marcus was the reason his aunt had sent him to the Tribal Lands, instead of allowing him to remain at her side. She didn't want to look at anything that reminded her of the monster who'd slaughtered her family.

Most of what Quil had learned about his father had been stolen, overheard in conversation, or gleaned from history books before his aunt whisked them away.

The only person who had spoken openly to Quil about Marcus was his paternal grandmother. He'd sat in her kitchen as a boy eating almond cookies. He'd seen himself in her long lashes and gold skin, her dark waves and high cheekbones and the measured way she spoke.

Your father loved those too, she'd told him as he enjoyed the cookies. *He and your Uncle Zak—they were beautiful boys. Good boys. Until Blackcliff, anyway.*

So, this was what he knew of his father. The man's disastrous, short reign, and the fact that he'd loved almond cookies. No paintings of Marcus existed. No busts or sculptures. Certainly not here in Navium.

There was, however, a statue of Quil's mother, Livia Aquilla. He stopped before her, seeking a reminder, perhaps, that he wasn't just his father's son. Assurance, for he was sick to death of dreading his future.

"Is this my fate, then, Mother?" He took in the high forehead he'd inherited, the full upper lip. "To take the throne? To never be free of it?" His skin crawled at the thought. Not just because of the unending constraints of the crown—his aunt hardly had a minute to herself. But because he'd read enough history to know that power corrupted. His father, who ruled before Aunt Helene, was evidence of that.

"What if I end up exactly like him?"

Power doesn't have to corrupt. Not if you're wise about it, instead of thoughtless.

Tas's words. Quil wished for his friend now, for Tas helped Quil untangle his thoughts. Tas, an orphan like Quil, was father and brother and blood in a way that few others were.

Years ago, after Elias and Laia married, Tribe Saif adopted Tas and he grew up with Quil. The prince's first memory was lying on a woven mat next to Tas as the elder child pointed out constellations above.

That big bird-looking thing? That's the falcon. Aquillus. That's your family's symbol. When Tas realized how much Quil hated his given name, he'd started calling him Aquillus—Quil—and refused to stop no matter what Aunt Hel said. Eventually, everyone else followed.

But Tas was gone, off on another mission for Aunt Helene. *Going through half the treasury,* his aunt had grumbled. Tas did have expensive taste. Charming, quick with a blade, and wickedly clever, he was the consummate spy, appearing not quite Scholar nor Martial, but a bit of both. Quil missed his irreverent humor, the stories of his adventures. He hadn't heard from Tas in months.

In truth, Tas's presence wouldn't make a difference. Quil wouldn't abdicate, no matter how much he wished to. Not after everything Aunt Helene had endured to secure the throne. Not after all she'd lost because of him.

"Cousin! I've been looking for you."

Quil stepped away from the statue, though the speaker would not judge him for talking to it.

Throughout Quil's life, Aunt Helene had tried to engender a closeness with Marcus's many family members. One of them was the girl approaching with a mallet tucked under one arm and a miniature catapult in the other.

"Cousin Arelia." He reached out a hand in greeting, but she rolled her eyes and gathered him in a hug, promptly dropping the mallet on his foot.

She wore dark blue engineers' coveralls, the pockets filled with all manner of rattling objects; her loose, brown-blond curls were pulled back into a bun. Quil was taller and broader than his cousin, and her skin was warmer—closer to Sufiyan's coloring. Quil tended toward contemplation and control, whereas Reli was forever muttering to herself and experimenting with dangerous ideas, chaos trailing. But they both had the hallmark strong jaw and pale hazel eyes of Gens Farrar.

"Glad I caught you." Arelia released him. "I saw the oddest blueprint on your aunt's desk when I was giving her an update on the bridge restorations. Here, hold my trebuchet—" Reli shoved it at him and patted her coveralls, pulling out a silver hammer, a leather hair thong, and a foreign coin before shaking her head.

"Had a sketch. Gone now. It could be a weapon, but I hope it's a form of transport because skies know livestock and barges are too slow. In the south, the Kegari travel by air. Air!"

"What good are aircraft if they're only used to raid and pillage?" Quil said. His aunt had expressed worry about Kegar, a nation so troublesome that even though they were thousands of miles to the south, their warmongering was affecting Empire allies.

"If we could get a look at their transports—"

"Good luck," Quil said. "They only talk to the Ankanese. Any time the Mariners have sent a ship down there, it disappears. They're worse than the bleeding Karkauns."

The smile dropped off Reli's face. "No one is worse than the Karkauns." Like most Martials, her hatred of the Empire's southern neighbors ran bone-deep—a savage occupation would do that to a populace. "Your aunt would agree—which reminds me. She's looking for you. What did you do to irritate her?"

"I'm sure she'll tell me," Quil muttered.

"You should apologize. Rumor is that she had a report from the Ankanese ambassador, warning her about Kegari unrest. Scant on details, but it put her in a foul mood. And a Jaduna Raan-Ruku arrived this morning, so she's antsy, too."

Arelia shuddered at the mention of the Jaduna, a group of magic-users so powerful, so shrouded in mystery that even Aunt Helene treated them with caution.

Quil frowned. The Raanis—the six women who ruled the Jaduna people—did not usually leave their lands. Instead, they sent their Raan-Ruku—*Wolves of the Mother*—as emissaries. *Strong in magic*, Aunt Hel told him years ago. *Never to be crossed. You will know them by the shape of their coins, triangles flanking a circle.*

But they didn't visit the Empire often. Usually only in times of emergency.

Quil and Arelia both turned at the tinkle of metal behind them. The prince's blood went cold at the sight of a blond Jaduna, wearing a heavily embroidered robe with bell sleeves and a golden headdress. It was decorated with triangle coins and a single circle, in the center.

She fixed her kohl-lined eyes on Quil as if she wished to bore into his brain. Sweat trickled down his back. He'd once read an old folktale about a substance that suppressed magic. He wished the stories were true, wished he could wrap himself in it so the Jaduna sorceress wouldn't know what lived inside him.

Now it was too late. The Jaduna must be aware of his magic. She'd have told Aunt Hel. And he'd be forced to train with them—

But she merely inclined her head and walked on. Quil bolted for his room, glancing back to make sure the Jaduna hadn't followed. Arelia kept pace, as keen to escape the Jaduna as he was. Magic perplexed her, as she couldn't take it apart.

"Oh." Arelia pulled a small book out of her coveralls. *Recollections* by Rajin of Serra. "Stole this from you a few days ago. I knew it would take you another three years to finish."

Quil winced as they turned into the passageway that led to his quarters. "I only got it from the library a week ago." He nodded a greeting to the Masks guarding the hall.

"If you spent less time bashing shields with that scim-happy friend of yours—"

"His name is Sufiyan, as you well know, and he's more healer than fighter—"

"Then maybe"—Arelia pushed open the door to Quil's room and offered him the book—"you'd have finished it faster. Too much ancient lore and navel-gazing for me, but I did find the drawings of his war machines enlightening."

BOOM. A door slammed distantly and footsteps thunked down the hall.

"Right," Arelia said. "I'll take my leave."

"Coward!" he called as she slipped away. A minute later, Aunt Helene strode through his door, kicking it shut behind her.

"Aunt," he said. "I saw a Jaduna Raan-Ruku—"

"Routine visit. Sit." She pointed at a posh settee. "Now."

She spoke with the toneless frigidity of a Mask—something she reverted to when she was giving orders or tamping down her anger. Quil's own frustration rose. He wasn't in the mood for another lecture.

Still, he sat, watching Aunt Hel pace. To the distress of the court clothiers, Empress Helene mostly wore plain black fatigues, with a scim strapped across her back. The only indication of her rank was a silver circlet pinned to her crown braid—one that Quil had seen flung to the side of a training field, tossed in with the laundry, and once, most strangely, sitting atop the head of a particularly ugly gargoyle on the roof of the palace in Antium.

They'd laughed when he'd found it up there, but the Empress was the furthest thing from laughter now. She crossed her arms and pinned him with her pale blue gaze.

"You were overheard in the market today," she said. "Speaking with Sufiyan about abdication."

"Were you spying—"

"I didn't have to spy on you. Half the city heard you. Including the Paters of Gens Candela, Duria, and Visselia."

"We were only talking, Aunt Hel. I didn't mean—"

"Those men rule their Gens with iron fists. Their heirs don't so much as sneeze without their permission. Yet here I am, Empress and Mater of my own bleeding family, and I can't get my nephew to show decorum in public. You cannot act like some ranting revolutionary plotting to bring down the government!"

You used to be that revolutionary, Aunt. You and Mother and Laia and Elias. Twenty years ago, when a jinn known as the Nightbringer tried to wipe out humanity, Aunt Helene defied the powerful families of the Empire and took her troops into battle. Quil wanted to remind her. But that was as wise as flashing a scarlet centurion's cloak in front of a cranky bull. He kept his mouth shut.

"You are the crown prince. You're to be Emperor, Zacharias."

The sound of that name was as pleasant as the shriek of an axe splintering wood. It reminded him of his demon of a father and the twin brother he'd murdered—and then named his son after.

"How could you be so careless?" The Empress stopped pacing. "You know what this throne has cost. You'll throw it away because you don't want responsibility?"

"It's not about responsibility," Quil said. *I don't want to be like my father. But if I tell you that, you'll dismiss it because you hate talking about him. So, there's no bleeding point.* "Abdication isn't unheard of. The crown princess of Sunn—"

"Abdicated because Sunnese rebels threatened regicide," Aunt Hel said. "They still killed her, and now the country is starving. They've been begging us for grain and could barely muster up a defense force when the Kegari raided them last year."

"The Ankanese—"

"Have a representative government overseen by a single spiritual leader."

Though he was nearly a half foot taller than his aunt, Quil felt small suddenly. Cut down to a schoolchild who hasn't remembered the day's lesson. This was why he hadn't spoken to her about abdication. He wanted to research. To come up with legitimate arguments and explanations. He wanted to make a case so effective she'd be forced to consider it.

"I've managed to silence any word of your . . . misstep," the Empress said. "But that brings me to another matter. Your guard captain said you first ordered him to leave you and then rushed toward an altercation."

Finally, an opening. "Something awful happened in the square—"

"Yes. A dead child. Before you ask, I won't discuss the details."

"Why?" Quil shot back. "Why, when other children have died and you're doing nothing about it?"

"This is exactly why you need guards," Aunt Hel said.

Her blatant evasion was so bleeding infuriating that he almost threw something at her head. But she'd only storm off and he'd never get any answers. Quil pitched his voice low, so as not to sound petulant.

"I don't need guards."

"Just because you've been trained to fight—"

"By the greatest warrior in the Empire."

The Empress's lips thinned. "I wouldn't call him *the greatest*—"

Quil snorted. "Every year you and Elias have that ridiculous duel and every year he beats you."

"I beat him three years ago! And stop changing the subject." The Empress's cheeks turned red, and the pale ghosts of two scars appeared on her face.

They were the only remnant of her mask, the liquid metal that once covered her face and marked her as an elite soldier of the Empire—a Mask. Whenever Quil wanted to whine about his duties as heir, he'd remind himself that Aunt Hel trained and suffered for fourteen years at Blackcliff Academy. She'd revered the Holy Augurs who founded the school, and whose predictions had guided the Empire for centuries. She'd knelt as the Augurs had laid the handcrafted mask of living metal upon her face.

Aunt Hel had trusted the Augurs even though they deceived her. Quil was glad he'd never have to meet them. They were dead now. But Blackcliff still trained its recruits rigorously, and the Masks lived on, their face coverings taken from soldiers who had fallen and refashioned for new troops every year.

As Aunt Hel touched her scars, Quil knew she was fighting an urge to bellow at him, even as he suppressed his own glare. His aunt loved him, true. But some days it felt like it was because she had to, and not because she wanted to. Some days, Quil thought Aunt Hel would never stop seeing her dead sister in his face and his father in his eyes.

Deep in Quil's chest, a familiar sensation. An unfurling—warm, as if he'd taken a draught of hot, spiced cider amid a snowstorm. It was his magic responding to his frustration, eager to be used, to read Aunt Helene's emotions, her memories, to sway her the way he wished.

Quil shoved the unwanted inclination back into a box. Memories were private, meant to be offered—not taken. Emotions were meant to be experienced or shared—not stolen and manipulated. Quil couldn't bring himself to sink into someone's mind without permission. It felt like something his father would do if he had possessed magic. The violation was unconscionable.

The Empress cracked her knuckles and walked to the window. Her gaze roved the balconies and parapets of the royal residence. She was always vigilant; it was a habit that would never die.

"I'm sorry I got so angry," she said after a minute, her voice almost subdued as she turned and sat beside him. "Listen. Please."

A chill rippled across Quil's spine at the shift in her demeanor. Whatever she was going to say, she sensed he would hate it.

"You are twenty," she said. "Old enough to assume the throne. We are to have a fete in five days to mark Rathana. I plan to use the occasion to announce your coronation in the spring. You're ready. And I . . . I am finished with this." She gestured to her circlet, to the royal residence. "I've given up enough of my life for the Empire. Long ago, I swore to see you on the throne. It's time to keep my promise."

Quil felt as if hands were dragging him down into a cold ocean, holding him deep beneath the surface. He couldn't find words, only a well of denial choking the breath out of him.

"I know you don't want this, nephew," the Empress said. "Skies know I didn't want it either. But it will be good for you. You hide it well, but you've walked with shadows these many months. You loved Ilar and Ruh. Their loss—"

Helene shook her head, and Quil knew she remembered her own lost love, dead twenty years now.

"I understand. Of all people in the world, I do. The business of ruling will give you purpose beyond grief. You were born to a Plebeian and an Illustrian. Brought into the world by a Scholar. Raised among the Tribes. You are the best of the Empire. And she needs you. Remember the words of your Gens." *Loyal to the end.*

The Empress stood smoothly, shoulders thrown back, eyes burning like blue fire, as if she didn't hold the weight of millions of souls upon her shoulders. Quil wondered if he'd carry the crown so effortlessly. If he'd move through the world with the knowledge that he was exactly where he should be.

Perhaps he would. Or perhaps his heart would turn cold, his face hard. Perhaps he would become resentful and bitter like his father—or any number of Martial emperors who were more monster than human.

"Why didn't you tell me?" Quil asked again when she was at the door. "About the dead children?"

His aunt paused, her back to him. "Grief is a strange beast. Some battle it, their souls scarred from its abuse. Some bury it, and live life waiting for it to reemerge. And some tread water, the grief a weight about their necks. Every reminder makes the weight heavier." She turned halfway, her face in profile. "You and I tread water, nephew. And I would not see you drown."

A moment later, the Empress was gone. Quil thought of the wide spaces in the Tribal Lands. Of racing across those long flat deserts, sleeping beneath that crystalline night sky. Since he was torturing himself anyway, he allowed his thoughts to stray to Ilar, the way she'd walk for hours at night and return to him, a half smile on her face, the scent of wind and roses in her hair.

He missed her. He missed that life. He wanted it so badly he could smell the heat and feel the stars between his fingers.

But it didn't matter what he wanted. *Remember the words of your Gens.* The Empress had spoken.

And he was loyal. To the end.

Five days later, Quil found himself awaiting his aunt in a long stone hallway outside the palace's throne room, searching for serenity and failing to find it.

He pulled at the collar of the tunic, which fit him about as well as an assassin's garrote. At least it was blue and silver—Gens Aquilla colors. The imperial clothier tried to force Quil into a black-and-gold outfit—

a nod to Gens Farrar and an unsubtle reminder of Quil's Plebeian origins.

But Quil wasn't stupid. This party was going to be bad enough without his foes muttering about his unworthiness as heir.

With his guards looking on, Quil paced back and forth. He'd brought Rajin of Serra's *Recollections* with him—Arelia was pestering him to finish it—but he couldn't focus, and eventually shoved it in his pocket.

Two winters ago, he'd spent Rathana with Tribe Saif in Nur. They celebrated midwinter with fire-throwers and acrobats and spit-roasted deer. Laia, the Tribe's Kehanni and storyteller and history-keeper, told a dozen tales. Sufiyan's little sisters won a dueling contest, and Sufiyan and his little brother cleared out the moon cake stall.

It was the happiest Rathana that Quil could remember.

Now he was here wearing ill-fitting clothing and with shadows beneath his eyes. His coronation would be announced tonight. His fate sealed.

The steady clip of boots was a blessed distraction, and he looked up as his aunt rounded the corner into the hall. She wore her ceremonial armor and dented coronet, her silver-blond hair tucked into a crown braid.

"Have you heard anything from Tas?" Quil asked before his aunt could speak. Better to find out now, before she got swept away by every member of court who wanted a piece of her.

"The Blood Shrike is to arrive tomorrow from Antium," Aunt Helene said, speaking of her second-in-command. "We'll ask her."

Quil knew Aunt Hel well enough to sense she was dissembling. He'd overheard her fighting with Tas nearly six months ago, the day before Tas left on a mission he never returned from. Most of the court heard it, as it had happened in the bleeding throne room.

What the hells is the point of having an adviser if you never listen to the advice? Tas accused the Empress.

Say something worth hearing, you drunken lout, Aunt Helene snapped, *and maybe I will.*

Certainly, Tas was a libertine. He found whatever perks there were in espionage and enjoyed them to the fullest. But he'd spent years carrying out missions for Aunt Hel. And still, she kept him at arm's distance.

"Tas is a brother to me and I'd like the truth," Quil said. "Even if you two don't always get along."

His aunt's eyebrows shot up. "Tas is a loyal servant of the Empire," she said. "And I'm deeply appreciative of all that he's sacrificed. As I said, we'll ask the Shrike."

So diplomatic. And cryptic. That was Aunt Hel, always implying something without saying it. It made Quil want to shout, but he bit back his discontent.

His aunt took his arm and they walked to two huge doors—carved with the falcon of Gens Aquilla—that led into the throne room. Aunt Helene stopped to take a breath, as she had the very first time he'd joined her at a public event. He'd been seven, solemn and poker stiff beside her, smoothing down his shirt over and over because he'd wanted to make her proud.

Do you mind if we wait a moment? she'd asked him. *Sometimes I'm nervous before I go in. If I take a second to breathe, it helps.*

"It's a battle on the other side, you know," she said now, voice soft. "But not the kind I spent my youth training for. Your mother was so much better at this."

"You're better at it than you think, Aunt Hel."

She smiled faintly. "You'll be better at it still. Ready?"

For a moment, the distance between them dropped away, and he smiled back, his lone dimple a mirror of hers.

"As I'll ever be." He gave the answer he always did. She nodded to the guards, and the doors swung open. Every head turned as a herald announced them.

"Empress Helene Aquilla, High Commander of the Martial Army, Imperator Invictus, and Overlord of the Realm, and her nephew and heir, Zacharias Marcus Livius Aquillus Farrar, Lieutenant Commander of the Imperial Army and Crown Prince of the Realm."

"What a bleeding mouthful," Aunt Hel muttered as the room bowed. She gave an imperious half nod in greeting, then gestured to the musicians, who promptly began to strum their instruments. Almost before she'd stepped into the room, she was surrounded, a dozen voices clamoring for her attention.

Quil stepped back and took in the party. Hundreds of colored Tribal lamps cast a soft light over the room. A groaning table was filled with Scholar delicacies like sugared nuts wrapped in paper-thin pastry, minced meat enrobed in spiced tea leaves. The musicians were Scholars too. Quil didn't see much about the gathering that was Martial. The way the Plebeians kept to the edges of the crowd, perhaps. The way nearly every person was armed.

Distantly, through windows opened to keep the room temperate, Quil heard the drums echo, marking the change of the city guard.

"Greetings, crown prince."

Quil bowed his head to the green-robed, white-haired woman who'd finished speaking with the Empress. The pear-shaped jewels edging her robe flashed in the lamplight.

"Ambassador Ifalu," he greeted her. "You are to return home tomorrow, yes? We will miss you at court. My aunt especially."

"I will miss the Empire—and the Empress. She has been a good friend to me in my years here." The ambassador glanced at the Empress with affection. "But I long for Ankana. You have seen the beauty of our capital. My family is there. My parents and cousins. My duty to them calls me home."

The ambassador was the only child of a high-ranking Ankanese family. They expected she would be named High Seer one day.

"Congratulations are in order, I hear," the ambassador said. "Are you happy?"

A question Quil couldn't answer honestly. "I am the heir," he said.

"I see." The ambassador's brows dipped in sympathy. "You do not wear the mask, but you were trained as one. *Duty first, unto death*—is that not their motto? It always spoke to me, for I, too, am dutiful. Fear not, prince. You will do good for this world. Emifal Firdaant." She offered the traditional Ankanese words of parting—*May death claim me first*—and faded into the crowd.

Moments later, a voice spoke up from behind Quil.

"Skies save me, Quil, but who tailored that tunic for you? The fall is all wrong."

Quil smiled and turned to the tall, dark-haired man emerging from the crowd of partygoers. Musa of Adisa. To most here, he was the ambassador of Marinn, a seafaring kingdom east of the Empire. The Empress referred to Musa on some days as "beloved," on others as "you jinn-touched demon of a man." To Quil, he was simply a friend.

"Didn't think you were coming," Quil greeted Musa.

"Your aunt asked me." Musa shrugged. "I am, as always, her humble servant. Unlike the castle clothier, who clearly has it in for you. I swear to the skies, that old man wouldn't know fashion if it bit him on the arse. Here." Musa loosened the top button of Quil's tunic and draped his own scarf about the younger man's neck. He caught Quil's eye. "How are we feeling about today? Not planning anything reckless?"

Quil laughed, though it sounded hollow. "When have I ever been reckless?"

"Maybe that's your problem." Musa tracked Helene as she moved about the room. "You're a model prince, Quil. She tells you to attend a party, you arrive early. She tells you to fight Karkauns, you seize their cities and expand the Empire in her name. She tells you you're going to be Emperor . . ." He shrugged.

"I know my duty, Musa."

"Yes, duty." Musa snagged a deep-fried potato cutlet from a nearby server. "Your family makes much of duty. But you're twenty, Quil. You shouldn't be chained to the throne. Or to your aunt's wishes. You can tell her I said that." Musa winked and took a bite. "She and I are due for a good, long . . . argument."

Quil gagged audibly at the insinuation as Musa walked away, laughing. Only a moment later, the prince, still disgusted, was accosted by a Pater who'd finished speaking to Aunt Helene.

"What do you think of your aunt's plan, Your Highness?" Pater Vissellius oozed forward, clapping the younger man on the shoulder. "No objections?"

"Do shut up, Vissellius." A woman with massive rings in her ears and ghas stains on her fingers appeared at his side: Mater Andricar, a wily old creature whom Quil had always liked.

The old woman took a thin cigarillo from her bodice and lit it on a nearby brazier.

"The boy supports his aunt. The Empress is only being reasonable." Mater Andricar blew ghas smoke into Vissellius's pale face. "She must secure the line."

Vissellius coughed, waving the smoke away. "A bit rich, seeing as she never had children herself. Why does it have to be a foreigner?"

"To make a strong ally! The girl's highborn, I hear. If it's done before the coronation, all the better. The prince's bride will—"

Quil, who'd begun to inch away from the two gossips, froze. "I'm sorry," he said. "What's this about a bride?"

Vissellius and Andricar exchanged a glance. The former quickly took a large sip of wine to hide the barely repressed glee seeping from every pore.

"Why, my dear prince, didn't the Empress tell you?" Andricar, to her credit, appeared genuinely shocked. "You are engaged to be married."

6
Sirsha

The man was surprisingly polite for a client—if enigmatic. He was evasive about the details of the job, and while some might see that as dishonest, Sirsha saw it as intelligent. Anyone trusting enough to put all their cards on the table with a stranger was too naive to work with.

Sirsha held her hands up to the fire that the man kept burning despite the accursed damp. After he hauled her up from the maw of the Jutts, they'd gone to his camp on the south side of the Roost, in one of the many caves that pitted those hills. On the way, he explained the job: To track a murderer. One who targeted young people.

"How did you know where to find me?" she asked the man now.

He kept an eye on the storm outside, his back to the wall as she awaited his response. His wariness was oddly reassuring. For the first time in weeks, maybe months, Sirsha didn't feel like she was about to get stabbed between the shoulder blades.

"I asked around," the man said. "Overheard your dead nemesis plotting against you. Figured you'd have to escape into the Jutts eventually. The path you took is the one I'd have used."

Sirsha supposed that was his version of a compliment, but she didn't like being so predictable. Then again, she didn't like dealing with fools either. She'd have to tread carefully.

"Migva wasn't a nemesis. Just a greedy Roost rat."

He ripped off a piece of the flatbread he'd warmed over the fire and took a bite. Then he handed the rest to her. She considered him as she ate. There was something familiar about him. Something that nagged at her. It would come to her, eventually. What she needed to know now was how much he was willing to pay—and whether it was worth it.

He was a Martial, that was clear. Built like a soldier and in fighting shape, with a touch of silver threading through his dark hair. Finely made boots, a single, well-crafted scim strapped across his back. He was likely Illustrian—a member of the highest Martial class. Whatever he offered, she decided she'd ask for double.

"You're not telling me everything about the job," she said. "Or yourself. I'd like to know who I'm working for. Do you have a name?"

The man shrugged. "Not one that matters. I've told you what you need to know."

"You feed me dribbles of information and I suss out the rest?" Sirsha laughed. "I don't like games."

His face went still then, and there, in the sudden bleakness of his pale eyes, Sirsha saw all his dead. All his ghosts. The fire flickered and the wind screamed into the cave, an eldritch warning.

"It's not a game," the man said softly. "Sixteen children are dead. Perhaps more."

"I'm not a bounty hunter," Sirsha said. "I track down cheating spouses. Traitorous business partners. The odd jewel thief. If the children were missing, I could help you. Tracking killers seems like a quick way to get a knife in the eyeball. In any case, I can't drag a murderer all the way back from whatever hidey-hole—"

"Rodinius Lucius."

Sirsha started at the name before recovering. "I don't know who—"

"He tricked an entire village out of its gold, up in Marinn. He and his gang killed a family on their way out of town. Authorities couldn't help. The village headman traveled to Taib looking for someone to seek justice and found you. You hunted down Lucius, recovered the gold, and dragged him back to face the villagers. Killed three of his associates in the process. You were what . . . fifteen at the time?"

"Now, look here, they tried to kill *me* first—"

"I won't judge you for killing someone in self-defense." The man's face went hard, and Sirsha glanced at his scim. It looked well-worn.

"Don't act like you can't handle this job," the man went on. "Doing so is beneath you." He leaned forward. The fire made his eyes glow orange. "Track down this child-killer. Shove a knife through his throat or bring him to me alive so I can do it myself, I don't care. I'll pay you a thousand marks either way."

Sirsha nearly choked on the flatbread. A thousand marks would get her out of the Empire for good. Set her up with a nice little guesthouse in the Southern Isles. In time, she could hire help. She might be able to avoid tracking entirely.

Freedom, she thought desperately, *finally*. She knew her hunger was written all over her face, but was unable to care.

"Two thousand," she haggled, more out of habit than because she felt she was being underpaid. "And it's a deal."

"Thirteen hundred," the man said. "And I'll throw in enough for transport and supplies."

Sirsha raised an eyebrow. She hadn't expected him to budge quite that much. A voice inside her head, one that had kept her alive since she'd struck out on her own at the age of twelve, whispered at her. *Careful, Sirsha.*

Sirsha's skill lay not just in tracking, but in tracking magic—and binding it. But she didn't do that anymore—on pain of death. Such were the conditions of her banishment from her people.

A Martial wouldn't know all that. Still, Sirsha didn't want to directly ask if the killer had magic. Her client would want to know why she cared. She'd have to lie. And he was obviously not the type of man who suffered liars.

"This killer," she said carefully. "There's nothing . . . unnatural about him, is there? He's not a jinn, say? Or some kind of otherworldly entity that will rip out my innards?"

The man furrowed his brow, incredulous. "Of course he's unnatural.

He kills young people for sport. And jinn keep to themselves in the Forest of Dusk. They want nothing to do with the world of man."

Can't say I blame them. "Half the money now," Sirsha said.

He scoffed. "And have you run away with it? I'll give you a hundred marks now, plus twenty more for supplies." He pulled a small leather pouch of coins from his cloak and tossed it at her. It landed in her palm with a satisfying *clink*. There were at least one hundred twenty marks in here. Maybe more. It was a third of the amount she'd saved up over the last eight years. Sirsha checked the gold with her teeth. Real.

"Before I forget, take this." He pulled a ring from his right hand, flat and silver, with an X etched onto it. "When you find the killer, bring it to any Martial garrison or Tribal or Mariner embassy. They'll help you get him—or his head—back to me. I'll pay you the rest when the job's done."

"I don't walk away once I've taken a job." Sirsha examined the ring before tucking it away. "Ask anyone I've worked for."

"In that case, you won't mind swearing on it."

Sirsha didn't see him draw the blade. She only realized he'd done so when he cut a line into his hand, flipped the knife around, and offered it to her.

She considered him over the fire. He was wily. Cunning. And he knew more about her than he let on. Among Sirsha's people, blood oaths were not made lightly.

"Who are you?" she asked him.

"A man looking for justice." He held the knife out again, but she still didn't take it.

"You managed to track me, so you're clearly capable," she said. "I wager you're good in a fight. Why not kill this murderer yourself?"

"I've tried to hunt him," the Martial said. "For months. He's eluded me." He looked away, jaw tightening. "I can hunt no longer. I must return to my family. I'll travel with you until you catch the trail. Then I'll be on my way. I need you, Sirsha Westering. I don't have time to dicker anymore." He offered the knife a third time. "Will you help me?"

Thirteen hundred marks on one hand. On the other, a blood oath that she could never break—not unless this fellow died or spoke words to release her. If she tried to walk away, the oath would bend her body and mind back to her vow. Eating, sleeping, bathing—it would all become secondary to hunting down this killer and either sticking a knife in his gut or dragging him back to her client.

Ah well. It wasn't like she had any other prospects. From what the Martial described, the killer was human, which meant a relatively quick chase.

She took the blade, cut open her hand, and pressed it against his before she could second-guess herself. Before the warning in her head became a screaming howl.

There was a brief chill between their palms, like they'd plunged them into snow. A moment later, it was gone. Cold flared near Sirsha's neck, and the thin gold chain she wore grew heavier. She fidgeted. It had been years since her magic conjured an oath coin. She felt the ice of the vow she'd made sink into her very marrow, and wondered what in the skies she'd agreed to.

They made their way out of the Roost on horses the Martial had procured. The sky loomed low and threatening. To the south and east, thick bands of rain smudged the horizon. The horses would be ankle-deep in mud by midday. Sirsha glared at the heavy clouds.

"The entire reason I moved to the desert was so I wouldn't have to deal with the bleeding rain," she said.

"It must interfere with tracking."

"Mmm," Sirsha grumbled unintelligibly. The Martial didn't need to know that she wasn't one to paw at the ground looking for boot prints. Sirsha's skill lay in reading the language of the natural elements: The way the sand shifted and the wind whispered and the rain fell, the way the land warped to give her a picture of the past. Of what had passed through and when.

The earth, wind, and water were always speaking. Sirsha was one of the rare few who knew how to listen.

Her people called it Inashi. *Scenting.* But she didn't use that word. It made her think of hounds, bound to the will of their masters. No, she called it tracking, and it allowed her to hunt down her quarry faster than those relying on traditional methods. Which meant with any luck, this job would be done before the end of the week, her vow fulfilled, and she'd be on a ship heading far away from the Empire with a fat sack of gold.

If the land deigned to tell her its secrets, anyway. All magic—no matter who wielded it—required two things: an emotion and an element. Sirsha had emotion aplenty. Desire, curiosity, anger, annoyance, greed—with enough focus, any of them would work.

The elements, however, were wide-ranging and capricious. Like toddlers or goats, they didn't always cooperate. Reading the earth was simple. It projected a map of nearby terrain in her mind, and told her where her quarry was. But wind and water were a different matter.

Speak to me, she called to the elements. *Who walked here? What violence did they carry with them?*

"It rains a great deal in the west, yes?" Her client's question pulled her from her work, and she frowned in irritation.

"I wouldn't know." Sirsha refused to confirm anything he might have heard about her origins. She didn't like to think about it, and in any case, it was none of his damned business. Besides, she *didn't* know. Eight years had passed since she'd seen the Cloud Forest near her home. Maybe the rains had stopped.

"If you wouldn't mind," she said, "I'm working. A bit of space would be appreciated. And silence."

She turned away before he could respond, and pondered the details of the killings that he had been willing to share. The number of dead. How they'd died. When she was sure the Martial was well ahead and couldn't see or hear her, she began to whisper what she'd learned. The earth was always listening.

Around her, shadows emerged from the landscape. Shadows she knew the man couldn't see. Slowly, a figure took shape. She expected it to be marred by violence, trailing the dead. But it appeared alone. It was strangely skittish and she strained to see it better, but it sat at the edge of her vision. When she tried to look at it directly with her mind's eye, it disappeared.

Unusual. Her power was reliable, for the most part. Sirsha told the elements what she wanted. One or all of them provided a trail. She used common sense and poisoned blades to keep troublemakers in line. In a pinch, she could usually wheedle aid from the earth or wind. Most contracts took no more than a week.

Sirsha slowed her horse and peered around, waiting for a trail to emerge, for the earth to show her something else.

"We can head west, to Serra," the man said from ahead of her, and Sirsha realized she had no idea how long he'd been talking. "The last few victims were there, so the killer might be as well. He might even—"

She. Not he.

To Sirsha's surprise, it was the wind who spoke. The wind was taciturn, and despite witnessing practically everything that went on, it preferred to observe, not aid.

Which way should I go? Sirsha asked it, unsurprised when no answer came. She supposed it didn't really matter. She hadn't gotten quite what she needed, but she'd learned enough to realize she shouldn't head west.

"—he's ruthless in his attacks. He—"

"First of all"—Sirsha gave her mount a nudge so she could catch up to the man—"the killer's not a *he*."

At the man's surprise, she scoffed. "You don't think women can be so brutal. Or that it might not be a he or a she?"

"I know very well that women can be brutal." The man's shoulders tightened. "*He* was a general term. The former ambassador of Ankana is a friend. They are a dona'i and their people have multiple classifications for gender—"

"No need to get huffy," Sirsha said. "Your killer isn't male or dona'i. She's a woman. Second, she didn't go west. She went south. If it's all the same to you, I'll go my way, and you go yours. I know how to find you."

The man brought his mount around and considered her from beneath his hood. She stared boldly back, but was again struck by a sudden familiarity. She knew she'd never seen him before. He was a big man, with a face and form not easily forgotten. And yet . . .

She eyed him, looking for a telltale warp in the air that would indicate the presence of magic. Nothing. But that didn't mean he didn't have it. Occasionally, the strong-minded could bury their magic deep enough that not even a rivulet leaked out.

"If you know an ambassador, you have friends in high places," Sirsha said. "Why not ask them for help?"

"There's only so much they can do. And this is personal."

Sirsha pulled her mount to a stop, though the rain was closing in and she knew she'd regret a delay.

"How personal?" she said.

"South, you said." He stared out at the desert. "I must bear west, to Serra, so I'll be on my way."

"Not yet." Sirsha nudged her mount in front of his. "Why are you keeping so many secrets?"

"I've told you what you need to know," the man said flatly. "Anything else would only put you in danger."

"You can't ignore my questions! You hired me to track for you—"

"Track," the man cut her off, hands knuckled tight around the reins of his horse. "An interesting word. But not the right one, I think."

He knows. Whoever he is, he knows what you truly are.

When Sirsha was a child, one of her aunts had been shunned by Kin Inashi—Sirsha's family—for reasons the girl never learned. Like most of those cast out, Auntie Vee was ordered to give up her magic or face the consequences.

Kin Inashi was vast, made up of scores of smaller families. But Auntie Vee's immediate family was renowned for their tracking. Auntie Vee thought she could use her magic to hide her trail.

Sirsha's older sister, R'zwana, helped hunt Auntie Vee down days after she was banished. She was drowned, her body left as carrion that she might never return to the earth that nourished her.

Years later, when Kin Inashi cast Sirsha out, her mother had unwittingly—or perhaps wittingly, Sirsha never could tell—left a loophole. The girl was told to never again use her magic to hunt *as your Kin had hunted*.

Since they hunted dangerous magic-users by employing skills that Sirsha possessed but avoided using, she figured she was in the clear.

Still, she waited a year—until she was thirteen—and a thousand miles to use her tracking. And even now, seven years after that, she wouldn't take a job if she risked running into a member of her Kin, no matter how lucrative it was. None of her employers knew where she was from or how she tracked. If she caught the slightest whiff of magic, the deal was off.

But this fellow knew more about her than he'd let on. He could use that against her if he wished. Because while she could still officially use her magic, Sirsha had no doubt that if certain members of her Kin found out she tracked at all, they'd kill her on the spot and ask for forgiveness after.

Her hag of a sister would be first in line.

"*Not the right one*," she said. "What is that supposed to mean?"

"It means, Sirsha Westering, that I'll let you keep your secrets, if you leave me to mine." He gestured at the empty land to the south, and the boiling purple clouds gathering along the horizon. "South, you said. Best be on your way if you want to beat that storm."

"South," Sirsha ground out before wheeling her horse away and putting heel to flank.

7
Aiz

Among Aiz's people, the Tohr was the hunched wolf of bedtime tales, a fetid maw from which few emerged unscathed.

The prison was built into a great granite mountain that abutted the western edge of the capital. Two huge slabs of black and purple stone stood sentinel on either side of an iron gate, with a third slab resting across the top. As Aiz passed through the doorway, her windsmithing, already skittish, faded into nothingness. The mountain's rock dulled magic.

Tale-spinners said the bones of Mother Div's enemies were ground into the dust of the Tohr's lower levels, their spirits haunting the prison's depths.

Not long after Aiz entered, she began to suspect those stories were true. As the jailer walked Aiz, Sister Noa, and more than two dozen other clerics through the low hallways, the rock seemed to close in, whispering, *You will die here. Those you love will die here. It is your fault.*

Aiz glared back at the rock. "Perhaps I will," she muttered. "But I won't let them die."

One of the jailers, a short, bearded man with skin like a rotted fish's, grinned at Aiz. Half of his teeth were missing. "Already talking to ourselves, are we? You'll fit right in."

"Aiz, my love," Sister Noa murmured. "Do not fear. Mother Div is with us."

"Shut it!" barked the other jailer, a broad-shouldered woman with a scarred face. "Don't you invoke Mother Div. *Accursed are the traitors, those who forsake me.*"

"You can quote the Nine Sacred Tales," Sister Noa said. "That is heartening."

"Nine," the jailer muttered. "Never understood why they called it Nine Tales if there's only eight."

Noa smiled, a flash of light in the gloom. "I used to ask that too. What is your name, child?"

Aiz prepared to step in front of Noa, expecting the jailer's whip to come down. The woman lifted it, a vein pulsing at her temple; but then she looked between Aiz and Noa and shoved the latter forward roughly.

"We've got a special cell for you, hag," the bearded man said. "Shut your gob and move."

Aiz considered Sister Noa's words. *Mother Div is with us.* But she wasn't, was she? Not anymore. Mother Div let Aiz fail. Did nothing as Tiral's men beat and imprisoned her loyal clerics, those who shared her Sacred Tales.

If Aiz wanted to get the clerics out of here, she'd figure it out without divine aid.

They wound through long hallways lined with cells, dirty faces staring out at them, lit spectral blue by the lamps. The jailers stopped at a large, dark chamber, and the woman shoved Aiz, Noa, and Olnas inside. They'd left anything resembling sunlight long ago. Aiz could barely make out the cots and slop bucket in the corner.

The jailers disappeared with the rest of the clerics, and Aiz turned to Sister Olnas, who was pale and sweating.

"Her leg." Sister Noa gestured for Aiz to take Olnas's shoulder, and they helped her to a cot. "She needs to get off it."

"I'm so sorry, Sister Noa," Aiz said. "I didn't know they would—I didn't think—"

"It's done, child," Noa said. "Mother Div had trials too. She survived. So will we." She tilted her head, a bright-eyed bird, even in such darkness.

"Tell me a dream, little love."

Vengeance, Aiz thought.

"Getting you and all the other clerics out of here," she said.

"May Mother Div make it so." Noa's eyes went over Aiz's shoulder and widened. The girl turned, scouring the shadows near the other cot.

Shadows which, Aiz realized with horror, were moving.

"Sister Noa," she said. "Get back."

But Noa took a careful step toward the cot. "Come out, little ones," she said. "We won't hurt you."

Three children emerged from the dark, emaciated and covered in dirt and filth. Aiz stared in disbelief.

"Why—why are there children here? What could they possibly have done—"

"We didn't do anything," one of them, a girl, said. She was small, a half foot shorter than Aiz, her head too big for her body. But her eyes were a keen blue and Aiz noticed that she pushed the two other children behind her protectively. "It was our parents who did wrong. They're dead now."

"How long have you been here?" Aiz asked.

"There's scratches there." The girl nodded to the wall behind Olnas's cot. "I mark every day so we don't forget. You better not hurt us." She looked back at her two charges. "You might be bigger, but we bite."

"We would never hurt you," Sister Noa said. "I'm Sister Noa. That's Aiz. That's Sister Olnas. Will you tell me your names?"

"I'm Hani," the girl said after a long, appraising pause. "This is Jak, and Finh." Jak was smaller, but both boys had dark eyes and shorn red hair. Jak smiled shyly at Aiz, revealing a few missing teeth. Finh, Aiz noticed, had a significant limp.

"They're brothers," Hani said. "And I protect them." She looked at Aiz challengingly. "You're not a cleric."

"No," Sister Noa said. "But she tells beautiful stories. Better than me, even. Would you like to hear one?"

"Is it a scary story?" Finh asked. "I want a scary one."

"You can't have a scary one," Hani said. "Jak's too little."

"I'm not!" Jak piped up. "I like scary ones too!"

"Maybe you shouldn't tell a story." Hani glanced nervously after the jailers. "Kithka leaves us be—she's not so bad. But the other jailer, Gil—he'll throw you in the Hollows if you cause too much trouble." The girl shivered. "People aren't right if they ever come back."

"They won't throw her in the Hollows for a little story," Sister Noa said gently before turning to Aiz. "Tell them the First Sacred Tale. It was always your favorite."

I can't tell tales! I must get you out of here.

"Sister Noa"—Aiz dropped her voice—"you always said that to speak the Sacred Tales when one didn't believe was sacrilege. I am too angry. At Tiral and the Triarchs and myself. At Mother Div, most especially."

"Anger is still belief, Aiz," Sister Noa said. "Tell the tale. Not for yourself, but for the children. Div knows they must get precious little instruction here."

Aiz dug her fingers into her thigh, anger nipping at her mind, demanding to be fed. But the only person who deserved her ire was herself, so she sat on the dirty stone floor and gestured for the children to join her.

"Gather, gather and listen well, for Mother Div's voice must not be forgotten." She started the tale as all the Sacred Tales began. "Long ago and across the sea, there was a fair gold and green land that was ours alone. It had at its heart a Fount of golden light, and that was the source of our magic."

She told the children then of the cataclysm that struck the old country ten centuries ago. Of Mother Div's desperate search for a new homeland for her people. Of her elation when she discovered Kegar, a spit of land ringed by soaring rock spires.

The children listened, and Aiz heard rustles from the cell next door, saw movement through the bars as other prisoners edged forward. Once, someone called a warning and Aiz ceased until Kithka—slapping her whip against her leather pants—had stalked by. When the story was over, Hani, Jak, and Finh watched Aiz with open mouths. Prisoners murmured up and down the cellblock.

"That was beautiful," a rough voice said from across the hall—a Dafra Snipe, judging from his rounded vowels. "Tell another, would you, girl? Passes the time for the littles."

Aiz wanted to say no. But the children in her own cell looked at her hopefully.

"One more, then," she said. To her surprise, her heart lifted. Perhaps the stories that meant so much to her as a child weren't useless. "Gather, gather and listen—"

"Ssst!" a voice hissed. "Questioners!"

Panic whipped through the air like shrapnel as prisoners receded into the dark of their cells. Children cried out and were hushed as quickly. Prayers of *"Mother Div, please"* echoed through the cellblock as the tha-*thunk* tha-*thunk* of the Questioners' boots grew louder.

And louder. Until finally, the boots stopped in front of Aiz's cell. She looked up, summoning her anger. She wouldn't let these bastards break her.

The Questioners were cloaked in blue and black, faces hidden. One stepped forward, a hand on the whip at his belt.

"Clerics." His voice was menacing in its softness. "Rise."

Aiz's anger transformed into panic. "No," she said. "They didn't do anything. I'm the one who—who thought of this plot. I'm the one who—"

"The more you talk," the Questioner said, "the worse it will be for them."

Aiz held her tongue, hands shaking as Sister Olnas stumbled to her feet, Noa by her side, as the Questioners grabbed each cleric by the wrists and led them out, down the hallway to a place Aiz could not follow.

The Questioners brought Noa and Olnas back to the cell a few hours after taking them. They could hardly walk, their clothes soaked with blood and tears and grime.

"Turn away," Aiz ordered the children. Jak and Finh obeyed, covering their little faces. Hani grabbed a box from the corner, offering it to Aiz. Inside, she found a bottle of spirits, gauze, and a few clean cloths.

"Kithka gave it to me," Hani said. "Said it was to keep us from squealing too much."

"Thank you, Hani." Aiz turned to Olnas, but she waved her off.

"Hani can help me." Olnas winced as she ran her fingers through her tangled hair. "Noa took the worst of it. Tend to her first."

Aiz cleaned Sister Noa's wounds: bruises that would take weeks to heal, cuts and lacerations that would take months. *Mother Div, let her heal. Mother Div, let it be quick.*

"Aiz," Jak whispered, having broken away from Finh. He stared at Sister Noa. "Will she die? When Mam died, she looked yellow and sick like that. I—I'm scared."

Aiz took the boy's hand, her heart clenching at the way his body shook. "It's all right, little love," she whispered. "Do something for me, yes? Tell me a dream. A hope."

"A dream?" Jak appeared to have forgotten the word.

"Well . . . I dream of shoes. Thick, warm ones, with fur on the inside." Aiz wiggled her toes in the dark, and Jak's mouth turned up, just a little.

"I dream of sugar," he said. "Da brought it once. From the market."

"I dream of chicken." Finh limped over. "A big, juicy one, with red pepper and lots of salt."

Next to Olnas, Hani spoke without looking over. "I dream of the wind," she said. "I miss the sound it makes in the spring."

"May Mother Div hear you," Aiz said. "And bring you all of your beautiful dreams."

"Aiz, love." Noa's voice was a weak croak. Aiz trembled with relief that the cleric lived, followed by rage that she might have died.

"I'm sorry, Sister," Aiz whispered, trying to temper her anger. "I'm so sorry—"

"No!" Noa glared and gripped Aiz's wrist so fiercely that she flinched. "Don't you give up, girl," Noa whispered. "Hold on to your anger."

Aiz stroked the cleric's short curls. "You're never angry, Sister."

Noa smiled. "I'm angry all the time. At the world and the Triarchs and us Snipes for accepting our lot. I'm angry for myself and for you. Better anger than despair. Anger will get us through this."

She collapsed back and Aiz shook her head. There was no *through this*. There was only the Questioners finally understanding the clerics had nothing to do with the assassination attempt. The quicker Aiz could get them to take her, the quicker she could convince them of this fact.

But at sunrise, the Questioners took two other clerics. Two more each dawn after that. Again and again, Aiz watched as they dragged the clerics, tormented and beaten, back to the cellblock after their interrogations. Once, the Questioners took Olnas to the Hollows. She was only gone for a few hours, but when she returned, she didn't speak for days.

"Take me," Aiz begged the Questioners, then reasoned, then screamed. "I'm the one who tried to kill him!"

They ignored her as if she were a dead beetle, too insignificant to even be kicked out of the way.

"What can I do?" Aiz held Noa after the second time she was taken. The cleric felt so frail, as if a little pressure would wither her bones. "How do I fix this?"

"Tell the stories, my love." Noa squeezed Aiz's hands. "We all need to hear them. Tell them with wrath. Tell them with hate. But do not give up. Despair is death."

When Aiz told one of the Sacred Tales that night, her voice shook with fury. She did not care if the jailers heard and punished her.

"Gather, gather and listen well," she snarled. "For Mother Div's voice must not be forgotten!"

Aiz had told the Nine Sacred Tales often, and by now the cadence of her voice quieted all who heard her. As her anger roared out of her like a great wave, faces peeked through bars up and down the cellblock. Snipes who were sick and wounded and hopeless, yet listening.

So it went, day after day. Week after week. When the clerics returned from interrogation, beaten and broken, Aiz took her place near the cell door and preached, the Sacred Tales imbued with a fiery righteousness that made even the weakest prisoners sit up.

The girl's anger grew to an inferno, something beyond her control. The storytelling helped, but it wasn't enough. After weeks in the Tohr, Aiz felt her ire press for release. She found herself snapping at Hani, Noa, even at dear old Olnas.

Curse Tiral for keeping the clerics here, when the Questioners must know they were innocent. Curse the Triarchs, who were descendants of Holy Div and did nothing as Div's disciples were tortured. Curse the jailers who kept children like Hani and Jak and Finh locked up in the noxious dark for the crime of being born Snipes.

One day, after Aiz finished the Eighth Sacred Tale, Hani interrupted her.

"Aiz, why are there only eight tales when they're called the Nine Sacred Tales? What's the Ninth?"

"It has yet to be revealed," Aiz said. "Mother Div whispered the Ninth Sacred Tale to the wind in a faraway land. When the wind circles the earth and returns to Kegar, we will finally hear the tale. Its telling will herald the Return to our homeland."

"Until then," Olnas said from the cot where she brushed Jak's hair, "we start back from the beginning to see what we missed the first time."

Aiz smiled. "Long ago and far away . . ."

She was midway through the tale when a figure stepped from the darkness. Kithka. Aiz didn't know how long the woman had been lurking in the shadows, but it didn't matter. Aiz refused to stop.

"And Mother Div ordered the early builders to lay the foundations of our capital, first and foremost the cloister in Dafra."

As Aiz spoke, Kithka gripped her whip, gaze darting from cell to cell, clearly uncertain what to make of the sheer number of prisoners listening to Aiz.

"What the bleeding Spires is going on?" Gil barreled through the door at the far end of the block, behind Kithka. "What's the racket?"

As if his voice had shaken her out of her indecision, Kithka wrenched open the door to Aiz's cell. "Enough yammering from you." The jailer grabbed Aiz by the scruff of her neck and shoved a rag in her mouth. "You're going to the Hollows."

8
Quil

Married.

The word rang in Quil's ears like a screech of a dying wraith. It was only a lifetime of court training that kept him from grabbing Mater Andricar by her silk-clad shoulder and demanding to know what in the skies she was talking about.

"Mater, Pater," he managed through numb lips. "Whatever the Empress has arranged for me will be for the best. Her only concern—and mine—is the prosperity of the Empire. If you'll excuse me." He offered an anodyne smile as he moved away, fingers tingling from the sheer effort of appearing unruffled.

A few others approached him, but he begged off, scanning the room for his aunt. He needed to find her, talk to her, get answers out of her.

Usually, he'd rue the height that made him stand out in a crowd. Now he was grateful. He spotted a flash of silver-blond hair. She was surrounded, but she must have sensed his anger because she looked up, directly at him.

For a moment, they were the only two people in the room, bonded as blood often is. She nodded toward a back door that led to a private balcony, and lifted her hand.

Five minutes.

Quil nodded and turned away. The room spun.

Though he tried to stop it, his magic, leashed like a rabid beast at the back of his mind, rose up. He took a shuddering breath and shoved the magic down. *Not now! Not here!* The effort of it was immense, and for a moment he thought that he'd pass out and drop straight onto his face, humiliating himself, his aunt, his entire Gens.

Then Sufiyan was at his side, shaking Quil's shoulder, and the magic receded.

"You look like someone's yanked your knickers around your neck." Sufiyan pulled him to the edge of the party, shoving people out of his way.

"Talk," Sufiyan said when they'd gotten clear of the crowds. "What's happened? Is it Tas?"

Quil shook his head. He'd forgotten about Tas entirely. "The Empress arranged a marriage. Mine."

"*What?*" Sufiyan nearly shouted, and the partygoers nearest them turned to stare, scandalized.

"Shut it," Quil hissed. "Mater Andricar told me. Maybe she's mistaken."

"She's a meddlesome old bat, but she's not usually wrong," Sufiyan said.

"Maybe Aunt Hel was going to tell me," Quil said. "Maybe she didn't get the chance."

"*Get the chance?* What about when she was shouting at you last week for saying the word *abdicate* in public?" Sufiyan said. "I hope you'll tell her to stuff it."

Quil sighed. "I'm not going to tell her to stuff it."

"Why the hells not?" Sufiyan stared at his friend like he'd agreed to marry a cabbage. "You might have to marry someone you've never met. She could be exceedingly violent. Or stupid. She might have an unnatural obsession with goats. Don't you care?"

Ilar's smile flashed in Quil's head, the song of her laughter. "Of course I care." Quil pushed her memory away. "But an arranged match was always a possibility. For the stability of the Empire."

Sufiyan put his hand to his temple, as if to call on untapped reserves of patience. "I'm not saying the Empire isn't important. But you do realize that I'm heir to one of the most powerful Gens? Yet my parents aren't demanding that I marry some horse-faced Illustrian to keep the line going."

"Not all of us have three siblings to carry on the line if—"

"Two." Sufiyan's voice was soft as he glanced away from his friend.

Quil flinched, realizing his mistake. Of course. Ruh was Sufiyan's baby brother. And he was dead. "Oh skies. I'm an idiot."

"Look, there's Arelia."

"I'm sorry—"

"Stop." Sufiyan shoved his hands in his pockets and looked down, dark hair obscuring his eyes. "Makes it worse. It's fine. Really."

Quil cursed himself for not thinking before he spoke, thankful when his cousin appeared. She wore a narrow-waisted gown that was a riot of green, her curls loose down her back. Quil glared at the knot of besotted fellows trailing her, scaring them off. He didn't need anyone eavesdropping.

For her part, Arelia ignored her admirers. Her gaze had snagged on Sufiyan, half in shadow, his dark gold eyes glittering appreciatively. He nodded a greeting.

"Nice dress," he murmured.

Arelia's skin flushed ever so slightly. "I hate it. It doesn't have pockets. But the dye is quite rare. Stone-ground from Ogfaso shells and left to dry for three months before it can be mixed with squid ink to form a dye this pigmented. Smells like rotting eggs."

Sufiyan nodded with bemusement or perhaps mockery. It was hard to tell. Arelia huffed in annoyance, likely assuming it was mockery.

"Mater Andricar says she upset you." Arelia turned to Quil. "She wouldn't tell me more than that."

"Ah . . . well . . ." Quil considered what to say. As a court engineer,

Arelia went all over the city, and heard things others didn't. But if she knew about his betrothal and hadn't told him—

Sufiyan let out a sound of impatience. "Mater Andricar told Quil he's going to be betrothed and I'm trying to persuade him to tell the Empress to stuff it."

"Betrothed?" Arelia's gasp was so genuine that Quil knew she'd been as ignorant as he. "There must be some explanation. She wouldn't ask you to do anything that wasn't within the scope of your duties."

"You Martials," Sufiyan muttered, "and your bleeding duty."

"*May* I remind you that you are half Martial yourself." Arelia's pale eyes flashed, a rare show of temper.

Quil caught a glimpse of his aunt's armor. She was heading for the balcony.

The prince left his friends to their argument and edged through the crowd, keeping his face stony to discourage further conversation.

Once outside, he wished for his cloak. Winter's chill had penetrated even this far south, and Quil shivered. The palace gardens stretched beyond the carved stone of the balcony, lit by hundreds of tiny lamps.

Quil knew three ways into the gardens, four ways out, two of which only he and the Empress used.

Back when they were close, she'd shown him. That was when she told him everything. He'd enjoyed his visits to Navium, Serra, Antium—all the cities where she had residences. The Empress moved constantly. Quil used to think it was because she got bored.

It's because every city has ghosts, she'd told him once, when they walked along the shores of the River Rei. *If I stay too long, they grow angry, and bother me.*

He'd not understood how his fearless aunt might be bothered by a few ghosts. After all, she'd taught him how to escape a room with one door and a dozen guards blocking it. How to traverse a city's rooftops and disappear in a crowd, height be damned. How to navigate by starlight and raise a sail and shoot a bow and ride seventy-five miles in a day without killing himself or any horses.

Your best and most reliable protection is this. She'd tap his head when he was a boy. *And these.* She'd take his hands, so much smaller than hers. *Never depend on anyone else to keep you safe, nephew. You keep them safe instead.*

Together with Elias, she'd made him into a Mask without him having to spend a day in Blackcliff Military Academy.

Yet she still had guards trailing him. She made decisions for him. She didn't talk to him. Not anymore.

"Nephew." Aunt Helene appeared out of the darkness. "What troubles you?"

She was so calm. It made him want to scream. When Sufiyan and his sister Karinna were bickering incessantly a month ago, Laia lost her temper and told them that if they didn't shut it, she'd put a nest of Ankanese jumping spiders in their boots. Would that Quil could shout at his aunt without caring who heard, and she could threaten him with poisonous beasties, the way normal people did.

"Were you going to tell me that you're marrying me off?" he said.

His aunt stared at him with her mouth half-open, and Quil was briefly hopeful she would laugh and ask him where he'd heard such a ridiculous rumor. Then she did the oddest thing. She glanced first to the doors of the balcony, and out into the lamplit shadows of the garden. Her mouth hardened.

"Indeed, I received a dispatch from the Kegari Triarchy. One of the Triarchs has a daughter who—"

"Were you going to tell me?" Quil cut her off. "Or drag me to meet my bride the day I was to marry?"

"You're being dramatic. How long have you known?"

"I— That's what you ask me? After planning this behind my back?"

"I am asking," the Empress said, each word edged in exasperation, "because the Kegari stopped responding to us in the fall, and we can't get any information about what's going on. Tas was trying, but—" She shook her head. "How long?"

"I found out today," Quil said. "Mater Andricar mentioned it. Of all the people you could choose from, Empress, why the Kegari? All we know about them is that they enjoy internecine massacres and stealing their neighbors' grain."

"Zacharias." Aunt Hel's voice was low, urgent, and she stepped closer. "This isn't what you think. The Kegari—"

"How did we get in touch with them? No one knows their language, Aunt Hel, because there are hardly any texts to reference. How will I communicate with my future wife?"

The Empress ran a hand over her crown braid. "I do not wish to discuss this with you. It is not the time or place."

More secrets. "Then when is?" Quil asked. "Tas said that the Kegari—"

"Tas cares more about you than he does his duty as an agent of the Empire."

Quil took in his aunt's words. "Tas defended me." He felt a surge of gratefulness for his friend. At least someone cared about what Quil wanted. "Because not everyone is like you, Aunt. Willing to throw their family members to the wolves for the sake of duty."

The Empress stepped back from him, the scars on her cheeks livid white against her already pale skin. Quil opened his mouth, words at the ready, waiting to explode out of him. Years of things he'd wanted to say. Years of fear and anger and frustration. Years of hiding what was inside him because that was what his aunt taught him to do.

The air shifted. The songs of the night creatures tripped, the breeze slowed.

Aunt Hel stiffened as a drumbeat echoed across the city, sudden and frantic.

Attack—

The sound cut off and Quil met his aunt's eyes. All was silent.

And then the sky burst into flame.

9
Sirsha

The murderer felt slick and clever as a greased eel. Unlike anyone Sirsha had hunted before.

Perhaps she should have been vexed. Instead, she was intrigued, the way she hadn't been since she was a child first discovering her skills. After Sirsha's people had cast her out, her jobs were simple. Too simple. She often took a second job while doing the first, because she was so damned bored.

Now, six days after she and her client had parted ways, Sirsha knelt in the winter-yellow foothills a day outside Navium, the Empire's southernmost port city. She'd successfully avoided the small settlements along the River Rei, where people might ask her questions. From afar, she would look strange: a girl with golden-brown skin and black hair piled high, staring off into space as if thinking of a lover or a dream.

In fact, she was puzzling out the trails winding through the air and earth around her. For the past few hundred miles, she'd followed the path of a single woman meandering south. It grew thin at times, but it eventually led her here.

Now the trail appeared to split. The killer could have met someone here. But if that was the case, Sirsha would have been able to see their spoor and wherever they came from. Unless they appeared out of thin air.

Even still, her magic would have revealed a trail.

Sirsha surveyed the land ahead. A harsh mountain wind flattened the scrub, powerful enough to have long ago swept away normal tracks.

"Talk to me," she said. "Tell me what I'm looking at." But the air merely yanked at her hair, taunting her before racing off. All her senses felt utterly befuddled.

Her magic lived in her blood. Had since birth. It was as steady as breathing or having skin. Or it had been, until now.

Sirsha walked farther down the hillside, leaving the horse her client had given her to graze on the sparse winter grasses. She put her hand to the earth. Nothing. A thousand threads, a thousand trails—none of which mattered. The wind spun dead leaves around her, swirled dust into her eyes.

"If you're not going to help"—Sirsha coughed and batted the dust away—"then piss off."

A low, sullen hiss. *Follow the bones.*

She scanned the scrubby land, which was filled with ravines and gulches. The wind's hints were never idle. If the bones weren't near, it wouldn't have said anything. She walked across the dead, snow-dusted grass to a spot that dropped away into a gully. There, at the bottom, she saw a flash of dull white.

"Got you," she muttered, and shimmied down for a closer look.

The bones were picked clean. Smaller than an adult's, though not by much. A young person, but not a child. Sirsha knelt beside them, closed her eyes, and touched the earth.

Her vision narrowed and went white, then coalesced into a figure running—racing, desperate to escape the killer following him. A roar. A scream.

Soul crumbled. Rotted. Monstrous. Killer of tender saplings, death in the blood, death in the bones, an ocean of death—

Sirsha gasped at the earth's rage. She'd heard the earth growl before, and whisper. Occasionally, it laughed and teased Sirsha. Once, long ago, she heard it weep. But she'd never heard it roar.

A series of impressions crossed her mind. A gray cloak. A canteen and a cap fallen into the dirt, dropped by a shaking hand. A shadow. Human? Fey? The earth shriveled away from the memory of whoever had passed here. It gave her nothing more.

But Sirsha had the trail now. Strong and clear and heading directly south—to the city of Navium.

It was dawn before Sirsha joined scores of other travelers on the main road leading into Navium. She'd buried the bones because she hadn't lost all semblance of decency. As a result, she was exhausted and grumpy, in sore need of a meal, a bath, and a nap. And perhaps new clothes.

But as Navium came into view over a rise, her hopes were dashed. The front gate was a tangled throng of adults, children, horses, carts, even a herd of cattle.

A young man carrying a baby across his chest rode nearby, and Sirsha called out to him. "What's happening in the city?"

"Rathana." The man pointed at a single dark blue flag flying high on the gates. "That's the standard of Gens Aquilla. Our Empress is in residence. The guards only have one gate open, so they can properly check everyone."

He gave her a dark look then, as if she might personally stick a knife in his precious ruler. "She's a good woman, Empress Helene. I for one am pleased as pie that she's spending Rathana with us."

"Good for you," Sirsha muttered when he'd turned back to the road.

The Empress being in town was a complication she hadn't anticipated. This had happened before, more than a year ago when Sirsha was in Sadh. Tracking had been a nightmare, the city so busy that she couldn't get a clear sense of the trail she'd been following. The dock agents were stricter, the city patrols more vigilant. There were Masks, horses, and healers at all the gates, in case the Empress was wounded or needed to escape an assassination attempt. The docks—even the tiny one with a fishy that sold the best fried cod in the Tribal Lands—were all shut down.

It was a mess. Navium was no different, it appeared.

By the time Sirsha persuaded a gate guard that she wasn't planning to assassinate the Empress or her nephew, the crown prince, it was past noon. She smelled of cow dung and thought she'd faint from hunger.

A novice Inashi would collapse at this point. But Sirsha had trained at her mother's knee, and few could match her stamina. She used her magic to skim through the city, searching for signs of her Kin. She found traces that were a few days old—but nothing current. When she'd assured herself that she was safe, she went looking for an inn.

Usually, she laid low at the Torius Arms near the massive, key-shaped cothon on the east side of Navium. The Empire kept their fleet there, and the merchant ship docks were the largest outside of Marinn. It was an easy place to go unnoticed.

But her client had given her gold for supplies—more than she could use in the time that this mission would take. So, she headed to Navium's posh central district, the streets turning from packed mud to neatly tended cobbles. The stench of the gate crowd faded and Sirsha began to enjoy her walk, slowing as she passed an enormous mural.

The Battle of Sher Jinaat. The words were emblazoned at the base of the mural. On one side, the Empress of the Martials and the storyteller Laia of Serra stood, backed by an army of Scholars, Tribespeople, and Martials. In the shadows, with scims in hand, lurked the hooded figure of the famed warrior Elias Veturius, who'd persuaded the Empress to take up arms in the war. Opposite them, on the other side of the mural, the Nightbringer loomed, a gray-white vortex of agonized faces at his back, his sun eyes glaring.

Sirsha searched the rest of the mural, but her people weren't represented at all, even though none of these vaunted heroes would have had a chance against the Nightbringer without them. It irked Sirsha to see them ignored, even if she wasn't one of them anymore.

She walked on, stopping at a lovely inn with a front window depicting an ecstatic-looking stained-glass mermaid.

The innkeeper at the Mermaid's Rest did not appear pleased to see—or smell—Sirsha. But he grew more amenable when she paid him a gold mark and didn't ask for change. By the time the daylight faded, her horse was stabled, she had a belly full of chicken curry, she'd procured a better pack, supplies, and new clothes, and she was neck-deep in a bath that smelled like lilies.

Now this, Sirsha thought as she closed her eyes, *is how all jobs should go.* It had been ages since she'd had the coin for a proper bath. Mostly, she scrubbed herself off in cold water and hoped the beds she slept in didn't have fleas.

A far cry from her life in the Cloud Forest. Her mother was a Raani of Kin Inashi, a woman who'd ruled over scores of families with Inashi leanings. She was a scenter, like her daughters, one of the strongest. While Sirsha hadn't lorded that fact over the other children like her sister, she had enjoyed the finer things her mother's position afforded her. Silks, dresses, gorgeous weapons—and her own bathing pool.

Her sister mocked her for it. *You're lazy and stupid and slow. You'd rather hide in the bath than serve the Kin.*

Sirsha groaned. That was the second time today that she'd thought of her family, and it was two times too many. She pushed those memories away. They never led to anything good.

She turned instead to the job. She'd sensed the trail when she'd entered the city, but as before, it felt muted. It was possible the killer had passed through long ago. Or maybe she was still here, skulking about.

The wind rattled Sirsha's window. It was a chill, clear night, and she was glad not to be out in the freezing—

Crack.

The window flew open, shattering the glass in one of the panes. The air that blew in stank of a fresh-opened grave, icy and putrid. It curled around Sirsha and spoke.

Death and pain, blood and screams. Follow the bones.

The world spun and a wave of nausea washed over Sirsha. She clutched her stomach as she staggered out of the tub.

"How many dead?" she asked the wind. "And why do you care so damned much?"

But the wind swept out, tugging at her to follow.

Sirsha threw on fresh clothes and her boots. After a moment's consideration, she grabbed her newly stuffed pack, braided her wet hair, and made her way outside. The earth tugged at her, pulling her south through Navium's crowded streets, until the ocean appeared ahead, its waves a thundering roar.

When she reached the wide stretch of sand beach, she looked around. There were no bones here. She knelt and put her hand to the sugar-soft sand.

Follow the bones.

It wasn't the wind screaming this time, but the earth. The two so rarely echoed each other that Sirsha didn't know what to make of it. Her client had told her that sixteen young people were murdered across the Empire. But Sirsha felt the bones, even if she couldn't see them. In Navium alone, dozens of lives had been cut short. So many that if she found every body and buried it, she'd be here for weeks.

The bones were hidden deep in the earth, in the sewers that carved another world beneath the city.

Sirsha rose, perplexed. The wind had shoved her here; the earth had spoken. There must be a reason for it. Behind her, a row of seaside businesses bustled.

Shopkeepers lit blue-fire lanterns, illuminating the night with a cerulean glow. To Sirsha's left, a long dock stretched into the sea, dozens of vessels tethered to it, their masts undulating and creaking with the winter tide.

They were pleasure boats, mostly, those used by Navium's elite. Each was emblazoned with the crest of an Illustrian Gens. Sirsha frowned as she surveyed them. Perhaps the elements were telling her that the killer was a wealthy Martial. She wouldn't put it past a bored Illustrian to start murdering children.

To her right, another dock disappeared behind an outcropping of rock. Two Masks loitered near it. Perhaps the killer was a Mask. Skies knew Blackcliff bred them violent, even if their skill was legendary.

But no—there was no trace of the trail around the Masks. She edged toward the seaside eateries—though she'd just had dinner—lured by the scents of almond cake, stewed apricots, and hot tea. But as she was about to open the door to a bakery, the air shifted to reveal a glowing white filament: the killer's trail. Her relief at seeing it so clearly was overshadowed by the fact that it led not to the docks or the city, but directly out to sea.

"Ten hells," Sirsha muttered, drawing a look from one of the velvet-clad Illustrians behind her. She couldn't tell if the trail led east, west, or south. It didn't matter. A sea journey meant a longer job. Sea winds were harder to read, and water was her weakest element. The trail she was following was so strange, she didn't know if she could track it over the ocean.

But she'd caught it now, and even if she hadn't made that damned vow to the Martial, her curiosity had taken hold. Sirsha *wanted* to find this woman. She wanted to understand how in the hells she was hiding her trail without magic. So, even though a warm room awaited her, Sirsha pulled her fur-lined cloak closer, ignoring the frost in her wet hair, and made for the merchant harbor to the east to hire a ship.

The wind nipped at her as if irritated, and even the earth twitched beneath her feet. "Yes, yes," she said to the elements. "You want me to leave Navium. But I can't fly, so we must go to the docks."

The streets were aglow with Tribal lanterns and food stalls. It seemed as if everyone was out in the streets for Rathana. Even the docks, usually quieter at night, were packed with families and friends celebrating the Empire's midwinter festival.

The tracker made her way through the crowds, passing massive Mariner schooners and Ankanese dhows, their sails emblazoned with an enormous eye. She spotted a Thafwan ship, but Thafwans were sticklers for rules. What she needed was something small, fast, and discreet.

The wind nudged her and she walked quickly. It was a clear night, though cold enough to make her teeth hurt. Unease gnawed at her. An agitation came upon her the longer she spent at the docks.

A strange aura tainted the air. A presence that did not belong. Sirsha glanced up at the black night sky. It was patchy, as if from the weather, but there were no clouds. Instead, it looked as if the stars were blocked out.

The wind howled in Sirsha's ears, sudden and unmistakable.

Run, swiftly, the wind hissed. *Run, little one.*

She bolted without thought, without consideration. In seconds, she'd left the docks and turned up one of the few alleyways that wasn't packed with people. She looked back over her shoulder.

Musicians played and families danced, and jugglers threw up torches lit with flame as children shrieked in delight. All appeared well. Except for a sound—the strangest sound. Like a bee buzzing, but more penetrating and growing louder by the second—until it felt like a shriek burrowing in her brain.

She clasped her hands over her ears. The music stopped. Others covered their heads too. And then, in a dreadful chorus, everyone around her began to scream.

10
Aiz

Kithka dragged Aiz down deep into the prison's depths, where there was hardly even a rumor of light. The cells were icy and hellish—holes in the ground with a latched door on top and a latrine ditch in the corner.

Aiz thought her jailers would leave her inside for a day or two. She'd survive. She had her anger to soothe her, fuel her, strengthen her for whatever came.

But almost immediately, she was gripped by nausea and confusion. In the Hollows, the only light came from the twisting purple ore veining the gray stone. The ore seemed to pulse like the fading heart of a fresh-felled deer. When Aiz touched it, she felt infinitely worse.

Aiz heard no sounds at all. No whispers from other prisoners, no passing footsteps. Not even the scurry of rats. There was only silence so profound that she would scream on occasion to remind herself she was alive.

A day passed. Three. Perhaps more, but after a time, Aiz couldn't keep track. The walls pressed in on her, and she struggled to breathe.

In Dafra slum, Aiz had sharpened her wrath on the ever-spinning grindstone of misery. But here, in the deepest bowels of the Tohr, her anger faded into hopelessness. She didn't know what would happen to Sister Noa or Olnas. The children or the other clerics.

She tried to tell herself the Sacred Tales, tried to take inspiration from Mother Div's strength during her flight from Old Kegar, when she hadn't known if she would find a new home or crash into a merciless sea. But Aiz heard Cero's voice in her head, caustic. *Mother Div won't be reborn as the Tel Ilessi, Aiz. She won't save us.*

Perhaps Tiral had figured out that Cero had the book. If so, Cero would die. It would be Aiz's fault. Her impetuousness would have deprived the world of his creativity, his dark humor, his dreams, closely held but beautiful. *What if we harnessed the sun to grow plants in the winter? What if we transported goods with our Sails for other countries and got food in return?*

I'm sorry, Cero, Aiz thought. *I wish you were here. I'm lost. I don't know what to do.*

Kithka brought food at uneven intervals, and when Aiz stopped eating, she yanked the girl out of the hole, beat her, and shoved the food in her mouth.

"The Triarchs don't want you dead, girl," she said. "They want you to suffer. You'll eat. If you don't, I'll shove it down your gullet again."

After the beating, Aiz lay on the dirt floor, body shaking and vision blurry. How naive she'd been to believe in Mother Div! *Death is honorable in the service of belief.* That was from the Eighth Sacred Tale, and it was rubbish.

This ugly, stinking, humiliating fade into nothingness—*this* was death. Not noble. Not in service of anything. But forsaken and forgotten in the depths of a jail where Kegar's most hated criminals disappeared. *You were right, Cero. It was all lies.*

Aiz.

The voice was distant, a whisper on the wind. Aiz tried to sit up, but her body felt weighed down with stones. Around her, the dim light of the cell shifted. It faded and transformed into the night sky, dancing with bands of purple, red, and green light. The silence in the Hollows was no longer the menacing quiet of death but the soft hush of a gentle snowfall.

Aiz's mind was a Sail, flying far away. She thought of her mother. How tired she always looked. Strange—it had been years since she remembered her mother's face, thin and sharp like Aiz's, but still soft somehow. She'd died during a raid after being forcibly enlisted. Aiz had tried to hold on to her as soldiers dragged her away. But she was too small.

Aiz, hear me.

"Who—who are you?" She batted at the air.

Aiz, my daughter, finally I come to you, in your hour of great need.

"Ma? Who is there?" Aiz called, bewildered, for she saw no one.

Do you not know me, daughter of Kegar?

A figure appeared above her, tall and hooded, face veiled, a crown atop her head. Aiz couldn't make out her features, but that silhouette was familiar from statues, friezes, and coins. Aiz knew her as sure as she knew her own face.

"Mother Div?"

Have you lost your faith so swiftly, Aiz bet-Dafra?

She knew people had visions before death. When the orphans in the cloister burned, Aiz heard many calling out to their mothers as they died. Not in pain or terror, but in greeting.

"There's no faith here," Aiz whispered. "Only death. Only darkness."

Darkness perhaps, for there is beauty in the dark, and strength. But not death, daughter of Kegar. Not yet. Listen well. Corruption eats at the heart of our land. It grows most virulently among those who rule our people. A traitor to my blood seeks to fulfill my prophecy of a Tel Ilessi. A vile pretender to whom Kegari lives mean less than a mote of dirt.

"Tiral," Aiz whispered.

The figure came in and out of focus. Aiz tried to shake away the torpor that weighed down her bones. She needed sharpness now. For this could not be real.

It is real, child. If it wasn't, how would I read your thoughts? My blood alone held the power of mindsmithing. If I was not real, how would I know that Tiral bet-Hiwa plans to claim the mantle of the Tel Ilessi before the next full moon?

Aiz's disgust penetrated the haze in her mind, her hunger for vengeance rekindling. Heartless, faithless Tiral as Tel Ilessi? The killer of orphans—who were most precious to Mother Div—playacting as the vessel of her spirit? It was repugnant. A desecration of Div's kindness, her love. But before Aiz could protest, the figure spoke again.

Heed me. The Triarchy is corrupted and cannot help our people. Only you can.

"How?" Aiz asked.

The highborn call the wretched poor Snipes, but we are Starlings who move together as one. The low, the broken, the forgotten, the hungry—they will be your shield, your sword, your army, the heart that beats within you. Look to them for strength. Do not let Tiral's blasphemy stand. For as long as it does, we cannot return home. We cannot leave this accursed spit of land for the golden shores of our forefathers.

Aiz gasped. Mother Div spoke of the Return. The tantalizing promise at the end of every Sacred Tale. *Mother Div will return in the body of the Tel Ilessi, the Holy Vessel. And the Tel Ilessi shall deliver us back to the homeland from whence we fled, so long ago.*

"I failed to kill Tiral," Aiz said. "Even if I succeeded, we don't have enough Sails or Loha to leave Kegar."

Do you know what Dafra, *the name of your home, means?*

Aiz shook her head.

It was the name of the evening star, the brightest in our sky far away, in the land to which I was born. Aiz bet-Dafra, you are a daughter of the evening star. You are not meant to be caged. Despair is death. Crush it. Stoke your rage instead. Escape. Kill the pretender. Take our people home.

"The clerics—"

I will not leave my most loyal servants unaided. Escape. Swear it.

"I—I swear."

Mother Div touched Aiz's hand, the cool slide of the cleric's skin as real as if she was in the room. Aiz felt sudden pain. She looked down to find a *D* cut raggedly into the skin between her thumb and forefinger.

I mark you, daughter of the evening star. You are my anointed. Do not fail.

Mother Div took one step back, then another, until she faded, the light surrounding her dimming, leaving Aiz alone in the dark.

Kithka returned Aiz to the main prison block hours later, hissing impatiently as Aiz limped along the Tohr's serpentine halls behind her.

"Thought she had another week." Gil glanced up at Aiz from his post at the end of the cellblock, picking at a flea in his beard.

"Orders," Kithka said. Aiz watched her, wondering whose orders. Wondering if her early release from the Hollows was the work of Mother Div.

Aiz ran a finger over the letter carved into her hand. Perhaps she'd been hallucinating. Her nails were bloody. She must have clawed the mark into her own skin.

Or Mother Div did it and you aren't meant to die here. Find a way out, Aiz.

Before, she'd thought the ceiling of the cellblock low, the shadows teeming with nightmares. But after the dark and silence of the Hollows, the spitting torch at the far end of the hall felt like a miracle. Prisoners peered out at her from their cells as she passed. They were crowded with more people, including clerics who weren't from Dafra cloister.

Whispers trailed as Aiz passed.

"It's the tale-spinner."

"Aiz. She's alive."

"The tale-spinner lives."

"Shut your holes," Kithka snarled, voice echoing. "And you"—she shoved Aiz in her cell—"the next time you open that rat trap, I'll stick a rusty knife up it."

The moment the jailer was out of sight, Noa, Olnas, and little Hani swarmed Aiz, helping her to a cot, pulling a threadbare blanket over her shivering body. She wanted to weep at their careful hands, their warmth.

Jak hung back, shy, but Finh, the red of his hair barely visible beneath the dirt, offered Aiz a wrinkled apple.

"I saved it," he said. "For you."

Aiz took it gratefully. "I was so worried. I thought—"

"We're fine," Noa soothed Aiz, though the bruises across her arms said otherwise. "Tiral sent nearly a hundred more clerics here. The ones who asked the Triarchy to release us. Our people have been rioting. A highborn neighborhood was burned down."

The low, the broken, the forgotten, the hungry—they will be your shield, your sword, your army . . .

"Aiz," Jak whispered, rubbing her shoulder the way Hani did when he had nightmares. "Shall I tell you a story?"

Aiz kissed the boy on his forehead. "Another day, Jak."

"Let her rest." Olnas herded the children away. "A good night of sleep is what she needs."

But Aiz did not sleep, even when everyone else in the cell did. Instead, she relived her strange visitation until every word was etched in her mind. She felt so consumed with confusion that she finally called out to Noa.

"In the Hollows," Aiz said when the old woman had settled next to her on the cot. "In the darkness, I—I saw something."

As she told the cleric of what happened, Aiz felt certain that her desperate mind must have conjured all of it.

"I know it sounds like a Spires-forsaken lie," Aiz said when she was done. "But, Sister, it felt so real—"

"Because it was." Noa took Aiz's hands with gentle reverence to drive home what she said next. "*To step into the abyss and know Mother Div will catch you—this is faith.* The Seventh Sacred Tale. You have been chosen, Aiz. I know this in my heart, as sure as I've known anything in my life. Look, child—"

Sister Noa shifted her rags to reveal a long pin. "It fell out of the Questioner's hair last night. I took it, thinking to give it to Olnas. But—" She glanced at the lock of the cell. She knew well that Aiz had learned to pick locks and pilfer food as a child. "It was a gift from Mother Div. A sign. You're not meant to wait. You're meant to leave. Now, Aiz. Tonight."

Aiz shook her head. "I'd never make it."

"Where is your faith?" Noa drew herself up, and Aiz saw once again the woman who'd survived the toil and hardship of Dafra and still had enough strength to be kind. "Always, you believed. And now that you are called to act upon it, you falter?"

"I believe the stories," Aiz said. "It's my own heart that I doubt."

"Do not!" Noa grabbed Aiz's hand and forced the hairpin into it. "For it is the same heart that remembered the dead children all others had forgotten. The heart that gives first, takes last. I know the strength that lives within your heart, Aiz bet-Dafra. It is time you learned too."

"They will punish you for this."

"The Mother will care for us. If Tiral plans to declare himself Tel Ilessi, that is a sacrilege that demands an answer. *You* are Mother Div's answer. *Go.*"

If Noa died for helping Aiz escape, it would be the first of many deaths. If she fell apart every time, nothing would change for her people. Tiral would win. The Snipes would keep starving, keep dying in the raids that seemed to feed only the highborn. The Kegari would be bound to this merciless place, never to return home.

Sister Noa tilted her head as if she knew Aiz was on a precipice.

"Tell me a dream, little love."

Aiz drew a sharp breath in. "I dream of freedom from tyranny," she whispered. "A better life for us all."

"Mother Div will make it so," Noa said.

Aiz nodded, took the hairpin, and thought, *Mother Div, if it breaks to make two picks, then I will pick the lock.*

It broke easily. Aiz rose gingerly from the cot and made her way to the door. There, she thought, *Mother Div, if I can open the lock, then I will walk through the door.*

The lock was ancient and heavy. But after only a minute of fiddling, it opened. Aiz's hands shook. She took a breath and stepped through. She moved then as if drawn forward, as if some great cord pulled her. As she passed her brethren, voices whispered.

"Light of the Spires."

"Light go with you, tale-spinner."

"Mother Div bless you."

"Tale-spinner of the Tohr. Hurry. We'll keep your secret."

Each voice was a push at her back, urging her onward. She reached the end of the hallway and paused. One iron-banded door led to the Questioners' chambers—they'd slithered out of it too many times for her to forget. The middle door led to the Hollows. Aiz pushed through the third door, entering a low stone hall.

The hall was silent, the air weighty, as if charged by a storm. A nearby torch illuminated an open door, and Aiz peeked in to find a poorly stocked pantry. A rat scurried away at her approach.

Forward, instinct told her, and she understood why a moment later. The Tohr was built into a mountain, but its layout reminded Aiz of Dafra cloister. Mother Div had built both, after all.

Kitchen's ahead, she thought, and sure enough, the next open door led into a darkened room where Aiz made out the gleam of an enormous cooking pot. But that was when Mother Div's blessing appeared to run its course.

Two jailers stepped out of the dining room to her left—a room she hadn't seen. Gil, stocky and well armed, and Kithka.

Mother Div's first true test of my mettle.

Aiz's body ached from the beatings. Her muscles were weak and atrophied from lack of movement. But she was still a child of Dafra's hard streets, and the guards were so surprised to see her out of her cell that they stared in shock.

Aiz leaped upon Gil, snatching his knife from his belt and shoving it into his throat before she could doubt herself. She felt queasy at the way his flesh gave, at the drag of steel against bone. She ripped the knife out, bringing meat and sinew with it. Gil collapsed and Aiz barely evaded Kithka's fist as the tall woman lunged for her.

"You'll die for this." Kithka whirled, circling Aiz with her daggers out. "You and your clerics."

The jailer leaped again, fast enough that Aiz couldn't get out of the way. The back of her head hit the tunnel wall and her knife fell. Aiz blinked rapidly, trying to clear her vision as Kithka grappled with her. She let her body go boneless, and then slammed her palms as hard as she could into Kithka's belly.

The jailer doubled over, shrieking when Aiz wrenched her knife away and stabbed her in the shoulder. Aiz shoved her into a pillar and put the blade to the woman's throat.

"Do it then, you Snipe bitch," Kithka spat out. "Make it quick."

Aiz stared at Kithka, taking in the emaciated frame, the sallow skin, the bruises on her throat and the tattoo on her wrist, a circlet of four flowers, each with a slash through it to mark the children she'd lost. It was a common tattoo in Dafra slum. Stillbirths, fever, illness, starvation. There were so many ways for children to die in Kegar.

Mercy, Mother Div seemed to whisper.

"I won't kill you." Aiz eased the knife back. "I am you. We are daughters of the evening star. You do not deserve death. You deserve safety. Your babies in your arms. Food on your table. A warm hearth."

"I—" The woman looked not angry but confused. Her eyes filled.

"My mother said that we were daughters of the evening star. How did you—"

"We are meant for more than this." Though Aiz's childhood in Dafra told her to keep the dagger, the voice within told her to offer it to Kithka, who took it, perplexed.

"You've heard the Sacred Tales," Aiz said. "You listened the other day. Our people are meant for better. I aim to give it to them. Let me go. Tell me how to get out of here."

The guard gazed down at her dead companion.

"He was cruel to the prisoners," she said. "Especially the little ones. I hated him for it. But what can I do? My family must eat."

Aiz held her peace. One wrong word, and that dagger could end up in her chest. *Give her a moment*, the voice within said. *Give her grace.*

"You speak to Mother Div, yes?" Kithka said. "You tell the stories like a cleric even if you don't wear the robes."

A guard called out at the end of the hall. "Kithka? Gil? I heard something."

Kithka lowered her voice. "Ask Mother Div to guide the spirits of my children to the Fount, girl," she said. "That they might spend the afterlife bathed in its light." The jailer shoved her toward a door in the dining room. "Through there. Down the hall. Last chamber on the left. Looks like a storage closet, but there's a door. Go through it."

"Thank you," Aiz said. "Kithka—"

"Go." The jailer moved toward the voice that had called out. "Before I come to my Spires-forsaken senses."

Aiz limped through the door. She had no plan if she emerged from the prison. She would freeze in her rags. She had no food or shoes. No way of getting in touch with Cero or anyone at the cloister. If there even was a cloister left.

But exhilaration still buoyed her. She could have been stopped, killed, caught. But she hadn't been. *Daughter of the evening star.*

She stumbled into the closet, which was crowded with manacles and chains. Aiz shuddered as she moved them aside to find the door.

Go. Go. Go. Voices behind her, in the hallway. She scrabbled at the handle, stiff with grime and disuse. The voices grew louder, but the door did not budge. She braced her feet and pulled with her whole weight. She was so close.

"Mother, please," she murmured. "Be with me once more."

The door squealed open to a tunnel of pure darkness. Fear burned through her veins, a memory of the Hollows.

There is beauty in the dark, and strength. Aiz closed the door behind her and staggered forward, a hand outstretched. She walked until her feet burned, then went numb. With each step she felt weaker. She realized why when purple-black veins began to appear in the rock walls of the tunnel. Aiz reached her hand out to touch the substance and flinched back. It burned.

A faint whistling echoed through the tunnel. It grew louder the farther she went. Stronger.

Wind.

She was on her knees now, crawling because her feet couldn't support her. And then it was not Mother Div who Aiz thought of. It was her loathing of Tiral and the Triarchs, a lightning bolt that lit her veins aflame with outrage. They were the reason Kithka mourned her children and Cero his father. They were the reason the cloisters didn't have food and the Snipes didn't have hope.

And Aiz swore on the Mother that if she survived, she would destroy them all.

She turned a sharp corner. Blessed light poured into the tunnel. Aiz sobbed, knees bleeding, and burst out of the cave into a raging storm, the wind howling around her like a thing possessed.

Perhaps she should have been afraid of the cold or starvation. Of death. But a figure emerged from the darkness, catching her as she fell, and she smiled when she saw green eyes burning into hers, brown hair swirling about his face.

"Did you hear her, Cero? Did she visit you, too?"

Cero shook his head and pulled off his cloak, the same gray as the rocks around them, and tucked it in about her shoulders. "Come, Aiz. We must hurry—we're dead if we don't get to shelter."

"There is beauty in the dark." Aiz reached up and touched Cero's face. "And strength. But not death. Not yet."

11
Quil

The explosion at Navium's docks was so massive, the plume of smoke and flame shooting so high, that Quil struggled to make sense of what he was seeing. His mind cycled through the possibilities—fire in the lumberyard; explosion on a Sadhese oil ship; experiment gone wrong.

Then the shock wave hit, knocking him and the Empress to their backs, and he knew in an instant that it was none of those things. That his old life had been a castle made of sand and sticks on a shoreline, and the explosion was a wave crushing it with unfeeling finality.

The Empire was under attack.

He crawled toward the Empress, who lay crumpled against the wall of the palace. She was still and panic gripped him.

"Aunt Helene!" He knelt beside her, shaking her shoulder. "Empress!"

She couldn't be dead. The last thing he did was pick a bleeding fight with her. Why the hells hadn't he taken a second to think? Why—

His magic surged and screamed for release, incited into a frenzy by his own panic. It felt as if a part of his mind was completely out of control. *Take her thoughts*, his magic urged. *Her memories. It is the last chance for you to hold on to any part of her.*

His aunt's voice brought him back and the magic faded.

"Qu-Quil—" She opened her eyes. Her voice was thick, slurred, but she was alive, and Quil would have hugged her if she wasn't clawing his arm, trying to stand.

"Thank the bleeding, burning skies, Aunt Hel."

The balcony door burst open, and Musa, his fine tunic covered in dust, staggered out. Arelia and Sufiyan followed close behind, halting at the sight of the immense fireball.

"The—the docks," Arelia said. "Must have been a munitions explosion."

"Munitions?" Musa stared at the plume of fire. "You mean firepowder? Firepowder wouldn't—"

BOOM.

The next explosion, from the cothon where the military ships were moored, knocked all of them to the ground. Screams erupted from the ballroom, and Aunt Hel's guards emerged, scims drawn. Foremost among them was Rallius, a Mask who'd been captain of her personal troops for nearly twenty years.

"Empress." His gaze raked the gardens behind her, looking for threats. "We must get you to the safe room."

"Send units to every drum tower," Aunt Hel said. "Our heads should be aching with their thundering by now. I want to know what happened to our drummers. Get a message to my Blood Shrike," she said. "She's to remain—"

"The Shrike will know better than to come here," Rallius said. "The Gens leaders are already gathering in the safe room."

"Musa." The Empress turned to the tall Mariner. "Get me answers. Whatever you can."

Musa nodded and disappeared over the balcony and into the garden below. Aunt Helene didn't spare him a glance, nor her nephew, nor the city burning behind her. She pushed past Rallius into the ballroom.

"Come." Rallius gestured Quil, Sufiyan, and Arelia inside. "Quickly."

"We should go down to the city," Quil said to Sufiyan over the pandemonium of the ballroom. "To the docks. People might be injured. They'll need help."

Sufiyan's face was blank. It was Arelia who regarded Quil as if he'd suggested they chop their own heads off.

"The city guard will see to them." She glanced at the cracked ceiling. "We need to move if we want to live."

Another rumble shook the ballroom, and a chandelier above rocked wildly, its tapers flickering and falling to the floor twenty feet below. The earth groaned.

Rallius pulled Quil away from the flames now spreading across the ballroom, and they entered a long, pillared hallway.

"Wait, my prince!" Rallius eyed the high windows lining the hall, the glass spiderwebbed with ominous cracks. "I'll go first."

Rallius was ten steps ahead when a deep hum sounded from above them, like the sweep of a bird's wings but a hundred times louder. Deeper. The ground shuddered so violently that the windows shattered.

Quil grabbed a pillar, but Arelia slammed into Sufiyan, knocking him to his back and tumbling over him.

"I'm sorry—"

Sufiyan silently pushed Arelia off and stood, unmoving, which was when Quil realized his friend was in shock.

"That blast was closer," Quil said. "It's not a munitions ship, Arelia. Suf, let's move—" The cries outside intensified, a new wave of pain exploding with every attack.

The doors behind them burst open and a herd of guests rushed past, no doubt hoping to escape the palace and make it home.

Quil took two steps after them, wanting desperately to go into the streets of Navium and do whatever he could. The screams of his people swirled and echoed like a hellish wind. The prince's hands shook in rage and sorrow.

"Move, you three!" Rallius staggered toward them. "We're under attack and you're making it easy for our enemies!"

Something's coming, the Bani al-Mauth had said. Quil had felt the truth of that statement in his bones. But he'd never imagined this.

"It can't be an attack." Arelia limped beside Quil. "Our watchtowers would have seen ships. Bombs this big wouldn't fit on sea trebuchets. It's not possib—"

"Quil!"

Sufiyan yanked him backward, his mouth open in a silent scream as another blast shook the palace and one side of the hall crumbled, stone tumbling into the space where Quil was just standing. Freezing air blew in from the black winter sky. The sculpture garden was below, its priceless carvings shattered to dust. The balcony where Quil had stood with his aunt was gone entirely.

Quil had a clear line of sight to the outer gate, thronged with guards and party guests all trying to escape. Beyond, the city burned and the sky glowed a lurid orange. Something flashed above.

The world turned to white fire as the glimmering object smashed into the palace gate and exploded, leveling everything for a hundred yards around it. Quil's ears screamed and his vision went dark.

When he opened his eyes again, he didn't understand whether he was standing or on his back, whether he was staring up into a dark sky or down into one of the hells. His chest seized in terror. The last time he'd felt like this was a year ago, after walking into a blood-soaked chamber.

Don't think about it. Don't.

His ears made a strange, high-pitched *eeeeEEEEEeeee*, then went silent, then shrieked again.

Sufiyan's face appeared above him, bloodied and soot-stained. "Not again," he muttered as he frantically shook Quil. "Not another brother. I—I can't—"

Quil coughed and grasped his friend's shoulder. "I'm all right, Suf," he said. "Where's Arelia?"

"Here." Arelia staggered toward them, her dress ripped from waist to hem. Quil blanched at the blood trickling down her face. "It's nothing," she said, and lodged herself under one of Quil's shoulders. Sufiyan took the other, and with Rallius leading, they lurched down the hall.

By the time they reached the safe room, Quil had shaken Arelia and Sufiyan off, limping but able to walk, astonished, in a way, that he could do so. That his body still functioned as if the world around him wasn't falling to ruins.

A phalanx of Masks barred the door but, upon seeing Quil and Rallius, moved out of the way. The prince entered to find a crowd of generals bleating at each other about the defense of the city. Runners dropped missives with breathless panic, each one convinced that their message was the most urgent.

One look at his aunt told Quil that she was on the verge of lopping off heads.

"Nephew." She nodded when he entered, but if she was relieved to see him, she didn't show it. Instead, she looked over his shoulder, where Musa had followed him in, blood running down his cheek. Quil caught a flash of something iridescent moving near the man's head. The wings of a wight—tiny humanoid creatures who were notoriously mistrusting and shy, except with Musa. They'd spied for him in the war on the Karkauns twenty years ago. He'd used them only in emergencies since. But their presence explained why he'd returned so quickly. They must have brought him news.

Musa glanced pointedly at the Paters.

"Everyone out," Helene said. "Rallius, get the generals to safe houses outside the city. Take the tunnels. The Fourth Legion is stationed to the north. Its sole purpose is to get our government to safety. See it done."

The Maters and Paters began protesting, but Rallius nodded to his guards, who, after bodily dragging out a few of the Paters, persuaded the rest into docility. Rallius was about to herd Quil, Suf, and Arelia out when Musa spoke up.

"Wait," Musa said. "Sufiyan, Arelia, stay. Quil, you need to hear this."

"He does not," the Empress snapped at Musa. "He—"

"—is heir to a throne you're about to lose," Musa said.

Aunt Helene looked away from Musa to Rallius, who was staring at them, jaw agape, probably wondering the same thing Quil was: why the Empress hadn't taken Musa to task for saying something so treasonous.

"Rallius, go. Don't"—she shook her head when he began to protest—"worry about me. I'll find you, after."

As soon as Rallius closed the door behind him, Musa spoke.

"The Kegari force numbers above thirty thousand—"

"Kegari?" Quil said. "But the marriage—"

Aunt Hel held up a hand and Quil fell silent.

"They flew those infernal Sails here," Musa said, and Quil attempted to remember what Arelia had said about the Kegari transport, other than that it was airborne. "The wights say they've split their forces. A third for Navium. The rest divided throughout the Empire. They're outside the city."

"Thirty thousand isn't nothing, but our army is several times that," Quil said. He didn't understand why they hadn't engaged the Kegari already. "We have two legions in Navium, a hundred Masks—"

But Musa kept his gaze fixed on the Empress. "They have two hundred Battle Sails."

Aunt Hel's face drained of blood.

"Two—two *hundred*—"

"That's for Navium," Musa continued. "They've sent at least a hundred to Silas and Serra. Two hundred more to Antium. That the wights could spot, anyway. Each can carry a significant payload. They know your cities, Empress. Better than they should."

"They went from fifty to five hundred in a few months," Aunt Helene said. "And our scatter spear defenses aren't complete. We didn't get the firepowder shipment."

"You knew?" Quil stepped in front of his aunt so she had to look at him. "About this attack?"

"Not for certain," Aunt Hel said. "We'd heard rumors. I— Tas spent nearly a year trying to learn more, ever since . . ." She trailed off, and Quil wanted to scream at all the things she wouldn't say.

"You knew," Quil said, "and you still tried to arrange a marriage—"

"The marriage wasn't real. There was a spy in our ranks." His aunt lowered her voice and Quil could barely hear her. "There *is* a spy. Someone telling the Kegari everything about us, our defenses, our cities. Tas suggested we announce a marriage to draw the bastard out, but—" She waved Quil away. "Musa, can the wights tell us anything about the Kegari reserve troops? If we're forced into an insurgency, we need to know what we're dealing with long-term."

Quil exchanged a glance with Arelia. An insurgency meant that the Martials would be rebels in their own Empire. Which meant the Empress was entertaining the possibility that this attack would succeed. The Empire had stood for more than five hundred years. The prince couldn't fathom that it would collapse in a matter of hours.

"I don't know yet where their primary camps are," Musa said. "But there are reserves to the southwest, in Jibaut. How many is unclear."

Aunt Helene laughed bitterly. "They promised those pirates first crack at our coastal cities, no doubt. How fast can the wights get us more information?"

"Weeks, at the soonest. I haven't asked for their aid in years."

"Empress!" The door burst open and a runner entered, guards flanking her. "It's urgent." Aunt Helene tore the missive open once the girl was gone. She handed it to Quil.

> *Eastern and northern reach drummers slaughtered. Eastern wall breached. Send aid.*

"Aid," the Empress said. "We have no aid to give."

"You have a plan." Musa squeezed Aunt Hel's shoulder. "It's better than nothing."

"How—" Aunt Hel shook her head. "I let this happen. For five centuries we have weathered every tempest from within and without. And I'm the one watching as we fall."

The palace shuddered, and screams echoed from beyond the safe room. The roof cracked.

Musa glanced up. "You might want to move before that comes down. Ridiculous way for an empress to die, getting crushed by her own palace."

The ground trembled, and a crack shot up one of the walls. The Empress threw herself at her nephew, knocking him to his back as the wall smashed down. Most of the lamps in the room shattered on the floor, and the sudden darkness was suffocating. Quil coughed as Aunt Hel pulled him up.

She turned to Musa, who relit one of the lamps. "Tell me true," she said. "Without the scatter spears, can we hold?"

Musa shook his head and Quil didn't think he'd forget his aunt's face then, a detached sort of calm taking over as her hope leached away, as her world—their world—crumbled into heaps of rubble.

But Aunt Helene had survived the death of her mother. Her father. Her middle sister. Her youngest sister. The love of her life. Her comrades in arms. One after the other, taken from her. She'd seen her capital city fall, her people decimated. She'd clawed it back. She would again. He was certain of it. She'd give some order to turn all this around.

The Empress turned to Quil. "You need to get out of the city, Quil. Leave the Empire. I need you to—"

"Aunt Hel, you can't send me away while our city burns with no explanation."

"The Kegari will be after me, nephew. Take Sufiyan and Arelia. They'll be safer with you, and skies know I don't want to face Elias and Laia if anything should happen to their boy."

Quil shook his head, glancing up at the ceiling. It wouldn't hold for much longer. "I'm not leaving you."

"I'm not going if he's not," Sufiyan said, the first time he'd spoken loud enough for anyone but Quil to hear.

The prince glanced at Arelia, who was peeling her curls off her face. "Me neither."

But Aunt Hel didn't look at them. Instead, she met Quil's eyes with the same sadness as when Quil was returning to the Tribal Lands and she was saying goodbye. For a moment, he saw everything she'd been hiding. The well of feeling that drove her from city to city, that left her in deep silences—sometimes for days.

"I will fight," she said to him. "Skies know I will. But, nephew, if I fall—"

"You won't—"

"If I fall, you will be Emperor. It is your destiny. You *must* survive."

"I—I don't—" *I don't want it.* Quil felt the words clawing up his throat, but he could not say them, not when his aunt was so clearly willing to die for the Empire and the people in it. To die for him.

A shrill shriek and another detonation. The roof above began to crumble. Aunt Hel reached over her shoulder, unbuckling the strap across her back. The blade that came free had a distinctive hilt made by only one blacksmith in the Empire.

"It's a Teluman scim." She shoved it into Quil's hands. "One of Elias's. I asked for it—for your coronation."

At any other time, he'd have marveled at such a gift. The scim was a work of art, and Elias's twin swords had been with him for twenty years.

"Empress!" Musa called. "There's no time!"

"Save us, Quil." Helene dragged him toward her so only he could hear, and now her voice was ragged. Panicked. "Save the Empire. Find out as much as you can about our enemies. But most importantly—" She looked around, as if she feared being overheard. "Bring—bring it back. It's the only thing that will destroy them."

"Bring what—"

"Tas!" she hissed. "He's with the Ankanese. Find him. You know where he'll be. He has it. Bring it back. As much as you can. I cannot say more. *This* is why you must leave. I trust no one else with this task."

"Let me stay with you. Send the Blood Shrike—send Tas a message—"

"I dare not. The spy could be anyone and we cannot risk a message to Tas being intercepted. The survival of the Empire depends on you, Quil. Do not fail our people. We are Gens Aquilla. We are—"

"Loyal," he said. "To the end."

She touched her hand to his brow. "My boy. My heir. My blood. You are the best parts of me. I know you will not fail."

The earth shook so violently that Quil's bones rattled. Sufiyan steadied him as Arelia charged ahead, picking the safest way through the rubble. Quil stumbled after, turning back once. But the Empress and Musa had disappeared into the wreckage of the falling palace.

12
Sirsha

Sirsha lay atop a tree branch, gazing at the wide blue sky through the canopy. Her mother stared down, stern as ever. But her face held none of the hatred Sirsha remembered from the day she was cast out of her Kin.

Come back to me, little one, her mother whispered. *I miss you.*

Sirsha tried to move her mouth. Tried to say *I miss you too, Ma.* But a rushing filled her ears, like an immense cataract, only distorted somehow. She grasped her head, staring dully as her mother waited for her response. "Sirsha," her mother said. "Wake up."

Sirsha opened her eyes to a sky set aflame. Her ears rang with the screams of injured people, and her clothes were stained with blood—her own, she realized with a wince. A glass shard the size of her thumb was embedded into the soft flesh above her hip. Shaking, she tore off a strip of her cloak and yanked out the glass, not bothering to muffle her scream.

She bound the wound quickly and rolled to her side, growling as the debris that littered the street cut into her arm, gawping at the catastrophe before her.

Navium collapsed before her eyes. The docks were a solid wall of flame. If the wind hadn't warned Sirsha when it did, she'd have been roasting on a mass funeral pyre with hundreds of others.

All those families. Joyful only a minute ago.

Something heavy and dark swooped overhead, illuminated for a moment. A Kegari Sail. She'd seen one before, long ago, when she was still tracking for her Kin. *Magic keeps them aloft*, her mother had told her. *Wind magic.*

She'd later puzzle over why the Kegari were dropping bombs on an empire thousands of miles from their homeland. The knowledge of what that thing above her was, of what it could do, brought her staggering to her feet. She stumbled through streets carved in new, deadly ways by Kegari missiles, stepping over dolls and dancing shoes, food that would never be eaten, skin that would never be warm.

She ran until the merchant harbor was well behind her. A telltale whoosh of a Sail flying overhead, the buzz of a missile falling, and Sirsha knew she had to get out of Navium—out of the Empire. Whenever and wherever the Kegari attacked, they left only death in their wake.

Think! An overland path out of here would leave her in a countryside swarming with refugees and Kegari troops within days if not hours. Besides which, the killer's trail led to the sea. Going overland would delay her mission by months if the Kegari seized the nearby ports.

Even considering an impediment to her mission made her oath coin itch. She had to follow the killer.

She needed a ship small and fast enough that it wouldn't be noticed by Kegari air patrols, but strong enough to handle a sea voyage.

Of course, those thieving bastards had bombed the military and merchant docks first. They weren't stupid. Judging from the flames rising in the south, the Kegari had destroyed the docks where the pleasure boats were moored too.

They couldn't have gotten every vessel in the port. There were too many docks. Fishing boats, smuggling ships, a moldering log. There had to be *something* she could steal.

A memory surfaced: the city of Sadh more than a year ago. Shut down, just like Navium was, because the Martial Empress was visiting. Sirsha had wanted to go to her favorite fishy, but the Masks at the dock sent everyone packing. The ship they were guarding had no flag. No markings at all, other than a screaming bird as its figurehead.

Now that Sirsha considered, she realized what that boat must have been. A safeguard. An exit in case the Empress needed to scarper and couldn't get out by land.

If she had a boat in Sadh, she'd have one here. Probably in an unusual place. A smaller but well-guarded dock.

Like the one she'd seen near her inn, where a couple of Masks had been loitering.

The wind shoved her south, as if to say: *Finally, you figured it out. Halfwit.*

Of course, she still had to steal the damned thing. From a pair of Masks, no less. And that's if the boat was still there.

Ah well, she'd figure it out as she went. Like usual. At least she'd grabbed her pack.

The pitted cobbles smoothed out, and warehouses gave way to fountains and wide boulevards, still intact.

"Run!" Sirsha shouted as residents tumbled from their homes, bleary-eyed and confused. "Flee the city! It's under attack!"

The fire at the cothon was so enormous that despite the cold, sweat poured down Sirsha's back. Finally, when she thought her lungs would burst, she caught the glimmer of ocean ahead. It glowed like lava, reflecting the massive fire at the pleasure boat docks. The smoke was so thick that Sirsha had to crouch beneath the fug to keep from choking to death.

She really did pick the most skies-forsaken jobs.

When she broke free of Navium's buildings, she headed for the small dock she'd seen earlier. Both Masks guarding it were dead, their faces torn to shreds. The air around felt strange and warped, but Sirsha ignored it; she hadn't been hired to avenge the Masks. She raced up the dock, heedless of anything but getting to the vessel, cursing in relief when the two-sailed shabka came into view. *EF II* was emblazoned on the side.

The captain appeared too, a broad-shouldered man who looked like he could knock Sirsha over with one swipe of his massive paw. He lumbered to the edge of the gangplank, eyes wild, a scim in one hand and a wet handkerchief in the other to protect him from the billowing smoke.

"Who the bleeding hells are you?"

"Ah," Sirsha rasped, coughing. "I've come from—from the palace." Guilt nibbled at her, but she needed out of here. The Empress probably had a million paths to escape. Besides, if she was running from the Empire at the first sign of trouble, she wasn't much of a ruler. "I've an—urgent mission. The Empress said you must take me."

As far as lies went, it wasn't one of her stronger ones. Still, the captain nodded. "Show me the order and we'll be on our way." He put out his hand expectantly.

"You think she had time to write me an order in this chaos? Just take me on the fastest route out of here or else—or else all is lost."

The captain peered at her. "You don't even know where we're going?"

Sirsha scoffed. "I couldn't possibly tell you until after we left, in case there are spies among your crew."

"Crew?" The captain narrowed his eyes and nodded to the aft of the shabka. "This ship is powered by a Mehbahnese ore engine. It doesn't need a crew. Who—"

He went suddenly, deathly quiet. A second later, blood poured from his mouth. Sirsha saw the thin blade embedded in his throat just in time to duck as another passed over her shoulder and into the captain's heart. He toppled forward off the gangplank and dropped like a stone into the shallow waters of the Southern Sea.

"Dilitali unsiva va tuus!"

Kegari. When Sirsha's mother had her track a Kegari magicsmither years ago, she'd spent weeks in the mountains at the arse-end of the Southern Continent. Sirsha recognized the language, though she couldn't decipher the meaning.

But as both raiders were running at her in full armor with teeth bared and swords flashing, she didn't exactly need a translation.

"Va tuus, beh!"

Sirsha ducked below the ship's rail and crab-walked toward one of the masts. She could take on a Martial soldier or three, and Roost rats were nothing. But she knew little about Kegari fighting tactics. Judging by the skin-curdling screams coming from the city, she'd rather not find out.

"Rue la ba Tel Ilessi!"

She flattened herself against the mast, just wide enough to cover her lean frame. Then blades flashed on either side of her like murderous falling stars, and she drew her daggers.

Some people, like Sirsha's sister, could never get enough blood. But Sirsha didn't much like killing people. She'd had her fill of it long ago.

Still, she'd deal with a bit of gore on her boots if it meant her life.

They were almost on top of her. From her hiding spot, she tried to suss out weaknesses in their armor.

When their boots hit the deck, Sirsha emerged and let three of her blades fly. Two of them bounced harmlessly off the bigger raider's armor, but the third sank into his chest.

The smaller raider surged forward with uncanny speed. Sirsha yelped, barely ducking the silver whip that flashed toward her face.

"Rue la ba Tel Ilessi!" The woman leaped for Sirsha, teeth bared. She knocked Sirsha to the ground and the knives from her hand, closing her fist around Sirsha's neck.

The woman's wrist glinted with a crawling white substance that dripped down her skin like paint. It oozed toward Sirsha and wrapped around her throat with the cold slide of metal.

The woman smiled and released Sirsha, holding her down by her shoulders as the band grew tighter.

In terms of hand-to-hand combat techniques, Sirsha hated strangulation. It took so damned long—a few minutes, at least, and you had to be in your enemy's face the entire time, watching the blood vessels burst in their eyes. But this woman appeared to enjoy it, grinning as the murderous metal she wore pulled with inhuman tightness. Lights popped at the edge of Sirsha's vision. Every sound narrowed to a strange gurgling—her own desperate struggle for air.

She should have left the Empire long ago, money or not. Ankana was beautiful. Warm water, good food, handsome men. She'd always liked it, even if it was too close to—

A sound—a squelch, really—and Sirsha's attacker stiffened and was yanked away, taking the accursed strangler with her. Sirsha gasped for air as a big hand grabbed hers and pulled her to her feet. She stared up into the face of a tall, broad-shouldered Martial wearing a fancy tunic and holding a fancier scim. His dark hair fell across his cheekbones, almost obscuring the yellow of his eyes, the thick black lashes.

"Are you all right?"

Sirsha responded by yanking him down to the deck as a hail of Kegari knives came flying through the space where his head had been. He nearly landed atop her, stopping himself inches away, forearms on either side of her head on the deck, muscles taut as the knives passed over them. Sirsha stared at his pulse racing in his throat and then glanced up to find his pale eyes on hers. Her heartbeat quickened and she felt oddly flustered. *Probably because you're about to die.* She wrenched her gaze over his shoulder; a half dozen more Kegari surged toward the dock, chasing two other people.

"Bleeding hells," she said to her erstwhile savior. "Did you bring the entire damned army with you?"

"You're welcome." He leaped up to meet the attackers with all the subtlety of a rabid bear.

"Are you stupid?" Sirsha shouted, certain he'd get himself skewered. "What are you—oh—"

The Martial tore the Kegari apart, cutting through them so fast that she struggled to follow his blade strokes. Another fighter whirled toward him, movements similarly graceful—a boy who was younger and leaner than the Martial, but as deadly.

The younger man—a Tribesman from the looks of his clothing—sheathed his blade and drew his bow, seemingly in the same motion, and a volley of arrows sliced through the air. He threw himself into the fight with seemingly no care for his own body.

"You're going to get yourself killed, Sufiyan!"

A curly-haired girl in a shredded green dress shouted at the archer as she dashed past, though he didn't appear to hear. She leaped onto the shabka, panting. When she spotted Sirsha, her relief was palpable.

"Sailor, thank the skies," Green Dress said in a rasp, her throat damaged from the smoke. "We feared that they killed everyone. Where are the ropes? The anchor?"

"How the bleeding hells—" *would I know*, Sirsha nearly said, before realizing that if the girl thought she was a sailor, she and her brawny friends wouldn't throw Sirsha off the shabka. Not yet, anyway.

"There." Sirsha pointed to a rope that appeared to be tethering them to the dock. "And that's the crank for the anchor, which, since it's the anchor, probably needs to be, um, on the ship—"

Luckily, Green Dress didn't notice that the supposed sailor was babbling like a chatty drunk. The girl lunged for the rope, while, on the docks, the tall Martial battled two Kegari.

"Sufiyan, help Arelia!" the Martial called to the archer. "Sailor! Engine!"

Skies, the man was bossy as a general. Though he wasn't wrong. The problem was, Sirsha had no bleeding clue how to start a Mehbahnese ore engine. She'd never heard of one until about seven minutes ago.

Sufiyan leaped onto the boat and hauled up the anchor. Upon closer glance, Sirsha realized that he was only dressed like a Tribesman. He had the sharp features and height of a Martial, but the dark eyes of a Scholar. She realized she was staring at him but couldn't stop because there was something familiar about his face.

"Quil," Arelia shouted at the bossy Martial, who was still locked in a scim battle. "Hurry up!" She turned to Sirsha. "Sailor, where's the engine room? What happened to Captain Tanlius?"

"Ah—he—he died," Sirsha said. "Kegari got him. I'm . . . I was second mate." Or was it first?

Arelia gave her a skeptical look, but Sirsha pointed to the aft of the ship, as poor, dead Tanlius had when he was speaking of his special engine. "Do you mind . . . turning it on?" Sirsha said, hoping to the skies the girl knew something about the engine. "I'm going to—*bleeding hells, Martial, on your left!*"

As a Kegari raider lunged from the boulders along the dock, the Martial called Quil spun his scim, knocking his attacker's metal whip away. A moment later, he'd ripped a knife across the raider's throat.

Quil then leaped onto the deck, kicking away the gangplank and finding Sirsha with that singular, cat-eye gaze.

"Well?" he said impatiently. "Let's go!"

"Yes!" Sirsha said. "Because I'm a sailor." The metal around her throat must have addled her brains. She felt a sudden thrum—the engine—and hurried up a set of stairs to the quarterdeck, having traveled on enough ships to know that she needed to find the damned helm.

She'd just gotten her hands on the big wheel when her spine prickled. She caught the scent of death—old death—and bones.

She's here.

The sea, which rarely spoke at all to Sirsha, whispered so quietly that she froze, uncertain if she'd heard it at all. The air changed, going still and noxious. Distantly, Sirsha heard Quil calling to her. She saw more

Kegari approaching, their whips snaking out from their wrists like living white chains.

It all faded beneath the choking blanket of malevolence that settled over Sirsha's mind. *The killer is here.*

But no—Sirsha realized almost instantaneously that this wasn't true.

To the elements, the past, present, and future can blend together. You must learn how to tell them apart. It was one of the first lessons her mother taught her about tracking and was burned into her mind.

Sometimes, a person left an imprint so powerful that it felt fresh, even if it was months old. Sirsha had a knack for sussing out when she was looking at an old trail versus a fresh one. It's why she'd been so valuable to her Kin.

This trail was old. And yet the flavor of death that Sirsha had been hunting for a week now was close. Slowly, Sirsha swung her gaze to Sufiyan and Quil. A boy with dark eyes and a laughing mouth that reminded her of someone, and a young man with cut-glass features and clothes spattered with Kegari blood who was saying something she couldn't hear.

The killer had been near these two men—marked them somehow with sorrow or violence. Sirsha felt dizzy and reached out a hand to the Martial, grabbing his taut shoulder. Images flashed through her. A woman with short, dark hair currying a horse; a child who looked like Sufiyan, his features soft and round. And then . . . then—

—a shadow with teeth and claws—

—a killer, drenched in blood—

—compressing and contracting—

—exploding and snaking its way through the countryside in a way no human was capable of—

Sirsha finally understood how the murderer had cloaked herself. Why the trail had split outside Navium. She wasn't some especially cunning killer. She had magic.

It was strange, skillfully concealed, and unlike anything Sirsha had ever tracked. But it was still magic.

And Sirsha was not allowed to hunt magic. Not unless she wanted to die a violent death at the hands of the people she used to call family.

She wondered why she hadn't sensed the killer's power from the beginning of this accursed hunt. Magic was difficult to hide, let alone from as skilled an Inashi as Sirsha. But then, it had been years since she hunted a magical entity. She must be getting rusty.

The ocean—which rarely showed interest in Sirsha—surged, and the boat lurched away from the dock. Sirsha caught the trail now, clear as if it was illuminated in starlight. It led west, toward the Southern Continent. The place Sirsha had spent the last eight years trying to avoid.

Now she'd have to head straight for it. To hunt a magic-wielding murderer, of all the bleeding luck. The exact thing she was forbidden to hunt, and of course, being an utter fool, she'd made a blood vow to catch it, if not kill it. She couldn't even take the money and run. The damn vow wouldn't let her.

She thought of her silver-eyed client—of his response when she'd asked if the killer was unnatural. *Of course he's unnatural. He kills young people for sport.* Curse him, he must have suspected the nature of this killer. And he *had* known about her magic. Only an Inashi had the skill to track a magical entity. More importantly, only an Inashi could bind a magical entity.

If they could identify it, anyway. Sirsha had no idea what she was hunting. Normally it would be fellow Inashi who would work that out. But as she didn't have that, she'd need help . . .

"*Sailor!*" Quil shook her, and Sirsha realized she was on her knees, body trembling. The Martial knelt before her, his visage dark, as if he was ready to thrash whoever had done this to her. Behind him, Sufiyan had taken the helm, his face soot-streaked and dull-eyed.

"Sorry." The Martial took his warm hands off her shoulders. The cold gripped her in his place. "Are you all right? Your eyes . . ."

"Quil, get back." Arelia pulled him away from Sirsha, and she knew that for the moment, the killer was the least of her problems.

"Your eyes," Arelia said, "went completely white. An unusual and rarely seen phenomenon known to occur when one is possessed by a ghost. You are *not* a sailor. Where is Captain Tanlius and who are you?"

"A traveler." Sirsha raised her hands, wishing she'd kept a blade in her sleeve. "Desperate to get out of that hellscape, same as you."

Quil put his scim to Sirsha's throat, his mouth thinning to a forbidding line. "Did you kill Tanlius?"

"No!" Sirsha said as he dug the scim in deeper. "I swear, it was a Kegari!"

Quil peered at Sirsha's face, searching for signs of perfidy. "Are you one of them?"

"I was fighting them!" Sirsha said. "And in any case, have you ever *seen* a Kegari? Sickly and sallow as corpses, most of them. Wouldn't know a hot day if it burned them to a crisp." Sirsha held out one strong brown arm. "I'm not Kegari. I'm a traveler and I happened to see the ship."

"No one *happens* to see this ship." Quil drew himself up. "It belongs to m—"

"The Empress of the Martials." Arelia cut off Quil with a look Sirsha couldn't read.

"If it belongs to her," Sirsha said, "then you have as much right to it as I do. Unless one of you is the Empress in disguise?"

"Suf, search her things," Quil said. "I'll bind her up."

He tried to truss her up quickly, but Sirsha shoved him away, wincing as the wound above her hip reopened. Eventually, he was forced to wrap one muscled arm around her shoulders while Arelia tied her hands.

"Bet you enjoyed that." Sirsha grinned at Quil, because she suspected he was the exact type of righteous prig who would find enjoyment of such a thing repulsive.

As predicted, he seethed and turned away. And because Sirsha wasn't above petty joys, she found his outrage deeply gratifying.

Arelia took the helm as Sufiyan silently rifled through Sirsha's pack. Though Sirsha tossed her head, seemingly unconcerned, she grew increasingly uneasy.

"Stop worrying about me and get us away from the coastline," Sirsha said. "We're too close to the city. If the Kegari spot us, we're done for."

Quil ignored her and behind them, Sufiyan cursed in surprise. Sirsha sighed, expecting him to have found the stash of gold that her client gave her for supplies. She'd have to part with it, but at least she'd had the sense to keep the rest of her gold on her body. She'd fight to the death before anyone took that away.

But Sufiyan wasn't paying attention to the gold. Instead, he held up her client's ring.

"Where did you get this?" She heard his voice for the first time. "*How* did you get this?"

"That's none of your—"

Sufiyan leaped faster than Sirsha thought possible, knocking her back, putting a dagger to her throat. He wasn't blank-faced any longer, but shaking in rage, as if the sight of the ring had yanked him out of his shock.

"Answer me." He dug the knife into her skin, and she could barely swallow. "Or I'll cut your throat. How did you get this?"

"Get him off her!" Arelia called from the helm in alarm. "Quil, he's going to—"

"Sufiyan!" Quil attempted to pry him away. "Sufiyan Veturius, stop—"

"A client gave it to me!" Sirsha said as Quil finally pulled Sufiyan back. "I'm a tracker."

"A tracker," Sufiyan said. "But why would my father—"

Sirsha saw it then. The wide shoulders, the laughing mouth, the dark hair and symmetric features. No wonder he'd looked familiar. This was her client's son.

Whose name was Sufiyan Veturius.

Veturius.

"Bleeding, burning hells," Sirsha said. "Your father is Elias Veturius? Hero of the Empire? *That's* who hired me?"

And at the bewildered expressions on their faces, at the utter, ridiculous unlikelihood of the situation, Sirsha began to laugh.

PART II
THE HUNT

13
Aiz

Aiz and Cero stumbled down the mountain, the cold cutting through them like a knife. Aiz hunched forward, tucking her hands beneath her arms protectively as Cero pulled her under his cloak. A lifetime in Dafra slum taught her that in a storm like this, one could lose their fingers in a matter of minutes.

"Left," Cero called from behind her, barely audible over the screeching gale. "There's a Sail."

"We can't fly in this!"

"We can if we're both smithing," Cero shouted. "You call the wind. I'll direct it."

Aiz had never heard of such a thing, but she trusted Cero. She spotted the lump of canvas beside a hulking overhang of rock and staggered toward it.

Cero brushed past her and hoisted the Sail onto his back. It draped around him like an enormous brown cape.

"Made it myself," he said, and Aiz wanted to ask a dozen questions about when and how, but there was no time. "Come on!" He strapped Aiz in on his right, then plunged his hand into the Loha box. The metal flowed immediately, flashing white as it wound around Cero's arms, triggered the engine, and shot up the empty reed scaffold of the Sail. The canvas went rigid and the engine hummed to life.

"Call the wind," Cero yelled, and Aiz pulled the wind to her, holding it tight in her grip, even as it tried to yank away like a skittish horse. Aiz's heart sank. Her inability to control her accursed smithing would tear the Sail apart.

But then Cero calmly braided their wind together to create a clean updraft. His power and control were breathtaking in their elegance. Within seconds, the earth beneath was indistinguishable from the sky.

The Sail dipped and dove in the blizzard, the snow so thick that Aiz could no longer make out Cero's face. She hoped he could keep them from crashing into a mountain; she peered below, trying to make out any signs of pursuit. But the dark hulk of the Tohr was lost in the storm.

They touched down hours later in a coastal cave south of the capital. Aiz's legs crumpled beneath her as soon as her feet met the wet rocks of the beach. She must have passed out, because when she awoke hours later, she was on her back and the light had shifted. The angry pink snow clouds had rolled north, giving way to a soft gray drizzle. Aiz couldn't bring herself to move, even as she shivered.

"C-Cero?"

He was nowhere to be seen, and Aiz looked around at the seaside cave. It was immense, with a sandy half-moon beach and tunnels that branched out behind it.

Aiz sat up, staring at her hands, her feet. They were filthy—the Tohr had always been so dark that she'd not gotten a good look at her own limbs in weeks. She tried to get her bearings. They weren't far from the docks of the city. She could see the masts in the distance. They must be west of the harbor.

A soft whoosh drew her attention as a Sail passed in front of the cave. A few minutes later, Cero trudged in on foot. His dark hair was still a mess, his pale gaze hooded.

He set a pack before her, and a pair of thin shoes. He didn't look at her. Perhaps because she'd treated him so terribly before being captured. Now she didn't know why she'd been so angry. It was *Cero*. Unpredictable as mountain weather and about as friendly—to most people, anyway. But Aiz had seen him feed alley cats scraps before eating himself, had felt his cool hand at her brow when she was fevered. In the blooming spring of the new year, he lit candles for his dead father, for

Aiz's mother, and for the parents of all the orphans in the cloister.

And she'd turned on him. Her skin burned in shame, thinking of it. Perhaps if she'd asked for his help with the assassination, they would have succeeded.

"You don't have much time." He offered her the shoes, and she laced them on. "Tiral left for the north a few days after you went to the Tohr. He was sick of raiding Struri and Diyane and wanted a bigger prize."

"How many Snipes dead?"

"Too many. He's had the army wreaking havoc for weeks. The enemy has fallen, and he's left most of the army up there. He's on his way back to crow about his victory, and he's ordered a gathering at the Aerie. He's insisting the clerics attend."

"It's to announce that he's the Tel Ilessi." Aiz was certain of it.

"The clerics would have to declare him so," Cero said. "And the Triarchs would never agree. He'd have to prove his power—that he was bloodsmither, windsmither, and mindsmither. He could never—"

"He won't need the Triarchs. And he wouldn't have to prove his power," Aiz said. "Not if High Cleric Dovan vouches for him. Which she will. He jailed a hundred more clerics in the Tohr. A quarter of the clergy. He's left her no choice, and when she declares for him, the people will believe her. Because she's their High Cleric."

Understanding dawned in Cero's eyes. "No one can manipulate those with faith like a person who has none," he said. "We underestimated his cunning."

"I have to stop him," Aiz said. "I failed before, but Mother Div is with me now. This is my calling. Can you get me a Sail big enough to challenge him?"

"You can't face Tiral." Cero paced in agitation. "Especially not on a Sail. You saw his power. You nearly died because of it."

"Holy Div did not let me die in the Tohr. She will not let me die now."

"I know you think Div communicated with you." Cero spoke more carefully than Aiz was used to. It irked her. "But you got yourself out of that prison, Aiz. You're stronger than you think."

"You must believe me, Cero. I have been chosen. Mother Div came to me and to you. How else did you know to meet me on the mountain?"

"Just a feeling. Never mind that now." Cero knelt before her. "Look at me, Aiz," he said, and as she met his gaze, she lost her breath. She had not looked openly into Cero's eyes in so long that she'd nearly forgotten their strange color, a deep green that mirrored the sea on days when it appeared calm but was something else entirely.

"I believe you heard Div's voice," Cero said. "I will help you however I can, but you must leave Kegar. I do not think it is Div's intention that you remain here. The Lady of the Air was many things, and a fool wasn't one of them. The legends say that she, too, left our people for a time."

An old story the clerics rarely told, as it was not in one of the Sacred Tales. Aiz couldn't recall it in full. She was surprised Cero even knew of it.

"I'm meant to save our people from Tiral's machinations, Cero. Not run away. Mother Div said—"

"We don't have time to argue." Cero looked out at the sea. "I should be patrolling the northern border right now. If I'm discovered missing right when you escape, they'll assume I helped you. Tiral knows that I—that we're friends."

"Friends," Aiz said softly. In the months before Cero had been chosen as a pilot, her relationship with him, as solid and reliable as the walls of the cloister, had changed. Touches that had felt casual no longer were; she'd found herself watching him more, and when his stormy eyes locked on hers, she felt heat ripple through her marrow.

And then the night before he became a pilot—that kiss. She still felt it. Aiz thought if they were both selected to fly, they could talk about it. But that never happened.

Cero pulled Aiz to standing and she followed his attention to the coast. Through the gloom, a ship approached.

It was preternaturally silent, as if the creak of rigging and groan of wood had been swallowed up. It appeared nameless, the deck looked empty, and Aiz couldn't tell if the vessel was real or if exhaustion had her hallucinating. But then she saw the ship's sail, a deep forest green with an enormous eye painted on it.

An Ankanese ship.

"There's a seer on that ship," Aiz said. The Ankanese only flew a green sail to warn off pirates. Any approach by any nation would be viewed as an act of war.

And no nation would be thoughtless enough to test the Ankanese. Their navy and siege machines were powerful, their seers even more so. Most attacks on them had been turned away before they began. The Kegari didn't cross them—the Ankanese were the only foreigners they traded with, and their language was the only foreign language spoken in Kegar. Aiz had learned it fluently, like all the other cloister children.

"I know the seer." Cero nodded at the ship. "She's visited Kegar for years. A few days ago, she sent me a message. Told me I'd have need of her. Just now, I went to find her. The ship was waiting, ready to depart. I made sure Tregan was aboard."

Aiz spun toward him, heart leaping in hope.

"You would come with me?"

But Cero shook his head. "I wanted you to have a friendly face. Treg always liked you better."

He handed her the pack. "Some supplies and enough Ankanese silver talas to start you on your journey. I put Tiral's book in here too. Tried to destroy it, but the damned thing won't burn. Maybe you can reason out why he was so obsessed with it."

A splash sounded from the sea. A rowboat with a lone figure draped in green approached. The boat moved slowly—slower than it should in the rough surf. It stopped near an outcropping of rock jutting from the right side of the cave, a natural dock. Aiz caught a glimpse of pale skin within the green hood. The figure watched her, unmoving.

The reality of what Aiz was facing suddenly hit her. Tiral would be searching for her. She'd be adrift in foreign lands. She couldn't speak Kegari because it would be a dead giveaway. She'd have to only speak in Ankanese.

"Tiral might hire a Jaduna to hunt you," Cero said. "Don't windsmith; they can sense magic. You'll know them by—"

"I saw one, once." Aiz remembered the shine of her coins, and the fact that the woman spent so much time with the orphans at Dafra. "I will return, Cero." Her surety was thunder in her blood. "I will defeat Tiral."

"Aiz, there are things I'm supposed to say." Cero took a deep breath, cracks showing on his usually composed face. "But I can't bring myself to say them. You don't owe Kegar anything. No matter what you saw. You have a chance to make another life, a better one far away. One day, I'll get out too, and I'll find you. All of this"—he nodded to the distant hovels of Dafra slum, a dark smudge in the sleet—"will be a bad memory."

He slipped something onto her hand—her aaj. "Keep it," he said. "Don't use it unless you're dying—the Jaduna can track this magic. If you truly need me, I'll be listening."

They'd reached the boat, for Cero had walked her toward it, ever so slowly. Now he pushed her into the arms of the green-robed seer, who held Aiz with a vise grip. The boat lurched away from the rocky dock.

"Wait— Cero—"

Sudden fear gripped her. The farthest she'd gone from Kegar was a pilgrimage to Mother Div's cloister at the base of the Spires. Suddenly, the days ahead felt vast and unknowable. She wanted to dive into the water and swim back to Cero, to her people, to Div and the holy labor she'd entrusted to Aiz.

But the rowboat reached the dhow and hands pulled her onto the deck. The ship moved away from the shore impossibly fast. By the time Aiz ran back to the rail to look for Cero, the cave, her friend, all of Kegar, had faded into the rain.

14
Quil

Quil composed his face as he wiped his hands and scim—wet from the blood of so many dead Kegari—on the scarf Musa had placed earlier. The prince was skilled at walling off his emotions. He'd learned through the gauntlet of court life, his every expression dissected and analyzed.

So, even as Navium burned and the roar of fire marked the destruction of the world he knew, he forced himself to focus on what was before him: A girl with bitter laughter. A friend so terrified of losing the people he loved that he was willing to kill her. And the very real possibility that the Kegari would swoop down and blow this shabka to pieces if they didn't get the hells away from Navium.

"Quil." Arelia scanned the ocean and skies. "We need to pick a direction."

The tracker stopped laughing. "The next time you talk to dear Da"—she glared at Sufiyan—"tell him I don't appreciate him chaining me to a mission he wasn't honest about. When my family finds me and subjects me to a brutal death, tell him my ghost will follow him around wailing and tormenting him until the end of his days!"

Sufiyan hadn't released his knife, and Quil stepped between him and the tracker. More death wasn't going to solve anything.

"What did you do to him?" Sufiyan demanded.

"Nothing! As if anyone could take that ring off your father." The girl rolled her brown eyes and shimmied back to put distance between herself and Sufiyan. Despite her bindings she moved with grace. "Do you even know the man? He could crush my skull with his bare hand. I told you, he *gave* it to me."

Quil eased the dagger from Sufiyan's hand and pulled him a few steps away, toward Arelia. "I don't think she's lying, Suf." The prince glanced at the shoreline, where Sails patrolled. "We'll get more answers later. Right now, we need to get the hells out of here. I'm thinking we head south."

He didn't elaborate. He'd told Suf and Arelia about Aunt Hel's orders as soon as they left the palace. If they were to find Tas, then they needed to get to the Ankanese capital, Burku.

Arelia understood Quil's intent and spun the shabka's wheel. The tracker shook her head.

"You understand geography, yes? The Kegari are coming from the south."

While Quil didn't think the girl was a spy, he didn't trust her enough to tell her anything significant.

"We have friends there," Sufiyan spoke up. "Though—maybe we should head to the Tribal Lands. Take shelter. Or ask the jinn for help."

Arelia spoke up from the helm. "They won't help," she said. "The palace engineers wished to visit their capital. Their ruling council told us to get stuffed. They want nothing to do with humans."

"Head west." The tracker fidgeted, not-so-surreptitiously pulling at her bonds. "To Jibaut."

"The Kegari are using Jibaut for their reserve troops." Sufiyan was calmer now, though still cautious of the girl. "We can't go straight into the maw of the beast."

"No one will expect anyone fleeing Navium to head west," the girl said, and Quil wondered if he was imagining the slight desperation in her voice. "I have friends in Jibaut. Kade, a rare books dealer. He knows everything that goes on in that city—he'll know how to avoid the Kegari."

"That's not worth our lives." Sufiyan turned to Quil and Arelia. "If we go east, we can get a proper ship, clothing, weaponry." He looked down at his finery in disgust. "We don't even have armor."

The tracker groaned. "You can get those things in Jibaut! I could—"

"Jibaut is too dangerous." Quil spoke firmly, lest the tracker think she had a say in where they went. "The Tribal Lands aren't safe. If the Kegari attack—"

"We should be there," Sufiyan said. "Tribe Saif is wintering in Sadh. We must warn them."

"Musa will have done it already." Arelia lowered her voice. "With the wights. Quil's right."

"You should untie me," the tracker called out. "Whichever way you're going, we need to move faster. I can help."

Quil met her gaze, trying to read the intention behind it, trying to glean any information at all. She spoke Serran with a slight lilt, but Quil couldn't place where she was from. One might say she had the long lashes of a Scholar, or the high cheekbones and square jaw of a Martial, and yet on closer inspection, she looked like neither. She wore tight-fitting leathers and deep red boots, and though she was tall, Quil was taller. She was striking, and from the smirk on her face, Quil suspected she knew it.

"Like what you see, Martial?"

Quil flushed and looked away.

"What do we do with her?" Arelia lowered her voice. "We can't keep her tied up all the way to Ankana."

"If Aba hired her," Sufiyan said, "I want to know why. He's been traveling for months looking for . . ."

The murderer. Sufiyan didn't say it, but they all knew.

"But Ama asked him to come home," Sufiyan said. "You know he can't say no to her. Maybe he hired this tracker to continue the hunt."

If that was the case, Elias wouldn't want the girl anywhere near Sufiyan. He'd wanted to join his father and hunt his younger brother's murderer—had fought for days with his mother and sisters about it before acquiescing to their wishes and staying behind in the Tribal Lands.

Quil put a hand to his head. Skies, he needed time to think, to consider all the implications of keeping this tracker on the ship.

Far ahead, the land curved and Quil could make out a thin white band of beach. In the sun, the water would be pale blue.

Aunt Helene taught him to swim in those shoals as a boy. He'd feared the deeper water, the way the ocean dropped away and he couldn't feel anything beneath his feet. *You must learn*, his aunt insisted. *You can't trust someone else to save you. You must do the saving. Do it enough and you'll develop a knack for it. An instinct you'll learn to trust.*

He wouldn't throw this tracker in the sea. That instinct his aunt had tried to drill into him now told him that he needed to give her a chance to prove herself.

"She'll stay on board," Quil said.

"Oi. Martial," the tracker called out beside the shabka's rail. "As much as I enjoy being tied up by you, I *really* think you should unbind me."

"Quil!" Sufiyan grabbed his arm. At first, the prince couldn't make out what he was pointing to, but then he caught a flash of movement in the distant skies behind them.

Kegari Sails. Heading straight for them.

"They can't possibly see us from that far away," Arelia said, but she didn't sound particularly sure of herself.

"They're coming right at us." The blood drained from Sufiyan's face. "There's nothing else out here."

Quil's stomach lurched, the way it used to when he had to face a room of courtiers. But with Sufiyan and Arelia staring at the Sails in stark terror, he forced himself to speak calmly.

"Can you make this thing go any faster, Arelia?" he asked.

"Maybe if I had a few days to tinker with the engine. But I've only ever seen schematics."

"You can't outrun them," the tracker said, staring at the Sails. "Even if you had ten engines. Untie me. I can help."

Sufiyan and Arelia ignored her, the latter scanning the shore. "We won't make it to land," she said.

"You should jump." Sufiyan's voice was flat. "You and Quil. I'll stay here, distract them—"

Arelia frowned. "That serves no purpose. The odds are that—"

Quil clenched his fists as Arelia and Sufiyan argued. They couldn't run. They couldn't hide. They couldn't even fight, because the Kegari would rain down fire and death.

"Martial." The tracker spoke, low enough that only Quil could hear her. She squirmed, panic creeping onto her features. "I'd say we have seven minutes before they start circling. Another three before they drop one of those infernal bombs on us. Let me go—I swear, I'll get us out of it. You can trust me. I'll prove it."

Quil approached her warily.

"Lift up my shirt. I want you to see something," she said, and at Quil's scandalized expression, she sighed. "Not that. Lift it!"

He did as she asked, her skin warm against his fingertips. She had an injury above her hip that had bled through a binding. He winced at the sight.

"I'll deal with it later." She flicked her gaze down to a pouch strapped at the flare of her waist. "Untie it," she said. "Quickly."

At the surprising heft of the pouch, the prince realized what was inside.

"Bleeding hells," he said. "How much—"

"That's the ten percent Elias paid me to take on this mission." She spoke with an intensity that startled Quil. He wasn't used to it. Probably because so few people were willing to meet his gaze for an entire sentence.

"You don't know me. I understand that," she said. "But consider: Sufiyan's father and the hero of the bleeding Empire trusted me enough to hire me for a job. To pay me for it."

If Quil reached out to touch her, if he let his magic out of its cage, he'd see her memories. He'd know in an instant if she was telling the truth.

Yes, his magic whispered.

No, Quil growled back. He had no intention of digging around someone's mind.

"Your friend was right—I'm tracking a murderer." Sirsha glanced over Quil's shoulder at the swiftly approaching Sails. "Elias trusted me because he knew my reputation and because I gave him my word."

Quil quashed his sadness at how desperate Elias must have been to hire an unproven tracker from skies-knew-where to hunt down the fiend who killed his son.

"Trust me, like Elias trusted me," the girl said. "Cut me loose. Please."

Never depend on anyone else to keep you safe, nephew. You keep them safe instead.

Sometimes, that meant fighting, defending. But right now, instinct told him to trust this tracker. Quil cut her bonds, two swift slices of his dagger.

Sufiyan glanced over. "What are you doing?"

"She has a plan," Quil said. "Which is more than I can say for us." He turned back to her. "Perhaps you should tell us your name."

"Sirsha Westering," she said, and he might have imagined it, but as their eyes met, he felt a shift in his skin, a flash of something in her face that wasn't disdain. "Tracker and ship's malcontent. The pleasure is all yours. You," she called to Sufiyan. "Take off your shirt. Arelia, cut the engine. If we look like we're trying to escape, it will only anger them. Check the servants' cabin for something nondescript to change into."

Arelia flew down to the cabins and Sufiyan stripped, eyeing Sirsha with something between curiosity and mistrust.

"Get oars in the water." She pointed Sufiyan to the rowers' bench. "Quil"—she regarded the prince—"tear off the sleeves of your tunic," she said. "And turn around."

"I don't trust you enough to turn my back," he said.

She raised her eyebrows as she dug a bundle of cloth from her pack. "Fine," she said, and began to pull off her clothing.

Quil spun around, cheeks heating, trying to rid himself of the brief but potent image of her bare skin. A light, metallic ringing sounded, like wind chimes. It was strangely familiar, though he couldn't place it. The ship slowed, and moments later, Arelia emerged from the engine room wearing the wrinkled blue uniform of a palace maid. When she looked past Quil's shoulder, her jaw dropped, and despite himself, Quil turned.

Sirsha was no longer the scrappy tracker who'd tried to steal their ship. She was clad now in the unmistakable, heavily embroidered formal robes and gold chain headdress of a Jaduna.

Quil understood then that Sirsha was either far stupider than she seemed, or far more reckless. "Did you rob a bleeding Jaduna? How in the skies did you survive?"

"No one robs a Jaduna and lives to tell the tale."

Quil thought the frisson in Sirsha's voice was fear, before realizing that it was pride. He understood then why she appeared familiar. She bore the hallmarks of her people. That surety of gaze, the haughty walk, the confidence that comes with knowing you're the most powerful person in the room.

"You *are* a Jaduna," he said. Of course. Elias wouldn't trust anyone less skilled to hunt for Ilar and Ruh's killer. "Why haven't you broken free yet? You could've taken our heads off."

"We have two minutes before they can see us clearly. Three before they land. Don't spend it asking doltish questions." Sirsha raised her voice so Sufiyan and Arelia could hear.

"I'm a Jaduna sorceress, traveling from Adisa, where I've completed a contract. You"—she pointed to Arelia—"are my maid and have taken a vow of silence. Sufiyan, I picked you up in Navium after my engine failed. And you, Quil, are my bodyguard and manservant."

Sufiyan stifled a guffaw at the crown prince's demotion to "manservant."

"Don't get your knickers in a bunch," Sirsha said as Quil bristled. "You're the best fighter here, and if it comes to it, I'll need you on the deck stabbing people."

Quil struggled to hide both his pleasure at Sirsha noticing his skill in combat and his discomfort at being reduced to a mere killer.

"I'm trusting you," he said. "Don't make me regret it."

"The rich boy has teeth." Sirsha purred at him, her smile flashing in the darkness. "I like it."

The Kegari hovered directly above them now, the metal of their great dark Sails flashing. Quil tucked clenched fists into the pockets of his tunic to hide his rage. *I spend most days angry,* his aunt told him once. *But that doesn't mean I have to show it.*

Sirsha drew herself up, face hardening into the imperious lines of a Jaduna sorceress. Quil, standing behind her, took a step back. The magic-users were legendary. Even the Empress approached them with great care, insisting that Quil learn the intricacies of Jaduna law and etiquette so he could treat with them appropriately.

Ropes dropped from the Sail, and two Kegari soldiers rappelled down, spry as acrobats. One was lanky and dark-haired; his female companion was light-haired and freckled. They wore sleeveless flight leathers and shining white wrist cuffs.

Quil tried not to stare at those cuffs, but after fighting the Kegari in the city, he knew what they were. Weapons that stretched and moved with a life of their own. Weapons that had torn through Empire soldiers.

"Light of the Spires," Sirsha greeted the Kegari in Ankanese. Arelia exchanged a glance with Quil. Of course a Jaduna would speak Ankanese—

it was the primary language of the entire Southern Continent. Aunt Helene insisted Quil speak it fluently, and Arelia had a knack for languages. *Light of the Spires* was not a phrase either of them had heard.

"Long may it guide us." The dark-haired Kegari lifted his brows at Sirsha. "The Jaduna have ever been courteous to the Kegari. We didn't know your people to sail these waters."

"I am on a sacred mission," Sirsha said. "Of an urgent nature." She didn't add more, and the Kegari didn't ask, possibly as leery of the Jaduna as the Martials.

"Do the Jaduna not have their own transport? Why use an Empire vessel?"

"I will not explain myself to you." Sirsha spoke slowly, as if to a child. "Our people don't interfere with each other. Let's not upset centuries of tradition."

The Kegari tilted his head, assessing. "You're caught in the middle of a war, Jaduna. It would be within my rights to have you held until I confirm you're not spying for the Martials."

"Do you own the ocean as well as the land, Kegari?" Sirsha snapped, and the boat rocked, seemingly in response. The other Kegari shifted from foot to foot, uneasy.

"You have no rights here." Sirsha stepped into the man's face, chin high, so much a Jaduna sorceress that Quil wondered how he'd missed it. "And your *war*"—she spat the word—"has already delayed me. Go your way. And perhaps I'll not mention to Raani Inashi-fa Ima S'rsha iy R'zwana that you dared to suggest a Jaduna would serve as a spy for any nation."

Bleeding hells. Perhaps Sirsha *was* reckless. The Raanis were the highest-ranking Jaduna. The six women led their people as a unit. Quil couldn't imagine one would take kindly to having her name bandied about as a shield.

The Kegari stepped back. "Where is your ship headed, honored

Jaduna?" He was considerably more polite. "I will provide you an escort, so you are not harassed further."

"No Jaduna needs an escort—"

"Nonetheless," the Kegari said with a bit more steel in his voice, "I am honor bound to provide it. At least for a few days. Revna will accompany you." He nodded to his companion.

The bastard had trapped Sirsha. If she rejected him, he'd suspect something was wrong and their deception might be discovered. If she accepted him, they'd be stuck with a Kegari looking over their shoulder, possibly for weeks.

Sirsha was apparently making the same calculation as Quil.

Say Ankana, Quil willed her. *Say we're going south*.

"Jibaut," she finally said, naming the city where the entire bleeding Kegari reserve force was stationed. Damn her to the hells.

"I travel to Jibaut," she went on. "And I would be delighted to have an escort."

15
Sirsha

The Kegari sky-rat flew far above the little Martial shabka, disappearing at night but always reappearing around midday. On the first day out of Navium, Sirsha saw a few pirate ships approaching the Empire's southern coast. By the third day, she'd seen dozens. She braced for an attack, but the Kegari Sail above served as a warning. The pirates stayed away.

They weren't the only ones. Quil, Sufiyan, and Arelia had steadfastly ignored her. Still angry that she'd taken them west instead of south, as they'd wished.

From Sirsha's position at the helm of the Effie, as she'd taken to calling the ship, she could see the whole deck. Including Quil, mending a ripped sail, and Sufiyan and Arelia, arguing about whether fish should be caught with a line or the trap Arelia had rigged up.

As she watched them, a strange feeling crept through her, like smoke filling her chest.

Guilt.

She harumphed. Why in the skies should she feel guilty? If she'd listened to Quil and his friends, they'd have sailed into Kegari territory. Sirsha would have lost the killer's trail.

Even thinking about it made her oath coin burn, a reminder that she had to see this hunt through.

Sirsha resolutely looked west. Just ten days left in the journey. She'd simply ignore them right back.

Except at that exact moment, Quil approached.

Rather stupidly, she looked over her shoulder. Was he intending to talk to her, or did he have some other business on the quarterdeck?

"Tracker." He stopped before her, arms crossed. A bracelet on his wrist caught the sun, flashing in her view. "I need to discuss something with you."

Sirsha refused to look at him. He was too tall, for one. Sirsha was only a few inches shy of six feet herself, but she still had to look up at him. His very body, beautiful and hard and graceful, seemed to issue Sirsha a direct, insouciant challenge. *You might not like me, but try to look away. I dare you.*

"Finally willing to chat, are we?" She sniffed. "Sorry, not in the mood."

"You said Elias gave you a mission to track down a murderer."

Ugh. His voice. Deep and warm and sure, belying those unreadable eyes. She hated him a little.

"I wanted you to unbind me. I told you what I had to." Eight years alone had taught Sirsha it was best not to discuss her jobs too much. She didn't need anyone blabbing about her mission to the wrong ears.

"Why are you fidgeting like that?" Arelia came up behind Quil, regarding Sirsha suspiciously. "You don't have lice, do you? Sufiyan, tell me you know a cure for lice."

"Nolgh root and ground sap beetle wings. Stinks like horse dung," Sufiyan said as he joined from Quil's other side. "Who's got lice?"

"She does—"

"I do *not* have lice," Sirsha snapped. "I am fidgeting because—"

"Because you're lying," Quil said. "Elias *did* give you a mission to hunt down a killer."

"What's it to any of you?"

Sufiyan looked surprised. Then desolate. "It was my brother who died." His voice was horribly flat. "My little brother. The killer murdered him first."

There was a long silence, and Sirsha told herself to count to three before speaking, instead of shoving her foot in her mouth. "I'm very sorry," she said. "Elias didn't mention that." She sighed. They already knew. She might as well admit it. "He hired me to hunt down the murderer. Didn't tell me it was because his son was killed. Nor that the killer was magical in nature."

Sirsha took in the shock on their faces. "You didn't know that either."

"You hunt magic, then," Quil said. "How? Can you . . . sense it in people?"

"Not exactly," Sirsha said. "It doesn't matter. I'm not *supposed* to hunt magic-users. That's the arena of the Jaduna. For me, it's forbidden, and if they find out that I took this mission—"

Arelia—thankfully no longer looking at Sirsha as though she might have lice—spoke up. "I thought you were a Jaduna."

"Not anymore." Sirsha attempted to say it like this wasn't a loss she'd spent eight years mourning.

"Why are you heading to Jibaut?" Quil said. "Do you think the killer is there?"

"Could be," Sirsha said. The sea had been silent since Navium. The only way to tell if the killer was in Jibaut would be to pick up the trail there. "But mostly I have a friend there. I'm hoping he can help."

"The bookseller," Quil said.

"Don't let him hear that." Sirsha grimaced, imagining Kade's face. "He's a dealer of rare and one-of-a-kind manuscripts, enchantments, charmed goods, and information. Books are the least of what he does. If a killer's been active anywhere in Devan or Odista, Kade will know."

And Sirsha might get a better sense of what the hells she was hunting. A wraith perhaps, or an efrit, one that had been cursed or ensorcelled. She doubted it was a jinn—they tended to their own troublemakers for the most part—but it wasn't out of the question.

Whatever it was, she needed to know. Binding a magical entity required an understanding of their weaknesses. Trying to bind a monster you couldn't identify was like trying to aim a bow while tied upside down to a tree after you'd been slapped a few times.

Quil cleared his throat and considered Sirsha, thoughtful. "Thank you for telling us." Sufiyan and Arelia nodded, and Sirsha suspected that whatever Quil was going to say next he'd already discussed with them.

"We're traveling together for at least another week and a half. I thought it might be good if we made peace."

Sirsha smiled tentatively. "A truce, then."

He offered his hand. Sirsha meant to shake it firmly to seal their agreement. But as her fingers found his, a spark leapt between them and her breath caught. Her lips parted in surprise and Quil's gaze flickered to her mouth before he met her eyes, some dark emotion flashing across his own.

"Truce," he said, before releasing her and walking away.

After that, the mood on the shabka was easier. Sufiyan made Sirsha a tea for cramps and shared remedies for headaches and sore muscles. Arelia explained Mehbahnese engines in impassioned and incomprehensible detail.

The two of them, at least, had softened toward her. Quil was a tougher nut to crack.

Even though he'd been the one to suggest a truce, he hadn't spoken much to Sirsha. When she attempted conversation, he responded with variations of: *Just a moment. Please, excuse me. Sorry, I should trim the jib sail.* The message was irritatingly polite and very pointed: *Piss off.*

Right now, he was at the other end of the ship—as far away as he could get without jumping into the bleeding sea. While Sirsha took the helm, he'd spent most of the morning fixing a storm-damaged windlass. The day wasn't too hot, but he'd doffed his shirt.

Which Sirsha didn't necessarily mind. It's just that it was distracting. All that rippling skin. The Martial was a beautifully built man, and Sirsha was a dedicated admirer of beauty.

Still, she'd kept her eyes to herself. Mostly. As she glanced up, she noticed that he'd dropped his tools, and was examining something in his hands. Could be a weapon he was planning to sharpen and stab her with. Could be a poem he'd written about how she was a treacherous viper.

Not that she cared what he thought.

Sirsha gazed at the speck barely visible above them. Their Kegari escort had kept herself scarce, never descending, never speaking to them at all. Just as well. Sirsha thought she'd have to tie Quil up if that sky-hag came down. Every time he looked up at her, the wrath fairly radiated off him.

But he kept it bottled up. It was fascinating, the way he suppressed his emotion, forced it down and killed it dead.

"Tracker."

The girl jumped.

"Sorry to startle you," Quil said, and she was minorly disappointed to see he was fully clothed. This close, she saw that his light brown skin had freckled in the sun, and his dark hair had glints of gold in it. "Will we make it into Jibaut by tomorrow?"

"I have a name, you know." She tried to stare him dead in the eye, but, as always, he looked away, unwilling to show how much she vexed him.

"Sirsha," he said quietly, almost patiently, and there was something about *how* he said it, low and intimate without meaning to be, that made her wish he'd say it again. "Will we make it into Jibaut by tomorrow?"

"Should be in by evening." She glanced down at the scroll in his hand. So that's what he'd been looking at. He tucked it away quickly.

"What is that?"

He shook his head and glanced up at their escort, jaw hard. "Nothing good."

Quil disappeared into the crew's quarters shortly after, no doubt to find Sufiyan and Arelia.

Sirsha smiled. The earth still lived in the wood of the shabka, and her magic always allowed her to hear the earth most clearly. In cities and over long distances, eavesdropping using her skill was difficult, or at least time-consuming. But here on a ship, with no other conversations? Child's play.

"—are we going to do once we reach Jibaut? Go south? Go back?" Sufiyan asked.

"I don't know," Quil said. "I— Let's see what this says, and we can decide."

"Give it to me," Arelia said. "In case it's been tampered with or poisoned."

"I'll open it," Sufiyan said. "If anyone deserves to get poisoned, it's me."

"Sufiyan." Arelia's pragmatic voice was surprisingly considerate. "That's not true."

"That wasn't an invitation to converse about my feelings." The *crack* of a seal breaking. "Lo. I am not dead."

Silence. A gasp. And then Quil staggered out onto the deck and retched neatly over the side. She thought at first that he had been poisoned. But then she read the contents of the note he'd dropped.

> *Navium has fallen. Silas at risk. Serra and Antium under attack. Floods in the spring. The Butcher lives, the Orphan roars. Death to the east, the north, and the south. They search for you. Find him. Stay away. Stay alive. —AH*

Some of it made sense, but the rest was in code. Sirsha didn't pay attention to Martial gossip or politics, but Elias Veturius—and his son—were heirs to a powerful Gens. They would have powerful friends. Quil might be the son of a high-ranking military official or ambassador.

Or he might be a spy.

She watched him. Spy seemed likely. It would explain how he'd gotten so good at controlling his emotions.

Though he wasn't doing so now. He looked oddly vulnerable with his back bowed, his fists hanging over the side of the shabka and the sea winds tousling his black hair. He looked as if he bore a yoke around his shoulders no one else could see.

"Here." Sirsha offered him a stick of what looked like cinnamon. "Lilangia," she said. "Helps with nausea."

He took it, and looked moderately less green after a few moments of chewing. The wind tore at Sirsha's hair, pulling it free from the knot atop her head. Her gaze fell upon his bracelet—a medallion strung tight on black leather, a gold sun against blue lapis. That and an etched band of silver on his middle finger were the only adornments he wore.

Sirsha sniffed experimentally. Something about the bracelet spoke to her. It had an aura. She glanced up at Quil. It would be easy enough to nick it off him. Kade taught her the basics years ago. She made to touch Quil's wrist as if offering him comfort—

He snatched his arm away.

"I hope you weren't thinking of stealing that." Quil's tone was more musing than chiding, but Sirsha still felt like a schoolchild who'd been reprimanded. Her face heated in embarrassment.

"I hope you aren't accusing me of something untoward. Just because your bracelet is precious to you doesn't mean I give a fig about it."

She waited for him to stalk off. To find something else to do, as he had whenever she said more than two words to him. Instead, he stared at her. Long enough to make the scowl fade from her face. Long enough that she wanted to look away, but found she could not, caught by the sudden storm of feeling in his eyes, which faded almost as swiftly as it had appeared.

He stepped toward her, but there was no anger in his expression. Only curiosity.

"Why do you do that?" He sounded strange—careful. Almost gentle. "Distract. Deflect."

She shoved her hands in her pockets, vexed at the way he could read her so easily. "Why do you keep your anger so bottled up when it will feel better to let it out?"

"Because I have self-control."

"Or," she said, "because you're so afraid if you feel something, you'll actually have to *do* something. And that if you *do* something, it will be the wrong thing. Now, if you'll excuse me, Effie needs steering."

"Effie." He looked confused. "Who—"

"The ship." Sirsha spoke to him like he was a child. *"E-F two."*

"That's not—" Sadness flashed across his face. "That's not what *E-F* stands for."

Well, what does it mean, then? She didn't ask. Instead, she turned on her heel and walked away, knowing she'd frustrated him yet again.

Strangely, she took no satisfaction from it.

The next morning, the verdant line of the Southern Continent appeared on the western horizon, growing thicker and greener, until the city of Jibaut was before them. The strange hodgepodge of wooden buildings drooped in the heavy drizzle that began when they were still out at sea.

The rain was miserable, but it dampened the sewer stench that pervaded the port, at least. Jibaut was new, with the coltish sprawl of something unplanned. Only twenty years before, it had been a fur trading outpost for the Karkauns. But since those idiots had attacked the Empire and been routed by Empress Helene, they'd withdrawn from the port and no nation claimed it.

Despite the stench, Sirsha loved Jibaut. She loved its ever-changing nature, usually reflecting whichever gang or family happened to be strongest. She loved the way the edges of the city disappeared into the misty, pine-drenched hills. She loved that by day, Jibaut was languid, but by night, the lamps flared and knives gleamed and the real business took place.

But her favorite thing about this grubby little city was that, unlike the rest of the south, the Jaduna hated visiting it. Which was why it was the perfect place to learn more about the killer she hunted.

If Kade was still in the city, that was. There was a crater in Jibaut's outer wall, and one sector of the docks was destroyed, littered with the splintered masts of half-sunken ships. Jibaut had not escaped Kegari violence. Atop a tall wood-shingled building in the center of the city, a white flag of defeat fluttered. Night approached, and many of the buildings that should have been lit up remained dark. Either a fair number of Jibaut's residents had fled, or they were lying low.

Sirsha counted on the fact that Kade had fought too hard and sacrificed too much to leave his business. He'd be here. She just had to find him.

The Jaduna girl bounced on her heels, anxious to get away from this little crew. It wasn't that she disliked them. Rather the opposite. The three of them had an easy camaraderie that Sufiyan and Arelia, at least, had extended to Sirsha.

But that same affection set her on edge. She looked forward to it. Craved it, even. But she was a tracker, and trackers needed to move swiftly and selfishly, with no thought of anything but the hunt.

Now that Jibaut approached, the hunt was on again.

As Sufiyan angled the boat into its slip, Quil appeared. He wore a set of dark fatigues and plain leather armor he'd found in the shabka's stores. His hood was pulled low, but as he peered up to the skies, dotted with Kegari Sails, rain dripped down the hard line of his jaw.

"Where is she?" Sirsha eyed the Sails. "They all look the bleeding same."

Quil nodded to a now-distant speck, heading north. "She wheeled off a half hour ago," he said, hand tight on his scim. "Shame she didn't say goodbye first."

Sirsha eased his hand off his scim with a light touch. "Don't draw attention to that." She nodded to the Kegari in their blue-scaled flight leathers, weaving through the few dockworkers loading cargo in the downpour. "Those sky-pigs will take no prisoners."

"You saved us. Outside Navium," Quil said, and Sirsha looked at him in surprise. He was staring out at the city, taking in the Kegari damage. "Whatever your reasons, if we'd headed directly south, we'd probably be dead. Or imprisoned. Thank you."

About time you showed some appreciation. She nearly said it, suppressing it at the last instant. He was being sincere. It wouldn't kill her to return the favor.

"You're welcome."

The boat lurched as it hit the dock, and Sirsha stumbled, catching herself on Quil's arm. His peppery scent washed over her and she pulled away quickly. As she straightened her pack, she looked up. His hazel gaze was guarded but softer than it had been the past two weeks. She wished she knew what he was thinking. Or that he'd talked to her more. She wished—

The gangplank landed with a thud onto the dock when Arelia unhooked it behind them.

"This is good riddance, then." Sirsha stepped away quickly. "Good luck in Ankana."

She didn't wait for his response. In moments, she was down the gangplank and lost among the blue-inked Karkauns and fur-clad Mariners, the dour-faced Kegari, and the green-clad Devanese. She made herself push away any thought of the rich boy and his voice, his body, the way his skin felt under her hand.

As she walked, she squared her shoulders, threw back her hair, and glared at any who dared look at her with disdain. The only way to survive Jibaut was to make sure everyone knew you were smarter, meaner, and better with a blade than them.

Which was why it was a shame that at that exact moment, Sirsha felt a presence so oppressive it was like a great hand squashing her head. Her steps faltered, and she looked frantically for a place to disappear and collect herself. But the crowd tightened around her even as the earth screamed that a monster had walked these streets, left cracks in the bones of the earth.

Someone scrabbled at her pack, and despite her disorientation, instinct had her smashing the thief away and snarling, knives free and spinning in her hands.

The criminal retreated quickly, but there would be others. She needed shelter. Fast.

Once she'd made her way past the main thoroughfare, Sirsha stumbled into a side street, catching her breath against a wall. She wasn't sure how long she waited for her breathing to slow, for the awful feeling to recede. But it lingered at the back of her head, a sustained buzz that made her nauseated. She knew she should search for the presence of Jaduna, as unlikely as it was. But it was all she could do to remain upright.

Sirsha glanced around, expecting, at least, to see a trail somewhere in the air, bold as if painted in blood. But there was nothing.

She jumped when she felt something brush against her leg, but it was only a cat, brown and white, one eye shuttered from some old battle. Sirsha knelt and stroked the creature's soft head. It nuzzled her hand, purring.

Sirsha shook herself—she wouldn't be safe on the street for long.

Especially if anyone had trailed her from the docks. Kade's quarters were halfway across the city.

She hurried down the alley, surveying the flat brick of the buildings on either side, the empty windows above. The killer's presence had hollowed her out so thoroughly that she struggled to muster enough will to draw on her own magic. But she didn't need magic to know that something was deeply wrong with the city.

When she was nearly to the end of the street, her neck prickled and she stopped. Turned.

The cat still watched her, eye gleaming green in the shadows. But other than that, the street behind her appeared empty, so Sirsha walked on.

16
Aiz

The Southern Ocean boiled and raged, and the Ankanese ship should have been nothing but broken boards at the bottom of the sea. Instead, it cut a steady path south, riding the frothing waves the way Sail pilots rode the winds of a blizzard.

Aiz fixed her gaze on the southern horizon, welcoming the slap of wet on her face and the wind tearing at her hair. The ship's captain had shown her to her quarters, given her soap and a bucket of water to wash, and fresh clothing. Kegar was behind her. She must now determine what lay ahead.

"You have the rhythm of the sea."

The seer spoke from beside her, still in her deep green robes. Aiz stepped back, watchful.

"I am Dolbra." The seer inclined her head. "We promised Cero to take you wherever you wished to go after we round Cape Timdra tomorrow. Consider well, for once you decide, we will not change course."

Aiz had expected to fight Tiral, not escape Kegar. But Mother Div's will had set her on another path, and it was not fully illuminated. Perhaps Aiz wasn't ready to face Tiral. Mother Div would want a worthy opponent for her foe—and Aiz wasn't that. Yet.

"Why did you decide to help me?" Aiz stalled for time. If there was one thing she'd learned from the Nine Sacred Tales, it was that Mother Div communicated her will in a myriad of ways. Through visions, certainly, but also through signs. One simply had to know how to interpret them.

Dolbra gripped the railing as the ship crested a large wave, and spray broke over the deck. The bones of her knuckles pressed tight against her skin. For a moment, within her hood, the seer appeared almost skeletal.

Around the two of them, the odd silence of the ship deepened.

"I saw you," Dolbra whispered.

"Saw me where?" Aiz said.

"They mustn't hear." Dolbra's gaze raked across her countrymen all over the boat. "They mustn't know, for our people are to remain neutral in all things. But you appeared in my visions, Aiz bet-Dafra. You grasped an ancient wind in your hand and swallowed it. It bloomed through your chest and took form as a woman with her hands raised. Your cleric, Div."

"Your people," Aiz said. "They know of Mother Div?"

Dolbra nodded. "She visited centuries ago. Much of what she said was lost. But she told us her Nine Sacred Tales. She is not a holy figure for our people. But she is respected, for she knew the power of foresight. Look—"

Dolbra gestured up to a star burning low on the horizon.

"That is Malitha, which rises for rebirth and for destruction," she said, before drawing an invisible line to another star. "And when Jiragh is in direct line, that is a return. A change."

A chill swept up Aiz's arms. It was a star that led Mother Div to a new homeland long ago—the evening star.

"But there are other stars I see," Dolbra breathed. "In dreams, the seers delve beyond what the human eye can perceive and into the empyrean. There, constellations beyond our sky emerge." The seer stepped closer to Aiz now. "The Reaper rose once before, more than one thousand years ago. It rises again. When I look at you now, I see—"

"Holy Seer."

Aiz started, for she'd been so fixated on Dolbra's words that she hadn't noticed the ship's captain approach. She was small and fair-haired, with a stony gaze.

"Holy Seer, it is time for the sunset orison." The captain settled her hand on the seer's shoulder. "The crew awaits."

Dolbra seemed to come out of a daze at the woman's touch. She joined the rest of the crew, and they tipped their heads to the sky while Dolbra hummed. For a moment when everyone else faced the stars, Dolbra seemed to look across the ship at Aiz.

Her gaze pierced through the Kegari girl. Haunted.

Aiz wondered what Dolbra saw.

That night, Aiz pulled out the book she'd stolen from Tiral.

It was written in Ankanese and she'd read through it once already. The stories within appeared simple: "The Demon at the Wedding," "The Storm and the Storyteller," "The Wise Man and His Dutiful Daughter," "The Dragon of Wit and Wile." The types of tales you told children to ensure they didn't wander alone into a dark forest.

Certain words snagged in her head: *Demon. Dusk. Wind. North. Song.*

Tiral wouldn't have been so attached to it if it didn't mean something. There was a message in these words, and Aiz was determined to find it.

She finished one of the stories she'd enjoyed, about a monster who sneaks into a wedding. The setting alone beguiled her—the descriptions of lamps and food, of the bride's wedding dress embroidered to reflect the vivid purples and blues of the desert sky.

Aiz turned the page to see a new title:

THE VESSEL OF THE FOUNT

Aiz stared in astonishment. She'd read the book thrice now. She'd never seen this story. There, in the first paragraph, was Div's name.

Gather, gather and listen well, for Mother Div's voice must not be forgotten. Hear her in the wind which stirs in your blood. Forget her not, for she has not forgotten you.

No, this story was certainly not here before, else Aiz would already have it memorized. Almost without realizing it, she'd devoured half the story. Despite its unusual start, it otherwise mirrored the First Sacred Tale almost to the letter. The calamity across the sea. Div's desperate search for a homeland. The stars leading her to the valley below the Spires, where she settled her people.

But the First Sacred Tale ended at the cloister, with Div caring for animals and orphans and vowing that one day, the Kegari would return to their homeland. In this book, the story went on.

In time, Div felt the call of the wind again. She left Kegar and the burden of rule to her three children, Oona, Ghaz, and Hiwa. Div walked weaponless into the wind and let it carry her aloft to lands unknown, far beyond the Spires of Kegar.

She formed alliances with the Seers of Ankana and the Kins of Jaduna, the Ghost Men of Karkaus, and the Sun Lords of Firan. But the wind pulled at her still, until one day she met betrayal and imprisonment in the lee of a giant's fangs. Div wept, for no creature of fur nor feather dared to tread near her prison. No rain penetrated its shriveled hollow, no wind blew in to freshen the stale air.

There, in a place of unending death, Mother Div's spirit abides, trapped as she awaits one of the Blood to set her free. Only then can she return in the body of the Tel Ilessi, the Holy Vessel. And the Tel Ilessi shall deliver her people back to the homeland from whence they fled, so long ago.

The book fell from Aiz's hands, landing with a leaden thump on the deck. She closed her eyes, not quite believing what she'd read.

The clerics never spoke of Div's death. Only of her passing rulership to the first three Triarchs—her children. Aiz heard the story of Div leaving Kegar once. *More rumor than fact*, Sister Noa had said. *Div was devoted to her people.*

But that didn't mean that this story was false. It had the rhythm of a Sacred Tale.

Aizzzzz.

The voice—Div's voice. Aiz knew it instantly, and she spun, desperate to see the apparition of the Holy Cleric. To ask her if the story was true.

But the voice was different than when she heard it in the prison. More distant.

Help me, daughter. Find me. Release me and I will give you power beyond what you could dream. Power to do anything. Power to save your people.

"Power," Aiz whispered. "Windsmithing?"

Yes. You have the skill. You need only to control it. Windsmithing is the beginning. I can give you more than that. Whatever power you have, I will multiply it one hundredfold.

"Can you—can you help me destroy Tiral?"

As if he never existed. But first you must free me. The road will be hard, Aiz. There will be great sacrifice.

"What—kind of sacrifice?"

You may have to trade the few for the many. You may wish to turn back. But if you hold to the course I set before you, the poor and wretched of Kegar will never suffer again.

"Yes," Aiz said, and she could see it. See Noa and Olnas and Hani free. The cloister thriving, the orphans fed. And she, Aiz, would be the reason. "Tell me what to do, Mother Div."

Read the story. Find me. We will be unstoppable, child.

Mother Div's voice faded and Aiz reread the passage. *A place of unending death.* Aiz had not heard of such a place, but then, she'd never left Kegar. Dolbra might know, or the ship's captain, who was widely traveled.

Something occurred to her then. Dolbra's vision. *You grasped an ancient wind in your hand and swallowed it.* Aiz saw Hani in the dark of the Tohr asking why there were Nine Sacred Tales. *Mother Div whispered the Ninth Sacred Tale to the wind in a faraway land. When the wind circles the earth and returns to Kegar, we will finally hear the tale. Its telling will herald the Return to our homeland.*

Could this be the Ninth Sacred Tale?

Aiz flipped to the front of the book. There were numbers and letters inscribed there. *1006PF.* Only nineteen years ago. A thousand and six years after the cataclysm that drove Aiz's people from their homeland. Below, the author's name.

If it *was* the Ninth Sacred Tale, it had been recorded by a foreigner: *Laia of Serra.*

Excitement flared in Aiz's chest. This was the sign she'd been searching for. The book wasn't old, so Laia of Serra might still live. If so, Aiz would find her, learn how she'd come across the tale. She would find the prison, set Mother Div free, and prove herself worthy.

And then she would become something more than a gutter Snipe, fated to die cold and hungry and worth less than nothing.

The girl hurried to the deck, the book wrapped in oilcloth and bound to her body.

As she emerged, dawn broke, a sudden, brilliant explosion in the eastern sky, made more beautiful after the rain that had followed them out of Kegar. Far ahead, plumes of spray shot into the air as the ocean slammed itself against the high white cliffs of Cape Timdra.

Dolbra was on deck, singing her dawn orisons. Her voice was low, rising and falling like the mournful call of seabirds, the tide a sustained chord beneath. Aiz waited until she was done before speaking.

"Serra," Aiz said to the seer. "I wish to go to Serra."

Dolbra raised her eyebrows in surprise. "The Martial Empire? Why?"

In truth, Aiz knew little of the Martials. According to the clerics, Ankana considered the Empire to be a backward society, as the Martials had only recently freed their slaves, and still thought of the dona'i—those who were neither male nor female but ascended—as oddities.

Aiz straightened her spine. She would learn what she needed to. "I am on a holy mission," she said. "Of the utmost importance. I must meet someone in Serra." She pulled out Tiral's book, skin tingling at the slickness of the cover. "This book has a tale in it that could be significant to my people. The author is someone named Laia of Serra. She's the one person who could tell me more about the tale, if she's still alive."

At this, the seer observed Aiz thoughtfully. "Laia of Serra does not live in Serra," she said. "She is a Kehanni, a storyteller and history-keeper for Tribe Saif, of the Tribal Lands, a vast desert east of the Martial Empire. If you wish to see her, you must disembark in Sadh. Someone there could give you more information about her whereabouts."

"Then that is where I wish to go," Aiz said. "Sadh."

"I will tell the captain." The seer stared at the book, fists clenched. "Beware, daughter of Kegar." Her voice was soft again, as if she feared being overheard. But her eyes were bright. "What you carry"—she put her hand to her heart—"it is powerful. But it casts a shadow too."

Aiz looked down at the book. She'd felt a certain unease when reading it, as if some of its words were lodged in her brain like tiny splinters.

It is *powerful, child*, Mother Div whispered, and there was a tremor in her tone, something like impatience. *Only the weak fear power.*

"Not all shadows are bad, seer." Aiz remembered the darkness of the Tohr. "Without them, there can be no light."

Four weeks after the Ankanese vessel rounded Cape Timdra, Aiz woke to the smell of earth instead of sea. The dhow bumped lazily against a dock.

With her meager belongings on her back, Aiz arrived on deck and was immediately hit by a blast of hot air and a blazing sun. They had arrived in Sadh.

Aiz, first confused by the heat, realized the seasons were switched—in Kegar, it was early spring by now. In Sadh, autumn. That was the beginning of the differences between the two.

If Kegar existed in shades of obsidian and salt, Sadh was soothing umbers and browns, rendering the blue of the sky and the white walls of the houses more vivid. The entire city seemed to be moving at once: Purple and red curtains billowed from open windows. Clouds of creosote-scented dust rose from brightly painted caravans snaking into the desert. The harbor teemed with humans and animals. Wooden pulleys creaked beneath the weight of enormous crates.

Aiz wished she could show Cero. Noa. She wished they could hear the air, cacophonous with conversation and laughter and ebullience. Until Aiz heard it here, she didn't realize—there were as many shades of joy in Sadh as there were suffering in the slums of Kegar. A spike of bitterness curdled her awe. Hani and Jak and Finh did not have this kind of joy. No, her people were cursed to misery.

But not forever. Not if Aiz found Laia of Serra and through her, set Mother Div's spirit free.

"Aiz bet-Dafra." Dolbra spoke from behind the girl, gesturing to the gangplank. "Our oath is upheld. Your mount awaits. I've given you my own saddle." She nodded to a lower ramp, where one of the Ankanese crewmen coaxed Tregan onto the dock.

"Thank you for all you taught me," Aiz offered, for Dolbra had told her much of the Tribes that would be useful. "Perhaps I will see you again one day."

"If you have need of me, find one of my fellow seers, and ask for Dolbra. They will know the name. Emifal Firdaant." The seer offered the traditional Ankanese words of parting. *May death claim me first.*

Aiz reunited with Tregan, who appeared as happy as Aiz to finally be off the ship. They lurched together down the long dock and into the harbor crowds, Aiz feeling as if the ground still swelled beneath her.

The throng parted, with more than a few people giving Aiz a second glance. Likely because her tangled brown hair was styled in the Kegari way, the long strands pulled into braided knots. The clothing the Ankanese had given her looked ragged against even the simplest Tribal garb.

A lithe Tribal woman swathed in scarlet approached. Aiz gaped at her mirrored pants and the jeweled scarf wrapped around her hair. She must be wealthy to wear such beautiful clothing.

Or perhaps such finery was commonplace. In the distance, another woman wearing identical garb greeted a group of passengers disembarking from a ship.

The first woman peered over Aiz's shoulder at the Ankanese vessel.

"I am Neita—of Tribe Sadh," the woman said in accented Ankanese. "Welcome to our city. I am here to aid you, as my Tribe aids all newcomers. How may I assist?"

"I need clothes," Aiz said. "A place to stable my horse." She glanced around. She was drawing too much notice. "And a haircut. I can pay." She'd hidden Cero's coins under her shirt. She didn't want to get robbed. "But I would like to get out of the street."

Neita nodded, gesturing for Aiz to follow.

They made their way to a broad avenue lined with date palms and wagons, shops and restaurants. A rainbow of clothing fluttered on lines above them. Each storefront had a different colored awning, the merchants within trying to out-shout each other and draw in customers.

But it was the wagons lining the street that slowed Aiz's steps. For they were filled with food.

Vegetables she'd never seen before glistening with oil and herbs. Skewered meat, fat dripping in mouthwatering rivulets onto mountains of rice. Baskets of steaming golden bread shaped like half-moons.

A child ran past Aiz carrying a stick of roasted vegetables. In his excitement to follow his playmate, it slipped from his hands. He hardly looked at it before running off, and Aiz snatched it up without breaking stride, though her heart thudded. She waited for someone to stop her. To demand the food.

But no one noticed. The children here had full cheeks and glossy hair. They weren't fighting for fallen food, because they weren't hungry. A few months ago, she'd opened the cloister's front gate to the body of a man who'd starved to death in the night.

This place was miraculous. And obscene. Aiz wanted it for herself. But more than that, she wanted it for her people. She wished she could steal every last morsel and take it to Kegar. Feed the cloisters for months.

In time, Div's voice whispered in her mind.

"Come!" her escort, Neita, called out, and Aiz hurried to follow. "I apologize for the crowds. But you're lucky you didn't come a fortnight ago! The Martial Empress was here with the crown prince, and it was madness. Everyone in the city was trying to get an audience."

Aiz listened carefully as Neita spoke, surreptitiously shoving bits of vegetable skewer in her mouth. The strangeness of this place was almost intimidating. But Mother Div had sent her here for a reason. She must learn all she could about these people.

By noon, Tregan was stabled, and Aiz inhaled an enormous meal at an inn. The innkeeper, who introduced herself as Neita's wife, cut Aiz's hair to just below her ears with a delightful lack of sentiment, and then drew Aiz a bath.

When she finally emerged, clutching her book, it was to find a new leather pack on the bed, along with a pouch to wear against her body. Aiz ran her fingers along a soft, split riding skirt with a matching green and fawn-colored top. Inside the pack, she found a sand-colored cloak, its edges lined in green, and on the floor beside it, brushed riding boots. They were big, but still the finest shoes Aiz had ever owned.

Again, Aiz thought of Kegar, but Mother Div spoke: *Do not weep at the injustice your people face. Else you will not have the strength to change their plight.*

Aiz jumped at the suddenness of the words. At the bite in them. Perhaps she'd disappointed Mother Div by focusing on the material pleasures in front of her, instead of her holy mission.

She moved her possessions into the new pack, threw it over her back, and made her way downstairs, twirling her aaj around her finger.

"Now you look as though you have received a proper welcome to my city." Neita gestured for Aiz to take the seat beside her at the common room fire. "What brings you here, child? I don't even know your name!"

"I'm looking for someone," Aiz said. "Laia of Serra."

It was as if all the lamps went out at once. The woman's face closed, suddenly forbidding. She exchanged glances with her wife, running a rag along the bar.

"What would you want with Laia of Serra?" Neita said. "I warn you: as a Kehanni, she's well protected by Tribe Saif."

"Neita!" the innkeeper snapped, shaking her head.

Kehanni. Dolbra had told Aiz of the different roles in the Tribes: the Zaldars, who led each Tribe; the Fakirs, who tended to the dead; and the Kehannis, who kept its histories.

"Tribe Saif," Aiz said. "Are they here in the city?"

It was the wrong question.

"No one who would seek the Kehanni for unwholesome reasons

is welcome here." Neita's fists clenched and Aiz raised her hands in alarm.

"I don't mean her harm!" Aiz nearly took out the book to show them, but some instinct within quailed against it. She could not risk them coveting it and taking it from her. And she certainly couldn't tell them that she needed Laia to help her find the trapped spirit of Mother Div. They would think her a madwoman. "I'm interested in a story she told. I wished to ask her about it."

Neita's lips thinned and her hand strayed to the blade at her waist. "Sadh is a long way to come for a story."

"Look at me." She held out her skinny wrists. "I couldn't do her any harm."

"Trouble comes in strange packages." The innkeeper exchanged another glance with Neita, and they appeared to come to a decision without speaking.

"We thank you for your custom," Neita said. "But you'll wish to find lodgings elsewhere for the night."

In moments, Neita hustled Aiz out the door and back to the dusty streets of Sadh. Tregan was shoved out too, and they both stared at the courtyard gate, latched and locked against them.

Tregan whinnied, sensing Aiz's irritation, and she rubbed the mare between her ears. "We'll have to go about this another way."

The day was swelteringly hot, enough that Aiz was tempted to call the wind—only a trickle, to cool her brow. But there might be Jaduna in Sadh's streets, so she resisted, sweating her way through the city, into markets and caravanserais, looking for those who spoke Ankanese. She wasn't fool enough to bring up Laia's name again. Instead, she made small talk, learning of the desert beyond Sadh. She listened to a Kehanni tell a tale in a market square and paid a young merchant's assistant a few pennies to translate for her.

"I was not given this tale by a stranger, nor was it overheard around the fire. I speared it in the far west," the Kehanni said, "after searching out one of the blue-painted warlocks of Karkaus." The woman spoke as if the story was alive, as if she'd hunted it; Aiz filed the information away.

She bought spare clothing, oats for Tregan, a canteen, flint, tinder, dried meat. She listened and watched, learning that each Tribe sold a little of everything. But most had specialties. Tribe Nasur was known for its rugs. Tribe Nur for its lamps and rugs.

And Tribe Saif for its medicines and cures.

"Do you speak Ankanese?" Aiz asked a woman selling an array of herbs and poultices. The woman nodded—Aiz knew she would. She'd been watching her for the better part of an hour.

"My mother has an ailment of the lungs." Aiz let desperation seep into her voice. "I've tried bloodroot, green iris, and hallowrose sap. Nothing works."

The woman perused her own goods doubtfully. "I have basic cures, miss. I'd suggest a posset of fennelflame. But you'd need to go to one of the caravans for it."

"I've come from the south—I don't know anyone here."

She let a tear fall and the woman patted her kindly on the shoulder. "You could try Tribe Salah. They're on the east end of the city, near the gate. I'd suggest Tribe Saif, as their cures are the best, but they left Sadh a few days ago."

"I'll try my luck with Tribe Salah," Aiz said. Then, feigning an afterthought: "If they don't have it, can you tell me where Tribe Saif might be? My mother is the last person I have in this world. I'll do anything to help her, travel any distance."

The woman put her hand to her heart. "She is lucky to have a daughter like you." Her voice was thick with emotion. "Tribe Saif went north. They try to get to Nur before the winter storms. But beware on the road. There are coyotes and efrits."

By the time the sun set, Aiz had everything she needed. She and Tregan fell in with a large wagon train also making its way out of the city. The gate guards let her pass with hardly a glance. As soon as she was through, she nudged Tregan into a trot, and soon left the caravan and the city of Sadh far behind.

17
Quil

The Kegari were everywhere in Jibaut. In the skies, but also creeping along the docks in their blue-scaled armor, muttering to each other in their own language while barking orders in Ankanese to everyone else. The dock agents and stevedores and corsairs watched the newcomers with churlishness instead of challenge. The savagery of the Kegari attack had quelled even the bravest of Jibaut's residents.

Most of the pirates had left to raid the Empire's southern cities. The only ships in the port were from Marinn.

"No Martials, either." Arelia eyed the city with Quil, chewing on one of her curls. "The Kegari will be rounding up our people, to question or kill. Keep that hood low, cousin."

"You'll be all right, alone?" Quil asked. Worry ate at him as he pondered his aunt's message. *The Butcher lives. The Orphan roars.* Old codes referring to Aunt Hel and Laia. Musa sent the wight, so he'd be alive too, but Navium's fall haunted Quil. When he considered that something might also happen to Arelia or Sufiyan, he felt almost frantic. But his cousin waved him off.

"The dock agent will make sure no one steals the ship," Arelia said. "I need to understand this engine. If it's to take us to Ankana, it must last. Fear not, if I get bored, I can reread Rajin's *Recollections*."

Quil smiled. The little book was the only thing he'd carried with him from Navium, other than his clothes and scim.

"Don't forget my coveralls." Arelia looked distastefully at her dress. "Or the willadonna."

Not likely. The herb naturally dilated the pupils, which would allow Arelia and Quil, with their distinctively pale Martial irises, to avoid drawing attention. Quil hated the idea of using it. Of sneaking and skulking to survive, while back in the Empire, his people fought.

Arelia nodded to Sufiyan, who was paying off the dock agent. "Keep an eye on him. He appears to have a death wish."

Quil raised his eyebrows. "Is my *scim-happy* friend growing on you?"

"Days spent with a small group of not-awful people breeds tolerance. I put up with you, don't I?" Arelia disappeared below and Quil met Sufiyan at the dock.

"You seem upset," Sufiyan observed, and Quil glanced at him in surprise—he'd buried the feeling deep enough that he'd almost forgotten it was there.

"The Kegari," Quil said. "Seeing them . . ." His fingers itched for his scim, and he took a deep breath to quell his temper, as he always did with strong emotions. Then he heard Sirsha in his head:

You're so afraid if you feel something, you'll actually have to do something. And that if you do something, it will be the wrong thing.

Perhaps her words shouldn't have hit so hard, but they reminded him of the night Ilar died. She'd fought with Quil because he hadn't spoken to Aunt Helene about her. The Empress wouldn't approve of the crown prince falling for a no-name Ankanese girl. They had no future.

You say you want to be with me, Quil, but if you did, you'd tell your aunt about me. You'd take me with you to the capital. You'd let me meet the Empress.

He'd responded to her accusation with silence, worried that the wrong words would drive her away forever. Didn't matter. Later that night, she was dead anyway. Torn into pieces by the same murderer who burned out Ruh's heart.

"You going to say anything, or just stand around looking murderous?" Sufiyan eyed him askance, and Quil realized that he was stock-still, white-knuckling the hilt of his scim.

"I've already run from Navium." Quil was almost choked by a sudden wave of self-loathing, and here, in a sopping pirate's port with his best friend, it poured out of him. "I abandoned my family and my duty and the Empire—and *do not*"—he held up his hand at Sufiyan's protests—"say I didn't, because I'd hate to hear you lie. I did it because my aunt ordered it, and I'm good at following rules. But that's not going to help us now."

He looked out at Jibaut, at the lamps gleaming dully through the downpour as night drew closer.

"Musa will send another wight soon," Quil said. "This time, we send information back."

"About what?" Sufiyan squinted at the beaten faces of Jibaut's residents. "How even the pirates are afraid of the sky-pigs?"

"The Kegari reserve forces are here. The more intelligence the Empire has about them, the better. But Aunt Hel knows almost nothing." He met Sufiyan's eyes. "Let's change that."

Sufiyan led them through Jibaut's slick cobbled streets; with his features, he wasn't as conspicuous as Quil. The rain fell heavily enough that it was difficult to catch conversations in full. But the attack on Navium and the destruction of the Empire's navy was on everyone's lips.

After hearing it a dozen times, Sufiyan's fists were clenched as tight as Quil's. "How long do you think Serra will withstand the onslaught?"

"A few months," Quil said. "Spring, Musa's note said. But Elias knows the way out of there—in case."

"He knows the way out of every place," Sufiyan said with a note of pride. "I miss him and Ama. Nan was always telling me to appreciate what we had." Sufiyan spoke of the Bani al-Mauth, for he was one of four people who dared to call her anything but her title. "Wish I'd bleeding listened."

"Old people know things we don't because long ago, they didn't listen to their elders either," Quil said as they ducked into a darkened lean-to filled with moldering hay. "It's tradition."

Sufiyan snickered—not quite a laugh, but close enough. Better than nothing, anyway. Suf hadn't laughed in ages.

"Wait here," Suf said. Light flared from a tavern across the street as the door opened, and a pair of patrons tumbled out. "Someone in there will know where the Kegari are camped."

Quil waited in the rain, hating Jibaut more every time another pirate passed. He used to *want* to visit this place. Especially after Laia and Elias had come to the city with their youngest son, Ruhyan, in tow.

When Ruh returned from the trip, he'd been brimming with stories of emerald boats with ruby sails, markets bursting with smugglers, jugglers, and sorcerers. He'd brought Quil a gift—the bracelet Quil still wore.

Ruh loved Quil as a big brother, demanding lessons in archery and rides on his shoulders. He didn't care that Quil was the crown prince. Sufiyan groused when Ruh tagged after them, but Quil laughed at Ruh's stories, answered his questions. In return, Ruh never minded when Quil was quiet.

It was Quil who'd found Ruh and Ilar. Or what was left of them, anyway, in the recesses of a place he hoped to never see again. He'd never told anyone that he'd fought with Ilar before she died. He knew they'd say it wasn't his fault, and he wanted the guilt. He deserved it. If he'd done what Ilar had asked, she wouldn't have ridden off, brokenhearted. She wouldn't have been torn to shreds by a killer. And Ruh—

Dash that thought from your head, boy. The Bani al-Mauth had given him an order, and he'd tried his best to follow it, but it felt wrong to forget Ruh. Now, in the shadows of Jibaut, the prince reached for his wrist, for the bracelet he'd worn since then in honor of his young friend.

Only to find that it was gone.

He checked his cloak and pack before remembering this morning. Sirsha, stumbling. Touching his arm. Skies above. He was a fool. His aunt had taught him the finer points of thievery to prevent this exact thing from happening. He'd caught Sirsha once and thought himself clever, but this morning, she'd looked at him with her big brown eyes, batted those sooty lashes, and he'd been so busy mooning over the ring of smoky gray around her irises that he'd dropped his guard.

Wherever she was now, she must be laughing at how naive he was.

Someone staggered out of the darkness, pulling Quil's thoughts from the treacherous Jaduna. He'd drawn his sword halfway when he realized it was Sufiyan, bottle in hand. He was putting on a rather impressive act. Like many Tribespeople, Sufiyan didn't drink.

He reached Quil quickly. "Found our mark," he said. "Speaks Ankanese and has rank. He should be emerging in four . . . three . . . two . . ."

The door to the tavern opened, and a pasty-faced Kegari soldier tripped out and vomited into the street before staggering away.

Quil shook his head in disgust. "He's too drunk to be of any use."

"A little more faith in me, brother." Sufiyan clapped Quil on the shoulder. "I gave him Iltim. Excellent for headaches. Causes nausea with cheap ale. His friends will assume he's drunk. He needs to empty his stomach a few times, and then he'll be ripe for a little interrogation."

The two followed the stumbling Kegari soldier, and when he finally turned into an alley, Quil and Sufiyan quickened their pace. The prince spotted a large wooden rubbish bin and nodded to it. It stank, but it would hide their activities from anyone passing. Sufiyan, who'd been singing tunelessly, raised his voice, speaking Ankanese.

"Oi—you there. Sky-pig!"

The Kegari soldier spun around, groping for his weapon—which Sufiyan had already relieved him of. Suf shoved the soldier against the wall, a knife at his throat.

"We have some questions." Quil spoke in Ankanese and pulled his hood low as the rain poured down. His accent was Marinese because that's where his tutor had been from. All the better to throw the Kegari off. "You're going to answer them."

"Rue la ba Tel Ilessi! Kwye asti falli!"

"Speak Ankanese," Quil snarled, and Sufiyan dug the knife into the man's neck.

"I don't speak to Martial-loving snakes," the Kegari spat. "I will tell you nothing."

"Oh, but you will, cat bucket." Sufiyan's Ankanese was rougher than Quil's, but when he drew a long line of blood from the man's throat, his meaning was clear enough.

"How many reserve troops are there?" Quil asked.

The Kegari snarled. "Rue la ba Tel Ilessi!"

Voices echoed from the street beyond the alley. If they turned this way—

"*How many reserve troops?*" Quil growled.

"Rue la ba Tel Ilessi," the man whispered, though with fear instead of defiance.

He lunged for Quil, and Sufiyan lifted the dagger in defense, sinking it deep into the man's throat. Sufiyan jumped back, cursing as the man dropped to his knees, blood waterfalling from his neck. In mere moments, he fell face-first into the mud. Dead.

"Come on." Quil grabbed Sufiyan as he stared in horror at the dead man. "Move, Sufiyan."

His friend had never killed anyone. Quil had, of course. Killing didn't get easier. But nothing was worse than that first time, and Quil wished he'd had the bleeding sense to consider that before he'd dragged Sufiyan into the streets of Jibaut.

"Suf, walk." Ahead of them, near the next cross street, the group of people they'd heard talking hurried past, unaware of the body steps away. Sufiyan's gaze was wild, his hands shaking as he lurched back from the pool of blood spreading beneath the body.

"Walk!"

They made it to the end of the alley and through the nearly empty square on the other side. A Kegari patrol approached, blue armor flashing in the rain, but Quil and Sufiyan were out of sight before the soldiers could call out.

Quil wanted to punch a wall. They'd failed to get information and killed a man—for nothing at all. Best to cut their losses, get the supplies, and get the hells out of Jibaut.

Most cities had order to them—neighborhoods, business districts, markets, and squares. But Jibaut was laid out willy-nilly, as if a child playing with blocks had spilled them all at once and called it a city. Quil took a dozen wrong turns past dilapidated neighborhoods half-overtaken by the forest, shuttered shops, and a crowded shipbuilding yard before lights blazed ahead and voices echoed. A night market.

The market took up both sides of a wide boulevard and was packed so full of hooded buyers that Quil worried less about being recognized as Martial, and more that he and Sufiyan wouldn't be able to shove their way through. The thick flow of humanity hardly noticed the rain. Merchants beneath canvas tarps sold their goods with shrill vigor; tavern rats spilled into the crowded streets, ales in hand.

"An apothecary." Sufiyan nodded to a building a hundred feet away, its mortar and pestle sign illuminated by a sputtering lamp. "Let's get the willadonna."

Sufiyan's voice was flat, like it had been after Quil had found Ruh. Like after Karinna—Sufiyan's fifteen-year-old sister—had screamed at her big brother, *You were supposed to watch him!*

"Suf—"

His friend whirled on him. "I don't want to talk about it!" Sufiyan snarled. "He was going to kill us. I beat him to it. Your aunt did it a thousand times in the war. So did my parents. And you—in the border skirmishes. How old were you? Thirteen? I'm eighteen, for skies' sake."

"That's *why* I'm bringing it up. Aunt Helene talked to me about it, and it helped."

Sufiyan pushed ahead and Quil wanted to leave him be. He didn't want to fight with Sufiyan, least of all while hurrying through crowds of Jibaut's denizens, many of whom would happily sell them to the Kegari for the price of an evening meal.

But he took Sufiyan's arm anyway.

"You don't have to talk about it now," he said before Suf could bite his head off again. "But you will, eventually. If not to me, to Arelia. You can't stick a knife in someone for the first time and pretend it didn't—"

"I hated it, all right?" Sufiyan said. "I feel like the only thing I've thought about for the past year is death and loss, and now killing, and all I want is to bleeding get away from it. But I've just killed a man myself and I can't reckon with it yet. Maybe one day, but—"

His voice broke, and Quil sighed. "I'm sorry, Sufiyan, I shouldn't have—"

"Quil—look." Sufiyan nodded at something beyond Quil, and the prince groaned at the paltry excuse for a distraction.

"I'm apologizing, all right?" Quil said. "It—it seems like you've been gone for months now, and I wish we'd talk."

"Quil—turn *around*. Slowly."

"Maybe you're angry at me, because I didn't protect Ruh, but—"

Sufiyan finally met Quil's gaze. "We clearly both have feelings to discuss," he said. "But for now, will you shut it and look?"

The prince turned and immediately spotted what had caught Sufiyan's notice. In front of a tavern with a raised wraparound porch, at a table brightly illuminated by a row of dangling lamps, a woman argued with a young blond man. The woman had dark hair swept into a pile atop her head. A sharp jaw. Full, heart-shaped lips and cheekbones as keen as a Teluman scim. High red boots.

Sirsha.

Without speaking, Quil and Sufiyan shoved their way across the street toward the tavern. Sufiyan nodded at a cobbler's stall ahead of them with a wide awning, a few steps from Sirsha's table. The cobbler was locked in an argument with a customer waving a broken boot heel at him.

Quil made for the left side of the awning, Sufiyan for the right. The shadows were deep enough that anyone looking over from the veranda wouldn't be able to make out much.

Once ensconced in the dark, the prince eyed the Jaduna at leisure. It was the first time he'd looked at her—really looked—without telling himself to look away. There was something different about her. No— Quil realized. It was the way people looked at her. With wariness.

Jibaut was a dangerous place at night. Sirsha, Quil realized, was one of the reasons why. She wore a belt of knives across her chest, daggers at both hips and in each boot—none of which she'd had on the ship. Her shirt was low-cut, her leather armor close-fitting and made to accentuate her curves. She had a silhouette that would draw the eye of most people with a pulse. Quil noticed a few people looking—all surreptitiously—for there was a boldness to her, a bite.

She didn't have that amused smirk that had frustrated and fascinated him so much while on the shabka. She was all business.

The prince tried to interpret the cant of her head, the flash of white as she bit her full bottom lip in what could be anything from anxiety to flirtation.

At the thought of the latter, annoyance swept through him.

Sufiyan, who'd sidled up beside him, glanced over. "Jealous?" he whispered.

Quil wasn't about to lie to Sufiyan, so he shrugged. "Let's get closer."

Together, they inched to almost the end of the cobbler's awning. Rain soaked Quil's shoulder. He could barely hear the conversation over the downpour.

"—too deep. Let this go, tracker."

"Not an option," Sirsha said. "What's *wrong* with you, Kade? You're acting strange. You look awful. Are you ill?"

"You cannot hunt this killer," the man called Kade said. Indeed, he had heavy pink shadows under his eyes, and the waxy skin of someone who'd been unwell. Still, he was handsome, and the way he looked at Sirsha told Quil that if they weren't lovers now, they had been in the past. "It's too dangerous, even for you, Inashi."

"A murderer is a murderer." Sirsha sat back, arms crossed. "With weaknesses like anyone else. There must be something in those books of yours about the killer's magic."

"I can't help you. Find someone else."

"The only person who knows the old lore better than you is a month's ride south in a bleeding swamp, and you *know* how I feel about swamps. Besides which, the last time I saw her, she told me not to come back—"

"Sirsha—"

"Give me something, Kade. For old times' sake."

"Don't be angry at me. I—I—"

Kade glanced down at his hands, as if considering. But Quil saw his gaze flick over Sirsha's shoulder to the building beside the tavern. It was so swift that if Quil hadn't been staring right at the man, he'd have missed it.

"He's stalling," Quil realized aloud. "Distracting her."

"Bleeding hells." Sufiyan looked to their left, where a shadow detached from a darkened building and moved swiftly toward the tavern. Another figure cut through the crowded veranda with the patience of a shark on the hunt. A third silently crossed the lane not three yards from Quil and Sufiyan.

Sirsha was so busy trying to persuade Kade to help her that she didn't see the shadows closing in on her. Sufiyan reached back for his bow, but Quil grabbed his arm.

"Those are Jaduna surrounding her," he said. "Her own people. They won't hurt her."

"Don't you remember what she said about her family?"

When my family finds me and subjects me to a brutal death . . .

Quil caught a flash of gold—a Jaduna headdress. The hooded woman wearing it looked forbidding. Not like a family member welcoming home a lost daughter.

Moments later, the shadows—who'd moved slowly until now—descended on the tavern with sudden, near inhuman swiftness. The patrons on the veranda sensed a fight and began to jeer, but someone called out "Jaduna!" and in seconds, the crowd was tripping over itself to get away.

"Come on." Quil tried to pull Sufiyan away. "It's not safe, Suf."

"She's hunting my brother's killer." Suf shook Quil off. "We can't leave her to them."

"She's smart. She'll figure it out—" But even Quil froze as he watched Sirsha stand. Watched her realize that she was surrounded. The look she cast Kade could have melted stone.

"I'm sorry, Sirsha." Kade sounded genuinely aggrieved. "I didn't want to—for whatever that's worth."

Sirsha snarled at him. "Less than a moldering rat carcass, you traitorous—"

"*Traitorous,*" the Jaduna in the headdress said, pushing back her hood as she sauntered forward. She was older than Sirsha, with the same straight blue-black hair and brown skin. But her countenance was cold, her lips thin. Her voice was low and melodious, like Sirsha's, but something unpleasant seethed beneath.

The woman's headdress had a central, dandelion-sized coin dangling from the part in her hair. The coin was linked to a half dozen chains on either side, each adorned with thin gold triangles that looked like teeth.

Quil's stomach sank at the sight. She was a Raan-Ruku. *Strong in magic. Never to be crossed.*

She stopped in front of Sirsha, and Quil held his breath as the woman looked Sirsha up and down, her lip curled.

"Traitorous," the Jaduna said again, drawing the word out, almost savoring it. She smiled, all teeth. "You'd know about that, wouldn't you, little sister?"

18
Sirsha

The Jaduna had ambushed her. Of course they had—they weren't stupid and they knew Sirsha wasn't either. But if they were here in Jibaut in force, they could have killed her already. Which meant that her sister either wished to make a spectacle of her death, or she wanted something.

Sirsha hoped it was the latter. But with R'zwana, you never could tell.

"Bind her up," R'zwana ordered whoever was behind Sirsha. "Quickly."

Sirsha groaned. "R'z—"

"Do not speak to me, traitor," R'zwana said, voice flat. "Everything out of your bitch mouth is poison."

Sirsha took a step back, face hot, as if R'zwana had slapped her. She'd almost forgotten the unpleasantly specific sting of an insult from an older sibling. Particularly one you used to worship.

With dawning horror, Sirsha felt tears welling as the Jaduna surrounded her. After the ignominy of first getting caught unawares, crying would be too humiliating. Sirsha forced herself to grin and offer her hands up mockingly to D'rudo, her old teacher and cousin, who refused to meet Sirsha's eyes.

"Didn't realize you missed me so badly, R'z," Sirsha said. "You could have just written."

"Gag her too," R'zwana said. "I don't want to listen to her drivel."

Before Sirsha could respond, the gag came around from behind her. Then the hood.

She tested the stretch of her bonds—barely any room to twitch her hands. Her gag was so tight it might as well have been shoved down her throat. Bleeding D'rudo. He always was excellent at following orders. She listened carefully. There were at least three Jaduna here. Possibly four.

If Sirsha wanted to escape, her best chance was now, before they marched her into their compound on the other end of the city. Not for the first time, Sirsha wished she'd been born with one of the other Jaduna leanings. A Deshma with battle magic. A Khind who could slow the blood. A Bij who could call fire or lightning to her aid. A combination would be ideal.

But she was Inashi, a tracker, and could only read the earth, wind, and water. Bleeding useless. Especially since she was so accustomed to Jibaut's Jaduna compound being empty that she hadn't checked for her people, thinking herself safe.

Sirsha called to the earth, the most helpful of the elements. *A little quake, please. The tiniest rumble?* The earth didn't answer. Almost as soon as Sirsha asked, the Jaduna closed ranks around her, and her magic was choked off. She couldn't feel a single element. The trail she'd sensed, the one that had left her dizzy hours earlier—it disappeared too.

So, there was a Deshma with them. One strong enough to smother Sirsha's power.

"Please come along quietly, Sirsh."

At first, she didn't recognize the young male voice. But then a cool hand wrapped around her arm, kinder than R'zwana would ever be.

"J'yan?" she mumbled, though through the gag, it sounded more like *Jrrggh?*

"Quiet now," he said, softly enough that R'zwana wouldn't hear. He loosened the gag so Sirsha could talk. "Or R'zwana will hear."

A welter of confusion and joy and anger churned inside her. J'yan was a year older than her and trained in battle magic. When he was born, a Jaduna soul-seer, a Songma, predicted he would be the strongest battle Jaduna in eight generations.

That same soul-seer had attended R'zwana's birth, two years before, and said nothing of note. But when Sirsha was born, the soul-seer had a different message.

Rejoice, Raani, the woman told Sirsha's mother, *for your second daughter will shake the world.*

Within hours of Sirsha's birth, she was promised to the heir of the Deshma: J'yan.

It wasn't an oath to be taken lightly. A marriage in most places was an exchange of vows. But the Jaduna joined couples with magic, not as spouses but as Adah—*soul halves.*

Sirsha and J'yan played together, trained together, hunted together. He'd been sweet and kind and laughed when Sirsha wound him up. Neither understood they were sworn to each other, not until they were older and overheard their mothers speaking of it. They'd stifled their laughter by stuffing scarves into their mouths until they'd run far enough away from their village that they could howl without anyone hearing.

And then when she was twelve, Sirsha was banished. Her mother had nearly been unseated as Raani, and the Deshma Raani had threatened to pledge her Kin's loyalty to one of the other four Jaduna Raanis—preferably one who could keep her children under control.

Sirsha had last seen J'yan at the borders of Jaduna lands, standing behind a jubilant R'zwana, face wet with tears.

She'd thought about him a great deal in the months after she'd left. He'd been her friend—her only friend, it sometimes felt like.

"You were a fool to come here," he whispered to her now. "And trusting a Devanese pirate? It's a miracle you've survived this long."

"How was I supposed to know you lot would turn Kade?" Sirsha muttered, lest her bloodthirsty sister overhear. "He's been trustworthy until now."

Though upon consideration, that wasn't exactly true. Sirsha and Kade had been friends—sometimes more. But Kade's obsession with obscure languages and more obscure lore meant he trafficked in stolen things. The Jaduna could have bought him off with a few rare scrolls. Hells, Sirsha had done so herself a time or two.

"R'zwana's changed," J'yan said. "She'll show no mercy, S'rsh—Sirsha."

She winced at the sound of the old honorific that had marked her as Jaduna, a glottal stop that came from deep in the throat. *S'rsha* was the name that fit her. *Sirsha* was what had been foisted upon her. The reminder hurt.

J'yan quickened his gait, and Sirsha nearly tripped trying to keep up. She heard voices nearby but didn't bother calling for help. No one in Jibaut was brave enough to cross a group of fully coined Jaduna, two of whom were Raan-Ruku.

She snorted at that. When she was a child, a Wolf's magic oozed out of them. J'yan was strong in battle magic and deserved the title.

R'zwana did not.

They arrived at the Jaduna compound after a half-hour march. The air shifted, growing quiet and smelling of sap. Sirsha had seen the compound before and could imagine it now, the moss-covered boards blending seamlessly with the thick green forest of the mountains.

"Stairs," J'yan muttered. The Jaduna moved silently, but Sirsha's boots clanked loudly against the wide wooden planks. She smirked, knowing the racket would grate at R'zwana's nerves.

Once inside, J'yan nudged her into a wooden seat. Her hood and gag were finally removed, and she squinted despite the dim light. No windows. One door. A suspicious-looking stain on the oak floor. Sirsha's back was to the wall with three kohl-eyed Jaduna arrayed in a half circle in front of her.

D'rudo had the same thick black hair and barrel chest as when he was a younger man. He had more scars on his forearms and his hairline was higher, but his exasperation was familiar.

J'yan, with his curly hair and lean build, was still beautiful as a jinn, but with the stern mien of a Raan-Ruku. His rank was a testament to his power. The Wolves were nearly always women.

What did J'yan see as his dark eyes roved over her face? He gave nothing away—that *had* changed. The J'yan she remembered was an open book.

And then there was R'zwana. Cold, superior, *dangerous* R'zwana.

"Watch the hall, D'rudo," R'zwana ordered.

D'rudo gave Sirsha a warning glance before parting. *Don't cross her*, it seemed to say. R'zwana paced in front of her, headdress jangling softly.

"What are you doing in Jibaut?" she asked.

"Got sick of candle-making in the Empire." Sirsha smiled. "Thought I'd try my luck here. Better wax. Longer—"

Sirsha expected a blow. R'zwana always had a rubbish sense of humor. She *didn't* expect for it to smart quite so badly.

She spat on the floor. No blood. "Longer wicks," she finished.

"The conditions of your banishment were that you never return to Jaduna lands," her sister ground out. "That you never use your Inashi magic again. The punishment for breaking the banishment is—"

"Death by drowning, my body left as carrion that I might never return to the earth that nourished me, yes, I know." Sirsha yawned expansively, though even thinking those words made her stomach clench. "I think you'll find that our darling mother's exact words were: *You will never again use Inashi magic to hunt as your Kin had hunted.* You lot hunt human magic-users who are a threat to society, yes? Karjad? I hunt other quarry."

Another slap. Harder this time.

"Address her as Raani, cur. She is our sovereign and a thousand times the Inashi you are—"

Sirsha felt a heedlessness come over her, born of a sorrow she'd buried deep—the knowledge that her only sibling would never respect or love her. And there was nothing she could do to change it.

"Actually"—Sirsha spat again, and a red-tinged blob splattered wide against the floor—"she's one of *six* sovereigns and a thousand times the Inashi *you* are. She and I—we're equal, at least. That's where the problem started. Or don't you remember?"

The next blow was less a slap and more of a punch—straight at Sirsha's eye. Her head snapped back and stars burst in her vision. For a moment, everything went white.

Outside, the wind howled. The walls of the Jaduna compound rattled.

"Does our mother even know you're here, wasting your time with me?" Sirsha said. "Don't you think she'd disapprove of you hunting her favorite chi—"

"Enough!" J'yan stepped between Sirsha and R'zwana, something he'd had much practice with. "Sirsha," he said, "you hunt a killer who uses magic. We know this because we hunt him too. We've been scenting the Karjad for six months, and the trail led us here."

"Bleeding hells," Sirsha couldn't help saying. "It took you six *months* to track a mark so far?" *It only took me three weeks.* She quashed the retort when J'yan frowned at her—he'd clearly picked up on the direction of her thoughts.

"He's killed many, Sirsha," J'yan said. "He'll kill more if we don't destroy him."

She! Sirsha bit back the reply. "Destroy away," she said. "Just leave me be."

"Perhaps you could aid us," J'yan said, and Sirsha tried to hide a smile. So *that's* why they hadn't killed her. They needed her. "This murderer—we don't understand his magic."

R'zwana shoved J'yan away from Sirsha.

"She is a traitor and an outcast," she hissed. "I'll be reporting this defiance to the Raani. And you—" R'zwana turned on Sirsha, who cringed, hating herself for it.

Wrath between blood runs deep, D'rudo said when, as a child, Sirsha confessed R'zwana's cruelty. *When she looks at you, she looks in a mirror, and sees everything she was meant to be.*

"R'zwana," J'yan said. "Don't. Please."

Sirsha's skin prickled with familiar fear as R'zwana stalked toward her.

She had been vicious when they were children, a bizarre, one-sided rivalry that left cuts on Sirsha's skin, bruises in her mind. *I'll kill you*, her sister had said to her a hundred times for the pettiest of reasons: when Sirsha looked at her wrong or ate more than her share. *I swear one day, I'll kill you.*

The Raani had rolled her eyes at the threats. *Sisters!* she'd said. But Sirsha had seen other sisters. They didn't fear their older siblings the way she did. The best night of sleep Sirsha had in years was after she was banished, and she'd put an ocean between herself and R'z.

"You were told that if you used your Inashi magic to hunt as we hunt, you would die," R'zwana said. "We hunt a Karjad. So do you. Thus, you have flouted that law. As a Raan-Ruku, I have the right to mete out punishment in the name of our Raanis. Your punishment is death."

"R'z." Sirsha laughed, because for all R'zwana's viciousness, her threats to murder Sirsha had only ever been threats. "If you were going to do it, you would have already. What do you want? Help? Fine, I'll help." If the Jaduna aided her in rounding up the killer faster, all the better. They didn't need to know how well Sirsha was being paid, and Elias didn't need to know Sirsha had help.

"I don't want your aid," R'zwana said softly. "I want your death."

Sirsha opened her mouth to respond, but when she looked into the jagged glass of R'zwana's eyes, every retort she'd had fled her mind. Her sister was serious.

R'zwana *had* gotten worse.

"I would have killed you earlier," R'zwana said. "If I'd had my way, the gulls of Jibaut harbor would be feasting on your liver right now. But J'yan insisted I give you a chance to explain yourself."

"Wait a moment." Sirsha tried to leash her rising panic. "I never said I was hunting a Karjad. I said *other quarry*. You can't prove—"

"Gag her," R'zwana ordered J'yan. "I want this done by dawn. We'll take her to the southern part of the harbor. Speak with the harbormaster so her body isn't moved. Not until she's nothing but bones."

"You can't prove anything!" Sirsha said again as R'zwana made for the door. She thrashed against J'yan, who, like a good little soldier, was trying to get the gag on again. Sirsha would be damned if she let him. "This is wrong, R'zwana! J'yan, tell her—"

J'yan looked nauseous as he pulled her to her feet. "I tried to warn you," he whispered. "She's so much worse than—"

Voices in the hallway beyond the room silenced J'yan. His body tensed, and Sirsha felt him draw his magic as the door burst open.

"Forgive me, Raan-Ruku." D'rudo appeared out of breath. "I tried to stop them," he said, "but this boy—he says—"

A lean figure eased past R'zwana and into the room, and Sirsha had no idea why he wasn't yet dead, other than that he was Sufiyan Veturius, and rumor had it that death rolled off the members of the Veturius family like salt water off a seal.

"You have no business in the Jaduna compound." R'zwana tried to menace Sufiyan by shoving in front of him, but he sidestepped her so elegantly that she blinked in confusion.

"You're holding a citizen of the Martial Empire and we require her release." Sufiyan spoke in accented Ankanese, his handsome face reflecting a genial sort of boredom. He spotted Sirsha and winked. "Ah. Excellent." He called back over his shoulder, "She's here!"

Sirsha stared in bafflement as someone tall stepped past D'rudo into the room. Quil. But not the same Quil from the shabka. Certainly, he *looked* identical. His armor was a touch tight across the arms and chest—not that Sirsha minded—and he had the same silken, loose waves and light brown skin, the same hazel eyes and aquiline nose and broad shoulders. But something about the way he held himself was entirely different.

As if he owned the room, and everyone in it.

Quil's gaze raked over her, snagging briefly on her cheek where she was no doubt developing a nasty bruise. For a moment, his pale eyes flashed with fury—and Sirsha felt a tingling warmth roll up her spine. He was angry not at her, but for her.

A moment later, his aloof expression returned, and he fixed his attention on Sirsha's sister.

"Raan-Ruku-Ja'ira." *Honored Wolf of the Mother.* Quil addressed R'zwana in a tone that danced on the edge of threatening. "I require the release of this woman. In accordance with the Treaty of Nur, signed by Empress Helene Aquilla and representatives of the Jaduna Raanis in the first year after the Battle of Sher Jinaat, any citizen of the Empire found to have broken the law of a participating nation will be extradited to the Empire to face judgment."

R'zwana had by now gathered her wits and drew herself up, a hand on the dagger at her belt. "She is *not* a citizen of the Martial Empire. She is a Jaduna and—"

"She *was* a Jaduna. She has, however, been made a Martial citizen."

"Lies," R'zwana said, and Sirsha groaned, because Quil had picked absolutely the wrong Jaduna to argue jurisprudence with. R'zwana loved Jaduna law. She'd probably memorized every treaty the Jaduna made, including those inscribed on rock walls thousands of years ago.

"No Jaduna may be made into the citizen of another nation unless by marriage *and* sovereign decree," R'zwana announced in ringing tones. "The process takes months, if not years, and do not tell me"— she marched over to Sirsha and grabbed the thin chain around her neck as Quil opened his mouth—"that she is married, because Jaduna take vows very seriously. We are not husbands or wives or partners. We are Adah—*soul halves*. If she had bound herself to another, she'd have a coin veined with diamonds."

Sirsha's chain had one measly coin on it—the one that materialized when she made her vow to Elias, skies curse him.

Quil crossed his arms. He looked around at the Jaduna assemblage with supreme arrogance.

"By marriage *or engagement*," he said, and Sirsha realized that she was somehow being rescued by the one person on the entire Southern Continent who might know as much about the law as R'zwana. "No Jaduna may be made into the citizen of another nation unless by marriage *or engagement* and sovereign decree. And she is engaged. To me."

Sirsha tried very hard to keep her face . . . well, whatever it looks like when your so-called fiancé announces your fake engagement to the sister who wants to turn you into bird food.

Beside Sirsha, J'yan, who'd never released hold of his magic, went still and tried to catch Sirsha's eyes. She resolutely ignored him.

R'zwana laughed, a short bark, and held up Sirsha's chain again. "This is no engagement coin, Martial. And you don't have one. If you were engaged, you would."

"Martial traditions are different," Quil said. "She has a bracelet of mine. Black leather. Lapis stone with a gold sun. You have magic." He looked from D'rudo to J'yan, barely keeping the derision out of his voice. "One of you must be able to sense that it once belonged to me."

As Quil glanced at her, Sirsha felt her stomach twist in chagrin. She'd stolen the bracelet. And he knew.

She ignored her guilt and held up her still-bound wrists.

"It doesn't matter," R'zwana said. "I don't recall anything about engagement in the treaty. She's a traitor and you are a no-name soldier, certainly not sovereign enough to make *any* sort of decree—"

"Ah." Sufiyan cut R'zwana off, something that was so brave and foolhardy that Sirsha could only admire him for it while feeling a brief sorrow that he was probably about to die.

"Forgive me," he said. "I've been lax in my duties. He does, in fact, have a name. May I present Zacharias Marcus Livius Aquillus Farrar, future Imperator Invictus and Overlord of the Realm, current Lieutenant Commander of the Imperial Army and *Sovereign* Crown Prince of the Martial Empire."

19
Aiz

On her fifth evening outside of Sadh, with an early autumn wind nipping at her face, Aiz finally found Tribe Saif.

They had stopped their silver and green decorated wagons outside one of the many wells that lined the road from the coast. The stops were identical, with a small inn, a supply post, and two springs—one for animals and the other for humans. The desert beyond each well was cleared, with firepits for a dozen caravans. Every space was taken.

Laia of Serra is here, Mother Div said. *She is well protected.*

Night in the desert came swift and cool, a curtain falling over the sun. Soon, the only light was from the campfires scattered through the dark. One of the Saif Tribeswomen began strumming a long-necked instrument, while others joined around the fire, singing. Not long after, the smell of roasted vegetables and browning butter filled the air. Aiz's stomach growled.

Tregan whinnied when Aiz tied her up. "I'll be back, girl." She stroked the mare's head, and approached Tribe Saif silently, her survival instincts from Dafra slum kicking in. The edge of the camp was dark with shadow, and Aiz secreted herself between two wagons to watch, stroking the *D* scar on her hand, a reminder of her people. Of why she was here.

Aiz wasn't sure which Tribeswoman was Laia. There were multiple campfires, and everyone seemed to be telling stories or singing or cooking. Aiz watched one person in particular, a little boy with silver eyes and a ringing laugh, singing a tale to a group of children older than him.

Laia of Serra's child, Mother Div said. *The key to her trust. He sees what others do not. His mother knows this.*

The wind shifted, and Aiz slipped away from the wagon, studying the darkness behind her. She felt as if she was being watched. When she was certain she was alone, she untied Tregan and approached the camp, heart pounding.

Mother Div, be with me.

"Hail, Tribe Saif," Aiz called out in Ankanese, hoping a few among them spoke it. "I have searched for you for a long time. May I enter your circle?"

Laughter faded into murmurs. Steel hissed as fighters drew weapons. A flash in the dark told her someone had a bow trained on her heart.

"Come close to the fire," a woman spoke out in accented Ankanese, low but commanding. "Leave the horse."

Aiz approached, hands up, shoulders slumped, attempting to make herself as small as possible.

"I'm looking for Laia of Serra." She'd learned by now that it was best to hew as close to the truth as possible when it came to the Tribes. Especially this one.

"What do you want with her?" the voice asked.

Cold steel jabbed into Aiz's side. She looked to her left, alarmed to find a black-haired young man staring back at her, his sword gleaming in the dark. He was as tall as a highborn—taller, his face one of sharp angles. Aiz glared at him, unable to hide her surprise and anger.

All Aiz could hear was the pop of flame and scrape of sand. Faces stared out at her. Not hostile yet. But sober and alert.

Aiz focused her energy on tamping down the ire that made her want to slap the blade away. *Your anger will be the death of you.* Cero's advice helped not at all. She was exhausted and hungry, and she wished these damned people weren't so suspicious.

You never listened to Cero. Mother Div spoke in her head. *Because you don't care about yourself. But I understand you, daughter of Kegar. Heed me and stay your rage for now. Anger will be the death of your revenge on the pretender Tiral. It will doom your people to his weakness and spite.*

Aiz took a deep breath and found the calm within. While riding, she had concocted the story she would tell. The many layers of it she would use to keep her identity safe, to get what she needed.

Now was the test to determine if Aiz truly was fit to be Mother Div's chosen, or if all her plans were for naught.

"I have a question about a story," Aiz said. "One only a great Kehanni like Laia of Serra would know. The subject matter is of particular interest to me and my people, who are besieged and abused." She looked out at the faces of Tribe Saif. "I mean her no harm."

There was a long, tense moment, during which Aiz was sure the boy holding the blade to her side would run her through.

But then that same liquid voice spoke from the dark. "Step back, Quil. I will attend to her."

The blade dropped, its wielder nothing but a flash of yellow eyes in the darkness. Aiz released a slow breath as a woman emerged into the firelight, her dark hair pulled into a loose bun at her nape. She wore a simple green and silver dress, cinched tight around a narrow waist, and her wrists were intricately tattooed with geometric designs. Aiz had no skill with prescience, as the seers of Ankana did. But as the woman's dark gold stare bored into Aiz, she had a sudden desire to flee. To vault onto Tregan and ride away.

Aiz took a step back, and almost at the same moment, she heard the unmistakable *shing* of two dozen blades leaving their sheaths all at once.

"I wouldn't run," the woman said calmly. "You won't get far."

"You're her," Aiz said. "You're Laia of Serra."

The woman nodded in assent. "I don't know your name."

Aiz had chosen the name with care. Something that would never be linked back to that gutter Snipe freezing in the cloister. The ancient name of a star.

"Ilar," she said. "Ilar of Ankana."

"Welcome, Ilar," Laia of Serra said. "Take salt with us." She gestured to the fire, and Aiz joined her, taking a pinch of salt from a bowl that Laia offered. Moments later, the boy called Quil appeared with flatbread and bowls of lentils and greens. Aiz took hers warily.

"It's not poisoned." Quil's voice was quiet but sonorous. Even with the fire popping and conversation humming, Aiz heard him. He spoke Ankanese with hardly an accent—he must be one of the Tribe's linguists. With so much trade between these lands and Ankana, every Tribe had one.

He tore off a bite of flatbread, dipped it in Aiz's bowl, and ate it. "See?"

Beside Aiz, Laia tucked in with gusto as the other members of the Tribe settled nearby to eat. With Quil still watching, Aiz took a bite.

And nearly melted into the earth with bliss. She looked up at Quil to thank him, but he'd faded back into the dark. The Tribe trusted him—it was he who would have killed her if they'd deemed Aiz a threat. Yet he delivered food like a lowly servant. And he looked nothing like them. Nor did Laia.

Though everyone smiled and laughed around her, Aiz was under no illusion that they trusted her. *Breathe.* She dropped her shoulders and smiled. They'd let her in. Now she must win their trust and get answers about Mother Div's story.

"Forgive me, I do not speak Ankanese as well as Quil or my children," Laia of Serra said. "Tell me of—of you." As Laia spoke, tiny mirrors sewn into the borders of her clothing caught the firelight, making it seem as if her dress were aflame.

"Do you have . . ." Aiz could tell Laia was struggling to think of the word. "People?" she finally said.

"Family? No," Aiz said. "My mother died when I was young. I didn't know my father. I don't have siblings."

Laia's face softened. "Ah." She looked into Aiz's eyes, and touched her wrist, pulling back when Aiz flinched. "I am sorry. Where are you from in Ankana?"

The Kehanni's questions were gentle, but this was still an interrogation.

"The capital." Aiz had practiced this answer on the road. "A neighborhood called Bisker."

Laia of Serra shook her head. "I do not know it. My husband travels there regularly. Elias, love—" A big man with black hair appeared from one of the wagons. Two sword hilts poked up from behind his neck.

Elias dropped a kiss onto his wife's head before sitting down beside her. The little boy she'd seen telling a story before—a veritable twin of the man, down to the silver eyes—raced out of the dark and threw himself at his father, chattering in Sadhese until Laia said something to him. The boy glanced curiously at Aiz.

"Aba, listen." He switched to Ankanese so Aiz could follow the conversation—which matched what she'd learned of the Tribes during her brief time in this land. Hospitality was paramount—and that meant making sure your guests could understand you.

"Sufiyan says he didn't like the story I told about the Durani and the dust wall. Now he won't let me ride his horse. But yesterday he wouldn't let me ride because he said I'm half wolf and I'll spook her, but I'm *not* and he won't *listen*—"

"Ruhyan, love," Elias rumbled with a smile, lifting the child atop his shoulders as easily as one would a sack of feathers. "Your mother was speaking. Take in the view from up there, and after she's done, you and I can figure out how to outwit your brother, hmm?"

"Yes, Aba." The child patted his father's dark hair. "Sorry, Ama."

Laia gave the boy an indulgent smile before turning to her husband. "Bisker, in Ankana. Do you know it? That's where Ilar is from."

"I do." The man's smile faded, and he fixed his pale eyes on Aiz as if she were made of snakes. "You've a fine horse," he said softly.

Aiz's neck prickled. Elias knew Bisker was a slum. She'd chosen it on purpose. Aiz could never convince anyone that she was a noble. But Bisker was obscure enough—according to Dolbra, anyway—that Aiz didn't think anyone in the Tribal Lands would know it.

Least of all a man who could break her in half with one fist if she looked at his wife or child the wrong way.

"Tregan was a gift," Aiz said. "From someone with greater means than I."

Aiz's chest tightened at the thought of Cero. The cloister. She could not fail because of one man's suspicion. Mother Div had said something about Ruhyan. *The key to her trust. He sees what others do not.* Aiz looked up at the boy.

Ruhyan grinned impishly, reminding Aiz of Hani. Aiz couldn't help smiling back.

"That's my horse there." She pointed to where Tregan was staked. "Treg doesn't get spooked by anything, even little children who are part wolf."

"Half wolf," the boy said, but a shy grin bloomed on his face. "Can I ride her?"

"Certainly," Aiz said. "If your parents have no objection. She'd be happy carrying a lighter load. And she's faster than your brother's horse. Fast as the wind."

Ruhyan sighed longingly. "I want to go fast as the wind."

"Pffft." A voice came from beyond the fire. The boy who emerged was younger than Aiz and broodingly handsome, with Laia's dark gold eyes. "No horse is faster than Lili."

"Tregan is." Aiz focused only on Ruhyan. She winked at the child. "Trust me."

Ruhyan gazed at her for a few seconds, but it felt like longer. *I want to know where Mother Div is.* She let that truth rise to the surface of her mind. *I want to help my people.*

"I trust you," he finally said, his grin a flash of light in the darkness. "So can I race her?"

Something shifted in the camp with those words. Laia relaxed. Elias glanced up at his boy, smiling.

"In the morning, love." Elias stood, and Ruhyan swung down with a *whoop*. "I'll judge the race myself, and whoever loses folds laundry for a week. Now—where are your sisters?"

"Zuriya's with the Fakira—" Ruhyan said. *Those who tend to the dead*, Aiz recalled. "And Karinna is beating up that boy from Tribe Aish she hates so much. I told her not to, he's bigger than her, but you know Kari."

Laia looked stricken and slipped into Sadhese. "Pires?"

"Don't worry," Ruhyan said. "She's fine—"

"I'm not worried about *her*, Ruh," Laia said. "Elias—"

"I'll handle it," he said, stretching languidly before Laia glared at him.

"You don't seem to be in a hurry?"

He shrugged. "If my daughter sees fit to teach a smart-mouthed Aish boy a lesson, who am I to interfere?"

"Jaldi!" Laia said in exasperation, and her husband laughed, dropping down for a lingering kiss.

Their sons exchanged a glance, making identical faces of disgust before following their father into the night. The other Tribespeople fell into conversation with each other.

"My daughter Karinna," Laia said. "She's fourteen. Second-born, after Sufiyan. And she has more of a temper than the rest of the family combined."

More of a temper, perhaps, Aiz thought. *But her father is more deadly.*

"Ruhyan—Ruh—reminds me of a girl I knew back home," Aiz said. "Hani. She loves the wind too."

Laia tilted her head. Her expression was mild, but there was steel in the set of her jaw. "My family is protective," Laia said. "But I do not think you are here to kill me."

"I'm not," Aiz said, and she recalled what Dolbra had told her. "You are a history-keeper and storyteller for your Tribe. A story hunter. I imagine that means that you've told stories others don't wish told. And that makes them angry."

Laia looked at her in surprise. "Yes," she said. "You understand the role of a Kehanni well."

"I'm here about a story," Aiz said. "But only because I hope to learn more. You told this one many years ago, I think." Aiz reached for her pack to show Laia the book, but a voice shrieked in her head.

No! Holy Div cried out. *She must not see it!*

"Ah." Aiz froze. Laia had written the book. Asking her about it seemed the quickest way to learn more. As Aiz considered what to do, Laia quirked an eyebrow, the concern in her face transforming to caution.

"You were saying?"

"Forgive me." Aiz collected herself and left the book in her pack. Mother Div hadn't yet led her wrong. "There is a story you told long ago: 'The Vessel of the Fount.' I would like to learn more about it."

"'The Vessel of the Fount,'" Laia murmured, contemplating the middle distance. Aiz held her breath, wildly impatient to take Laia's knowledge and use it to find Mother Div's trapped spirit.

But Laia shook her head as her expression cleared. "I'm sorry, Ilar," she said. "I've not heard such a tale. Perhaps it was attributed to me, but I am not the source of it. However, the fire is warm. The stars are bright. Tell it to me."

While Laia didn't appear to be lying, Aiz couldn't be sure. Perhaps this was another test from Mother Div. The tale would not simply reveal itself. Aiz would have to prove she was worthy of it.

"If I tell you this story, I must ask that you not share it," Aiz said, considering the many ways Tiral might track her. "For my safety. My people are a small group. Persecuted for our beliefs."

"In Ankana?" Laia frowned, her curiosity evident. "The seers are known to respect the dignity of all. They weren't willing to open trade with the Empire until slavery was abolished."

"Every place has its outcasts," Aiz said.

Laia nodded and looked around the fire. She spoke one sentence and everyone who had been gathered moments ago cleared out, as if they had pressing tasks elsewhere.

"I will not share your tale without your permission," Laia said. "Speak."

Aiz recounted it with care, not mentioning Kegar, despite Laia's promise. Kegari were not known so far north, and the presence of one would be noteworthy. If Tiral *was* hunting her, he'd find her easily.

Instead, without using Div's name, Aiz told of a holy cleric fleeing a great calamity. Of finding a new land far away from her homeland for her people—and then leaving them behind and finding herself trapped.

Laia listened with such stillness that it was as if she was searing each word into her blood. To her, this wasn't simple fireside chatter.

"Her body is long dead, Kehanni." Aiz hadn't planned to speak of her holy mission, but the story brought fire to her blood, and she was sure the truth of her passion would persuade Laia to help her. "But her spirit is trapped. I cannot abide while that is the case. I must find her and free her. I know you'll say it's only a story—"

"I am the last person to say that a story has no power," Laia said. "Sometimes the power of a story is greater than anything else on earth. You say your Holy Cleric is imprisoned and you must free her. Describe her prison again."

"It is in the lee of a giant's fangs. No creature of fur nor feather goes there. It is . . . a shriveled hollow with no rain or wind."

The Kehanni traced circles on a wooden armlet she wore on her bicep, as if seeking a memory in its intricate etchings.

"A giant's fangs," she murmured. "Shriveled hollow—when you say it, I feel as if I have heard these words. But I cannot quite remember. This may be beyond me, Ilar. If my instructor Mamie was here . . ." Laia shook her head. "We lost her two winters ago. Every day I have a question for her. Let me think on it. You have taken salt with us. Until I have a solution, stay as a guest. Live as we do."

Resentment rose like bile in Aiz's throat. The Tribes had so much that they could share it with any stranger, while the clerics who cared for Kegar's weakest hardly had bread for themselves.

Jealousy would not serve Mother Div. Aiz made herself smile. "That's most generous, Kehanni. But I wouldn't wish to impose on you for more than a few days."

Laia no doubt sensed Aiz's impatience. "It may take months, Ilar," she said gently. "I do not mind hunting a story. Perhaps this was meant to be. But I will need to seek out other Kehannis who can advise me. I will send out messages—ask for meetings in Nur, where we travel for Rathana, the midwinter festival."

The woman stood and called out. A moment later, those who had disappeared from the fire returned, bringing with them a steaming dessert. Laia ladled a bowl for Aiz.

"This is khiram," she said. "Rice pudding with saffron, a specialty of Tribe Saif. Eat. Rest easy. You are safe with my Tribe. We will speak in the morning."

Laia left, and around Aiz, the members of Tribe Saif carried on their conversations.

Months. Aiz didn't have months. Sister Noa and Olnas and Hani were in the Tohr *now.* Aiz needed to destroy Tiral. And after—

The Sacred Tales said the revelation of the Ninth Sacred Tale would trigger the Return. Her people would finally go home. Impatience burned through Aiz. *Months!*

Mother Div spoke. *What is a delay of months when I have been waiting centuries? I did not bring you here only to free me. There is much you can take from the Tribes. You will remain here, and you will learn from living among them.*

Aiz shivered. Mother Div wasn't as understanding as she'd been in Kegar, or even on the Ankanese ship. She was disappointed. Aiz felt compelled to make it right.

Of course, Mother Div, she said in her mind. *I will do as you ask.*

Quil appeared by the fire, drawing the attention of most of the young people nearby, though they didn't approach him. He had high cheekbones, a square jaw, and the slightest ridge in his nose, with skin that was darker than hers, and imbued with a golden-brown glow, as if he spent most days outside.

The color of his irises was light and strange and shifting. One second as bright as a cat's, the next softer, like the shed leaves of a butterfly larch. Aiz had never seen eyes like his before.

He ladled himself a bowl of khiram—which was promptly stolen by a giggling Ruh. The child plopped down beside Aiz.

"My favorite food," he said. "No one makes khiram better than Quil."

The young man secured his own bowl. When Aiz glanced at him, he looked away quickly, cheeks flushed.

Interesting.

Aiz needed friends here. Anchors. People to help her make sense of this place—preferably without demanding too much of her in return.

She took a bite of khiram. The flavor was too subtle for Aiz.

"You made this?" She looked at Quil through her lashes. "Remarkable. Tell me how?"

Quil joined her, but before he could respond, Ruh spoke. "Do you like stories? You must, since you told one to Ama."

"I— You weren't supposed to—"

"I'm going to be a Kehanni one day," Ruh said. "I have a fine story to tell. But it's scary. You aren't very big." He eyed her doubtfully. "You might get too scared."

"Quil is here." Aiz glanced at him, hair falling in her face. "He'll keep me safe." Another flush. *Perfect.*

"Well then," Ruh said. "Not so long ago, on a cold night like this one..."

As Ruhyan launched into the tale, Aiz rested her head on her hand, lips parted, shirt slipping a touch off her shoulder as she listened and watched the stars, well aware of how her skin would look lit by the fire.

She'd purchased a bottle of Attar in Sadh, dabbed a bit on her wrists this morning. Aiz slung her magic down to lasso the scent, so that Quil might associate it with her. But it danced out of her fingers on a willful breeze.

Do not demand, Mother Div said to Aiz. *Coax. Then tether it.*

Aiz crooned to the wind in her mind. *You carry such marvelous fragrances. Come closer, please, that I might share this one with you.*

The wind resisted, but Aiz kept at it, only half listening to Ruh's story. Finally, Quil inhaled, gaze bemused.

"Roses," Quil muttered. "They're usually not in bloom."

Ruh raised an eyebrow. "What roses? I didn't say anything about roses. You're not paying attention!"

"Sorry, Ruh."

The boy continued with his tale. Quil tried not to glance over at Aiz and failed.

Half-hidden by the dark, Aiz smiled.

20
Quil

Sirsha, at least, appeared to have taken the revelation of Quil's title in stride, regarding him surmisingly while attempting to work herself free from her bonds. But as the prince edged toward her, R'zwana, initially rendered silent, finally found her tongue.

"We have no proof of your identity. Anyone could rattle off a ridiculous Martial name and say he's a prince."

"It's him, R'zwana," said the grizzled Jaduna who'd been guarding the door, peering at Quil. "I was part of the delegation to Antium eight years ago. I remember his face."

R'zwana could've lit the older man aflame with her glare. "Do not defy me, D'rudo."

"Seems like he's stating a fact," Sufiyan offered. "But you two can sort that out. We have a ship to catch, so if you could unbind her, we'll be on our way."

"You'll pardon her and let her go," the Raan-Ruku snapped. "After she has clearly flouted the very letter of the law by—"

Quil sighed as R'zwana rattled off a list of grievances. He'd been at court enough to know that if you let petty people argue, they'd never shut up. The Jaduna could probably turn Quil into a gourd with the snap of a finger. But Arelia was alone and the Kegari were crawling through the city like roaches. They needed to get out of here.

He was the crown prince of the bleeding Martial Empire. It was time these Jaduna realize it.

He recalled his aunt's flinty gaze when her council of advisers was being especially intractable, the way she'd tilt her head, and everyone suddenly thought thrice about crossing her.

Quil felt the change in his body, the iron in his spine, the press of his thumbs into his knuckles as his fists clenched. All of them sensed it, and R'zwana, still ranting, fell silent.

"Our two nations have a treaty." Quil silently thanked his droning pill of a tutor, who insisted on the prince memorizing said treaty. "Honor it. Or I'll be forced to draw my weapon. You'll call on your magic. And we'll have a diplomatic incident on our hands."

R'zwana's eyes were dark, like her sister's, but devoid of Sirsha's humor and warmth. What Quil saw instead was a festering insecurity that she worked hard to hide. Quil kept talking. Kept making her angrier.

"You hate your sister. That much is clear. But it's not my problem." Quil slowly let drop the blade in his sleeve, and drew closer to R'zwana, preying on her outrage, the way he'd seen his aunt do to others a hundred times. Until, in one swift motion, he had a dagger at her heart.

"Let her go. My patience grows thin."

A moment later, the young man named J'yan sliced through Sirsha's bonds, his knife flashing.

"I, too, am Raan-Ruku," J'yan said to R'zwana. "I don't relish telling the Raani that her daughter died in a knife fight with a Martial." He spat the last word like it was poison. Quil suspected that venom was because Quil had pronounced Sirsha his fiancée.

"She might be Jaduna-born," J'yan said. "But she's Jaduna no more. Let her go. We have a killer to hunt, and no time for foolishness."

A vein pulsed at R'zwana's temple. Then she smiled. The sudden shift was so unnerving that Quil grasped his dagger tighter.

"If they are engaged," she said, "then let him speak the words of fidelity. The *Jaduna* words, witnessed by the appropriate party."

"His Highness doesn't have time to wait for a member of the Jaduna clergy to show up," Sufiyan said, scorn dripping from every word. "He's a Martial prince, for skies' sake. His word is good."

R'zwana fixed her stare on Sirsha. "It's not his word that's the problem. Worry not. Any full-coined Jaduna can perform the ceremony with a few words."

"Enough." Sirsha's voice shook. "R'zwana, this is unnecessary—"

"I *knew* you were lying!" R'zwana grabbed Sirsha's arm and hauled her up. "Engaged! As if anyone would want to marry *you*." Sirsha winced, and at the sight of her misery, Quil's temper snapped.

He didn't know why he found R'zwana's contempt for Sirsha so repugnant. Perhaps because he couldn't imagine treating Arelia or Sufiyan this way. Or because, despite Sirsha's dissembling, there was something oddly endearing about how terrible she was at it, and it made him want to protect her.

Whatever the case, he was in R'zwana's face before he realized what he was doing.

Sufiyan stepped close, voice low. "Probably shouldn't kill the Jaduna, Quil."

"What are the words?" he said to R'zwana, dead quiet. "I'll say them."

Sirsha stared at him in surprise and R'zwana took a step back. Quil's initial dislike of the woman burgeoned into something like loathing. She had no interest in treaties or laws or logic. She just wanted to kill her sister. At some point, she'd think of a reason to justify it. The longer they dragged this out, the more likely it was that she would conjure another loophole, and the longer they'd be stuck in bleeding Jibaut.

He didn't know much about Jaduna vows—his tutor had focused on treaties. A Martial troth took some undoing because families and assets were involved. But they *were* dissolvable, and Quil had never heard anything indicating that a Jaduna engagement was any different.

"Make it quick," Quil said. "As Sufiyan said, we have someplace to be."

"Very well." R'zwana's surprise was evident. "J'yan, the words of witnessing."

The other Raan-Ruku hesitated, and Sirsha's sister gave the man a look so blistering that Quil was surprised his skin didn't peel off. J'yan sighed.

"I, J'yan Deshma, of Kin Deshma, bear witness to this union."

R'zwana cleared her throat at D'rudo. He shook his head, but still spoke. "I, D'rudo Inashi, of Kin Inashi, bear witness to this union."

Sirsha's face went pale as R'zwana smiled nastily at her, drawing a dagger and offering it to Sirsha. "You know the words, sister," she said. "You've heard them often enough."

"I—I, Sirsha W-W-Westering, name Quil as my—"

"His full name," R'zwana hissed. "Don't forget the blood."

Sirsha grimaced and cut her hand. ". . . Zacharias Marcus Livius Aquillus Farrar as my Adah, half my soul. I give my heart unto his keeping, a gift with no compare."

R'zwana took the blade and handed it to Quil. "You memorized a treaty, so I imagine you can repeat that?"

He cut his palm with the knife. "I, Zacharias Marcus Livius Aquillus Farrar, name Sirsha Westering as my Adah, half my soul." It was just a few words. It wouldn't mean anything. He tried to look comfortingly at Sirsha but shifted his gaze at her obvious distress. "I give my heart unto her keeping, a gift with no compare."

R'zwana looked between them. "Hands," she said, and Sirsha sighed, offering hers to Quil.

As he took it, as their blood mingled, his body flashed icy cold, then overly warm, as if he had a fever.

"Witnessed," R'zwana sniffed.

J'yan and D'rudo echoed her. Sirsha released Quil. A moment later, the air shifted, as if a window had been opened though the room didn't have one. Quil's neck burned, and he glanced down, alarmed. He expected to see a wound or a dart poking out of his skin.

Instead, he found a thin silver chain glimmering around his throat, with a coin attached to it.

"What in the bleeding hells," he said, "is this?"

"That is the mark of a *true* Jaduna oath," R'zwana said.

"Excellent," Sufiyan said. "Let's go."

Before anyone could protest, Sufiyan bolted from the room, Quil following. The prince grabbed Sirsha's hand, realizing that it would be odd for him not to at least try to touch her, since they were supposed to be affianced.

"Move, move," Sufiyan muttered as they hurried down a long hallway and up a flight of stairs. "Before they change their minds."

They pushed out the compound doors and into the rainy night. A figure reared up in front of them, and Sufiyan had his bow nocked and aimed almost before she could lift her hands.

"It's me!" Arelia was soaked through, her expression offended as she took in the murderous look on Sufiyan's face. "The Kegari boarded the shabka. Just when I'd finally started making sense of the engine, too. Barely escaped them. Caught up with you in the market, but you went after Sirsha and I got stuck in the crush."

She held up a bag. "Got some supplies. Since you forgot that bit of the mission."

Arelia glanced down at Quil's hand, still entwined with Sirsha's. He dropped it quickly, expecting the Jaduna to disappear with nary a thank-you. But she only looked worriedly up the street. Voices sounded.

"We need to get out of sight." Sirsha nodded to an alley.

They ducked into it and emerged on another narrow lane, only to spot four Kegari soldiers. They were dragging someone with them. From the clothing, it looked to be a Martial. Quil couldn't understand the soldiers' Kegari speech, but one of them was rubbing his jaw and glaring at their prisoner; the Martial had put up a fight.

Quil reached for his scim—*four soldiers, armor weak in the shoulder and neck*—but Sirsha grabbed his arm. "You can't fight them all, Quil," she said. "Not if you want to get out of Jibaut alive."

She pulled him back too late; one of the Kegari looked up, shouting in excitement.

"Run—" Quil said, but a sudden wind swept down from the sky, viciously dragging Sufiyan and Quil back into the street they'd been trying to escape. Arelia, still behind them, dove into a hedge.

"What the hells— Quil!" Sufiyan clawed at a nearby wall, but lost purchase and skidded to the center of the road alongside Quil.

Quil's nerves screamed at him to run, but he couldn't move. He couldn't even speak. *How is this possible? Another hellish Kegari invention?* He tried to see where Sirsha had gone—but found he didn't need to because his necklace burned and he *felt* her, hidden a few yards away.

He had no time to dwell on it, because a figure appeared out of the darkness of the alleyway. Tall and hooded, with broad shoulders and gray-scaled armor. His features were almost entirely in shadow, but Quil could make out pale skin, a sharp jaw, and a sneering mouth.

"Quil Farrar," the man said, his Ankanese uninflected. "The Martial crown prince himself. Long have I wished to look upon you."

He wore no markings of rank, but the way his soldiers fell back, the way he walked told Quil that he wasn't some no-name officer. The air itself seemed to crackle around the man.

Quil strained against the wind, breaking free for a moment before a tendril of white metal unfurled from the figure's hand and wrapped around Quil's shoulders.

"Hold still," the man said. "Let me look at—"

A thin blade flew out of the dark and sank into the man's shoulder. He hissed, flinching as three more whipped past his head, impaling two of the soldiers behind him.

Sirsha's face appeared at the end of the lane, more daggers flying from her hands. "Move, I'm covering!"

The wind faltered, and Quil and Sufiyan bolted into the alley, Sirsha and Arelia on their heels. The Jaduna overtook them quickly, and they followed her as she cut through a garden, vaulted over a wall lined with glass shards, and raced through muddy, winding streets before stopping in a narrow space between two stables. Within, animals moved. Arelia wrinkled her nose at the tang of horse dung.

"There are more patrols than before," Sufiyan said after catching his breath. "Now they know we're here. And we don't have a ship."

Quil turned to Sirsha. "Thank you," he said. "Consider us even. Good luck with the hunt." He glanced at Sufiyan. "We of all people hope you succeed. Though—" His gaze dropped to the bracelet she'd stolen. "I'd like that back."

"You can't leave." She looked at him as if he'd suggested she stab herself in the eye. "We're Adah now—soul halves. It's a deeper bond than a simple engagement. Until our oath is established, we must stay close to one another, or it will feel like our bones are on fire."

"How close?" Quil asked, alarmed.

"In Jaduna lore, *no farther than a cloud cat ranges to hunt*," Sirsha said. "Practically, that's a mile or two."

For a moment, he didn't understand. Then it sank in. *Bleeding, burning skies.* Why had he let Sufiyan talk him into saving Sirsha? And why, the one time he carried out a plan with no forethought, was this the result?

"You might have mentioned that the words of fidelity meant *chaining* myself to you—" Quil tried to pull the necklace off. It wouldn't break.

"R'zwana would have killed me on the spot! No Jaduna would get engaged without explaining the Adah oath. Besides, you knew our treaties backward and forward. I assumed you understood the oath, too."

"I—" Quil raked a hand through his rain-soaked hair, looking from a wide-eyed Arelia to Sufiyan, grimacing in sympathy. "You know who I am," he finally said to Sirsha. "I can't be saddled with—with—"

With a tracker who is far too intriguing to be good for me. He didn't say it, but from Sirsha's expression, it was clear she assumed the worst.

"I didn't *ask* to be rescued, mighty prince," she snarled. "Especially not by a *fiancé*. You saved my life but dragged me into yours in the process. I didn't *want* to say the words of fidelity. But it's done, so unless you want to enjoy the pain and suffering that comes with trying to outwit a Jaduna oath coin, you're stuck with me until we can find a Raani to break the link between us."

Relief swept through Quil. "It's not forever, then," he said. "We *can* break it."

"Yes." Sirsha rolled her eyes. "Eventually. And the longer we spend together, the farther apart we can get without causing ourselves any misery. For now, I'll come with you. Don't look so horrified. I'm good with a knife. I know the Southern Continent better than any of you. And I know someone who can help us get out of Jibaut. If we ever stop talking long enough to leave this alley."

As Quil studied her, his instinct tingled. The desire to use his magic, to understand her through her thoughts and memories, felt as powerful as the need to breathe when trapped underwater. He half lifted his hand, ready to touch her, to give in.

And then he remembered he'd be taking—stealing like a low criminal—and forced the magic to the back of his mind.

"You're hiding something," he said.

"I'm hiding many things, prince," she said. "Now that we're affianced, you'll learn all about them, I'm sure." Sirsha ran a finger down his chest, dark eyes fathomless as she looked up at him. Her pine-and-sky scent filled his senses and her gaze dropped to his lips.

For a moment, she was all he could see. Then she smiled and he remembered who he was dealing with.

"I hear another patrol coming." She shifted back to look at Sufiyan and Arelia. "You want to get out of here, right? Follow me."

Kade was not happy to see Sirsha. Perhaps because she had a knife to his throat. Or because Sirsha had punched him in the face about three seconds after breaking into his house—something Quil was sure he found as satisfying as she did.

Now, wild-eyed and panicked, Kade looked around the room as if for an escape. Quil took in the high windows, velvet settees, and intricately carved tables covered in rare books and scrolls. Pretty. But poorly designed for a quick exit, unless Kade wanted to defenestrate himself. Quil wasn't inclined to stop him if he tried.

"You're going to procure horses and supplies for me and my friends," Sirsha informed Kade. "You'll do it without making a fuss, or I'll hold your eyelids open as Reli here burns your life's work to cinders."

Kade released a short, panicked bark of laughter. "You wouldn't."

"I'd do worse," Sirsha said, "if I wasn't in such a hurry. Walk."

Kade stood, hands up. "Friends." He laughed. "I thought you said they were a pack of infernal Martials who probably wouldn't last the week."

Quil glanced at Sufiyan, who shrugged. The prince could tell Sirsha wanted to lie and deny it, as the *infernal Martials* were now essential to her survival. But, to her credit, she just lifted her chin.

"Horses, Kade." She tightened the knife against his neck. "Now."

Kade nodded and slunk ahead of them down the stairs, out a back gate and to a large stable. Sirsha whistled in appreciation as she took in the wealth of horseflesh. There were a dozen beasts here as fine as any mount a Mask might ride.

"You posh bastard," she said as Sufiyan and Arelia saddled the horses. "You don't need money. What the hells did my sister offer you that you'd betray a friend for it?"

"Get that away from me." Kade glared at her dagger. "I don't want you to trip and accidentally stab me."

"If I stab you, it won't be accidental."

She was trying to sound snide, but Quil could tell from the stiffness of her shoulders and the set of her jaw that Kade's betrayal had wounded her.

Which made Quil want to stick a knife in the pirate himself.

"Why betray me?" Sirsha asked Kade quietly, as if she'd forgotten Quil was a few feet away. "You know what my family did to me. I'd never have double-crossed you."

Kade looked down at his hands, ink-stained and scarred. "This . . . murderer," he said. "The one you're searching for. You don't know, Sirsha—you don't understand how—how awful she is."

Quil's gaze shot to Sirsha. *She?* The Jaduna hadn't shared that fact in all their days at sea.

"You've never taken an interest in my jobs before," Sirsha said. "Why now?"

"Because you're my friend," Kade said, and at Sirsha's scoff he sighed. "I don't want anything to happen to you."

"Is that why you sold me to my sister?" Sirsha said. "She was going to kill me, Kade. By drowning me and then leaving my body for the gulls' dinner. You'd have passed by your *friend* any time you went to the docks for the next three months!"

"You think you understand what you're dealing with. But you don't. You—" Kade went strangely pale then, the color of frozen milk. "I can't—" He turned away from her. Sirsha eased back, so surprised at his distress that she likely didn't see the point in threatening him. "I can't say more," he said. "Don't ask. Please—be careful."

"Ready," Sufiyan said. "Let's move."

Sirsha grabbed a length of rope from one of the hooks in the barn and tossed it to Quil. As he caught it, something occurred to him.

"You know this city," Quil said to Kade. "What do you know about the Kegari reserve forces?"

"Lose the ropes and I'll tell you."

Quil put his scim to Kade's stomach. "One more word that's not useful, and I'll gut you."

"They've got five thousand soldiers south of the city." Kade glanced down nervously at the scim. "Fifty Sails. They'll be doing sweeps, looking for you."

Quil nodded and dropped the rope, glancing back at Sirsha. "If he's tied up, they'll suspect we were here."

"Put them off our trail, Kade." Sirsha mounted her mare. "It's the least you can do."

Kade nodded. "I will. And I swear I won't tell your sister anything." His lips tightened. "She doesn't keep her promises anyway."

"What did she promise you?" Sirsha asked. "What did you need from her, Kade?"

"Sirsha." Quil glanced outside. They'd tarried too long. "It'll be dawn in an hour. If we want to get out of here without the Kegari seeing us, we need to leave."

Kade looked at Quil as if seeing him for the first time. "The Kegari are the least of your worries." He nodded to Sirsha. "Especially if you're with her."

21
Sirsha

By the time the sun rose, Sirsha had led the group deep into the Devanese woods southwest of Jibaut. When the port city was out of sight, she suggested they slow down, but Quil drove them on, clearing their path through the undergrowth and casting glances above, lest a Kegari scout spot them through the canopy of trees.

The powerful Kegari soldier—whoever he was—had seen and identified Quil. The sky-rats would be looking for him everywhere.

To make matters worse, Sirsha felt uneasy. Unpleasantly so. Perhaps it was R'zwana's slimy presence. Sirsha kept it from the others, but she knew R'z would follow her. They were hunting the same quarry, and Sirsha was the better tracker. R'z wouldn't risk letting Sirsha get too far ahead.

She shuddered at the memory of R'z's vengeful face. Though they'd always had a troubled relationship, R'zwana appeared to have disintegrated into the worst version of herself.

But the shadow in Sirsha's mind—it didn't *feel* like R'z. It felt like something else was stalking her. Every time Sirsha tried to track it, it disappeared.

They finally stopped well after sunset. When Sirsha spotted a cave she knew of, she refused to go farther.

"The horses need rest." She glared at Quil, who looked longingly at the path ahead. "And I'm starving."

She was cranky, true, but less because she was hungry and more because the killer's trail was faint now. With every mile in the wrong direction, Elias's oath coin burned hotter, as if to remind Sirsha that she wasn't carrying out her end of the bargain with him.

For now, it would only burn. But in time, the mission would supplant every other need, to the detriment of herself and everyone around her.

She'd worry about that when it happened. Right now, she needed food and sleep.

"Fine," Quil said as she dismounted. "Sufiyan, clear the cave. I'll make the rounds."

"Be careful." The words were out of Sirsha's mouth before she could stop them. "Don't do anything rash and give away our position," she added, lest he think she actually cared about his welfare. "In case—in case the Kegari followed us out of Jibaut."

Quil nodded, observing her keenly, and Sirsha squirmed and turned away.

"Are you all right?" Quil asked.

"I'm starving," she snapped. The truth, just not all of it. But he accepted it—to Sirsha's relief. He always looked so hurt when she lied, like a wounded puppy. And for reasons she didn't understand, deceiving him made Sirsha feel awful. Perhaps because of the accursed Adah oath.

When he was out of sight, Sirsha collapsed onto her back, exhausted. "Is he always like this?" she asked. A moment later, Sufiyan and Arelia leaned over her.

"You mean so protective of his friends that he'll double back to make sure they're safe," Arelia said, "even when he's as tired as the rest of us?"

Sufiyan offered Sirsha a wry smile. "You'll learn to appreciate it."

"I wasn't trying to be ungrateful." Sirsha felt small and petty as she sat up. "And I don't need a lecture from a couple of infants."

Sufiyan threw his hands up and walked away, but Arelia looked genuinely confused.

"I'm eighteen," she offered. "Suf is too. We aren't children."

"I didn't mean *literally*—"

"I realize you have spent much of your life alone," Arelia went on with a kindness one reserved for bumbling animals or aggrieved toddlers.

"But surely you learned not to be unkind to those who have only tried to help you?"

With that, she followed Sufiyan to the cave, which was just as well, because Sirsha's face burned in embarrassment. She tried to think of something pithy and biting to say and failed. Out of pique, she used her magic to eavesdrop on them, but they were merely discussing one of Arelia's inventions, and Sirsha felt ridiculous for spying.

She looked out at the dark forest, turning her Adah coin over in her hands. If she'd genuinely chosen Quil as her Adah, it would be a source of comfort, its gold surface intricately patterned to symbolize their vow. She'd be able to sense if he was safe or not, feel the beat of his heart in time with her own.

Instead, the coin was dull, flat, and unpleasantly heavy.

When Quil finally returned, he looked as weary as Sirsha felt, the freckles across his nose stark against blanched skin. He needed rest.

To appear *un*childish, Sirsha had offered to make dinner. What was left bubbled over a small fire.

"Didn't see any sign of pursuit." Quil spoke quietly, so as not to wake up Arelia and Sufiyan, asleep in the back of the cave. "But you clearly had someone in mind when you mentioned it. Might as well get it out."

Sirsha speared a piece of flatbread and balanced it over the fire to warm it up. "I don't know what you're talking about."

Quil's hair fell in his face and she couldn't quite read his expression. "You're not worried your sister followed us? Perhaps because you're tracking the same killer and she's terrible at it? So, it's easier for her to follow you, as you follow the killer?"

Damn him, he was quick.

"Condolences," Sirsha said. "You officially understand my sister's twisted mind." At his expectant expression, Sirsha sighed. She should tell him—he'd figure it out soon enough.

"Yes, she's following us. I can feel her and J'yan. Like a rash in my brain." She considered mentioning that *other* feeling but decided against it. Quil already thought she was trouble, and for now, she needed the farce of their engagement to keep R'zwana from feeding her to the local avian population. If Quil left her behind, R'z would assume the betrothal was fake, Adah oath notwithstanding, and murder Sirsha in a fit of umbrage.

"Next time, tell me," Quil said, and pulled at the necklace. "This oath coin. Does it . . . change behavior? Create . . . ah . . . emotions or feelings where normally there wouldn't be any?"

"The Adah coin is the seed of a bond." Sirsha wondered what emotions and feelings Quil was referring to. "But we decide how it will grow. It doesn't change our emotions. Only reflects them. Some among the Jaduna are oath-sworn as children and never become more than friends. Their vows are dissolved, eventually. Me and J'yan—we swore our pledge young. When I was—when I left the Cloud Forest, we recanted the vow. It was witnessed by three of our Raanis and our oath coin disappeared."

Sirsha said nothing of the desolation that followed. Of waking up every night after, grasping her throat, feeling as if she couldn't breathe. Jaduna oaths took their toll.

"In normal circumstances," Sirsha said, "the etchings on the coin grow intricate as the Adah learn to trust each other."

"And when that happens, they don't have to be in close proximity anymore?"

His disgust at being her Adah was so obvious that Sirsha wanted to kick him, and then kick herself for caring.

"Yes. There are Jaduna who fulfill contracts, traveling thousands of miles from their Adah. If their bond is strong, it doesn't matter," she said.

Whatever Quil thought about that—about any of it—he didn't say, instead nodding to the stewpot. "I'll clean up. Rest if you like. It's a long road to Ankana."

"What kind of fiancée would I be, letting you keep watch alone?" Sirsha batted her eyelashes at him, gratified at his too-brief smile. When she ladled him a bowl of stew, he looked at it askance.

"If I was going to poison you," Sirsha said, "you'd already be dead." She took a bite before handing it to him so he wouldn't be so wary. "Delicious."

He got a strange look on his face then. A sadness so fleeting that she wished she hadn't noticed. Because noticing was followed immediately by curiosity.

Sirsha did not want to wonder why the crown prince of the Martial Empire was sad.

"Thank you," he said, a bit gruff. It didn't take him long to eat, which Sirsha found satisfying. She'd always loved mixing ingredients to create something that made people smile. Even as a child, she'd taken pride in her roadside fare.

R'zwana mocked her for it, of course.

While Quil went to a nearby spring to wash up, Sirsha stared out into the darkness of the forest, asking the earth to show her where her sister camped. A sense of the terrain around her rose to the surface of her mind. She'd found R'zwana about six miles northeast when Quil returned and sat down in front of her. He glanced at his bracelet again—still on her wrist—and she started pulling it off.

"I should have given it back to you," she said. "I thought it might help me track the killer."

He stayed her hand, and she froze as his fingers—warm despite the chill night—traced the braided leather across her wrist. He shook his head. "If it helps you track, keep it. I brought you something."

He unrolled a wide, thick leaf and dipped his fingers into the orange paste within.

"Made it while I was scouting." His gaze fell on the left side of her face, properly bruised from R'zwana's beating. "That looks painful. This will help. May I?"

Sirsha was fully capable of applying the poultice herself. But she was tired, and he was offering, so she held still as he painted it onto her skin with a gentle touch. Slowly, the pain eased.

"Healing's an unusual pastime for a prince." Sirsha figured it was better to fill the quiet than linger on the way his skin felt against hers.

"Learned it from Suf," Quil said. "He has a knack for it."

The timbre of Quil's voice promised safety, even when he spoke softly. Sirsha wished he'd keep talking.

Don't be a fool. He probably spent years honing that veneer of trustworthiness.

"His mother—Laia of Serra. She's a healer too," Sirsha said. She knew the stories, though she was certain those she'd heard from bored traders at Raider's Roost had been embellished. "And a kedim jadu." *Ancient magic*, the Jaduna term for those who carried latent powers in their blood. "Did Sufiyan or his siblings inherit the magic?"

Quil shrugged. Sirsha wondered if she'd imagined the slight hesitation before he answered. "I don't think so."

"Your people have such an archaic view of the arcane arts. Even the Tribes. Jaduna trace our bloodlines through magic."

"Martials haven't made a study of it," Quil said. "It's not common in the Empire or Marinn or even the Tribal Lands. My aunt has no idea how hers works. Most Martials don't know she even has it."

Sirsha frowned, scandalized at his ignorance. "All magic has order," she said. "It comes from the same source."

"Mauth. Also known as Death," Quil said. "Sufiyan's grandmother is—"

"The Bani al-Mauth. Chosen of Death," Sirsha said. "All Jaduna know of her. She uses magic too, and like all of us, her magic has rules.

We must exert our emotion on an element. We can do this through speech, song, poetry, movements of the body. Some use objects, like a staff."

"What do you use? And what's your element?"

Sirsha hadn't spoken of magic to anyone since she was exiled. Even Kade didn't know exactly what she did.

"I talk to wind, earth, and water," she said, wondering what it was about Quil that made her want to tell him what he asked. "My emotion is usually desire or curiosity. I request help. For the most part, the elements offer it—as long as I tell them what I'm looking for. Sometimes they show me a trail only I can see. Or a warning. Sometimes the image of a place."

"You must be mentally flexible. Open," Quil said. "Maybe that's why you're good at tracking and your sister isn't. The older and more set in her ways she gets, the worse she probably is at it."

Sirsha blinked in surprise. She hadn't considered such a thing.

"The killer also has magic." Sirsha moved on, uncomfortable with how much she'd told him about herself. "She hid her trail. Not easy, but possible for those with particularly powerful mental control. If I knew more about her—"

She stopped herself. She'd shared a great deal already. Too much, perhaps. Trust wasn't wise in her business. If she'd gone it alone at Raider's Roost instead of trusting an adulterous jewel trader, she'd still have her money. If she'd kept her relationship with Kade professional, R'zwana would never have manipulated him into betraying her.

"Stop that," Quil said.

"Stop what?"

"Stop convincing yourself you can't tell me what you're thinking," he said. "I'm not like Kade. Or your sister. I won't betray you or judge you. You don't want to talk about your own magic? Fine, I won't ask again."

Quil had finished with her face and now took her wrists, his long lashes dark smudges against his cheeks as he examined her rope burn in the dim firelight. He worked slowly, methodically, his strong hands easing the paste into her raw skin, massaging the pain away.

"Oh. That feels—" Her whole body relaxed and the sigh that came out of her was halfway to indecent. Quil's pale eyes found hers. Heat bloomed across her skin, slow as a southern sunrise. She wanted to look away, but found she couldn't. His hands stilled and she started to pull back, but he held on to her.

"I'm not done," he said with a note of command that sent a shiver up her spine. Then, after a pause, "You said you needed to know more about the killer?"

"Yes," Sirsha said. "If I knew her emotion and her element, she might be easier to track. Elias said she burns out her victims' hearts with a poker. But that's all I know. Does she torture them first? Is that how they all died?"

"No," Quil said. "It's not."

Earlier that day, Sufiyan had told Sirsha that he and Quil had grown up together. Which meant Quil would know Elias's other son, too. Ruh.

"Could you—could you share anything more about the deaths?" Sirsha said. "How the victims were killed. Whether their bodies were . . . ah . . . arranged in a particular way."

Quil released her wrists, finished now, and was silent for so long that Sirsha felt flustered. "I'm sorry," she said after a minute. "I shouldn't have asked."

"The first person the murderer killed was also the first girl I fell in love with." Quil laced his fingers tightly, as if cleaving to something precious. "Her name was Ilar. I'm the one who found what was left of her."

22
Aiz

The next day, with a brisk autumn wind at their backs, Tribe Saif left the well, and Aiz accompanied them. As the caravan rolled out, Ruhyan dragged Aiz to his mother's wagon. He tied Tregan's lead to the frame, shouting out introductions to those of the Tribe whom Aiz hadn't met.

"That's my sister Zuriya." He pointed at a girl a little older than him riding at the front of a pitch-black wagon. She waved to Aiz shyly. "She likes talking about death. There's Karinna—"

Laia's second daughter led her mare over, looking Aiz up and down coolly. She was small—only a few inches taller than her youngest brother, but striking, with pale blue eyes and a raven-black crown braid.

"You like to fight?" she asked Aiz, lifting her chin. "I'll duel you when we stop tonight. Scims. Loser pays a mark."

Quil rode behind them. Aiz had spotted him currying Tregan that morning, speaking sweetly to the mare and sneaking her an apple.

"Leave her be, Kari," Quil said. "Even *I* don't like to duel you."

"Because you know you'll lose."

"Because I feel bad embarrassing you."

Karinna barked a laugh. "I'll beat you one day, biyah." *Brother.* "Race you to lessons."

Everyone in the Tribe was polite. But Aiz had spent a life welcoming orphans to Dafra cloister. The ones accepted as family were those who found a way to be useful. When the caravan stopped late in the afternoon, Aiz volunteered for dish duty with Ruhyan, and guard duty with Quil.

Her first watch was that night, and she found Quil at the edge of the encampment, speaking to Elias. Aiz hesitated a few yards away, wary of Laia's husband. His mien was assessing as always, but he nodded a greeting and offered her a small scim and scabbard—just her size.

"Quil's my best student by a mile," Elias said. "He can show you the basics, if you like."

Aiz watched Quil out of the corner of her eye as they walked. He was young—almost nineteen, Ruh said. Though he was raised with Tribe Saif, he didn't fit, exactly. It wasn't just his appearance, for Laia's family didn't look like the rest of the Tribe either. No, it was the way the Tribe treated Quil. Respectfully but carefully, too.

He'd been kind to her. Too kind. Aiz wondered what he wanted. And what she could get in return.

"When we're not riding, you're reading," Aiz said as they walked. *I've been watching you. I'm interested.* "Or writing. Will you be a Kehanni too?"

Quil laughed, but it was rueful, not mocking. "That path isn't for me. Tribe Saif is fostering me for my aunt, and there are many things she wishes for me to learn," he said. "Most of it is interesting. History. Statecraft. Philosophy. Astronomy."

So, he was wealthy. Though he didn't remind Aiz of any highborn Hawk she knew. "I will call you Idaka," she said. "In Ankanese, it means—"

"Philosopher." Quil smiled. "Thinker. That's appropriate."

"Your parents are . . ."

"Gone." In the moonlight, his face was expressionless, as if he was talking about the weather. "Like yours."

"I never knew my father," Aiz ventured. "Mother died of an injury when I was four. She liked to bake, though we never had much to bake with. Her hair was long and pale. And she smelled like snow."

Aiz had never told anyone that. Not even Cero. But it took trust to build trust and she waited, hoping Quil would share a similar memory.

"Does Ankana have the same stars?" His voice was cooler than before. "I never looked, when I visited."

Aiz found her curiosity piqued by his strange response. "Different, Idaka. But that one"—she pointed directly above—"is the same. Ilar. The evening star. I was named for it." Aiz looked up and felt unmoored, as if she would drift into the darkness and disappear. She put a finger to her aaj, taking comfort from the fact that she could use it if she wished to.

"Who gave you the ring?" Quil asked. "You play with it when you're restless. Which is . . . often."

So, he'd been watching her too. Her skin buzzed from his closeness, yes, but also from a sense of victory.

"A friend gave it to me," she said. *Let him wonder.* "And if by restless you mean impatient, then yes, I suppose I do," she said. "I need Laia's help to aid my people, but it will take time. Which my people don't have."

They hiked away from the rocky flats and up a ridge, until they reached a creosote-strewn cliff that was fifty feet higher than the land surrounding. The Saif camp was a dusting of sparkling lamps in the distance, swallowed by the great dark of the desert.

Quil offered Aiz a hand as they navigated the rocky terrain to sit at the edge of the ridge. He gripped her lightly, but some strange spark danced between them. It was a chilly autumn night and their bodies were close enough that Quil's heat sank into Aiz. He folded his big hands together and looked out at the land.

"Time is different here," Quil said. "Slow as a glacier and then suddenly galloping forward like Ruh racing his brother. Tribe Saif—they're good people. And I've known Laia since birth. She delivered me. Whatever she promised, she'll do."

Quil spoke with a calmness that both soothed Aiz and galled her. He could afford to be tranquil. It wasn't his people starving and dying. It wasn't those he loved suffering under Tiral.

"You weren't born to Tribe Saif," she observed. "Do you ever feel like you don't belong?"

"I have few close blood relations." He smiled wryly. "I take the family I can get."

"But your aunt. You're close to her?"

Quil shrugged. "Once. Not so much lately. She's been through the hells, but she pushes everyone away because of it. Laia says to be patient. That I wasn't there when—"

His head jerked up, and he grasped his scim as he stood. He went from relaxed Tribesman to soldier so fast that it was as if Aiz was looking at a different human. He was not Idaka, a thinker, anymore. He was Shigaf—a warrior. Every muscle in his body was rigid as he listened. It took Aiz a moment to hear what he did. The thunder of distant hooves. Out in the flats, a dust cloud appeared.

"Horses," he said. "Coming fast."

Quil pulled a horn from his belt and blew it. An answer sounded from down in the camp, and by the time he and Aiz reached the Saif caravan, a group of a dozen mounted Tribespeople formed a perimeter around the wagons. Elias and his son Sufiyan were among them, their attention fixed on the approaching riders.

The horses were close enough to count, and moonlight glinted off armor and weaponry. Aiz held tight to her sword, wishing she could wield the wind as a weapon.

You can, Mother Div said. *Lure it to you. Then tell it why you wish for its aid.*

Aiz hesitated but, feeling Mother Div's impatience, beseeched the wind to her. After dancing back and forth a few times, it came. *Help me,* she said. *Make me safe.*

Good, Div said. *Now shape it into a spear in your mind. If one of them threatens you, release it.*

Aiz broke into a sweat at the effort of bending the wind to her, then trembled with excitement when it flowed as she wished. Such power! She'd always known she had it, even if she couldn't control it. Now the wind felt as solid as any weapon, but biddable instead of chaotic.

She had not even freed Mother Div, and already, Aiz understood her magic better.

Imagine what it will be like when you do free me.

The horsemen drew closer and Quil relaxed suddenly. One of the men, brown-haired and dark-eyed, called a greeting and Quil laughed as he retorted. Aiz released the wind and it whipped away, startling a few of the horses.

The rest of the soldiers pulled in and—along with the dark-eyed man—dropped from their mounts and knelt to Quil. He waved them up almost before their knees hit the sand. Aiz couldn't help but stare at them, for they all wore silver paint on the top halves of their faces.

"They're masks," a voice beside her said. She looked down to see Ruhyan at her side. "Made of living metal. The soldiers get them at Blackcliff."

Aiz didn't know what Blackcliff was. "Ruh," she said. "Can you tell me what they are saying? I don't speak Sadhese."

Ruh stood up taller, happy to feel important. "First of all," he said. "That's Serran they're speaking. Tas—he's hugging Quil right now—he says he thought he'd have to wake Quil up with a bucket of water. Quil says not likely. Tas says that's good—because Quil's auntie wants to see him, and they need to leave. Now Tas is asking who you are—"

Aiz studied Tas—he'd picked her out of the shadows easily.

"Quil told him not to scare you. And Tas says Quil is only scared you'll like him better because he's more charming—"

"Why does Tas keep calling him Eppar?" Aiz asked.

"Eppar means *prince* in Serran," Ruh said. "I guess no one has told you, but it's only because none of us really care too much."

Aiz was about to ask what kind of prince when one of the masked men stepped into the light of the caravan's fires. His mask, Aiz realized, wasn't painted onto his face.

It was metal. Strange metal. Metal that moved. Shifted. Metal that lived. Ruh continued to translate, but Aiz could hardly hear him over the rapid thudding of her heart.

Before she realized what she was doing, she walked toward the man, hand outstretched, and it was likely only her small stature and the fact that he thought her unarmed that saved her from the edge of his blade. She touched his face. Touched the metal. It felt—

Like Loha.

Loha before it was refined by a Kegari metalworker. Aiz had seen the process when she was assigned to the forges outside the Aerie. Metallurgists took a ball of liquid silver the size of a thimble and turned it into enough Loha to power a dozen Sails.

And these soldiers had so much of it. Enough to power hundreds of Sails. Perhaps enough to carry the Kegari back to their homeland, back to the Fount.

Did I not tell you to have faith? Mother Div's voice curled into her ears like smoke. *There is much to learn here, Aiz bet-Dafra. Much to take. All your hopes will come to fruition if you but heed me.*

23
Quil

When Quil was ten, Aunt Helene took him to the Black Guard barracks in Antium, the capital. He struggled to hide his excitement, for he'd been born in the barracks.

Aunt Helene had never mentioned that fact to him, of course. It was Laia who told him the story of his birth. Or some of it, anyway.

The Black Guard were mostly elite Masks, and their job was to root out dissidents. While Aunt Hel and the soldiers conferred, Quil slipped away, hoping to find the room where he was born.

He remembered exactly why he wanted to find it. He thought he would remember his mother. He'd seen paintings of her. Sculptures. It wasn't enough. He wanted to recall her smell, her hands, her love.

The very center of the barracks, Laia had told him. *Up a set of stairs. There was a linen closet two doors down . . .*

The instructions should have been simple, but there were three sets of stairs. Quil got lost immediately. Eventually, he found himself in a nondescript passageway identical to a dozen others. Only this one had the seal of Gens Farrar emblazoned upon the wall. Two crossed hammers painted in black and edged in gold, about a foot and a half off the ground, and off-center.

Quil knelt by the symbol, perplexed. It would have looked better if it was bigger. Higher up. But then, maybe it was supposed to be overlooked. There were secret passages all over the royal palace in Antium. Could this be a passage too? Quil pressed his palm to the symbol, certain he'd hear the telltale grinding of rock that signified new adventures to be had.

Instead, he heard voices behind him, and turned to see his aunt heading toward him.

Quil opened his mouth to explain himself, which was when he noticed that Aunt Helene looked strange. Her face was silver—she wore a mask. Her braid, usually so neat, was askew. There was blood all over her.

It was pooled over the floor. The air smelled of smoke and death. Screams echoed. Where had all these dead soldiers come from?

"Shrike," a voice called out softly.

Aunt Helene ignored Quil entirely and made for the wall where the symbol was. Only there was no symbol there now. Instead, there was an armored man, bleeding from a dozen wounds and pinioned to the wall with a scim through his belly. Quil scrambled back, terrified.

But his aunt was calm. She knelt beside the man, speaking rapidly. At first, Quil was too afraid to get closer. But after a few minutes, he quieted his quaking heart and crept forward.

"Do it, Shrike," the man whispered, so softly that Quil barely heard him. "He waits for me."

Aunt Helene's hands shook—she was bleeding too. Quil opened his mouth to tell her but found he couldn't speak.

"Please, Shrike," the man whispered, and now Quil could see him. He was big and broad-shouldered, with dark hair, and brown skin that was lighter than Laia's. He had a square jaw, thin lips, and a sharp nose.

And his eyes—his eyes were the pale yellow of fall leaves. Like Quil's.

But that was impossible. Aunt Helene, Elias, even Laia had all told him his father had died in the battle of Antium, ten years ago. He died fighting, they said.

Not like this.

"The Emperor is dead," Aunt Helene whispered, and when she spoke again, her voice was strong. Cold. "Long live the Emperor."

Quil watched his aunt stab his father's throat. Watched the blood drain from his father's body. He closed his eyes to make the image go away, to forget, and when he opened them again, the world had shifted.

The man was gone. The blood. The bodies. And Aunt Helene—maskless and immaculate—knelt beside him.

"Are you all right, Zacharias?" He flinched at the name. It had never felt right. "What are you doing up here?"

"What is that?" Quil backed away from the symbol, frightened that if he touched it again, he'd go back to that nightmare place.

Aunt Helene pulled him up, her lips pursed—which meant that she was searching for the right answer to his question instead of telling the truth.

"It's a mark to remember the past, Zacharias," she said.

"Aunt Hel," Quil said. "How did my father die?"

Something passed across his aunt's face, like a fell bird blocking out the sun, leaving an impression of darkness.

"In battle, Quil," she said, and he knew she was lying because she only ever called him Quil when she felt guilty. "Don't think on it anymore, little one. The past will distract you from the now. And it's the now that matters."

On the outskirts of a Devanese town thousands of miles from Antium, Quil tried to remember his aunt's advice. *It's the now that matters.*

More than a week had passed since Quil told Sirsha of Ilar's death. Speaking of it had churned up so many memories that he wished he'd kept his damn mouth shut. Putting a blade to Ilar's side when she'd first walked into the Saif encampment. Hearing her voice, low and musical. The way her skin glowed in the firelight. Her half smile, rare and swift as a falling star.

It's the now that matters.

Quil hadn't told Sirsha everything. She'd asked about Sufiyan having magic—not Quil—and he hadn't volunteered the information.

After the vision of his father's death, Quil didn't comprehend the extent of his skill. It took the accidental leeching of other people's memories and thoughts—a language tutor, a palace gardener—to understand his magic. It spoke to him—urging him to use it. So one day, he did—on his aunt.

She'd fallen into one of her darker moods. Nothing Quil said pulled her from it.

Take her thoughts, the magic had whispered. *Then you will understand her.* One moment, he was wishing he knew how to help. The next, he was neck-deep in her sorrow and regret, which threaded through his aunt's mind like mold through a crop, spawned by the loss and heartache she'd experienced when he was a baby.

Quil couldn't extract himself from her thoughts or memories. That day, she dwelt on one especially: one in which she stood with a slender, dark-haired man in a cave, breaking stone after stone with a club, before falling to the ground, moaning. *I am unmade*, she'd said. *I am broken.*

The prince had never seen his aunt lose control. Her pain was raw and visceral, and he knew in his marrow that she would hate that he'd witnessed the innermost sanctum of her heart. He couldn't help her with what he'd learned. He couldn't do anything but wish she didn't carry such a weight.

After that, he vowed he'd never use his magic to read someone's thoughts again. But memories were different. So many seemed to have a will of their own. They *wanted* to be witnessed. Especially when filled with violence or pain. The older Quil got, the harder it was to resist their pull.

"Thank the bleeding skies," Sufiyan muttered when the town came into view, his voice wrenching Quil from his brooding. "I need a hot meal. And a bath."

"We shouldn't stop," Quil said. "It's not safe."

Arelia pulled her mount even with Quil's. She'd persuaded Sufiyan to buy her coveralls from a Devanese village they'd passed, along with a few basic tools, and her mood had been annoyingly buoyant. "Cousin, it's late. We're tired. We all need to bathe in something that's not freezing river water. We haven't seen a Sail in days."

Quil looked up. Devan's interior was a breadbasket for the Southern Continent, and thus ideal for invasion—if food and livestock were the goal. If the Kegari wanted this land, they could have taken it. But Arelia was right. They hadn't seen a sky-rat since Jibaut.

"I know an inn." Sirsha jerked her head toward a cobbled street on their right. "It's busy enough that no one will notice us."

She'd been quiet the last week too. Jumpy, forever looking behind them. Quil had scouted heavily, taking the most watches and ranging both behind and ahead. But with every day that passed, Sirsha seemed more ill at ease.

As she pulled ahead, Arelia watched her. "She's not herself."

"She's used to working alone," Quil said. "She doesn't trust people easily. Nor does she like to be indebted to people. But now she has to fake a holy Jaduna bond with me so her sister doesn't kill her. She's depending on protection from someone she doesn't much like. That would irritate anyone."

"You've made quite the study of her." Arelia lifted her eyebrows in interest. "But you're wrong. Not about the frustration bit. That makes sense. About not liking you. She stares at you all the time."

Quil's skin tingled. He couldn't tell whether it was a good feeling, or a bad one. "Because she's thinking of ways to kill me?"

"Or she likes what she sees," Arelia said. "The simplest answer is usually the right one, cousin." She rode off, leaving Quil flummoxed and a little pleased.

The inn they stayed at that night was a sprawling stone structure with three separate wings and a common room with four fireplaces. Almost every table and room were taken, as it was the only lodging for fifty miles. Left alone, Quil would have simply found a barn to sleep in.

Sirsha nixed that plan, and after a brief conversation between her and the bluff-faced innkeeper, they were seated beside the fire with two room keys, three roast chickens, and a pile of butter-soaked root vegetables in front of them.

"Your father was generous with his coin," Sirsha said to Sufiyan's admiring glance. "Probably because he felt uneasy about sending me to my death."

Sufiyan shifted uncomfortably, exchanging a look with Quil, but Sirsha rolled her eyes and slapped Suf on the shoulder. "No hard feelings. We aren't our parents, thank the skies. You'd know why that was a good thing if you ever met my mother." She flashed a smile that made Quil's chest lurch even as he glowered at Sufiyan for being the recipient of it.

Arelia frowned at Sirsha, equally irritated. Which was a surprise to Quil, since his cousin had sworn off men and women a few months ago, after a castle maid had broken her heart.

Sufiyan didn't appear to notice. He raised his glass to the table. "To good friends on bad days."

They dug in then, and after tearing through their meal, the four travelers huddled over a map that Arelia had stolen from Kade.

"It'll take us three weeks to get to the border with Ankana," Quil said. "Another to get to the capital—"

"Five weeks to the border," Sirsha said. "Two more weeks to the capital. We can cut our journey in half if we take the highways."

"Too dangerous," Sufiyan said. "The Kegari will be scouting the roads. The map—"

"—doesn't account for how bleeding long it takes to cut through the Thafwan jungle, which is crawling with bandits," Sirsha said. "If you want to avoid the roads, it's a seven-week journey. If we take the roads, three and a half, give or take a day."

She sat back, chewing on a sprig of rosemary, her nonchalance too obvious to be trustworthy.

Quil eyed her narrowly. She wanted to travel on the main roads. She wasn't sharing the true reason why.

Sufiyan's gaze drifted over Sirsha's shoulder. "Look who walked in."

Quil happened to be watching her face when she caught sight of a gimlet-eyed R'zwana entering the common room, trailed by J'yan. Sirsha's expression was unguarded for a moment, her haughty insouciance replaced by panic.

"Sirsha." He touched her wrist, and her wild eyes flew to his. "We're with you. You're not alone."

"I—" She looked confused for a moment. Then she turned away from him. He could see her putting on her mental armor as she shook back her braid and rolled her shoulders. As she wiggled her fingers mockingly at her sister. R'zwana stared back, inscrutable as stone.

Over the years, Quil sometimes wondered what kind of blood brother he'd have been if his parents had lived. His mother had been thoughtful and kind and wise. He'd have liked to have been like her. Someone his younger siblings could rely on. Someone they could trust.

Not like his father—who had stabbed his own twin in a bid for power. Or like R'zwana.

Quil's group wasn't the only one who'd noticed the Jaduna arrive. A table near them emptied out so quickly that the food was still steaming on the platters when they sat down, and a nervous hush fell over the common room before R'zwana turned to whisper something to J'yan, and conversation started up again.

"I thought we'd lost her," Arelia said. "I even used a spyglass—my own creation—"

"She's too clever to be spotted with a spyglass," Sirsha said. "She waits until someone feels safe and then she pops up like a bleeding ghul."

"You two will have to share a room," Arelia said to Quil with characteristic bluntness. "You're each other's soul halves, after all."

Beside her, Sufiyan elbowed Quil, smirking.

"Grow up. There are two beds," Quil muttered, further embarrassed at the heat rising in his cheeks. "And don't look so smug. You'll have to room with Reli and she takes *forever* in the bath. You'll be dust before she gets out."

Sufiyan's grin faded and he grabbed for the room key. Arelia was faster.

"I'm assuming she's not imprudent enough to try anything in a common room." Arelia glanced at R'zwana. "In any case, if she did, the most I could do is throw furniture at her. I'm still working on my self-loading slingshot. I'll excuse myself for the night."

"Wait a minute." Sufiyan jumped up to follow. "You can't *assume* you get the bath first. We'll flip for it—"

"Poor Suf." Sirsha watched them disappear. "Is she really that bad?"

"Worse." Quil chuckled. "But if he steals her reading material, she'll get out quick enough." He followed Sirsha's gaze to her sister, who scrutinized them with a hateful fixation that even Quil, used to the venom at court, found unsettling.

Sirsha shuddered, her fingers going to her face. Her bruise was gone—Quil had applied the poultice every night. But sometimes he saw her poking at where it used to be, grimacing. She pushed her food away, glancing up at R'zwana.

"Can't eat with her staring at me. I can practically hear her shouting that she wants to break my bones."

See what happens if she tries. The fierceness of the thought took Quil by surprise. He cleared his throat.

"Has she always been so . . ."

"Murderous?" Sirsha offered him a wry smile. "We laughed as kids too. I tagged along after her, got into trouble for her. I'd have done anything she said, but that wasn't enough. She got meaner. I was too naive to see it until it was too late."

Quil felt a flash of indignation, and then, looking back at R'zwana, inspiration.

"How do the Jaduna feel about public affection? They're more prudish than Martials, yes?"

"The only type of union is the Adah oath," Sirsha said. "A joined couple isn't supposed to even kiss until the ceremony is over. And behind closed doors, at that."

"Excellent." Quil spoke quickly, because if he didn't, he knew he'd analyze the idea until he talked himself out of it.

"We're going to persuade your sister to stop staring at us—and to think twice about doing it again." He took a tendril of Sirsha's soft, blue-black hair and pushed it behind her ear, before letting his fingers caress her cheek. Her breath hitched at his touch, and satisfaction flooded him.

"You'll have to trust me," Quil said. "Stand up."

"Bossy," Sirsha murmured, but she stood, and he took her fingers in his, slowly pulling her closer, inch by inch. His heart thudded strangely—something he tried not to think about—and he didn't look away from her. She smiled slowly, understanding his intent.

"Why, Quil," she purred, "is this an excuse to kiss me?" A few loose locks of her hair fell in his face as she leaned over him, and then her scent, pine and sky. He breathed it in slowly and looked up into her brown eyes.

"Too obvious," he said, and pulled her into his lap, wrapping an arm around her waist. The shape of her alone was enough to heat his skin, make him ache for more. Sirsha, not to be outdone, traced his jaw with a soft hand before tangling her fingers in his hair.

He was not prepared for how it felt to have her hands on him. For the way the curve of her waist—which he'd tried and failed not to think about after seeing it bare weeks ago—felt beneath his hands, just a thin layer of leather between his skin and hers.

This is an act, he reminded himself sternly. *Sell it. Don't believe it yourself.*

"We should establish a baseline level of affection." He cleared his throat. "This will do for now, I think—"

But Sirsha had ideas of her own. She took his hand, and his pulse stuttered as she stroked the skin of his palm, hardened from holding a blade but sensitive to her touch. Then she leaned forward, her breath tickling his ear and sending a spike of desire straight into the pit of his stomach. "Prince," she whispered. "You're assuming I've never seduced a man."

He wanted to assure her that, in fact, he made no such assumptions, hadn't even considered such a thing, because it was of little to no interest to him, except in regard to making her sister uncomfortable. But his attention snagged on her lips, full and berry-red and curved into the most enticing smile that was making it very difficult for him to focus on what he was supposed to do next—*kiss her . . . yes . . .*

No! He was to disentangle himself and make his way upstairs.

She pulled back and tipped his chin up. Her gaze roved over his face, like it was terrain she wished to know better, and her fingers traced spirals on his chest, his stomach, lower.

He caught her wrist. "Behave," he whispered.

"I never have," she said, her lips a breath away from his. "Why would I start now?"

She held herself there for a maddeningly long moment, nails scraping against his nape, before shifting away, dark eyes glinting. The necklace at Quil's throat grew pleasantly warm.

"Well then." She glanced over her shoulder. The Jaduna were gone. "That did the trick."

Quil shifted, suddenly very aware of how awkward he felt, of how close she was to him. After a week on the road, he couldn't possibly smell as good as she did, and why was he even noticing her smell and why hadn't any of this occurred to him *before* he'd put his hands all over her? "We should—ah—"

"Yes." She stood up so quickly that she nearly upset the table. "Of course."

They were quiet on the way to their room, and Quil was relieved, at least, that Sirsha appeared as tongue-tied as him.

Their lodgings were small but clean, with a separate bathing chamber and two beds. *Drat it,* Quil found himself thinking, before he squashed the thought into a ball and threw it out the window of his brain. It was *good* there were two beds. *Excellent,* in fact. Quil dropped his pack onto the bed closest to the door, and Sirsha wordlessly took the other.

"You can have the bath—"

"Why don't—"

They both spoke and Quil felt too big in his own skin.

"Why don't you go first," he said. "I'll make sure Suf and Reli haven't murdered each other."

Quil stepped outside the room to get a bleeding grip on himself. Yes, Sirsha was smart and funny and beautiful. He couldn't stop thinking about the warmth of her skin or the heat in her gaze. He wanted more. He wanted to undress her slowly and kiss her lips impatiently. He hadn't kissed anyone since Ilar—

With that thought, the tingling in his skin went cold, as if he'd been dunked in a snowbank. He'd known Ilar. She'd had her secrets, but she was inherently good. Honest. Sirsha, on the other hand, lied and manipulated to serve herself.

By the time Quil had checked on Sufiyan and Arelia—both alive, miraculously—and changed after his own bath, he felt calmer. A sensation that vanished the second a wight flew through the window.

The creature dropped a scroll on his head, and Quil stopped it before it disappeared.

"Wait." He handed the wight a message he'd written a week before, detailing what Kade had told him about the Kegari force in Jibaut. A flutter of wings and the wight was gone.

Quil opened the missive with shaking hands, crumpling it up only seconds later.

Silas destroyed. Antium evacuated. Serra stands.
We need what he has. Hurry. —AH

Silas *destroyed*. His father's ancestral home was there. Silas was where Quil met his grandparents. Where Gens Farrar was based. Where Arelia's parents still lived. And the Kegari had wiped it from the map. He didn't even know if any of them had escaped, or how many in Silas had died.

Quil felt helpless. Useless. Enraged. Which was, he thought later, the only explanation for what happened next.

He walked out of the bathing chamber. Sirsha had left his bedside lamp on, but put out her own and was a lump beneath her covers, breathing rhythmically. He was about to blow out his light when she spoke.

"Quil." Sirsha turned toward him and propped herself up, damp hair loose around her shoulders. "I— There's something I need to tell you."

He waited, apprehensive.

"I wasn't honest with you about why I wanted to take the highway to Ankana," she said in a rush. "It would be safer. But there's also someone I need to see, and she lives two days off the Palm Road, not too far from the border. She can tell me more about the killer's magic. But I—I think she can help you, too."

Sirsha leaned toward Quil, her scent washing over him. "You're trying to learn more about the Kegari. But you know nothing about the magic that powers their Sails."

"Magic—" Quil felt as if he'd been punched in the stomach. For if the Kegari had magic, the Empire was in worse shape than he'd imagined.

"What magic? Arelia said their Sails are remarkable feats of engineering. They have superior weaponry—"

"They keep the Sails aloft with magic." Sirsha bit her lip, sensing she was treading on uncertain ground. "I—I can feel it. The Martials don't know this?"

Quil gaped, his mind finally catching up to the dread pooling in his gut. "Why didn't you mention this? We've been traveling together for weeks."

She looked taken aback. "The man in Jibaut, the wind he used on you—that was magic. It didn't occur to me that you didn't know."

Of course. Quil had thought the wind was some unholy Kegari innovation. *The simplest answer is usually the right one.* "Maybe it did occur to you," Quil snapped. "But you couldn't use the information to your benefit until now."

Sirsha pulled her covers up. "No! I mean, yes, I'm telling you now because I want to go and see this person. But we could go together. I could ask her about the killer, and you can—"

"I watched my city burn," he said. "I watched my people die. I know that might not mean anything to you, as someone who doesn't *have* people. If we'd known the Kegari had magic—"

"How would it have helped?" Sirsha's face grew hard, her voice sneering. "You were running from them. You're *still* running. All you've done since I met you is run."

"And save your neck," he retorted. "Though I'm regretting it now."

He dropped into his bed and blew out the light, plunging them into darkness. His temper seethed at Sirsha's past subterfuge. At what the Kegari had done to the Empire. At himself for not stopping it. At his deceitful heart for feeling—whatever he'd felt for Sirsha, and forgetting Ilar so quickly.

"This person," Sirsha said after a long moment, her voice careful. "She can help. Think about it. Discuss it with the others."

"They'll be interested to learn you kept this from them too," he said, knowing it would sting. Sirsha liked Suf and Reli, and they her. They'd be as frustrated at her earlier duplicity as he was.

Though he kept a secret from them too. Neither of them knew about his magic. Or about—

Dash that thought from your head, boy. The Bani al-Mauth's order echoed, and Quil forced himself to focus on Sirsha.

"I suppose I should thank you for being honest now." He stared at the ceiling, numb. *Magic, bleeding hells. The Empress must not know.* "Though I can't imagine what brought it on."

"Something you said," she offered quietly.

He grunted in irritation. "And what was that?"

She didn't respond. But hours later, when he woke, he remembered a dream in which he heard her voice, a whisper.

We're with you. You're not alone.

24
Sirsha

Guilt, Sirsha decided the next morning as she saddled her horse, was a useless emotion. All it did was rob her of sleep that she richly deserved after riding like a jinn for a week straight without complaint.

Well. With minimal complaint.

She'd felt guilt too frequently of late. It was Quil's fault. Now she was finished with guilt, and him.

Her fingers were numb and clumsy in the predawn chill of the inn's stables, and she cursed when the buckles to her saddlebags kept slipping. She should have known that someone who was so sinfully skilled with his hands would be awful in every other way.

Quil had hidden it well, certainly. Acting noble and princely. Making that damned poultice for her and applying it every day. Looking at her in that way he had, like he felt nothing and everything and that he might want her the way she wanted him.

Ugh. There. She'd admitted it to herself.

But he was like every other man. Blaming his problems on others and too petty and narcissistic to realize that perhaps he, too, was occasionally at fault. It was insulting, really. Unforgivably rude.

Sirsha didn't need him anymore. Curse the bleeding oath coin. She'd take discomfort and pain over a single moment more with that—

"Sirsha."

She jumped, and glared at Quil, further irritated that he'd managed to sneak up on her.

"Don't worry," she snarled. "I'm heading out. No need to concern yourself with Sirsha, the awful, horrible liar—"

She glanced up at him and—*was that a bleeding smile on his face?*

"Stop." He put his hands on hers, and she went still. Not because his touch sent a thrill up her spine, but because his skin was lovely and warm and she wanted to leech his heat away.

"Sirsha, I owe you an apology."

"Oh" was all that Sirsha could think to say.

She looked down at his hands, which was distracting, because they were strong and quite beautiful, and they reminded her of how he'd pulled her close last night with more interest than seemed strictly necessary to drive R'zwana away.

"I shouldn't have gotten so angry," he said. "Usually, I'm in better control of my feelings, but I—" His hair fell into his face as he looked down. "I hate what they've done to us." His voice was low, but she felt the anger thrumming through it. "The Kegari. I hate that I'm not with my aunt, fighting. I hate that I ran."

He pulled his hands away, and Sirsha had to fight herself not to take them back. "Right before the Kegari came, I wanted to abdicate," he said. "My father was a terrible emperor—cruel and selfish and violent, and I suppose I feared that I'd end up the same."

"You won't," Sirsha said. "Enigmatic and bossy, perhaps. But vicious—that's not your style."

Quil smiled at that. "Doesn't matter now. I'd been reluctant to rule my whole life, but when the chance was taken from me—" He sighed. "I felt lost. I *feel* lost."

Sirsha's breath caught at the honesty of what he was saying. The familiarity. She knew what it was to be unmoored.

"None of that excuses me getting upset with you," Quil went on, and the words made her feel safe. Valued. As if she was worthy of the truth.

"I wish I'd known about the magic, but that's my problem. Not yours." He glanced behind him at Sufiyan and Arelia, who were not-so-surreptitiously eavesdropping.

"We chatted," Quil said. "We think it would be helpful to meet your friend—the one you suggested we speak to."

"On one condition," Sufiyan spoke up. "We don't keep secrets from one another. Not important ones, anyway. Obviously if you fantasize about becoming a Nevennes sheepdog and running howling into the woods, you can keep that to yourself."

"So, Sirsha," Quil said. "Is there anything else we should know before we get back on the road with you?"

Sirsha looked between the three of them, her irritation rising. She felt waylaid.

"We like you." Arelia cut into her thoughts. "A lot. But we must be able to count on each other."

At Arelia's frank words, Sirsha's anger fizzled. She didn't know how to explain the shadow in her head, the sense of being watched.

It must be R'zwana. Maybe her sister had simply changed her methods.

"No more secrets," Sirsha said. "Truly. And it's a dragon." At the trio's confused glance, she smiled. "I fantasize about transforming into a dragon. And flying howling into the wilderness, after crisping my enemies."

"I can support that," Arelia murmured. Sirsha laughed and looked Quil full in the face because she didn't want him to think she had anything to hide. Immediately, she regretted it because his gaze sharpened. For a moment, she thought he'd accuse her of deception. But he only shrugged.

"Alas that you aren't a dragon. We could use one. Let's get moving." He made for his horse, Sufiyan and Arelia following.

"A Nevennes sheepdog, really?" Arelia said to Sufiyan as they walked out of the stable. "Quite limited, wouldn't you say?"

"I wasn't saying *I* fantasize about it!"

"I don't know, Suf, it was rather too specific for you not to have at least considered it." Quil's voice faded as the three led their beasts away.

Sirsha put her face in her horse's coat to get ahold of herself, because quite suddenly she felt overcome with emotion.

"I don't deserve this," she whispered into the soft brown fur.

"No," a voice said behind her. "You don't."

Sirsha whirled to find J'yan in the shadows. His face was guarded as it never had been when they were children.

"That was quite a performance you and your *fiancé* put on."

"If you're going to tell R'z, get it over with."

J'yan grasped Sirsha's shoulder, and she had a hand wrapped around his throat before he could move another inch. But his magic surged so quickly her fingers went numb and she dropped her arm.

"I'm not trying to hurt you, Sirsh."

"Piss off!" She shoved him and he backed away, hands up, staring at Elias's coin.

"Who did you swear that oath to?" he asked her.

Sirsha tucked her coins into her shirt. "R'zwana sending you to do her dirty work, now that you're her dog?"

"I kept her from killing you."

"Quil kept her from killing me," Sirsha snapped. Her horse whinnied in irritation, and she stroked the mare's head, trying to calm her. "You were going to make sure no one disturbed my bones, remember? What's wrong with her, anyway? She didn't become extra murderous overnight. Something happened."

J'yan's face tightened. He said nothing, which told Sirsha she'd hit on something. She thought of Quil's words the night they'd left Jibaut. *The older and more set in her ways she gets, the worse she probably is at it.*

"Holy hells," she whispered. "R'z is losing her magic."

It happened sometimes. Jaduna who began life with a reasonable amount of power found that it faded with age. There was still a place for them in Jaduna society.

But not as a Raan-Ruku.

"Whoever hired you to track the killer bound you." J'yan resolutely ignored her assertion about R'zwana. "That's the only reason you'd come so close to Jaduna lands. How could you be so reckless, Sirsha? Do you even know what we hunt?"

"Do you?" she shot back.

J'yan eyed her with the same knowing he'd had when they were kids. They'd hunted together, after all. The perfect pair. "I don't," he said. "That's the problem. We've been on this trail for six months now, Sirsh. Whoever this killer is, he's like no one we've dealt with before. You don't seem to understand that."

"I understand I have a better chance of catching the killer than you and R'z." Sirsha led her mount away. "Which is the entire reason you're following me."

"Does your fiancé know what will happen to you if you don't catch this murderer?" J'yan said. "Didn't you think *that* was worth sharing?"

Sirsha walked away and didn't turn back.

For the next few days, Sirsha couldn't escape the feeling of being watched, however desperately she wanted to. Her oath coin had stopped burning because she was fixated on the killer again and fulfilling her vow. But that did not ease the itch in her mind.

Bleeding R'zwana. Perhaps her power was altered, but it was still oppressive. Sirsha jerked awake at night, certain that something malevolent was hovering over her, only to find the massive pines of the Devanese forest serene, the camp asleep, and one of her companions keeping guard.

Sufiyan spent most of his watches pacing and scouting materials for the medic bag he'd been pulling together. Arelia lit a blue-fire lamp and worked on her self-loading slingshot, shivering in the cold night air.

Quil was the only one who appeared to solely keep watch, walking the perimeter of the camp in concentric circles, ever vigilant.

He was also the only one who noticed Sirsha jerking awake, night after night.

One evening, after they'd made their way out of the Devanese forests and into the scrubland that rolled south into Thafwa, Sirsha shot into wakefulness, bolting upright. Her heart thundered, and she had her dagger in hand before realizing she was safe.

Quil walked over from the edge of camp, a tin mug of tea steaming in his hands. He offered it silently, and after taking it, she joined him for the rest of his watch. The next night, he made her a warm bowl of khiram and she ate it almost reverently, marveling at the balance of sweet and spice.

It became an odd nightly tradition. Nightmare. Wake. Drink or eat. Sit watch.

Sometimes they'd talk, or argue, but only about things that felt unimportant. Quil was intrigued by the politics in the Southern Continent, the way each country governed. Sirsha wanted to know what life with the Tribes was like. Once, she told him of her desire to buy an inn in the Southern Isles.

They didn't talk about killers or sisters or magic. Sirsha was happy to educate him—and to smugly correct his misconceptions about the south. Sometimes, they didn't talk at all. Usually, Sirsha felt a need to fill silence, but not with Quil. Not with the stars overhead, and the forest around them buzzing with life.

They spent hours together, and he even started chuckling when she inevitably linked the shapes of constellations to various carnal acts. But other than the moment their hands brushed as she took a mug or bowl from him, he kept his distance physically.

Maybe because of that girl he'd loved. Ilar. Sirsha shuddered when she thought of how Ilar died, of the bleakness in Quil's voice as he described coming upon her and Ruh.

Quil probably felt guilty developing an attraction to someone else. He was the type.

Just as well. Sirsha didn't need distractions. Still, she thought of his palms against her skin, the hard press of his muscled arm along her hip. The way he'd looked at her that night in the inn, not with his usual cool regard, but something heated and curious and *wanting*.

She relived that moment far more than was healthy. He had to have enjoyed it. She *felt* it in the fizz of her blood. What would be the harm if she led him away from the camp one of these nights? It wouldn't mean anything.

Then she heard J'yan in her head. *Does your fiancé know what will happen to you if you don't catch this murderer?* Skies, what would she even say? *Quil, if I don't find the killer, the need to hunt her down will take over my mind, driving me insane.* Not exactly teatime conversation.

The problem was, Sirsha did not entirely dislike Quil. He was hard to read and spent far too much time in his own head. He was irritatingly graceful for someone so big. But she liked the low thrum of his voice and the way he loved his friends and his people, and how he never did anything halfway. She liked how he was thoughtful without needing praise for it, and his quiet, unflappable confidence when giving orders.

He didn't deserve to be hurt. But she could tell he wouldn't take intimacy lightly. Which meant that she *would* hurt him, eventually.

So, she accepted his culinary offerings, accompanied him on rounds, and appreciated having a friend, for however long it lasted.

After ten days, they'd reached the border with Thafwa. The weather grew warm, the landscape lush, until they were making their way across roads that were unnaturally immaculate, despite running through miles of jungle.

The going should have gotten easier. Instead, Sirsha felt awful. Her skin burned. Her brain rattled with every step her mare took.

"The village isn't far." Sirsha focused on the task at hand to distract herself. "This person who can help us—her name is Loli Temba—"

"*Daughter of the Vine*, in Ankanese," Arelia translated. "She's not Thafwan, then?"

"Ah—" Sirsha knew she'd have to explain where Loli was from eventually, but hoped they could meet her first. "Not exactly."

"Are you sure there are bandits in the woods?" Sufiyan said, regarding the docile travelers passing them, the neatly cleared squares of grazing land, the bucolic village a quarter mile ahead. "This place is much nicer than Devan."

"The Thafwans are ruled by the army, and the army keeps a tight leash on the populace." Sirsha nudged her horse onto a narrow path that curved through the trees and up a densely forested hill. "Mostly by taxing them so they can't afford to stop working. If you don't pay in gold, you pay in labor."

The trees they passed under were thick-trunked and mossy. It was blessedly cool in their shade, something Sirsha only realized when she felt sweat trickling down her face. Strange, it wasn't very hot yet. Skies, her head hurt. She swayed in her saddle, lightheaded, and slowed her horse.

"Go—go on up the hill about a half mile," she called to the others. Or was it a mile? She didn't remember. "You'll pass a waterfall and—I'll be a minute."

Her mouth filled with water. Maybe it was the porridge Sufiyan made this morning. Should have checked the supplies they'd picked up in the last town. Bleeding Devanese selling secondhand grain—

"Sirsha?"

Quil knelt beside her, which was when she realized that she must have staggered off her horse—and that the others hadn't gone on but were arrayed around her. A brilliant green snake hung off a nearby tree, its color so bright that Sirsha's eyes hurt and she had to look away.

"Do you all really want to see me retch that badly?"

"You're gray." Sufiyan pulled something from his pack. Lilangia stick. "Chew on this. Arelia, canteen, please."

The Martial girl handed it over, then gasped. "Sufiyan—her eyes—"

The world spun. Sirsha felt a great weight pressing down on her chest. A sound then, wings slicing the air. It reminded her of the Sails, and she wanted to scream a warning. She should have told her friends to beware, but she couldn't explain what she felt and now Quil would think she was deceiving him, and she didn't know why that upset her so much, but it did.

A wave of pain slammed Sirsha in the stomach so hard that at first, she grappled for her knife. Why was Quil looking at her in horror, instead of at whoever punched her? *R'zwana*. Had her sister discovered a way to become invisible? Sirsha wanted to shout at them all that they were under attack.

But the pain doubled her over and she couldn't speak through her gasps. She caught a glimpse of something enormous—something that blocked out the sun. The world exploded in a burst of red.

She tried to grab for Quil, Arelia. Anything. But the last thing she heard was a voice out of her past, soft and paper-thin, creased with sadness and worry. Loli Temba.

"Sirsha, child, I told you not to return. Do you know what you have brought with you?"

25

Aiz

Aiz did not expect a ten-year-old child to teach her anything of the world. But over the next three weeks, after Quil left with Tas, it was Ruh who dulled the sharp longing for Kegar and Cero and the cloister.

The Tribe trundled its way northwest toward Nur, dropping off Elias's students or picking up new ones, trading for goods and collecting news, swapping tales around the fire at the end of the day.

Ruh taught her Sadhese, ate with her, kept her company on watch, and regaled her with stories. His favorites were about Duranis. "Chaos storytellers," he whispered to her one morning as the wind howled around his family's wagon. "They tell lies and pass them off as truth, seeding chaos wherever they go."

A fortnight after Quil left, Aiz sat with the child at the edge of camp, the steaming meat pies in their hands doing little to ward off the cold. Aiz had reread Tiral's book again last night, hoping for anything she could tell Laia, some snippet to jog the Kehanni's memory. But though Aiz had shared the story with Laia again, the woman still claimed not to remember it.

Aiz stared moodily out at the swiftly disappearing sun, only half listening to Ruh's story. The wind moaned and her neck prickled. She sat up.

There was something out in the sands. Something watching them.

"Ruh—" She put herself between him and the desert. "I don't think we're alone out here—"

"It's only the jinn." He smiled up at Aiz. "They watch me, sometimes.

Have for as long as I can remember. But don't worry. They won't hurt you."

"Jinn!" Aiz said. "The fire creatures, yes? How did you know they were there?"

Ruh shrugged, eager to get on with his tale, but an idea bloomed in Aiz's mind.

"Ruh," she said. "Could you help me with the story I seek? You hear things others don't. See things."

"I can try?" The boy sat up tall. "But you'll have to tell me what you're looking for."

"If I do tell you," Aiz said, "it has to be a secret."

Ruh hesitated. Aiz was certain he'd been told by his parents that anyone who asked you to keep secrets from them wasn't worth trusting.

"Your ama already knows most of this, Ruh," she said. "But she's busy and—and I think to help me, you'll need to know more than I told your ama. You'll need to know the stories that are special to my people. But they aren't shared with just anyone."

"I am not anyone!" Ruh said. "I'm your friend and the future Kehanni of Tribe Saif. I know how to keep a secret."

He fixed his silver gaze on her, his small chin set stubbornly, and he looked so much like Hani that Aiz's heart twinged. She wondered if Ruhyan and Hani would like each other. If in some world, they would ever be friends.

Aiz waited a moment to see if Mother Div would object. She did not.

"All right," Aiz said. "Gather, gather and listen well . . ."

Preaching the Sacred Tales again was a balm to Aiz's soul. Over the many days it took to tell the stories, her worry faded, overwhelmed by the resounding truth of her words. Ruh's questions and comments only deepened her faith, making her appreciate the Sacred Tales in ways she hadn't before.

One evening, a week after Aiz began sharing the Sacred Tales, she completed the Eighth Tale while she and Ruh walked a circuit around the Saif encampment.

"So, the Ninth Tale," Ruh said. "That's what you're looking for?"

Aiz nodded. "The Ninth Tale will tell me how to free Mother Div. I think your ama knows it, but for some reason, she doesn't remember."

Ruh scratched his chin, looking like a tiny, baby-faced old man considering a philosophical problem. "I'll check her story scrolls," he said. "Sometimes, she keeps notes there on tales she hasn't finished."

"Would your ama let you?" Laia hadn't so much as mentioned the scrolls to Aiz, nor offered to check them.

"No," Ruh answered. "But this is important to your people, yes?"

"The most important thing."

"Then I will look. Ama doesn't have to know. It's only stories. Ama tells honest ones, so they won't hurt anyone. It's the lies one must worry about."

Such a simple sentiment from a child, but it stuck with Aiz, and she had to remind herself that her lies had purpose. That they were for a greater good. *Get what you need. Forget the rest.*

In the encampment, Zaldar Shan blew the horn that signaled the changing of watch, and Aiz and Ruh returned to find Laia and Elias waiting.

Aiz's stomach clenched, the way it used to when she was a girl, and Sister Noa caught her filching extra helpings of food. *I've done nothing wrong*, Aiz reminded herself. *Only asked Ruh to help since his mother seems incapable.*

Laia smiled in welcome, and Elias gave his typical nod. Aiz wouldn't call it hostile. But it wasn't friendly, either.

"What's so funny, cricket?" Elias asked Ruh, who made a glowering impression of his father's face before laughing and darting away. Elias went after him, chuckling at Ruh's contagious giggles.

"Oi, Ankana!" Zaldar Shan shouted from beside the fire, where he was braiding his daughter's hair. The man called people by everything but their actual names. "Come decide an argument for me, will you? You're the only impartial one around here."

Aiz grinned. "I'll find you after dinner."

"You're settling in well," Laia said. "Zaldar Shan says you're an excellent listener. You'd have to be, to survive a conversation with him." The Kehanni raised her voice so that the Zaldar heard, and he made a rude gesture at her. Then he looked worriedly around to make sure Elias hadn't seen.

"The Zaldar has taught me much about inter-Tribal politics," Aiz said. "Especially how he trusts not a single member of Tribe Rahin. And I've enjoyed learning scim-fighting from Karinna."

Laia sighed. "You are kind, Ilar, to let her teach you. She is not the most patient instructor."

"But she is efficient," Aiz said, holding out her arms, bruised from Karinna's brutalist lessons.

Laia smiled. "You stopped a horse thief, I heard?"

"He wasn't a very smart thief." Aiz had noticed that Laia frowned on arrogance and was gratified at the woman's nod of approval. "I just yelled for help."

"You don't give yourself enough credit," Laia said, and then, after a pause, "I wanted you to know I've been hunting your story. I have a lead. I've asked the Kehanni of Tribe Nasur to meet us in Nur. She's one of the wisest among our number. She does not travel for many people, but she has agreed to see me."

Aiz turned to Laia swiftly. "She's heard the story?"

"She said she recognized the shape of it. We will see what she tells us in person. We'll be there in two months, a little before Rathana, to offload our fall wares and pick up stock for the winter."

Relief swept through Aiz, but it was brief, replaced by impatience. Yet another two months she'd be away from home. She was desperate to know if the clerics had been freed yet. If Hani and Jak and Finh still lived. She would give anything to be tucked under a fur with Cero in Dafra cloister, sharing a bowl of lentil stew.

"Ilar, you're sure the story isn't written down somewhere?" Laia furrowed her brow. "If I could see it, I sense that everything would become clear to me, but . . ."

Aiz didn't understand why Mother Div was so against showing the book to Laia. It was obvious that Laia wasn't a covetous type. Aiz was sure she wouldn't steal the book.

Do not question, Mother Div hissed.

Aiz chafed at the order, as she hadn't before. She knew Mother Div had her reasons, but—

You owe me, child. Without me, you never would have escaped the bowels of the Tohr.

"I'm sorry, Laia." Aiz traced the *D* on her hand—a reminder to herself of Div's wisdom. "I know only what I've heard."

"Of course," Laia said. "You did say so, but . . ." She shook her head, as if clearing it. "Quil will be back tomorrow. You met him that first night."

"I did." Aiz had wondered when the prince would return, had been preparing for it. "I'll look forward to seeing him again."

The Kehanni gave her a knowing smile and glanced to where Elias had caught up to Ruh. They were arm wrestling and Elias was losing quite badly.

"Funny, isn't it," Laia said. "How sometimes the first time you meet someone, your heart knows, even if your mind doesn't."

Laia might be smiling, but Aiz knew she needed to tread carefully. Quil was the crown prince of the Martials, and Aiz a stranger from a distant land. The Tribes knew Aiz was poor and they wouldn't look kindly upon anyone taking advantage of Quil for his position. The laws of hospitality only went so far.

"Perhaps one day"—Aiz turned her gaze down demurely—"I will be fortunate enough to experience that for myself."

Aiz excused herself then and made her way quickly to her tent. Not, as Laia might have suspected, to moon over Quil's return. But instead to plan exactly what she needed from the prince, and how she was going to get it.

The next morning, Aiz joined a group of other Tribespeople waiting for Zaldar Shan to give them their watch assignments for the day.

"Ilar," Shan said, "south side, moonrise watch—"

"I'll join her." Quil moved like liquid through the crowd, greeting other members of the Tribe with quiet words as they welcomed him back. His wavy hair was half pulled back and messy, his clothes dusty from travel. Still, there was something about him that drew the eye, and it had nothing to do with his noble blood.

He stopped before the Zaldar, but looked at Aiz. Her heart thudded faster.

"If she's all right with me tagging along, of course."

Aiz shrugged, seemingly unconcerned. "Fine," she said.

His responding smile lit up his whole face. Aiz's pulse hitched, and when she smiled back, it was spontaneous. He made his way to her.

"I hoped you'd be here when I got back," he said. "Is that all right?"

"I— Yes." What in the Spires was this sudden shyness that had come upon her? She'd known Quil was returning. She'd planned her questions, her comments—even a seduction if necessary.

But now that he was here, she wanted to know where he'd gone. What it had been like. And if he'd thought of her.

"Yes, it's all right," she said to Quil. "I'm happy you're back."

As responses went, it wasn't the most alluring, but Quil smiled again, and though others in the Tribe watched with interest, Aiz found she couldn't look away from him. For a second, she forgot about Kegar entirely.

Laia's words last night came back to Aiz, and she shivered. *Your heart knows, even if your mind doesn't.*

"Finally!" Sufiyan appeared from the encampment with impeccable timing, punching Quil on the arm. "Lessons have been bleeding boring without you. Where's Tas?"

"Here, little brother." Aiz jumped—she hadn't noticed the blond man in the crowd. "Ilar of Ankana!" He grinned at her with effortless charm. "Lovely to see you again. You made *quite* the impression on Quil here—"

"Hells, Tas, shut *up*—" Quil looked mortified, and Aiz found herself smiling.

"Oh, was I *not* supposed to mention that you—"

Quil dragged Tas off, and Aiz used the opportunity to slip away to her tent. She needed to collect herself. She felt discombobulated by Quil's return. By the anticipation she'd felt at the sight of him. She could imagine herself falling into this charmed life so easily.

She dropped onto her bedroll, twirling her aaj around her pinkie rapidly.

Cero had told her not to use the aaj except in an emergency, for fear of letting anyone who might be tracking her know where she was. But Tribe Saif was in the middle of the desert, and she'd seen no sign of a Jaduna. She needed to hear Cero's voice. She needed a piece of home.

"Cero." She grabbed the aaj and spoke. "It's—it's an emergency."

You better be dying, Aiz, he responded.

Aiz laughed at the acid in her friend's voice, familiar and beloved.

"Worse," she said. "I miss you. I miss home." She thought saying it would make her feel better. But the pain in her chest worsened.

Where are you?

"I'm—"

Don't answer if you haven't verified who I am!

Aiz searched her mind for a fact only Cero would know; there were so many.

"Who's the first person you fell in love with?"

Trick question. I'm too ice-hearted to ever be in love. Tell me everything.

Aiz swiftly caught him up on what had happened, impatient not to share her world but to know what was happening in his.

The clerics were released. Along with a group of Tohr inmates. But, Aiz—

"There were three children," Aiz said. "Hani, Jak, and Finh—"

Noa and Olnas made it out. And Jak and Finh and Hani. But then Tiral visited the cloister and Hani—Tiral killed her.

"What?" Aiz cried, her hand at her mouth. She thought of Hani's sweet face, of the way she never asked for stories even though she loved them, the way she tried to protect Jak and Finh.

Tiral knew it would hurt the clerics. He hoped they'd blame you, I think. He's Tel Ilessi now. Everything happened as you said it would. Dovan backed him after he threatened the clerics. The rest of the clergy fell in line. The Triarchy had to accept him or risk losing their heads. Especially since his raids brought in a fresh supply of food.

"Tell the clerics and orphans that I will return, Cero," Aiz said. "When I do, I won't come alone. I will bring the spirit of Mother Div with me. I will kill Tiral."

Cero was silent for a moment, and when he spoke again, he sounded tired. *Tiral never hunted you, Aiz. He didn't send pilots after you, didn't hire any Jaduna. He said he didn't need to, and while I can't untangle his twisted brain, it does mean you're free. Don't come back. Make a life for yourself. These people you travel with—they sound like good people.*

"They're a means to an end."

Even this prince you speak of?

Aiz found herself sputtering. "He— Cero, he's a prince. And I'm me."

Exactly. If he has any sense, he's half in love already.

He was smiling. Aiz felt it. But the expression wouldn't reach his eyes. He'd be looking at his hands or out at the Spires, jaw sharp as glass and just on the other side of clenched. Silence bloomed between them, heavy with what neither had gotten a chance to say.

Aiz took a deep breath. "Cero. I don't want to make a life here," she said. "I don't want a life with anyone else. I—I want you. And—"

The aaj went cold.

He was gone. And the hurt she felt, the longing for him and for home that she'd tried desperately to quell, grabbed her heart and squeezed.

Later that night, as Ruh and Aiz finished the last of the dishes, Quil appeared. He'd cleaned up, shaved, and pulled his dark hair back into a knot. *For her.*

"Who is this child?" He looked at Ruh in mock confusion. "Not Ruh, surely. *Ruh* attacks me the second I get back from Antium, demanding offerings. You must be someone else."

Ruh lifted his chin. "I'm mad at you. You were supposed to take me with you this time."

Quil knelt in front of Ruh. "If I tell you that all I did was listen to old people argue about very boring things, would it help?"

Ruh tried not to smile and failed. His demeanor brightened at the puzzle box Quil drew from his pocket.

"Aunt Hel hid something in here for you," he said. "Said it would take you two months to open. I said two weeks."

"Two days," Aiz said. She'd spent enough time with Ruh to know that his mind was unusually quick.

As Ruh disappeared with the box, Quil stood again. "Ready for watch?"

Aiz dried her hands and took off her apron. She'd dressed with care, her green dress flattering on her pale skin, the color bringing out the emerald flecks in her eyes. Quil breathed in as she joined him.

"That smell," he said—

"Desert roses." She smiled. "Too much?"

Quil shook his head, and she walked ahead, adding a sway to her step, satisfaction surging through her when she caught him looking.

She felt a twinge of guilt, too. She was misleading him for information. *For Hani*, she reminded herself. *For all the orphans Tiral murdered. For all those who still live.*

"Reports of wraiths out here tonight," Quil said. "Have you seen one yet?"

Aiz shook her head. "Karinna told me about them. You have to chop off their heads, she said." Aiz unsheathed her scim. "She's trying to teach me. But I don't think I have the way of it yet."

"Hold the blade with more flexibility in the wrist than you would a dagger." Quil slowed and came around to her side, wrapping his whole hand around hers and tightening her grip. "Like this."

She glanced up at him as he looked down at her. Aiz let her eyes drop to his mouth. She should have looked away quickly, kept him on edge. Instead, she found herself fascinated at the shape of his lips, the top one fuller, a stark contrast to his square jaw, his overly sharp cheekbones.

Quil cleared his throat. "We can practice tomorrow," he said. "With wooden swords." He pointed to a rocky hill ahead. "Good view up there. Better than anything in Antium, anyway."

Aiz suppressed a frown. She thought he'd kiss her. He must be shyer than she realized.

"Was Antium really just boring meetings?"

"Sort of. My aunt's pulling me deeper into the running of things. She wanted me to stay longer, but Tas and I convinced her to let me go."

"What's his job in the Tribe?"

Quil laughed. "Embarrassing me and breaking hearts."

"Breaking hearts. Not something I have to worry about with you, I hope?" Aiz looked up at him through her eyelashes, smiling to herself when he reddened and shook his head.

"Your aunt," she said. "She's young, no? Does she expect you to rule soon?"

"She never wanted to be Empress." They trudged up the hill along a well-trod trail. A ravine fell away to their left. To their right, the hill rose in a jumble of rocky crags, blocking the view of the Saif encampment. The wind prickled at Aiz, as if in warning, and she kept away from the edge of the ravine.

"She's told me since I was a child that she's holding the throne for me."

"Do you want it?"

"No one ever asks that." Quil looked at her in surprise. "I don't know. I—I suppose I don't have a choice."

"This makes you unhappy." She watched his face. "Because you will not be with the Tribes?"

"I'll be in the capital. Antium. Eventually I'll marry and have heirs, and . . . try to be as good a leader as my aunt. I'm afraid I won't be, though. I'm afraid I'm not even a fraction of the ruler she is."

It was the most honest thing he'd said to her, and she was both moved by the sincerity of it and determined to get more out of him.

"Because you feel unprepared?" she pressed. "Or because she was trained as a Mask, and you weren't?"

Quil looked at her in surprise and Aiz cursed herself. Perhaps the conversational leap had been too great.

"She trained me as a Mask, even if I don't wear one."

"They are strange," Aiz said. "Metal, but . . . not."

"Liquid metal," Quil said. "Elias always hated his. Took it off before it could join with him."

"The metal," Aiz pressed. "Where does it come from? And is it . . . alive?"

Quil nodded. "No one living knows where it's mined. And it's sentient, according to Elias. He might still have his mask. I'm sure he'd show it to you if you asked. I'm guessing Ankana doesn't have anything like them?"

Aiz shook her head. "We have seers. We don't need Masks."

"So, your people—your group is ruled by the Eye of Ankana?"

Aiz, like most who'd been educated in the cloisters, knew much about Ankana. Still, she felt a bead of sweat trickle down her neck. "The Eye is not to be questioned."

"Might the Eye be persuaded to help your people? I've met the High Seer. Maybe if I know more about what your people are suffering, I could talk to him. Try to help."

Aiz glanced at Quil in surprise, nearly tripping face-first into the ravine. Quil's hand shot out, warm on her wrist as he pulled her back from the edge.

"Careful," he said.

Her pulse quickened at his closeness. Then confusion hit. He offered his influence so freely.

Perhaps he did this out of kindness, and it was hard for her to recognize because she'd known so little of it. But the part of her that survived the Kegari gutters hissed that he must have an ulterior motive for helping her.

"Maybe the High Seer could help," Aiz answered his question. "Though in truth, I would like to speak to your Empress of my people's troubles." It was the Empress who had power here. The Empress who could help the Kegari, if she was willing to listen.

Aiz intended to ask Quil more about his aunt when a breeze nudged her in warning and her magic tingled. Something—someone—approached.

Aiz realized that she and Quil were in a perfect spot for an ambush. They couldn't escape up the mountain, nor into the ravine. She hunched quickly, knowing to make herself a smaller target, just as a volley of darts flew toward her companion. *Assassin!*

Quil stepped in front of her. "Ilar, run!"

Aiz lashed out with her windsmithing, thinking the word *shield*! The darts dropped to the ground. Along with Quil.

The assassin came surging down the trail. Aiz remembered what Mother Div had taught her before. To call the wind, hold it, and shape it into a spear. She did so now, flinging the wind at the assassin. The woman gasped as it hit, her boot slipping off the narrow trail and sliding into the ravine. She screamed, the sound fading as she dropped down the canyon. Distantly, Aiz heard a thump.

She was already turning to Quil. His eyes appeared glassy and unfocused, and she wasn't sure if he could even see her.

"Where are you hit, Quil?" She leaned over him, trying to make out his body in the moonlight. "Can you tell me?"

"N-neck. Poison. Could be Nightweed. Could be Anithas."

Aiz felt methodically along his throat, going slow. The darts were small.

"S-sorry I—I don't always know what to say to you," Quil continued gabbling. "I feel out of my depth when we talk. You smile and it does strange things to me. Which is odd because I've hardly spent any time with you. And Tas said to be careful, and I want to listen to Tas—"

Not on the left side of his throat. Aiz moved her fingers to the right.

"But Tas doesn't know anything about love—had his heart broken once and he's hopped from bed to bed since. Anyway, I'm not in love! Skies, I don't even know you. But you're good to Ruh and— Am I talking too much? Why am I talking so much?"

Aiz had no idea, but she'd found the dart. With careful fingers she plucked it out, thin and featherlight—almost impossible to see.

"Oh hells," Quil said. "It *is* Anithas. That's why I'm talking so much. Um—you'll—have to get the poison out." He looked away, and despite herself, Aiz smiled.

"Is the mighty Prince of the Martial Empire blushing because I'll have to suck poison out of his neck?"

She put her lips near the bite before he could answer and drew out the poison quickly, spitting the bitter liquid to the ground.

"Thank—thank you." Quil shuddered as if to shake off the poison's lingering effects. After a few moments, he stood with her help. Sudden horror dawned on his face.

"Oh hells," he whispered. "I don't know what I was saying. I'm sorry—"

"Nothing to worry about," Aiz said, relieved that he was all right. "We should get you back. Have the healer look at you. And Elias will want to do a sweep of the area—"

"No," Quil said. "I have an antidote in my tent. I don't need the healer. And I don't want Elias to know. He'll tell my aunt. What happened to the assassin?"

"Dead." She nodded to the ravine. Far below, a dark lump was splayed on the rocks, a pool of blood spreading out from her head. "Tripped coming down the hill."

"Huh. I thought I saw—" He shook his head, and Aiz spoke quickly.

"We should tell Elias," she said, because doing so would make her appear honest. "He'd want to know. And—perhaps deal with the body."

But Quil shook his head.

"Scavengers will take care of the body, and she tried to kill me, so she doesn't deserve any better," he said. "I've fought off thirteen assassination attempts in just the past few years. Sometimes, it's another Martial Gens. Sometimes a Karkaun. It doesn't matter who's trying to kill me. After every attempt, my aunt and I argue about whether I should have guards trailing me. I hate being caged, Ilar. I hate when choices aren't my own."

"I'd hate that too." She thought of the Tohr. "I won't say anything."

She told herself it was because he'd now owe her a favor. But some part of her also felt gratified at the relief on his face.

When they returned to camp around dawn, Elias, sharpening his scim and chatting with Tas before his own watch duty, approached them.

"Anything?"

Quil shook his head, and Elias shifted his gaze to Aiz. She felt pinned, and forced herself to smile.

"All quiet!" she said easily in Ankanese. Tas glanced up at her, head tilted as if she'd said something fascinating.

Elias's eyes narrowed ever so slightly, and Aiz felt a twinge of frustration. Somehow, he'd sniffed out her lie.

"I have a question," she said, hoping to distract him. "About—about your mask. Quil was telling me about them. Do you—still have it?"

Aiz smiled guilelessly, hoping Elias would think she was a breathless kid hearing stories from the boy she liked. Sweet. Foreign. Harmless.

"No," the big Martial said, sliding his scim into its scabbard. "Sufiyan's on breakfast duty," he informed Quil. "Get something to eat."

"Hells, Elias, don't scare the poor girl," Aiz heard Tas mutter as she and Quil walked away. "She only met us a few weeks ago."

Quil reached out and squeezed Aiz's hand as they walked away. "Thank you. I owe you."

Aiz shrugged it off, magnanimous. When she glanced back over her shoulder, Elias was contemplating them, a hand on the dagger at his waist. Aiz looked swiftly away, but the message was clear.

She was being watched.

26
Quil

The woman appeared out of nowhere. She wore shades of green that blended into the jungle so seamlessly that at first, Quil thought he was hallucinating a pale floating head.

Then she crouched beside Sirsha, the pelt of emerald feathers woven into her blond hair giving her the look of some delicate bird. Quil drew his scim, but Sirsha croaked, "Loli Temba," before her lids fluttered closed over her ghostly white irises.

Quil knelt and felt for her pulse, expelling a breath when he felt it, strong and rhythmic.

"She's alive." He'd no sooner said it than Arelia turned on Sufiyan.

"What the bleeding hells did you put in that porridge this morning?"

"Nothing!" Sufiyan crouched beside Sirsha, trying to figure out what was wrong with her. "We all ate it. Let me check her for injuries."

"Boy." Loli Temba spoke so quietly that it wasn't until she fixed her pale blue eyes on Quil that he realized she was talking to him. "When did it pick up your trail?"

To Quil's surprise, she spoke fluent Serran.

With a Karkaun accent.

Arelia noticed at the same moment that Quil did, and glowered. The temperature in the little clearing seemed to drop a few degrees.

Most Karkauns had the sense to stay away from Martials. Quil still remembered the day he'd learned about the horror they'd inflicted on Antium twenty years ago. His aunt had insisted on telling him herself.

They mutilated and murdered their own women and children, then used unholy magic to resurrect their spirits and unleash them on us. They brought us to our knees in mere days.

Quil had been born in the middle of that war, as the capital around him fell. He'd been spirited away to safety. But those left behind endured Karkaun atrocities that still haunted the city.

Loli Temba regarded Arelia dispassionately. "You hate my people," she said. "Good. I hate them too." She turned her full attention to Quil. "I ask again. When did it pick up your trail?"

"Sirsha's sister's been tracking us," he said. "But we haven't seen her for days. We were looking for you. We have questions—"

Loli hissed through her teeth as if in sudden pain and held up a hand to cut him off. She hummed and the air shimmered in a strange, diamond pattern, like a net made of dew.

Overhead, the clouds shifted and blocked out the sun. The jungle, dim from the thick canopy, grew darker.

Near the road they'd turned off, something moved.

Quil couldn't make out a shape, let alone a face. But the hair on the back of his neck rose, and he drew his scim. The familiar slide of metal against leather was small comfort. Beside him, Arelia stepped forward, peering at the road.

Loli Temba grabbed Arelia's arm, shaking her head.

A moment later, Arelia's surly frustration turned to fright. Quil tried to lift his scim, but terror crept into his chest.

The feeling was horribly familiar, though he'd encountered it only once in his life: when he was twelve and an assassin nearly got the best of him. He'd never forget her grinning face as her knee pressed down on his chest, squeezing the air from his lungs.

Now, in the Thafwan jungle, he felt that soul-deep fear again. Sufiyan's face went pale, his lips blue. He opened and closed his mouth the way he had that awful day a year ago, when he realized his little brother was dead. Quil tried to shake off his own dread and grabbed his friend's shoulder. "I'm here, Suf," he whispered. "I'm here."

Arelia's arms shook, her head tucked into her knees, and Quil reached for her hand. With Loli Temba hovering, the three of them crouched around a prone Sirsha, waiting, unable to countenance the terror in their chests, to explain it, other than that it felt as if the reaper himself whispered in their ears all the ways they could suffer. All the ways they could die.

The clouds shifted. The sun poured weakly through the trees, and whatever ill creature they'd briefly shared the jungle with appeared to have moved on.

"What in the bleeding skies," Sufiyan said, "was that?"

Loli answered no questions. Instead, she ordered Quil to pick up Sirsha, and faded into the jungle as swiftly as she'd appeared, expecting them to follow. When Arelia attempted to engage Loli in conversation, she responded with a forbidding growl.

Quil knew he should ask Loli Temba about the Kegari as soon as possible, but all he could think about was how light Sirsha was in his arms. How awful it was not to hear her wry mutter. Ilar's angry face rose in his memory. The last time he'd seen her whole.

Not Sirsha. Sirsha will be fine. But what if she wasn't fine? Skies, he couldn't even help her. He was depending on a Karkaun who didn't seem to want them there. *Stupid, Quil.* He should have noticed something was wrong with Sirsha. He should have *done* something.

They took a circuitous path through the jungle, toward a thunderous, white-water cataract. It boiled through a narrow slot before plunging into a shallow pool a hundred feet below.

Loli led them down a damp, vine-choked trail to a rock shelf at the back of the waterfall. There, she put her hand to the stone and sang a few low notes. Quil thought of what Sirsha said about magic. *An emotion exerted on an element.* The stone split right down the center, creating an opening wide enough for them to pass through.

Quil cursed. Arelia and Sufiyan still looked sick and weak, and he was holding Sirsha. If Loli had an ambush planned, this would be the ideal place to do it. But she merely closed the stone and motioned for them to follow.

The sound of the waterfall faded to a distant hum, and they emerged into a room with rough gray walls and thick columns of light pouring from above. A settee sat in one corner with a knitted blanket folded over it, and plush rugs lay on the floor. Beside shelves packed with cooking implements, a cold hearth vented into a chimney that disappeared through the cave's ceiling.

Loli Temba closed her door, passing her hand over it once. Then she nudged Quil toward a side bedroom—small, but lit like the rest of her home, with a broad beam of light.

"Stop gawping and lay her down." Loli pointed to a rope bed softened with thick, handwoven blankets. "It will take rest and quiet for her to come out of this."

"But . . . she will come out of it?" Arelia, at the door, whispered the question Quil was about to ask.

Loli didn't answer, and Quil didn't budge. "I'll stay with her," he said. He wouldn't leave her alone. Wouldn't let anything tear her apart the way Ilar had been torn apart.

Loli put a firm hand on Quil's arm. "I would die before I saw her harmed," she said. Quil was about to tell her to piss off, but something in the woman's uncanny stare assuaged his misgivings.

"Door stays open," Quil said, and Loli nodded and bade them sit on the settee.

"She is strong," the Karkaun woman said. "Even if she is a fool." She considered Quil. "You truly did not feel it tracking you?"

Quil's frustration finally burst out of him. He was worried about Sirsha, and he didn't know what the hells was stalking them, and he didn't want to answer questions—he wanted them bleeding answered.

"What do you mean *it*?" he snapped. "What was that thing? What did it want with us?"

Reli and Sufiyan exchanged a glance at his rare show of temper. Loli shook her head.

"I do not know. I only felt it when it breached the barriers I've put near my home. It stinks of death." Loli shuddered. "And guile."

"You have magic, then." Arelia leaned forward. "What is your emotion—and your element?"

"Sirsha has been instructing you, I see." Loli's voice was cold. "Did she not teach you that asking such a question is akin to asking the contours of your heart? Who you love? How it makes you feel?"

Arelia flushed and crossed her arms. "I'm trying to understand."

"You seek to understand the fibers that make the world," Loli Temba said, "but not your own pain, nor that of others. You'd be better served understanding the latter."

With that, Loli walked swiftly to a counter beside the hearth, above which hung copper pots and pans of varying sizes, as well as bunches of dried lavender and coriander, and strings of garlic and chilies. She grabbed a wooden bowl and brought it back to Sufiyan, handing it to him as he turned away from them and retched into it.

Quil was at his side immediately, patting his friend's back. He'd felt sick this way himself after the first time he killed a Karkaun. After he found Ilar and Ruh. "Get it out, brother," he said. "You'll feel better in a minute."

"Maybe it *was* the porridge," Sufiyan moaned.

"It wasn't." Loli took the bowl, waving away Sufiyan's apologies. A pump churned in a room beyond, and Loli returned a few minutes later with a tray of water glasses.

"I suspect that the more your soul hurts," she said, her tone kinder than it had been with any of the rest of them, "the worse you will feel when you're around it."

"We need help, not riddles." Quil didn't care that he was verging on rudeness. "Speak plainly. You must suspect what that thing could be."

For the first time, Loli Temba appeared surprised. "This is the first time you have seen it. But Sirsha must have felt it. She did not warn you?"

"She's been acting strange," Arelia offered, though her mistrust of Loli was still clear. "For days."

"She hasn't been well," Sufiyan said. "Yesterday I gave her Iltim powder for a headache. Do you think she knew and was hiding it from us?"

"If so," Quil said, "maybe she had a reason. Though—" He turned to Loli. "Is the creature following us? Or her?"

Loli dug through her pantry until she found a stack of plates. "Her, I think. When she left, I told her not to return. I told her she would bring something with her."

"Can you help her?" Quil said. "She said she came to you before. Long ago. That you healed her."

"I did not heal her," Loli Temba said. "I gave her time and love. Her own people offered neither. But that is her story to tell."

"We don't have time." Quil stood, pacing in impatience, peering at Sirsha's prone body through the open door. She was so still that for a moment, he thought she wasn't breathing and his own heart almost stopped. But then he caught the slightest flutter of her eyelashes.

"She will wake," Loli Temba said. "When she does, we will learn more of what she knew. You have more questions. Different questions. Ask."

He'd been so worried about Sirsha that he'd forgotten the reason he'd come here. He needed to get hold of himself. He was the crown prince of a shattered Empire. His people were depending on him.

"Sirsha said you might know about the Kegari," he said. "About their magic."

"Long ago"—Loli set four plates on her dining table—"the Martials attacked the Scholars. Took their lands. Enslaved their people. Why did they do this?"

"They were manipulated by the Nightbringer," Arelia said. Loli Temba's expression soured.

"They were greedy," Quil amended. "They wanted what the Scholars had."

"Greedy later, yes." Loli Temba pulled a long, dark fruit from the pantry, peeling back its thick outer skin and slicing up the soft pink innards. "But in the beginning, the Martials were simply poor and hungry. So it is with the Kegari. Their population is starving. Their leaders raid their neighbors to keep them fed. They cannot grow grain or raise livestock. So, they suffer."

"They didn't fly thousands of miles north to the Empire because they're hungry," Arelia snapped, sharper than Quil had ever heard her.

"Bah!" Loli Temba curled her lip. "Why should I tell you more about them when you do not listen? Perhaps, like the Scholars before you, you deserve to be conquered."

"For someone who hates the Karkauns," Sufiyan said, "you sound a lot like one of their warlocks."

"Shut it," Quil ordered his companions. "Both of you." He turned to Loli. "Please, tell us. We need the knowledge. My people—"

Loli Temba huffed in disgust as she washed a bouquet of thick green leaves. "Yes, your people," she said. "Your people barely knew Kegar existed. When they learned, the first thing your Empress did was demand the secrets of flight. When the Kegari failed to offer them, your people refused to speak with their envoys. *Your people* aren't as deserving as you think."

Quil's magic, quiet these past few days, warmed in his chest. A memory lived at the core of this woman. He could feel it. A pain that made her who she was.

He considered her. She was a loner. But she'd helped Sirsha. She understood abandonment. For the first time, Quil noticed the scars all over her pale skin. Tiny lines, as if she'd been cut repeatedly. He thought of how her lip curled when she'd said, *You hate my people. Good. I hate them too.*

"When I first understood that the Kegari were attacking us," Quil said, "I hated them. I still hate them. But hate doesn't fix anything." He leaned forward. "I must understand what they want from the Empire. If they have magic, why are they attacking us? If all they need is food, there are a dozen countries they can raid thousands of miles closer than the Empire."

Loli looked at him steadily. "You're an Aquillus, yes?" she said. "Nephew of the Empress?"

Quil was surprised—and unnerved—that she recognized him. Loli smiled, but there was no joy in it as she explained. "When my people attacked yours," she said, "twenty years ago, I was there as a sacrifice. I saw the Blood Shrike walking the walls. And another who walked in shadow with his other half behind him. The first ghost in the city."

"My father," Quil said, voice flattening like his aunt's did when she spoke of Marcus Farrar. "The ghost was that of the twin brother he killed." Or so the rumors said. Emperor Marcus was known to pace the city's walls, muttering to someone only he could see.

Quil shook thoughts of his father away, and sadness filled him at what Loli had suffered. "You were a sacrifice, you say. But the Karkauns killed their sacrifices, used spirit magic to chain their ghosts and unleash them upon the city."

"Indeed," Loli Temba said. "The warlocks wanted my ghost badly, for the ghost of a human imbued with magic, as I was, is far more powerful than one without. But I escaped them."

She gestured them to the table. The meal was fragrant and fresh—a salad topped with seeds, salted legumes, and a nutty oil; a thick, bouncy bread slathered in butter; and a mountain of the sweet pink fruit tossed with red chili.

Quil didn't realize how hungry he was until he'd demolished the plate, and Loli was heaping on a second helping and sitting down herself.

"You ask why the Kegari attacked you," she said. "You're a child of Gens Aquilla. Whatever your woes, they have not involved watching your people die from empty bellies. Hunger *is* part of it." She glanced at Arelia. "But perhaps this is only the beginning of the reason they chose you."

"Their magic," Quil said. "Is it spirit magic, like the Karkauns'?"

"Don't be foolish, boy," Loli Temba chided. "They keep their Sails aloft by manipulating the wind."

Arelia frowned. "That doesn't make sense." She'd softened her tone, though Quil could tell it was taking a great deal of effort. "Even if they could manipulate the wind, that would only provide lift. They'd need thrust, too, to maneuver the Sails forward. I didn't get a close look at them. But I didn't see an engine."

"And what about their weaponry?" Sufiyan asked. "Do they use magic for that, too? I've never seen weapons that appear to move on their own like that. As if they're alive."

"I do not know much of their weapons," Loli Temba said. "Listen to my words. Even with magic, the Kegari were nothing. Less than nothing. They raided and stole and barely subsisted. Then, many months ago, that changed. *They* changed. They began to rally around one man. A highborn leader, the rumors say. They call him the Tel Ilessi."

The words felt like thunder in Quil's ears.

"Rue la ba Tel Ilessi," he whispered. He'd heard those words over and again. He'd had no idea what it meant. Loli Temba nodded.

"An honorific or prayer," she said. "I do not know what the words mean. But I have heard they call upon him, invoke his name every time they kill. Or die."

"What does he want?" Sufiyan said.

"Maybe he wants what they've always wanted," Arelia said. "Food.

Security. But unlike the leaders who've come before, he knows how to get it."

"So, the Tel Ilessi is everything to them," Quil said. "Not just a leader. A—a savior."

"Yes," Loli said. "His people would follow him into the sea if he asked. Without him, they would be nothing."

"We met him," Quil said, turning to Sufiyan. "In Jibaut. The man who stopped us—who captured us with wind."

Sufiyan shook his head. "That could have been anyone."

"It was him." Certainty pounded through Quil's blood. "He knew me. He knew I was the crown prince and that I went not by Zacharias, but Quil." *Long have I wished to look upon you.*

"He's the one we have to talk to," Arelia said. "The one we need to treat with."

Treat. As if Quil could make peace with the man who'd destroyed Navium and Silas. Murdered thousands. As if anyone who had done such a thing, for whatever reason, would say anything that Quil was willing to hear. The prince shook his head. His hatred was stronger than his desire to understand.

"He's not the one we're making deals with," Quil said. "He's the one I'm going to kill."

Loli Temba disappeared into a back room, and Arelia and Sufiyan slept not long after. Suf tossed and turned, troubled by dreams. Quil put a blanket over him, and put his hand on his friend's shoulder, as Tas used to do for Quil. When Sufiyan finally went still, Quil slipped into Sirsha's room, unable to sleep knowing that she was alone.

Loli Temba had placed a low stool beside the rope pallet, and Quil perched on it, feeling slightly ridiculous. He thought about taking Sirsha's hand, but he wasn't sure if she'd want that.

"You should wake up," he whispered. "I have a plan. You might even like it."

He didn't mean to touch the pallet. In fact, he hadn't even realized what happened until he looked up, and noticed the light in the room had shifted drastically. The change happened so seamlessly that, like before, Quil didn't understand he was in the past until it was too late to leave.

The girl in the bed wasn't Sirsha.

Or rather, it wasn't the Sirsha he knew. This person was a child. Twelve or thirteen at most. Scrawny and short, with bruises on her arms and neck. She stared straight up, unblinking.

Loli Temba appeared behind Quil, leaning through him as if he wasn't there. She laid her hand on Sirsha's brow.

"You have to sleep, little one," Loli said with a quiet tenderness. "You cannot heal unless you sleep."

"When I sleep," Sirsha the child whispered, "I see the village. I see everyone I—I—"

Tears trailed down into her hair. Loli Temba's eyes were red-rimmed and her scars were darker. She looked much younger, barely older than Quil now.

"Tell me what you see," Loli Temba said. "Expel it from your mind."

"I see them," Sirsha whispered. "The mothers and daughters. The lovers and the s-s-s-sisters. I see everyone I killed."

"You are a child," Loli Temba said. "It is not your fault."

"Should have listened to the Raani," Sirsha mumbled, and Quil wondered if she meant her mother. "I deserve it, what's happened. Let me suffer. Let me feel the pain, Loli Temba. I deserve it."

"You don't, child—"

"You don't understand," Sirsha whispered. "I'm alone now. I'll be alone forever."

That shift again, like a breeze drifting past. Quil didn't know he was back in the present until he found himself staring into Sirsha's open eyes.

She reached out a hand, resting it against his cheek. His face was wet, he realized, but there was no question in her face about why.

"I'm here," he whispered. "You're not alone, Sirsha."

For once, she didn't have a quip or a comment.

At his throat, their oath coin burned.

27
Sirsha

Sirsha still had a raging headache when Quil stood to fetch Loli Temba. She felt the hum of her Karkaun friend's magic, which lay like a protective net over the cave.

Try to get through that, R'zwana.

Sirsha didn't know why R'z had attacked—or how she'd managed to creep up without Sirsha realizing it.

But for whatever time Sirsha was here, in Loli's home, she was safe from the Jaduna. More importantly, if anyone could tell her about the killer she hunted, it was Loli.

Loli Temba strode into the room then, one of her odious drinks in hand.

"Did you miss me?" Sirsha grinned weakly, surprised when Loli remained silent.

The Karkaun sorceress knelt by the bed, pushing the drink into Sirsha's hand. The girl sniffed it and winced. It smelled like rancid fruit. But she knew the power of Loli's concoctions, so she drank it down. Almost immediately, Sirsha's pain eased. She marveled yet again at Loli's skill. The woman had plumbed magic most Jaduna hadn't even heard of. She was so deeply in tune with the earth around her that plants and even animals came to her aid as if they were an extension of her.

"I told you to stay away," Loli said when Sirsha handed her back the cup. "I warned you."

"You know I'm rubbish at following orders."

"Do you know what you've brought with you?"

"An empty stomach and dirty laundry?" Sirsha struggled up from the blankets tucked around her. Sufiyan and Arelia stood at Loli's side, equally grim. She looked for Quil, and found him leaning against the wall behind them, arms crossed, unreadable as ever. Confusion shot through her. When she'd awoken minutes ago, he'd seemed open. He looked at her like her secrets were the sea, and he was at home in dark water.

"I've brought you a passel of Martials." Sirsha shifted her attention to Loli Temba. "Don't tell me you share those old prejudices. Besides, that one's only half." She nodded at Sufiyan.

Loli never smiled or laughed much. Not with humans, anyway. Right now, she had a stern furrow in her brow.

"You brought evil with you, Sirsha. I felt my doom in the weave of the earth, and I warned you not to come. Why did you not listen?"

Sirsha felt the sting of rejection in her chest. She'd thought Loli cared for her more than this.

"I— Of course. We'll leave. My sister isn't your problem."

"I would fight your sister a thousand times for you, child!" Loli Temba said. "I do not fear Jaduna. But I do fear the killer you seek. For that is what chased you here, to me. That is what hunts you now."

Quil looked sharply at Loli Temba. "You said you didn't know what it was."

Loli Temba kept her gaze fixed on Sirsha. "They told me you were acting strange." Loli nodded to Sirsha's companions. "But that you didn't tell them why."

Sirsha felt her fingers tingle in anxiety now that she understood why they all looked upset. They knew she'd been deceiving them. After promising she had nothing to hide.

"I—" *I did what I had to do*, she nearly snapped. But something in Quil's stance shifted and he didn't look angry or forbidding. He looked . . . curious.

"I felt strange, but I didn't know why," Sirsha said. "Hunted. Sick. I felt . . . something in my head. I thought it was R'z. I've no idea what she's capable of—"

"You know your sister's magic," Loli Temba groaned at her. "How could you be so stupid?"

"We've been on the run for weeks," Quil said, steady but with that flash of steel that Sirsha found intriguing. "She was tired, and J'yan suppressed her magic in Jibaut. I'd thank you to leave off insulting her. She thinks too highly of you to say it herself."

Loli looked Quil up and down and nodded her head a fraction of an inch. Which, from her, was practically a declaration of fealty.

"Tell me everything you know about this creature you hunt." She turned to Sirsha. "Spare no detail."

"Her magic isn't familiar to me. She murders young people, mostly. Teenagers. Children. Burns out their hearts with a poker. She's left a trail of bones in the Tribal Lands, the Serran Mountains—even Jibaut. I felt her in Navium—that's when I realized she wasn't human."

"That was the first time her eyes turned white," Quil noted. "The second was right before you found us."

"Spirit magic," Loli Temba whispered, and Sirsha's heart sank. She'd spent enough time with Loli to know she couldn't abide ghost magic.

"But why did Sirsha faint?" Arelia asked. "Reactive force? Rajin's fifth law says that every action evokes an equal and opposite reaction. Would spirit magic interact with tracking magic in such a way?"

When she was young, Sirsha enjoyed arguing about magical theory. But Loli's anxiety was catching, and Sirsha didn't see how Rajin's fifth law would help.

"Maybe the killer is Karkaun," Sirsha said. That might explain why Sirsha hadn't tracked the magic easily. The Karkauns dabbled in things the Jaduna forbade. It had been years since Sirsha hunted one.

"If the killer is Karkaun, you must leave. I feel it—her circling. I cannot be discovered by my people. They will take me back, and they will make me pay for my defiance, all those years ago. You know this, Sirsha."

Sirsha nodded. If indeed it was a Karkaun warlock she tracked—and if the warlock had begun hunting Sirsha instead—then Sirsha would find the bitch and bind her.

"We'll leave." Sirsha shoved the covers away and lurched to her feet. Quil offered his arm and she took it gratefully, head spinning. "We can't put her at risk, Quil. If I'd known, I'd never have come here."

Quil nodded tiredly, and Sirsha wondered if he'd slept at all while she'd been dead to the world. From the shadows under his eyes, she didn't think so.

"We learned what we needed to," he said. "Most importantly that the Kegari are led by the Tel Ilessi."

"Rue la ba Tel Ilessi." The hateful phrase came immediately to Sirsha's mind. "They kept saying it."

"He's a holy figure," Quil said. "We met him. In Jibaut."

The man Sirsha had held off with her blades, the one who crackled with magic. "Pity I didn't have better aim."

"No," Quil said flatly. "I'd rather dispatch him myself."

Sirsha had seen Quil fight in Navium. Hells, she had a body count of her own. Still, she was unsettled by the calm implacability of his words. But then, this was war and he was a prince of the conquered. Of course he'd want to kill the man who'd engineered so much suffering.

Her oath coin with Elias prickled unpleasantly, reminding her that she had her own mission.

"Let's get out of here," Quil said, as if he felt the same impulse Sirsha did. "We'll discuss what's next on the road. Join us when you're ready." Quil walked out, Sufiyan and Arelia following him into Loli Temba's main room. They spoke too low to hear, and Sirsha reached to the earth almost instinctively to listen to what they were saying.

Then she stopped. If Quil wished to tell her what he confided in his friends, so be it. If not, she'd focus on the job. She was done being duplicitous.

Skies, if she'd known she'd get so soft spending time with the Martials, she'd have swum out of Navium's harbor.

Sirsha dragged herself to the privy and splashed water on her face. One glance in Loli Temba's mirror told her she needed a bath, clean clothes, and a week of sleep.

She made do with a comb and the sweet-smelling balm Loli used on her scars. When she emerged feeling marginally human, Loli Temba waited, Sirsha's pack in hand.

"Subtle," Sirsha muttered.

Loli Temba ignored the dig. "Be on watch for the creature's magic," she said. "It comes quickly and without warning."

Sirsha reached to the earth, the rock. It remained silent. But as they made their way to Loli Temba's stone door, Sirsha's neck prickled. A whisper. A warning.

"Maybe you should stay here while I scout." She turned to Quil and the others. "It will be safer. If the killer wants me—"

"You have a better chance of survival with us at your back." Quil drew his scim, Sufiyan unhooked his bow, and Arelia held up a contraption that looked like a cross between a slingshot and a dagger.

Sirsha's eyes felt funny and hot. *Stop being ridiculous*, she told herself sternly. *Eventually, you'll part ways with them, so don't get attached.*

Loli whispered to the stone, and the roar of the waterfall filled their ears. Beyond it, a chorus of frogs sang an ode from the pool below, and evening bugs chirped and chittered. A brightly patterned lizard darted across the rock behind the falls.

Loli Temba slipped ahead, moonlight reflecting off her pale skin. Sirsha followed first, then Sufiyan and Arelia, with Quil bringing up the rear, jaw tight as he surveyed the jungle.

They made their way to a set of steps at the edge of the falls that led to a barely noticeable seam in the thick jungle underbrush. A trail. Loli listened, a breeze pulling at the feathers in her hair. She nodded once.

"Go," she whispered. "Quickly. The jungle remembers you, Sirsha. Let it aid you if you need."

"Thank you, Loli Temba," Sirsha said. "Forgive me for bringing trouble upon you."

Loli Temba rolled her eyes, and though her smile was but a twitch of her mouth, it changed her whole face. "Thank me by not returning, little one," she said. "At least not until—"

There was a moment of warning. An instant when the air seemed to moan in pain and the earth, so quiet, suddenly bellowed at Sirsha.

Run!

Sirsha's voice caught, and she shoved Arelia into Sufiyan, who staggered back into Quil. She turned to warn Loli.

But she was too late.

One moment, Loli Temba was lifting her hand to grasp Sirsha's in farewell. The next, she was screaming as a gray apparition appeared before her. It was roughly Sirsha's shape but in no other way human. The creature flicked one claw toward Sirsha's friends, knocking them onto their backs. Then it turned to Loli. A gash appeared in the Karkaun woman's chest as the killer slowly cracked her open to reveal her heart.

The creature hissed and Loli's heart glowed red, then orange, then white hot before collapsing into gray ash.

She fell to the ground, dead, the feathers still ruffling in her hair.

Sirsha tried to scream. To move. But every nerve was gripped by terror.

The apparition hunched over Loli, and Sirsha heard a vile sound. An obscene, greedy moan, as if the creature was ecstatically enjoying the most delicious meal. Then silence—and a sudden feeling of a monstrous attention rising, shifting, fixing on Sirsha.

The killer's stare felt as heavy as a harrow plowing furrows into the earth. Its consciousness seemed to scrape against Sirsha's mind. Its form solidified into a human wearing a familiar robe, patterned with the purple and gold embroidery of a Jaduna Raani.

The figure lowered her hood and Sirsha found herself looking at her mother.

No—Sirsha caught the creature's brown eyes and flinched—not her mother. Something wearing her mother's face. Sirsha hadn't seen the Raani of Kin Inashi in eight years—but she knew her mother's magic, her cool scrutiny. This *thing* was no Jaduna.

Beneath the murderer's skin, a monstrosity seethed, its vastness something Sirsha could scarcely fathom. It wasn't human, though it wore the guise of one. Perhaps that's why the wind had called the killer *she* all those weeks ago.

Sirsha chanced a glance behind her. Quil, Arelia, and Sufiyan were unconscious.

"They are weak of mind, weak of body," the killer said in a voice eerily identical to that of Sirsha's mother. "Not you, though. As I suspected."

"Don't you look at them." Sirsha stepped in front of her friends, daggers ready, though her hands shook so badly they'd be useless. "Why did you kill her?"

"A far better question," the killer said, "is why didn't you stop me?"

Sirsha's mind whirred as her gaze darted over the creature. She watched Sirsha with her head tilted. She didn't know Sirsha's name or who she was. And yet, the killer took on the form and voice of Sirsha's mother. The earth around her—the air—felt wrong. As if a gaping wound stood in front of Sirsha, manifesting in the form of a person.

The creature stank of the spirit world. But she didn't feel Karkaun at all. Sirsha thought she might be a projection from a source nearby. But how could a projection do so much damage?

"Oh, it is fascinating to watch your mind work," the killer breathed. "I'd like to get inside it." She dropped her voice, and there was something vulgar about how she spoke. About how she used Sirsha's mother's face and form to look at Sirsha like she was something to be devoured.

"Not sure why," Sirsha retorted. "Nothing in here but spite and lies."

"Your magic is . . . special?" The killer tried out the word, as if it were unfamiliar. "Yes. Special. I've never seen its like."

Sirsha didn't bleeding care. But while the creature talked, Sirsha felt, through the earth, a thread of magic the creature was working hard to hide. A cord tied back to her source.

Somewhere, the killer had someone pulling her strings. She had a master.

"What are you?" Sirsha asked, hoping to lure the creature into talking about herself.

"An interesting question." The creature smiled, an expression that looked somehow corrupted. "No one ever asks, you know. I have tried to talk to some of them before I eat them, but they are screaming, usually, and do not care what I *am* . . ."

While nodding along to the killer's prattling, Sirsha whispered to the earth. *Follow the tether to the source. Who is the source?*

Sirsha's mind filled with images. She moved south through a verdant, forested mountain range that yellowed to grassland. Then the earth took her east, skipping across an azure river and toward a vast coastal encampment. Soldiers patrolled in the shadows, beyond the light cast by hundreds of small cooking fires. Flags flapped in a stiff breeze, a blazing gold half-sun against a blue sky.

In the camp, a tent. And in the tent, a tall figure with broad shoulders and dark hair leaning over a table, speaking to a young woman. Behind them stood a group of men and women in familiar blue-scale armor.

"Holy Tel Ilessi," one of them said. "We cannot split the forces this way. If only you—"

The tent darkened. A human voice spoke. *Return to me. Now.*

Sirsha's consciousness was wrenched back to the jungle clearing. The killer shrieked at her, enraged at what Sirsha had done, and the apparition burst from her human skin and disappeared—yanked away by her master.

"Sirsha." She felt a hand on her shoulder, and turned to find Quil, stricken as he looked down at Loli Temba's body. Behind him, Arelia struggled to her feet, stunned. Sufiyan stared at Loli in a daze.

"Skies," Arelia gasped at the sight of Loli Temba's ravaged chest. "What happened?"

"Sufiyan," Quil said. "Don't look."

But Sufiyan had already seen, and he crawled toward Loli. When he found Quil's gaze, Sirsha felt her heart clench.

"This is how Ruh died, isn't it?" he whispered. "You never said. He must have—he must have been so scared—"

Arelia knelt beside Sufiyan, speaking quietly to him as Quil turned to Sirsha.

"We need to leave. If she comes back—"

Sirsha nodded. She didn't know why the killer had disappeared, but there was something terrifying in the way she looked at Sirsha—at her friends.

Yes, friends, she realized. She'd stood in front of them, ready to defend them with her life against that *thing*. They weren't fellow travelers or chance acquaintances anymore.

"Take her shoulders." Sirsha deadened any sentiment she might feel about Loli's body. "We'll drop her into the falls. The Karkauns burn their dead, and she hated them more than anything. She loved the river, though. The jungle. She'd—she'd want to be returned to it."

Quil lifted Loli's shoulders, Sirsha her feet, and they cast her into the falls, watching as her body disappeared into the darkness of the pool below.

"I'm sorry, Sirsha." Quil took her hand in his and squeezed. "I know you loved her."

"It's my fault," Sirsha said. "She told me years ago never to come back, but I didn't take it seriously because—"

She heard R'zwana's voice in her head, chiding her when they were children. *Everything is a joke to you, but one day, you'll stop laughing long enough to find you're a failure to your Kin!*

"Is the killer some Karkaun monstrosity?" Sufiyan stood now, hands fisted tight around his bow. His voice was flat. "Is that why she killed Loli?"

"No." Sirsha understood now why the killer had been in Navium, raining down destruction, and again, in Jibaut. "She's not Karkaun," she said. "She's not working on her own. That thing that killed Ruh and Ilar and Loli Temba—she's being controlled by the Kegari, by the man you want to kill. She answers to the Tel Ilessi."

28
Aiz

After the assassination attempt, Quil grew easier around Aiz, telling her of his aunt and the cities of the Empire. The massive, multi-masted ships in the port of Navium and the fortified walls of Antium. He told her of the webs of Gens politics, the beauty of Serric architecture, the drums that thundered out messages across the Empire.

Each story was an opportunity to know him—and his weaknesses—better. To embed herself deeper into his consciousness as the girl who understood his heart.

As the Tribe ventured west, toward a distant jag of mountains, Quil and Aiz often scouted ahead, the desert unrolling blue ahead of them.

"I talk too much, Ilo." Quil used a nickname Aiz had grown fond of. "You must be sick of me."

"Never," Aiz said, and to her surprise, it wasn't a lie. He *did* talk—but only with her. The rest of Tribe Saif took up their fair share of space and sound, whether it was Tas telling bawdy tales or Karinna cursing as she trained.

Quil, Aiz observed, didn't feel as if he had a right to that space. Tribe Saif was not his family, no matter how much they might love him. He kept his opinions to himself and, much like Aiz, always strived to be helpful.

With Aiz, Quil was more relaxed. Honest. It was useful, of course—he answered everything she asked about himself, the Empire, the Tribes. But deep in the night, when she hoped Mother Div couldn't see into her mind, Aiz also admitted to herself that his trust felt like a gift.

As did his attraction to her. Their glances became touches. Their touches lingered—his hand on her waist as he lifted her into her saddle. Hers on his shoulders when she passed behind him.

The Kegari girl often thought of what Laia had said. *Your heart knows, even if your mind doesn't.* Aiz wasn't sure about her heart. But her body was aware of the heat of his gaze, the thrum of his voice, the flow of his movements. It was easy to make him want her, she realized, because she wanted him in return.

Take, Aiz, Mother Div whispered in these moments of weakness. *Do not give. Not to him. Not to anyone.*

Ruh, meanwhile, pilfered a few of his ama's scrolls almost daily, secreting away with Aiz whenever he could escape from lessons and chores to translate them for her.

"I found one that's promising!" he said when they were only five weeks out from Nur. They were on horse duty—which was mostly Ruh giving the beasts treats while Aiz curried them. It was a good time to talk, as everyone was preoccupied with getting Tribe Saif's tonics and poultices and teas ready for trading.

Ruh glanced around them surreptitiously before speaking.

"The scroll had notes on a story about two people who fall in love," Ruh said. "They get married, but something goes wrong—a Durani emerges from her haunted castle, shrouded in dust—one of the strongest of her order."

"A chaos storyteller." Aiz finished up with an ornery gelding and moved on to Tregan. "Teller of lies, spreader of untruths. They have an order? And how is that related to Mother Div?"

"Mother Div was imprisoned, right? But who did the imprisoning? You say she's a cleric. Powerful in magic. Not just anyone could imprison her."

Perhaps the child had a point. Aiz had grown to respect his cleverness. *He sees what others do not.*

"Tell me more about them, then." Aiz snuck Tregan a lump of sugar before reaching for the curry comb. "These Duranis. You said they have an order—where do they live?"

"The stories don't say, but there's an entire area north of Nur where Zaldar Shan refuses to go because rumor says that's where the Duranis dwell. Even Aba stays close to the wagons when we're there. And Ama hates that part of the desert."

He launched into a tale then, one that culminated in the Durani enticing an unsuspecting child to a castle in the desert with the intent of feasting upon his flesh.

"Why is it always a woman doing the feasting?" Aiz scratched Tregan between the ears when the mare nudged her. "I've never heard of a male witch who gnaws on legbones."

"Kehannis are usually women, so Duranis must be, too. And it's not just a story. One of my friends met a Durani once." Ruh dropped his voice and Aiz strained to hear him over the wind. "From Tribe Nur. Do you know what he said?"

Aiz lowered her voice too, getting into the spirit of the story. "What did he say?"

"He said he was lured to the desert by this Durani. The archer constellation led them to the pinnacles in the desert. There, they found a hole in the desert that led to the sky."

"How can a hole in the ground lead to the sky?"

"I don't know, that's what he said. The Durani took him there, but she was so tired after the journey that she fell asleep. He was small in the hole she'd put him in, still as—"

The boy paused, his pale gaze shooting directly toward the desert.

"Ruh?"

A moment later, he raced into the sands.

Aiz dropped the curry comb, heart clutching in fear. There were coyotes out here, bandits—even wraiths. Quil pointed one out a week ago, drifting near their camp until Elias took its head off. Its otherworldly shriek echoed in Aiz's ears for hours after. There were even jinn, whose ability to manipulate thoughts, fire, stone, and blood made Aiz uneasy. Ruh wasn't safe alone, and when Aiz called his name again, her voice cracked in panic.

A thump out in the darkness, one body crashing into another. A raspy voice spoke.

"Have some decorum, boy. Remember my station, for skies' sake."

Beware, child, Mother Div whispered to Aiz. *This is a creature of great power. Bury your magic. Speak little.*

Moments later, a woman stepped out of the dark, her hand in Ruh's. Her white hair fell in thick waves to her shoulders, and she wore an embroidered tunic and loose pants in forest colors—traditional Scholar garb. The scars that clawed across her face made it difficult to make out any of her features beyond her dark, deep-set eyes.

As the woman approached the fire, every member of the Tribe stopped what they were doing, inclined their heads as one, hands clasped together. All but Karinna, Zuriya, and Sufiyan, who enveloped the old woman in a tumultuous hug.

Laia and Elias's children spoke at once to her, Ruh telling her of the puzzle box the Empress had sent, Karinna of a backflip she'd mastered, and Zuriya of her advancement in the Tribe's holy Mysteries. Even Sufiyan, more aloof at sixteen, gave the woman a tight hug. "You have time to lose a shooting contest with your favorite grandchild, Nan?"

His grandmother patted his cheek, gaze filled with affection. "Of course, my love," she said. "Though I'm only going to embarrass you again."

The woman didn't look at Aiz—she didn't have to. Though she kissed her grandchildren and laughed at their jokes, Aiz could sense her regard. It reminded her, in a way, of Elias, but more subtle, as if she were a lioness circling Aiz at a distance, nothing but a pair of cold eyes in the dark.

The girl felt something featherlight against her mind, like a whisper from across a room.

"Bani al-Mauth." Laia addressed the woman formally in Sadhese before embracing her. "Mother. Join our fire. Are you hungry?"

"No food, daughter."

Aiz looked down to hide her surprise. *This* was the woman who was almost as holy to the Tribes as Mother Div was to the Kegari? Aiz had expected someone . . . taller.

Ruh had told Aiz of his grandmother, the Bani al-Mauth: Chosen of Death. She lived in the Forest of Dusk, far to the east, and guided troubled ghosts to the afterlife. She took the pain and misery of the spirits and cast it into a place Ruh called the Sea of Suffering.

Do you mean Kegar? Aiz had chuckled darkly to herself, but didn't make the joke with Ruh. He was a child, after all.

According to Ruh, the ghosts came from all over—even Ankana. The Kegari had simple death rituals. A shroud, a prayer. *May Mother Div welcome you to the Fount.* Aiz wondered if the Bani al-Mauth had met a Kegari ghost. She had a story prepared in case.

The Bani al-Mauth said something in Serran, a language Aiz didn't fully understand. Laia's attention drifted to Ruh. She nodded once and disappeared into the outer edge of the caravan. The woman sent her other grandchildren off with promises to find them later, before prowling toward Aiz.

"Ruh's Ankanese friend," she said.

"A harder worker I've never met, Bani al-Mauth," Tas spoke up. "And she has a good sense of humor."

The holy woman snorted, well aware of Tas's idea of humor.

"Don't get many Ankanese spirits in the Forest of Dusk." The Bani al-Mauth turned her scarred face to Aiz. Whatever softness she'd shown her grandchildren was gone. "Your seers have a tight grip over the death rituals."

"The seers guide us." Aiz thought back to her time on Dolbra's ship. "The orisons we sing light the way to our own after."

The Bani al-Mauth grunted in agreement or disapproval; Aiz couldn't tell which.

"My daughter says you're seeking a story. Are you sure it's one that wishes to be found?"

"I don't know." Aiz's only choice was honesty. This woman would pick out a lie from a mile away. Even shading the truth was dangerous.

"Not all stories should be told, girl," the woman said. "Sometimes they cause more damage than good. I'd hate it if you brought harm to my family. For your sake."

The old woman excused herself, disappearing amid the wagons. Aiz warmed her hands by the fire, a placid smile on her face, as if the holiest—and most powerful—woman in the Tribal Lands hadn't just menaced her. Aiz's rage, so well controlled for weeks, stirred fitfully. But she tamped it down as always, for it would not serve her.

When it seemed as if everyone had moved on to their own tasks, she stood up, and followed the Bani al-Mauth.

Aiz crept past the wagons and tents closest to her to the more distant ones, where Laia and Elias had made camp. She moved slowly, until she spotted three figures standing around a fire near Laia's silver and green wagon. One of them was tall and broad-shouldered: Elias.

Aiz knew by now that the big man moved fast. Faster than was normal. She suspected he had magic of some sort. She walked with care, flitting from wagon to wagon until she could make out their conversation.

Which was in Serran.

A voice spoke from beside her, and Aiz clapped her hand over her own mouth so she didn't scream.

"The next time you want to spy," Ruh whispered, "bring me with you. I can translate."

"You scared me!"

"Nan is saying that someone . . . or something is tied to the Forest of Dusk." He translated line by line then, voice barely above a whisper.

"You're certain you've seen no sign of magic in him?"

"Nothing beyond what you already know." Elias's deep voice was soft. "What do the jinn say of it?"

"Very little." The Bani al-Mauth sounded angry. "Those few who pass the ghosts speak to me of our work, but not of their people. Something is afoot. Some change. And he is at the heart of it, but I cannot glean more than that."

Ruh looked suddenly abashed. "Now, ah, now they're talking about you."

"Me? Why would they talk about me?"

"Nan wants to know why Laia gives shelter to every stray who comes her way—" Ruh squeezed Aiz's hand. "You're not a stray," he whispered. "You're my friend."

Aiz didn't know why a lump rose in her throat. Maybe because she knew he was sincere. Maybe because Ruh was her friend, too, and she had grown to truly care for him these past few weeks.

"Ruh, you left the bleeding dishes!" Sufiyan's irritated voice called through the dark, growing closer with every word. "If you don't get your skinny behind over here, I'm going to dump them in your bedroll!"

The boy jumped up. "I have to go!"

Aiz stared after him, mouth open in protest, then turned back to Laia, Elias, and the Bani al-Mauth.

Only to find that there were two people at the fire now.

Elias had disappeared.

Aiz cursed, backing away from the wagon where she'd hidden. She hadn't noticed him vanish. She ducked around a small group of tents, raking the dark for the Martial. He was here somewhere, and likely to find her. She'd need to hew close to the truth: *The Bani al-Mauth told me I shouldn't look for this story. I wanted to ask her why.* Would he believe her? Bleeding hells, if he kicked her out of the Tribe now, when they were so close to Nur—

"Ilo?"

Aiz stumbled straight into Quil. He caught her, brows raised in alarm. At the same time, the hairs on her neck rose. Only a dozen yards away, she caught a flash of metal. *Elias!*

Aiz made a snap judgement, knowing Elias would likely see through any excuses. She took Quil's face in her hands and kissed him.

She'd expected surprise, a moment for him to consider, maybe even to pull away. She didn't expect the spark that had danced between them for weeks to roar into a flame. For him to kiss her back like he'd imagined it a thousand times in his head, for her own body to arch into his, hungry for more—

Or for her breathless embarrassment, moments later, when Elias's wry voice drifted out of the night.

"Perhaps find a better spot," he suggested before his footsteps faded.

Quil chuckled and Aiz did too, more relieved than amused. His lips parted and she could practically see the questions tumbling to the tip of his tongue. *What are you doing out here? Are you all right?* But she didn't want to answer those questions, because she didn't want to lie to Quil.

He is a means to an end. Div's voice sounded in Aiz's mind, but for the first time, Aiz didn't respond, didn't agree.

Instead, she put a finger to Quil's lips. She'd memorized the shape of them, and at her touch, Quil closed his eyes, taking a shuddering breath. Aiz felt power course through her, potent and delicious. He wanted her even more than she wanted him. It was written in every line of his body, and Aiz could use it to her advantage.

"Come, Idaka," she whispered, and led him away from their hiding spot and to the south side of the camp, where he always pitched his tent. His cheeks were flushed, his yellow eyes bright with desire as he gazed at her, as she pulled him into the tent and pushed him onto his cot. Then she kissed him again, reveling in the fact that whatever questions he might have had would soon be forgotten.

29
Cero

As Cero landed his Sail at Kegar's central airfield, the heady fragrance of Spire roses assaulted his senses. He grimaced, thinking of Aiz, for she dearly loved to chain them together and make crowns for the orphans. *They smell of life*, she'd say. Cero used to think so too.

Now everything stank of death, even Spire roses. Especially on the days when Cero came back from bombing runs.

Spires, he hated those runs. The cowardice of dropping explosives on a scrambling, screaming population made him feel as if he'd rolled around in excrement. Watching and listening as the Kegari ground forces swept in to steal food and goods, murdering any left alive, made it impossible to sleep.

He'd long since altered the missile chutes on his Sail, allowing him more control over bomb drops. When the Sail squadrons launched raids, Cero's payload landed on empty barns and evacuated town squares. The bloodlust of Tiral's other pilots meant there was never a shortage of casualties, so for months, Cero's questionable aim went unnoticed.

No longer. As Cero dropped from his Sail, Tiral stalked across the airfield toward him. Sweat plastered Tiral's pale hair to his head—spring was warmer than usual—and his cheeks were an ugly red. From the heat, perhaps, but more likely from anger. The so-called Tel Ilessi had a temper. Which was nothing new for Cero. He'd known Aiz since birth, after all.

At that moment, his aaj burned. *Cero!* Aiz called through it as she had for days now, weeks. He refused to respond. He didn't want her to come back.

Cero-Cero-Cero-Cero. His name echoed with such constancy that it sounded as if he had a ball of snakes living in his brain.

He *wanted* to speak to her. To know everything about this Tribe that had taken her in, the child Ruh whom she loved—even the damned prince she claimed not to care for. *Give your heart to him*, he wanted to say, *because it's precious and deserves to be cherished by someone kind.* But Cero also wanted her to guard her heart. To wait.

For him.

Utter folly to think these things. No child of Dafra would allow themselves such weakness. For in weakness lay death. *Then stop thinking about her, fool.*

"That is the fifth time you've missed the mark on your bombing runs." Tiral paced before him, spittle flying as he stripped off his flight leathers. "You destroyed a half ton of foodstuffs. Explain!"

"The channels on some of the Sails are faulty. I told you." Cero refused to grovel to anyone, least of all a false Tel Ilessi. Still, he kept his voice neutral. Tiral had already destroyed Dafra cloister. He could still hunt down its clerics and those few orphans left—just to teach Cero a lesson.

For the thousandth time, Cero cursed his own heart. Love was misery. Without it, he'd have deserted this hellhole years ago.

"I reported this failure to the head engineer," Cero said. "It's not my fault she hasn't fixed it." The head engineer was a two-faced Hawk hag who mistreated Snipe pilots for sport. Cero had no qualms about throwing her into the flames of Tiral's temper.

Though perhaps, Cero thought as he surveyed Tiral's expression, he should be more cautious. Tiral thought ruling was as simple as sitting on the high throne and calling himself Mother Div's chosen. But now that shipments of raid loot had dwindled, discontent seethed. Some called Tiral a false Tel Ilessi. The people's patience thinned and Tiral knew it. He'd massacred hundreds of Snipes who had protested against him in Dafra slum just weeks ago. He was more volatile than ever.

"The head engineer assured me your Sail is in perfect working order,"

Tiral said. "So tomorrow, Snipe, you will hit every target with precision. Or I'll pay a visit to those clerics of yours." Sensing Cero's trepidation, Tiral smiled. "They can't very well preach without their tongues, can they?"

No one greeted Cero as he left the airfield or while he made his way through the streets to Dafra slum. Aiz was the one who befriended every orphan and street sweep in the city. Cero preferred anonymity.

He found Sister Noa in Dafra's main market, passing out cups of grain to a long line of weary, hungry Snipes. He considered helping her and then dismissed the idea. He hated being thanked.

Cero drifted to the shadows, watching his people. Most looked worse off than the last time he'd visited Dafra a week ago. Before, they were hungry. Now, they were starving.

Sometimes, Cero thought that if he died in a raid, if some murderous villager split him open with a scythe, it wouldn't be organs that spilled to the earth, but a scream of hopeless fury. One whose seed had been planted when Cero was a boy who realized his people were doomed by the idiocy of their leaders.

It didn't have to be this way. If the bleeding Triarchs had an iota of creativity, they would see what Kegar had to offer the world—and all they could receive in turn. So much possibility lost because those three rotters had the collective imagination of a tree stump.

Sister Noa spotted Cero leaning against the crumbling wall of an old tavern called the Dead Man's Ale. She handed the grain cup to Sister Olnas and hurried toward him.

Cero! Aiz's voice again. More insistent this time.

"Thank Mother Div." Noa threw her arms around him. "Every time you go, I worry—"

"I'm fine," Cero said. "But you might not be, if Tiral has his way."

The blood drained from Sister Noa's face. "What now?"

"I've erred, and he's threatening the Dafra clerics and the orphans, again. We need to move everyone. I've got a place in mind. It's better anyway, the building you're in now has no back exit if—"

"No," Sister Noa said. "The children need stability. We can get the young ones out quickly, if Tiral comes. As for the clerics—he's jailed us, tortured us. He's destroyed—" Noa took a breath, chin quivering as she looked toward Dafra's skyline, bereft of the cloister's steeples. "Destroyed our home. Killed our fellow clerics. If he wants to kill the rest of us, too, so be it."

"So ready for death." Cero stepped aside for a drunk stumbling out of the tavern. "Wasn't it you who told me a few weeks ago that there was still so much to hope for?"

"For you, certainly." Noa patted his cheek. "You're young. Have faith in Mother Div—"

Cero sighed. Noa meant well. She was a kind woman, a hopeful one, with a backbone of iron. But she wasn't a realist.

Cero, talk to me. Aiz again.

"Sister Noa, please consider moving," Cero tried again. "If not for yourself, then—"

"Have you heard from her?" Noa glanced at Cero's aaj. Other than Aiz, only Noa knew what the aaj could do. When Cero first heard from Aiz weeks ago, he'd had a moment of weakness and told Noa about it, knowing how worried she'd been. The old woman had been so overjoyed she hadn't even asked how Aiz got the aaj. Noa didn't know of Cero's role in Aiz's escape. No one did, other than Aiz.

And even she didn't know the whole of it.

"Haven't heard from her," Cero said. Apparently telling fibs as a child—*I most certainly did not skip lessons, Sister Noa*—made him an effective dissembler as an adult.

"She will return." Sister Noa's face glowed with a familiar, beatific shine reserved for when she told the Nine Sacred Tales. "And she will be changed. Mother Div chose her—"

Not this again. Cero groaned and Sister Noa gave him a long-suffering look.

"How someone so faithless came out of the cloister is beyond me," she said. "Yet I do not fear for you, child. The cloister put a love of Mother Div in your heart, whether you acknowledge it or not. One day, you will turn to her for comfort. As we all do."

She kissed him on the cheek and went back to Olnas and handing out grain. Cero watched for a moment longer before making his way through the rose-scented streets of Kegar and back to the Aerie.

Cero, for Spires' sake, talk to me.

His Sail had been brought to a hangar, and Cero spent the rest of the evening tinkering with the missile chutes enough so that tomorrow, after he missed his bombing targets, Tiral could examine the chutes himself and see that they were defective. He'd never suspect Cero, because what would a Snipe know of the high art of Sail engineering?

I know you can hear me, Aiz called. *Why won't you respond?*

It was a nice night out. The kind he and Aiz used to spend by the docks, dreaming up another life. The stars clear above, the air cool, not yet summer-warm. Cero bunched the canvas of his Sail into something resembling a bed and lay back, hands folded behind his head. A gray fox ran across the edge of the airfield and heavy-bodied insects droned through the skies. Distantly, voices carried from the Aerie, arguing, laughing.

Cero. Cero. Cero.

He could remove the aaj. Give himself silence. Instead, he listened to her, and to the world around him, and all the other voices, and despised himself for how many innocents would die tomorrow.

30

Quil

Quil fled the jungle with Sirsha, Arelia, and Sufiyan, Loli Temba's brutal death fresh in their minds, lending them frantic speed. They didn't stop to eat or drink or rest their horses. Not after seeing what happened to Loli.

Even when Musa's wight arrived, Quil didn't slow, reading the message as he rode.

Much of Serra destroyed, but we resist. Fewer supplies, enough for five weeks. Sadh under attack. Tribes scattered. Nur rejected a truce. It is gone. Send word of progress. Everything he needs awaits him. —AH

Destroyed. Scattered. Gone. The devastation was unending. The prince wanted to write a letter in which he told his aunt all that had happened, and all that he feared. He wanted her wisdom and advice. For years, that hadn't been enough for him. What a fool he had been.

In the end, he responded curtly. *Alive. Almost to T.*

He knew his companions looked to him for their next move. But he couldn't reconcile that the killer who murdered Ruh and Ilar was also the puppet of the Tel Ilessi. Questions circled his mind like hungry crows: How had the Tel Ilessi learned of Ruh and Ilar? Why had they been his first targets in a war that would claim thousands?

None of this made any bleeding sense. Quil wanted to carefully sift through every scrap of information he had before deciding his next step. But he was also consumed by a volcanic fury that he didn't know what to do with. A grief-driven rage that obliterated all rational thought. He didn't want to cage it, as he did every other emotion. He wanted to shout, break, stab.

Instead, he channeled the wrath into riding harder, into attuning his mind and body to every possible danger he and his companions might face. They rode all night and the next day, not stopping until they were out of the Thafwan jungle and entering the highlands that marked the country's central region.

They'd long since left the road behind, and it was impossible to traverse the rocky terrain with so much cloud cover. Spotting a copse of trees and boulders that would shelter them from the rain, Quil finally called a halt.

"I could get a s-s-stew going," Sufiyan offered, teeth chattering from the cold. "If you can find something to burn."

"No fire," Arelia said. "We're too exposed. That thing saw us. It knows there are four of us, and if it's working with the Tel Ilessi, the Kegari will know too. You said the Tel Ilessi saw you in Jibaut. That he tried to capture you?"

Quil nodded. "Would have, if not for Sirsha."

"I have the killer's trail now." Sirsha's voice was strangely flat, as if she'd never laugh at the world again. "She's far from here, due south. As for the Kegari"—she tipped her head up to the rain-heavy sky, closing her eyes for a moment as it drenched her skin—"I don't sense anything. But the wind is difficult to read. I might not be able to tell if they are close. I—I don't trust my tracking right now. Arelia's right. No fire."

Quil felt her desolation, understood in his bones that even speaking took an enormous toll on her. She'd lost someone she'd loved. She blamed herself. Nothing he said would bring her out of it. All he could do was try to physically look after her and listen if she needed to talk.

He coaxed her down off her horse and asked Arelia to curry them. Sufiyan doled out the bread and cheese that Loli had packed, and after tucking an extra blanket around Sirsha, Quil checked the perimeter of the camp, looking for signs of pursuit and attempting to avoid copious piles of goat dung. At least there would be good hunting if they ever could make a fire.

By the time he returned to their shelter, the rain had stopped and Sirsha looked marginally less like a wraith. Arelia had lit a blue-fire lamp, keeping the flame low and hidden under a cloak, and she and Sufiyan rolled out a map beneath a tarp they'd strung up. They gestured Quil over. Sirsha lay back against a boulder, watching.

"We're here." Arelia pointed to the southern end of Thafwa. "A few days from the Ankanese border. The Empress told you Tas is in Burku, the capital." She pointed to a dot southeast of their current location. "Sirsha—how far is it now that we're off the roads?"

"Maybe ten days," Sirsha said, and at their looks of dismay, she shrugged. "The highlands are hard going. We can do fifteen miles a day if we push the horses."

Ten days to get to Burku. A day, at most, to find Tas. If he had whatever it was that Helene wanted—Quil assumed it was a weapon of some sort—they'd take the first ship north. Quil would have to persuade the High Seer to let them sail under an Ankanese flag, otherwise the Kegari would discover them. But if all went well, they would be back in the Empire within five weeks. Before Serra ran out of supplies.

The plan was solid. But Quil's mind and body rebelled against it, for a better opportunity had presented itself.

"I'm going after the Tel Ilessi," he said.

Arelia looked at him in alarm. "We have no idea where he is," she said. "And the Empress told you to—"

"The Empress isn't here," Quil said. "She told me to save the Empire. I finally have a clear way to do that." He turned to Sirsha. "You're tracking the killer. You said she was bound to the Tel Ilessi. How tight is that binding? How long is the leash?"

"She can't stay away from him for long." Sirsha gave Quil an appraising look. "A few hours. As for the leash—I have no idea. The encampment the earth showed me was near the sea." She leaned forward to examine the map, tapping on a broad swath of land to the east. "Thafwan prairie. The camp was massive—looked like it had been there for a while."

"Perhaps the Thafwans capitulated to the Kegari," Arelia said. "Like in Jibaut."

"Thafwa has miles of shoreline," Sirsha said. "The camp could be anywhere."

Arelia looked between Sirsha and Quil, shaking her head. "If we go after the Tel Ilessi, we can't go after Tas," she said.

"Yes, you can," Quil said.

Sufiyan understood first, knowledge dawning on his face, followed immediately by anger. "We don't split up."

"The Tel Ilessi has a Sail, Quil," Arelia said. "Use your head, cousin! He can go anywhere."

Sufiyan watched Quil, and when he spoke, there was a sharpness to his tone. "You could be tracking him all over the place. He could be in Ankana for all we know, and we'd have split up for no reason."

Quil shook his head. "Ankana is our trading partner. They've been honest and evenhanded in their dealings. They wouldn't harbor the man responsible for the Empire's destruction. The Kegari need a permanent base for their Sails and the Tel Ilessi will eventually visit."

"Yes," Sufiyan said. "And any idiot could figure that out, so you're playing into his hands."

"The last time we ran into the Tel Ilessi, we were heading west. And he knows Ankana is an ally. He'll expect me to go there. Arelia, you said yourself—he knows the four of us are together. We'll be safer if we split up."

Sufiyan paced, agitated. "We're *not* splitting up."

Quil hadn't wanted it to come to this. In all their years of friendship, Quil had never pulled rank. But the Empire depended on him, and though he hated what came out of his mouth next, he didn't know any other way of getting Sufiyan to cooperate.

"I'm not asking, Suf," he said. "You might have grown up with Tribe Saif, but your parents are a Martial and a Scholar, and you are still a citizen of the Empire."

Sufiyan's jaw dropped open. Quil wondered if his aunt had ever felt like sinking into the earth when she gave orders to her friends.

"Someone needs to find Tas." Quil hoped reason would help. "Tell him what's happened, procure a ship, and make sure everything is prepared for us to head back to the Empire with whatever he has that our people need."

"You're not wrong," Arelia said, and at Sufiyan's shock, she fidgeted. "He's not," she said. "It's the logical next step, though I hate it. We'll need a meeting point and time. And a plan for if any of us don't make it."

"This is ridiculous," Sufiyan said. "What if something happens to you? I've already lost—"

One brother.

"You will not lose another," Quil said. "You're heading south, we're heading east. This is a detour. We'll be a few days behind you."

"I can track you, Suf." Sirsha held up her Adah coin. "I'm stuck with Quil for a bit more, anyway. After he takes out the Tel Ilessi and I bind the killer, it will be easy enough to find you."

Quil watched Sirsha flip their gold coin between her fingers, and wondered if it had changed since their oath conjured it. His own coin had slight etchings on its silvery surface, and when he'd ranged ahead, he'd gone three miles and felt nothing but a warm sense of her presence, somewhere behind him. As if they were a few feet apart instead of miles.

Perhaps they didn't need to travel together anymore. Once the Kegari were dealt with, Quil could ask for a Raani to break the bond. Sirsha would collect her money from Elias and move to the Southern Isles. Buy an inn and never track again. He wanted that for her.

Even if it means you never see her again?

Quil pushed the thought away, though his chest tightened. *The Empire is first*, he reminded himself. *Loyal, to the end.*

"If anyone should go after the Tel Ilessi," Sufiyan said, "it's me. His pet murderer killed *my* brother, not yours."

"You seem to be forgetting—"

"Ilar. Yes. You knew her for what, a few months?"

"I was going to say that you seem to be forgetting that I loved Ruhyan too," Quil snapped, blood rushing to his face. "Skies, Suf, I know he was your brother. I know you loved him. But I'm the one who taught him to string a bow. I taught him to ride. To read. You never had the bleeding patience for him or his stories. He was my little brother as much as he was yours, so don't you dare say that I didn't care or that I don't understand."

Sufiyan fell quiet, his eyes haunted, and Quil knew he'd gone too far. He cursed himself. This was why his aunt had taught him control. This was why he'd worked so hard to keep a lid on what he felt.

"Ruh knew you loved him," Quil said tiredly. "He did, Suf—"

"But he didn't, did he?" Sufiyan said. "He attached himself to Ilar because she listened to him. She loved his stories. She understood him the way I never did. Maybe if I had made an effort, he wouldn't have gone with her that night. Aba never trusted her. He didn't say it, but I could tell."

Quil frowned. Elias had been reserved around Ilar. But he'd never warned Quil away from her.

"Enough," Arelia said. "Don't take the blame for something you didn't do, Sufiyan. The monster killed Ilar and Ruh. Not you. Now we can make sure she doesn't kill again."

"Fine." Sufiyan stared at the ground, black hair damp from the rain. "We'll leave for Ankana. Arelia and me. In the morning. That's what you want too, right?" He glared at Arelia, who stared right back, her jaw set.

"Because it's the logical thing to do. Yes."

"And logic is all that matters." Sufiyan sounded like he had in those months after Ruh had died. Like he couldn't care less.

He walked away from their shelter, down the hill, and into the woods. Quil made to go after him, but felt a light touch on his arm.

"Leave him." Sirsha stared out into the night. "You'll only make it worse. I'll track him. If anything threatens him, I'll know. Sleep. I'll take first watch."

He nodded and squeezed her shoulder. "I'm here," he said. "If you need me."

Sleep was elusive, but it must have found Quil at some point, because before he knew it, Arelia shook him awake for the predawn watch. By the time the rain-heavy sky lightened enough to see their surroundings, everyone was packed up and the horses were saddled.

Quil hugged Arelia goodbye and told Sufiyan how to find Tas. To this, his friend merely shrugged before turning his back. It was clear he'd be happy to leave without a further word exchanged. But Quil had made the mistake of parting ways with someone on bad terms once before. He'd never do it again.

"Look at me, damn you," he finally said to Sufiyan, who glowered at him, surly as an aging ox.

"Yes, Crown Prince Zacharias. Whatever you say, Crown Pri—"

"Oh, shut it," Quil said. "I wanted to say thank you for doing this. You and I both know that you're stubborn enough to ignore me if you wanted."

Sufiyan shifted from foot to foot, jaw stiff. "You're an idiot," he said. "But don't die. I don't give a fig, mind you. But Ama will kill me if anything happens to you."

"Same goes for you," Quil said, "as she'll kill *me* if anything happens to *you*."

"And if Laia kills you, Quil," Arelia said, "the only practical choice as your favorite cousin would be for me to kill her. Which means Elias would have to kill me."

"And then," Quil said, hand on his chin, "Aunt Helene would have to kill Elias."

"I'd have to kill her because she killed my father," Sufiyan said. "But she'd end up killing me, obviously. Then my father would have to come *back* from the dead to kill her—which, knowing him, he'd figure out how to do—"

"Well . . . who would I kill?" Sirsha said, and Quil was relieved to see that blank look was gone, replaced by the tiniest spark of mischief beneath the sadness. "It's not fair that you get to have all this vengeance, while I'm stuck watching from the sidelines."

"We'll have to involve your sister." Arelia put heel to flank, calling out from the bottom of the copse, "From what I can tell, R'zwana would inspire anyone to murder."

"Don't say her name." Sirsha's countenance went as dark as the clouds above. "Skies know she's demon enough that it might summon her."

PART III
MOTHER DIV

31
Aiz

The morning after Aiz spent the night in Quil's tent, he brought her tea.

"I'm grateful for the warmth, Idaka." Aiz shivered as sand scraped the outsides of the tent, kicked up by a bitter fall wind. "But it smells awful."

"It's—ah—to prevent pregnancy." Quil sat beside her. "I'm told it doesn't cause pain."

Aiz observed the murky green liquid. He'd clearly done this before. "I suppose it wouldn't do for the Martial crown prince to have a half-Ankanese heir," she said archly.

"You—don't have to drink it," Quil said, looking alarmed at the prospect of an heir. "If you don't want to—"

"I'm teasing you, Quil." Aiz pushed a lock of hair off his forehead. "I'm not in any hurry to have children. I doubt your aunt would approve, in any case. Have you told her?" Aiz asked. "About me?"

"Not yet." Quil kissed her hand. "But I will."

"I was thinking," Aiz said. "The next time you go see her, you could take me with you—not because of this." She gestured between them. "But she's the Empress. Perhaps she could help my people."

More specifically, Aiz wanted to ask the Empress about the liquid metal used to make the masks. Quil knew little about them, a fact that frustrated Aiz to no end. But the Empress would have a keen understanding of her people's resources. Perhaps there was some trade Aiz could make. Even a small amount of the metal could change the fortunes of Kegar. *And the Tel Ilessi shall deliver her people back to the homeland from whence they fled, so long ago.*

"I'm ashamed I didn't think of it myself," Quil said.

After that, Aiz rarely pitched her own tent. Tas grinned at Quil, eyebrows in his hair as he asked why Quil looked so tired all the time. Karinna and Sufiyan made vomiting sounds when Quil was affectionate with Aiz. But for the most part, the Tribe seemed to find their relationship sweet.

All but Elias. It wasn't anything he said, or even did. It was a feeling Aiz got when she and Quil were together. The way Elias's jaw tightened when he saw them. The way he always seemed to appear when she and Ruh were talking about Mother Div or the Duranis.

The day they were to arrive in Nur, Quil was gone when Aiz woke up. She shivered in the early winter chill, packed up their tent, and tossed it onto the supplies wagon. Ruh found her as soon as she began to saddle Tregan.

"Can I ride with you, Ilar? Quil left with Tas and Elias before dawn. Didn't say when they'd be back. But you get to see Nur today! It's called the City of Light for their lanterns . . ."

Ruh told her all about Nur as, far in the distance, a quiver of air on the horizon solidified into the gold buildings and green palms of the famed oasis. Beyond and around it, massive rock plateaus cast huge shadows upon the ground, giving the desert an ethereal aura.

Aiz didn't see Quil again until the evening, when they were nearly to Nur's gates, waiting in an enormous line of caravans to secure a camping spot outside the city's walls.

"Ilo," he said, breathless as he rode up, his face drawn. "I'm sorry I've been gone all day. I must leave for the capital tonight with Tas."

Aiz cursed internally. Of course her opportunity to speak to the Empress would clash with finally meeting the Kehanni of Tribe Nasur. Just her luck.

"Could we leave in the morning? I've been waiting months—"

She stopped as Quil scratched the back of his head and fidgeted.

"I don't think I can bring you," he said. All around them, the caravan pressed in, moving impatiently toward their camping spot, everyone eager to settle in for the night. Quil lowered his voice. "I can't say much about what's going on, but—"

"Who will I tell, Quil?" Aiz struggled for composure. "I have no one. Even if I did, why don't you trust me?"

"Forgive me." He reached out a hand to take hers. Almost immediately, her temper softened. "It's been a long day," he said. "Of course I trust you. Have you ever heard of the Kegari?"

The mention was so unexpected that Aiz was barely able to school her features.

"Just the name," she said.

"They live at the tip of the Southern Continent. Notorious raiders. Very secretive. Isolationist, almost. The Ankanese say they raid because they're starving. But our sources tell us something terrible has happened there."

"Why does it matter?" Aiz said. "Are you friends with the Kegari?"

"No," Quil scoffed. "They're . . . not friends with anybody. They live on a spit of rock with nothing to trade, nothing to offer. The world has ignored them for years, and they seem content being ignored."

Aiz bit her tongue. *They raid because they're starving. Nothing to offer . . . content being ignored.* How wrong Quil was! How horribly shortsighted—him and anyone else who thought so little of a people they knew nothing about.

"Recently, there was a massacre there. Hundreds dead, Aiz. Perpetrated by their own king."

"A—a massacre?" Aiz's heart began to pound, and she thought of Tiral. Of how he hated the Snipes. But she said nothing, for a refugee from an Ankanese slum wouldn't know anything about Kegari politics. "Why would this king kill his own people?"

"The Ankanese are the only ones who trade with the Kegari and they didn't offer any theories. We're sending someone to investigate, but he won't reach there for weeks. Perhaps they are like the Karkauns, and death allows them to harness magic. I don't know. The envoy said that religious figures were targeted along with children."

Noa. The cloister. Cero had said nothing—perhaps Noa and the orphans were fine, and this was a rumor. Aiz shivered. The land around them felt oppressive suddenly, the plateaus and the mountains seeming to cast everything into shadow.

"Your aunt." Aiz didn't bother to hide her worry—Quil would think she was reflecting his own concern. "Why does she care about what happens with the Kegari?"

"She doesn't. But Ankana is one of our biggest trading partners. The Kegari are biting at their southern borders. One of our treaties states that the Empire will lend soldiers and siege machines in case of a security threat to the Ankanese. My aunt needs someone to speak with the High Seer."

"So, she'll send you."

"Or herself. I'd run things in Antium while she was away. I'm nearly old enough now."

Aiz cursed the fact that she hadn't told Quil she was Kegari from the beginning. It would give her the perfect excuse to see the Empress. She couldn't tell him now—her lies would be revealed and no matter how fast she talked, he'd never trust her again.

"I can still come with you," she reasoned. "I'm Ankanese—"

"She doesn't know you, Ilo," Quil said. "But I'll present your case. Tell me exactly what—"

"What's so wrong with me, Quil?" Aiz snapped, weeks of pent-up anger salting her veins. "Do you think I can't handle myself around your precious Empress?"

"Of course I don't think that." The furrow in his brow said otherwise. "It's just . . . my aunt, she has certain expectations of me."

"You say you want to be with me, Quil, but if you did, you'd tell your aunt about me. You'd take me with you to the capital. You'd let me meet the Empress." Of course, he was silent. Quil had steel in his spine. Just not when it came to her.

Hoofbeats had them both turning in their saddles, and Aiz forced herself to smile as Laia approached, riding her husband's stallion. The mirrors on her heavily embroidered Kehanni robes caught the swiftly fading light. Already, stars twinkled on the horizon.

"Ilar." Laia held up a folded piece of parchment. "The Kehanni of Tribe Nasur awaits us. We're to meet her at her caravan north of the city after dusk. If we hurry, we'll make it."

"Ama!" Ruh rode up swiftly on his pony. "Take me, too! I'm Ilar's translator."

Laia shook her head. "I can translate for her. Kehanni Nasur is quite old, and you, my love, are quite spirited. Another time, perhaps."

"Kehanni Nasur likes me. She won't mind if I come! Last time she said I was such a good tale-spinner that I must be part jinn."

"Indeed, she did," Laia said. "But, Ruh—"

Aiz's own instinct prickled. *He sees what others do not.* Something about this story was hidden from Laia. But perhaps Ruh would be able to see it.

Yes, Mother Div said. *Take him.*

Aiz looked at Ruh, uneasy at Mother Div's interest in the child.

There is reason for all that I do. Take the child.

They were only going to see a storyteller. The boy would be perfectly safe.

"I—I think Ruh should come," Aiz said. "He can ride with me and Tregan."

Laia looked at her son's hopeful face and sighed. "Come along, then."

The Nasur caravan wasn't unlike Tribe Saif's, though it was smaller, the wagons older, their paintings less vivid. Aiz held Ruh close as she approached, reminding herself that she was not Aiz, the lowly Snipe, but Ilar, an Ankanese woman fighting for her people, and a guest of Tribe Saif.

"Let me speak, if you will, Ilar," Laia said in an undertone. "Kehanni Nasur is a traditionalist. But she is deeply learned and I'm certain she can help. Ruh—"

"Speak softly, watch, and listen," Ruh said. "I know. Ilar taught me."

They dismounted, and a young man picketed their horses and ushered them to the center of the encampment. The wagon waiting for them was adorned with images of desert skies and wheeling constellations in shades of gold and blue that reminded Aiz of the Kegari flag. A good omen, perhaps. It was the largest of the wagons, warmly lit, with the scent of creosote incense wafting from the door.

"Come in, come in!" The voice that boomed out of the wagon belied the tiny form lying on a cushioned bench within, tucked in a woolen blanket. The woman was so old that her face seemed more wrinkle than skin. She was small and brown, with a halo of curly white hair. Aiz had thought Laia's Kehanni tattoos were intricate, but Kehanni Nasur's tattoos wrapped all the way up her skinny arms.

Her wagon was packed with scrolls, books, drawings, and engravings, as well as a map of the Empire pinned to the wall behind her. The lamps that Tribe Nur was known for sparkled with every color Aiz could conceive of.

"Kehanni Nasur," Laia said. "You honor us."

"Laia of Serra. You and your family are very welcome, my child." The old woman held out a bowl of pink salt with a shaking hand, and Aiz followed Laia and Ruh, putting a pinch of it on her tongue. Once they'd partaken, the Kehanni bade them sit on the bench across from her. She had laid a table with two steaming cups of tea and a large glass of magenta-colored juice.

"For you, little one." She nodded to the juice. "Still telling stories?"

Ruh nodded and took the juice. "But not today. Today I'm here for my friend." He looked at Aiz with pride that made her forget her earlier anger at Quil.

The Kehanni shifted her regard to Aiz. "I hear you have a story to tell."

"Yes," Aiz said. "But . . . my Sadhese. I understand more than I speak."

"I will translate for her." Ruh nudged Aiz affectionately. "I'm used to it."

Aiz had told Ruh the story of Mother Div's entrapment so many times that he was translating almost before she was finished with the sentences. But the telling was smooth—she knew by now to focus less on Mother Div's travels and more on the description of her prison.

When she finished, Aiz could scarcely breathe, waiting for the old woman to respond.

"I have heard this tale," Kehanni Nasur finally said, and Aiz's blood surged in excitement. She wanted almost to shake the old woman, to demand to know if she had further details about Mother Div's prison.

"The version I heard was different," the Kehanni said. "It came from far to the south."

"Ankana," Aiz said quickly.

"Perhaps," the Kehanni said. "Perhaps not. In the telling I remember, the tale ends when the Holy Cleric names her three children the rulers of their land. How come you by this story, child?"

Aiz opened her mouth to say what she always said: that a storyteller in Ankana told her. But the words felt stuck in her throat. Hiding the truth had gotten her nothing.

"I see the story." The Kehanni looked *beyond* Aiz. "It lives in you, the whole of it, and yet it is trapped. Like your Holy Cleric. Tell me the truth of how you found this tale, girl, and I will hunt the story for you."

Laia and Ruh looked at Aiz quizzically. Aiz was reminded of the moment she escaped the Tohr. The moment she revealed herself to Tribe Saif. The moment she told Ruh the Sacred Tales. Each time, it felt as if she were on the cusp of something, and if she only stepped into the air, the currents would bear her. She felt that again now.

She reached for her pack and pulled out the oilcloth-wrapped book.

No, girl! Mother Div warned. But this time, Aiz didn't wish to listen.

Trust me, Mother Div.

"Laia did tell the original story. In this book."

Laia looked at the book in confusion. "What—what is this, Ilar? Why did you not show me before?"

The old woman whistled in a deep breath, silencing Laia with one hand. "Show me."

"You will not be able to read it—it is in another language." Aiz bet on the fact that the woman wouldn't recognize as obscure a language as Kegari and opened the book to the first page, with Laia's name, and then to the story itself: "The Vessel of the Fount."

As Ruh looked between his mother and Aiz, Laia shook her head. "The book is blank, Ilar."

"No." Kehanni Nasur peered at it. "The stories are in Sadhese. Your name is on the first page, Laia."

"I— No—" A sudden sheen of sweat gleamed on Laia's face, and she grabbed Ruh's hand. "I—I've seen that before. But there is something wrong. We cannot be here. And you—" She turned on Aiz. "You lied to me. You never said anything about this book. If you had—" She put a hand to her forehead, as if in pain. "C-come, Ruh."

"But, Ama—"

"We're leaving!"

"Wait, Laia, let me explain—" Aiz turned to follow, but Kehanni Nasur grabbed Aiz with a clawlike hand.

Her eyes were completely white.

"But the wind pulled at her still, until one day she met betrayal and imprisonment in the lee of a giant's fangs." The Kehanni groaned out the words in Kegari, a language that she had no business knowing. "Div wept, for no creature of fur nor feather dared to tread near her prison. No rain penetrated its shriveled hollow, no wind blew in to freshen the stale air. She had followed the archer north across the sky from the City of Light, only to be felled by his arrow."

The Kehanni fell back, gasping, her eyes clearing.

The door slammed, and Aiz could hear Ruh's protests fading as his mother dragged him away.

"That is a vile tome, child," the Kehanni said, speaking in Sadhese now, her hand flexing toward the book like a vulture's claw. "Not meant for creatures of our world."

Aiz bet-Dafra! Mother Div shrieked so loudly in Aiz's mind that she flinched. *Why do you not listen! Hide the book.*

The lamps in the wagon flickered as a malodorous wind blew through. Aiz backed away, tucked the book in her pack, the wind fading as she did so. The lamps dimmed for a moment, then grew bright again, and the old woman blinked, as if she'd woken up from a dream.

Aiz watched her in fear, waiting for her to call for her Tribespeople. To demand the book be taken away. But the old woman shivered.

"An ill dream," she muttered, looking foggily at Aiz, as if she didn't remember the past few minutes. "You—you were looking for a story. I cannot help. I am tired. I need rest. Please—the door—"

The woman shoved Aiz into the windy night. Aiz's mind reeled at the little she'd learned—and at everything she hadn't. *Mother Div, how?* Aiz asked. *How did you make the Kehanni forget? Why?*

I used every scrap of strength I had saved to empty her mind. Mother Div's voice quivered with rage. *I cannot help you now. I must recover. Until you find me, daughter of Kegar, you are on your own.*

I've been on my own! The wrath Aiz had spent so many months controlling, suppressing, denying now ricocheted through her mind. She wanted to shout at that useless old woman back there, to demand to know why Laia had recognized the book and yet seen nothing on its pages. She raged at Mother Div herself.

Why me? she screamed in her mind. *Why choose me if you don't trust me? If you don't think I can free you?*

Mother Div did not answer.

Aiz hurried through the streets toward Tribe Saif's caravan, shielding her face from the thick clouds of dust the wind had churned up. As the familiar wagons came into sight, she threw her shoulders back and lifted her chin. She'd been here for weeks now. Laia knew her—trusted her with her child. Already, Aiz was coming up with an explanation for the book. *It was holy, Kehanni. A gift not meant for outsiders. My beliefs are different from yours. Would you have me forsake them?*

As she passed the outskirts of the camp, a shadow fell over her, her arms were wrenched in front of her, and she was pulled to the shadows between two wagons. She looked up into the pale, assessing stare of Elias Veturius. The point of his scim dug against her heart as a desert howler raged around them. Her fingers twitched, but she knew she wouldn't be able to call the wind before he ran her through.

"Ilar," he said. "A word."

Nothing in Elias's mien resembled the father who threw his son on his shoulders, the man who taught dozens of children everything from history to archery with humor and patience.

This was the soldier. The killer. The monster.

"My wife returned to camp not two minutes ago," he said. "She was confused. She could barely speak. But she did say you couldn't be trusted."

"She's upset." Aiz's anger faded into alarm, and she fought to steady her breathing. "I understand. But I didn't do anything wrong."

The scim pressed closer. "I find that hard to believe."

"Aba, no!" Ruh came hurtling from the camp. Aiz wanted to hug him in relief. If this Martial brute would listen to anyone, it would be the ten-year-old child who had more sense than him.

"Ruh." Elias lowered his scim, but Aiz didn't dare move in case he decided to skewer her with it. "Go back to your ama's wagon. There's a sandstorm coming in fast, love. It's not safe out here."

"Let go of Ilar." Ruh grabbed his father's hand, and Elias clenched his jaw, marshalling his self-control.

"Ruh!" Elias said. "Your mother's not feeling well. You need to go to her. Tell her everything is all right. I won't hurt Ilar. I promise."

Ruh looked worriedly at his father and then ran away. Aiz wanted to shout at him to come back.

"Are you in the habit of lying to your son?"

Elias's jaw twitched. "Laia says you're dangerous. That you can't be trusted. She said we must send you away. But she won't say more. She's fuzzy—she doesn't seem to remember what happened in the wagon. Tell me why. Is my family in danger from you?"

She forced herself to meet Elias's gaze, but it was so merciless that she quickly looked away. Quil approached, slowing down as he took in the scene before him. Elias shook his head at Quil, his face forbidding enough that the younger man backed away.

Weak! Quil would never go against Elias. Certainly not for Aiz.

"Answer the question, Ilar," Elias said. "And do not make the mistake of lying to me."

"You're not in danger from me," Aiz said. "I am looking for my Holy Cleric. I found her story in a book, but she—she speaks to me in my head, and she told me not to talk about the book."

Elias nodded. "I believe that is the first fully honest sentence you have uttered in the entire three months you've been with us," he said. "You're not Ankanese. Where are you from?"

"I'm from a forgotten place," Aiz spat out, her anger turning her face hot, making her hands shake. "A place with no hope. I came here to find a future for my people. But you wouldn't understand that, would you, Martial?"

"My son Ruh," Elias said. "You involved him in the hunting of this story. He told me as much. Did you tell him to keep it a secret from us?"

Aiz nodded, looking around, hoping now that Quil could come back, or the Zaldar, even one of Elias's other children.

"We accepted you into this Tribe," Elias said. "We took salt with you. My wife hunts a story for you. We trusted you. And you told my child to keep something from me—in addition to whatever lies you told about who you are and where you're from. No longer. You will gather your things and your horse, and you will leave. You will not interact with anyone. You will certainly not say a word to my family—and that includes Tas and Quil. I will be watching. Go."

Aiz trudged toward her tent, Elias's gaze boring into her back. She wanted to turn and tear Elias's weapons from his hand, let the wind spin him up and into nothingness. How dare he speak to her like she was a common criminal? How dare he kick her out of the Tribe as if the past few months meant nothing?

As Aiz threw her things pell-mell into her pack, sand scoured the sides of the tent. The storm was nearly here—where would Aiz and Tregan take shelter? There must be someplace in Nur that would have her. Surely Elias wouldn't turn the entire city against her in one night.

"Ilar!"

A knife came through the back canvas of the tent, and Ruh's face popped in, his dark hair a haystack.

"No, Ruh," Aiz said. "You— I can't talk to you. Your father—"

"He's watching from the other side of the camp. Ilar—I heard what the Kehanni said in the end. *She had followed the archer north across the sky from the City of Light, only to be felled by his arrow.*"

"She spoke in another language," Aiz said. "How could you even understand—" It didn't matter. She didn't want Ruh to end up in trouble. "Go, Ruh. Before your father—"

The child lengthened the rip in the tent and pulled Aiz out. "Ilar. Look." He pointed directly upward. A wall of dust moved toward them, but it had not yet obscured the stars, and she saw the constellation he pointed to before it was swallowed up.

"Those stars," Ruh said over the wind, "that's the arrow—the archer's arrow." He looked toward the rock formations north of Nur.

"I never finished telling you the story." He spoke so quickly that his words tripped into each other. "About the Durani. And the boy from Tribe Nur."

It was weeks ago he'd mentioned it. "The chaos storyteller lured him out to the desert. They—they followed a constellation." Aiz's skin tingled as she spoke. "That constellation—the archer. And—and there was a hole that led—"

"To the sky, yes!" Ruh said. "The Durani wanted to eat him, but she was old and she fell asleep. He was small in the hole she'd put him in, still as the air itself. It smelled awful, like rotting things. He was scared of the mountain's shadows, but he waited until he was *sure* she was asleep and then he ran. But he wasn't the same after he came back. He was . . . empty."

"No rain penetrated its shriveled hollow, no wind blew in to freshen the stale air," Aiz whispered, quoting "The Vessel of the Fount."

Her gaze went west, to the immense mountain range that burst up from the earth. "In the lee of a giant's fangs . . ."

The wind screamed, as if in exultation. Suddenly, with the kind of knowing that could only come from beyond, from Mother Div herself, Aiz *knew*. She knew where her cleric's spirit was trapped.

32
Sirsha

Sirsha wanted one simple thing: to stop seeing Loli Temba die. But when she looked into a fire, she saw her friend's incinerated heart. When she boned a fish for a meal, she thought of the way Loli's body disappeared into the river.

The tracker's thoughts cascaded, and she found herself dwelling on older memories. Of the days before she was driven out from Jaduna lands. Of her failures, and the havoc she'd wrought.

Quil let her set the pace, and she pushed them hard and fast across the highlands, keeping away from trails so the Kegari sky-pigs wouldn't spot them. All her will was bent on tracking, on reading earth, wind, and water.

The earth offered its secrets freely, whispering of the monster and where she had walked. Who she had murdered. A young woman beside a river, a few miles from where they passed. A Thafwan child who'd wandered too close to a forest in the evening. Each time, Sirsha flinched, disgusted and enraged. Each time, the earth shrieked at the wound, and guided Sirsha east, toward the Thafwan coast.

Quil understood Sirsha's silence and gave her space during the day. But the first night they stopped, as she curled up against a tree trunk, he knelt beside her, dark hair falling into his eyes. Despite the highland cold, his hands were steady as he pulled her into his arms. For a second, she held herself stiff. But he was warm and solid, and in the end, she tangled her fingers in his and melted into his hard chest.

"I'm here, Sirsha," he murmured in her ear, and she couldn't help the heat that bloomed through her blood. "You're not alone."

Her Adah coin warmed, chasing away the cold. Its formerly flat surface was etched with thin, linked lines. The closer she and Quil became, the deeper and more intricate the etching. The harder it would be when they inevitably had to sever their connection.

Sirsha knew this. But in the dark nights, she didn't care.

On the fifth day of travel, as a storm rolled in, they took shelter in an abandoned shepherd's house overlooking a mist-shrouded valley.

The stone structure was bigger than it looked on the outside. It had a large main room with a dusty table and chairs shoved in a corner, two smaller rooms with no furniture, and a privy. Someone had long ago lit a fire in the hearth, and the privy had a pump, a tub, and a low stone pit for heating water.

Sirsha had dropped her pack to the floor when the wind curled into her senses, bringing a deeply unwelcome scent.

R'zwana.

She cursed loudly, and Quil turned from where he was laying the fire.

"It's R'z," she said. "She's close."

"No Kegari?"

Sirsha shook her head. "R'z will want to stay here." Sirsha rubbed her temple, agitated. "It's the only shelter for miles."

Quil tilted his head and there was sympathy in his regard. "She will, but not because of the storm. She wants to get to you. I'll deal with her when she arrives. Take one of the back rooms. Come out if you feel up to it—or not at all."

"I— We'll have to share again." She pulled at their coin, finding a strange comfort in rubbing her fingers against the etchings.

"I'll take the other room," Quil said. "You could use some time to yourself, perhaps. They can sleep in this room, and if they have an issue with that, they can take it up with me."

She wished to weep, to thank him, to hiss at him for knowing her when what she wanted was for him to be obtuse, so he'd be easy to leave behind. But he wasn't obtuse and that made her angry, so all she could do was glare at him and hope he'd flinch.

Instead, he stepped close, the proximity tightening something inside her chest. *Closer*, she wanted to say. As if he could read her thoughts, he lifted a big hand to her face, tipping it toward his with barely a touch. She channeled all her venom at her sister, at herself, into her gaze. He looked at her level, taking it in, aware of what lay at the core of it.

Until the loathing drained out of her, and she looked down at her hands—her useless hands that did nothing as Loli died.

"I've seen terrible things, Quil." Her voice shook, but she kept speaking, because she needed to expel the words from her mind. "Perhaps beyond what you could imagine. But even after all that, what stays with me is how it—it *fed* on her. Those sounds. I don't know how to get them out of my head."

"The more you try not to think about it, the more it will haunt you," he said with the surety of someone who lived with a bevy of his own ghosts. "And if you forgot, it would be an injustice to her. I don't forget what happened in Navium, even when I wish I could. I remember, and I mourn, and I rage at myself and then I vow to have vengeance."

The words were so unnaturally fierce coming from him that she glanced up, finding to her surprise that his venom matched her own. But she supposed it made sense, for who would hate himself more than a prince who didn't stop his Empire from falling?

He didn't look away, and she took it as a challenge, even when she knew this was exactly what she shouldn't be doing, staring into the eyes of a person she couldn't afford to care about, burning in his sunrise gaze.

Outside, thunder crashed, breaking the spell between them. Quil shook himself and walked to the back room, laying out her bedroll and lighting a fire for her bath. The rain had plastered his black hair to his head, his clothing to the taut ropes of muscle running along his shoulders and arms. She'd heard Quil joke that Sufiyan had gotten the looks and Quil the royal legacy.

But that's only because he didn't see himself clearly. Quil, with that aquiline nose and cut-glass jaw and magnificent body—Quil was addictive. Sirsha didn't think she'd ever tire of looking at him.

Something that was deeply inconvenient, she realized, as he was staring at her, saying something.

"Ah—what?"

"The fire is going." He nodded to the bath. "Your water should be warm soon. Are you all ri—"

"Fine!" she said, horrified when it came out more shriek than word. She pushed him out the bedroom door, shoved it closed, and marveled that she could find new and interesting ways to humiliate herself in front of the boy she wanted to kiss amid an emotional crisis. If Loli were here, she'd scoff. *Tup him and get it out of your system.* Sirsha chuckled, and the ache in her heart faded a touch.

After what seemed like an age, her bathwater warmed, and she stripped and scrubbed herself, her mind moving unbidden to thoughts of the creature she hunted. She shivered as she remembered the fixed, hungry way she had looked at Sirsha. The killer was far away—the earth told her as much. But Sirsha still felt disgusted, like there was a tentacle snaking along the deep reaches of her mind.

Eventually, she heard voices—R'zwana and J'yan had arrived. She rose reluctantly, throwing on clean clothes and braiding her hair. She'd greet her sister, so the hag wouldn't think Sirsha was afraid of her, then take her leave.

Easy enough.

She strode into the main room, and barreled into J'yan, who was pulling out a seat for her. He tried to steady her, but she slapped him away.

R'zwana, sitting across from Quil, smirked.

For his part, the prince looked almost bored. His legs were stretched out and he was slouched in his seat, like a big predator trying to put his prey at ease. He'd bathed too—out of a bucket, probably—and changed into dry clothing. His dark hair was still wet and pulled back from his face.

What a face.

"Sister," R'zwana greeted her, and Sirsha snapped her attention away from Quil. "Dawdling away your time in the bath, as usual."

"R'z," Sirsha said with a sugary bite. "Letting other people do the hard work because you're a shit Inashi, as usual. Why are you still following me?"

"Perhaps I don't trust you," R'zwana said. "Perhaps I think your engagement is a lie."

"That's not the reason," Quil said, and Sirsha heard that steel in his voice that made her weak in the knees. Skies, but she loved it when he was the hard, cool, disdainful prince. His pale gaze was fixed on R'zwana, and he didn't bother to hide his dislike. "You know what she's hunting. You're hunting the same thing, but can't manage it on your own."

"You admit it, then!" R'zwana's face lit with malicious glee, even as J'yan groaned in frustration. "You hunt as we hunt. J'yan, take her—"

"That is my fiancée you're threatening." Quil had a blade at R'zwana's throat—Sirsha hadn't even seen him draw it. "Touch a single inch of her skin and see what happens."

"She has admitted—"

"She could admit to lighting your arse on fire and you couldn't do anything because she's my Adah and a Martial citizen," Quil said. "For someone who claims to understand the law, you're remarkably forgetful when it comes to one you find inconvenient."

"Follow me if you want," Sirsha said, trying to quell her laughter at the image of R'zwana with her arse on fire, "but don't get in my way, sister. This isn't a normal hunt."

"It's a Karjad, like all the other Karjad—"

"You haven't seen it, have you?" Sirsha realized it as she was saying the words. No one who had seen that thing would compare it to a Karjad—a blanket Jaduna term for a dangerous magic-user. "You haven't seen what it can do. You have no bleeding idea."

"I have J'yan bleating in my ear a dozen times a day that it's dangerous," R'zwana scoffed. "I'm well aware that you two are frightened of it."

"It is worth being frightened of." Sirsha could hardly lift her voice above a whisper, thinking of how Loli had died. Of how dangerously cavalier R'zwana was. And though part of her wanted her sister to see for herself, come what may, R'z was still blood. Still her sister. No matter what lay between them, Sirsha didn't want her to get hurt.

"It's of another world, the spirit world," Sirsha said. "If you don't respect it—if you don't *realize* how dangerous it is—you'll get yourself killed."

"You're a coward, sister. Always have been."

"And you," Quil said, apparently bored of listening to them spar, "are pathetic. You're stalking us because you can't catch this creature yourself. You've never even bleeding seen it. When your sister tries to warn you, instead of thanking her, you insult her. For a Jaduna, you are stunningly weak-minded, Raan-Ruku. You shame your people."

He stood, as the rest of them, even Sirsha, stared dumbfounded at the insult. "My fiancée and I will retire now." He took Sirsha's hand, giving it a squeeze. "Take the night to think on whether we could be of aid to each other, or whether you'd rather continue acting like a skulking dog, yipping at the heels of your betters."

They walked down the hall and into the room Sirsha had claimed. When Quil closed the door, she whirled on him.

He sighed. "I'm sor—"

She cut him off. "I did not need you to defend me."

"She was so bleeding annoying—"

"I didn't *need* it," Sirsha said. "But it was glorious." She shook her head. "I can't believe you likened a Jaduna Raan-Ruku to a skulking dog."

"I can't believe she hasn't burst in here and turned me into a squirrel."

"If she had that kind of power, I'd be happily collecting nuts in the Cloud Forest."

"Hmm. You'd make a good squirrel, I think." Quil's grin was rare enough that when his lone dimple flashed, Sirsha's heart swooped. "You'd charm all the other squirrels."

"Have my own squirrel army," Sirsha said. "We'd stockpile acorns and pelt R'zwana with them."

The image was so ridiculous that she giggled, and Quil snorted, and then they were laughing until tears leaked out the corners of their eyes, the wild guffaws of two people who were dancing with the reaper and knew it. Fear and exhaustion and hilarity mingled, and Sirsha grabbed Quil's arm to steady herself.

Later, she'd wonder if that was the moment that lit the fire between them. Perhaps it had kindled earlier in the main room when she'd lost herself in his gaze. Or at that inn in Devan, with his hands tight on her waist, his pulse thumping beneath her fingers. Or earlier still, when he'd saved her life on the Effie in Navium.

It didn't matter. Because now, as if her touch had cut loose anything resembling restraint, he grabbed her by the waist, pulled her to him, and brought his mouth to hers.

Or had she leaned up to kiss him? She didn't care. All that mattered was his lips hard and demanding against hers, her frantic need to feel his skin, to peel away his clothes. She gasped when he pinned her arms to her sides and pushed her against a wall, pulling back, his kisses feather-light now on her jaw, her neck. At his withdrawal, a sound of protest came unbidden from her throat. She saw his lips quirk in a satisfied smile.

Some part of Sirsha's mind screamed at her that this was an appalling idea. Her dalliances had always been meaningless. It was better if they didn't matter.

But Quil, patient Quil, beautiful Quil, angry, enraged, yet always in control Quil, was making it matter. She should shove him away. Tell him this was foolish. Only he was turning her bones to liquid with these slow, languorous kisses.

"Bedroll," she panted, because it was the closest thing to a horizontal surface, and she wanted him so badly she ached.

"No," he whispered against her skin, pulling open the laces on her shirt, her pants, removing both, leaving a trail of fire down her neck and stomach, going slow, so torturously slow, like he was getting vengeance on her for her smart mouth, for all the times she'd argued with him or snapped.

"Quil—" His name rolled off her tongue, a prayer. "Please—"

"Mmm," he said. "You should say that more, Sirsha. I'd give you whatever you wanted."

"Then give me—"

"Not yet."

He sank to his knees, cradling her hips in his hands, whispering words against her skin that she couldn't hear but that sang through her blood like magic.

She ran her fingers through his soft hair with one hand, gripped his shoulder with the other, and thanked the skies she had purchase on something because he pushed her to breaking with his clever mouth, his big hands, the heat of his body against hers, the sure way that he held her, as if she belonged to him and always had.

Sirsha wanted to say, *Don't stop*. She wanted to say, *More*. She wanted to throw him on the floor and climb on top of him and claim him the way he was claiming her, but she couldn't think anything more than *yes*. As her pleasure crested, she clasped a hand over her mouth to muffle her cry and then sank into his arms, trembling and liquid.

Rain hit the small window, a *pat-pat-pat* that blurred the world outside, making the room their own isle. Quil looked far too pleased with himself, his cheeks flushed red, mouth parted in a lazy smile. He was, she noted with annoyance, still fully clothed.

She swung her leg over his waist and straddled him, watching the color of his eyes shift, shadows across gold leaves. His breath quickened as she slowly drew off his shirt.

"Now we're even." His hands tightened on her bare back. Sirsha tucked her fingers lightly into his waistband, drawing triangles on his skin.

"Not quite." She relieved him of all his clothing. With only lamplight between them now, she pinned his wrists to either side of his head and kissed him slow, all the while keeping the rest of her skin a breath away from his. Every muscle in his body was taut with desire and he groaned in impatience.

"Sirsha—" he said, his voice resonant, the low strum of an oud echoing across a desert.

"The way you say my name." She scraped her fingernails along his back, kissed a line down his shoulder. "It's indecent."

"Sirsha." He said it again, quieter this time, and took her face in his hands, his touch so tender that her chin trembled. When she tried to look away, he brought her gaze back, but she shook her head.

"I can't," she whispered. *Can't love you. Not when one day, we'll have to let each other go.* She hoped he could see. "Please."

He nodded, understanding what she didn't have the strength to say. When he kissed her again, there was no restraint, only need. She returned it in kind, melting into him. This—desire, lust, want—this she understood.

Later in the night, they lay together on her bedroll, staring out the broken window into a rainy sky.

"How long have you been planning that?" she asked.

"Since the second you told me that I'd probably enjoy tying you up."

"Would you?"

He turned toward her with a shadow of a smile that left her flushed. "Perhaps you'll find out."

She ran a finger along the sharp line of his jaw, letting him see in her eyes what she thought of that. He made a sound in his throat that made her hungry for him, again.

You're enjoying this too much, Sirsha told herself. *You will regret it.*

But by then he'd drawn her into another kiss, one that made her forget everything but him.

The next morning, Sirsha woke before Quil—before anyone—and slipped past the sleeping Jaduna and outside to the cabin's front porch. The rain had cleared, the mist burning away as the sun rose.

She was breathless for a moment at the beauty of the valley below. The mist had hidden it yesterday, but now, with the sun chasing away the night, its full glory was revealed—huge granite formations, and distant falls roaring from the onslaught of rain. A river ran through the base of the valley, its blue startling against the deep green hills. Sirsha wished she could make her way down there with Quil. While away the hours by the riverside.

She heard the scrape of a boot behind her and turned, smiling, expecting Quil.

Only to find R'zwana.

"Does he know what you did?" R'zwana asked. Sirsha was almost impressed at her sister's ability to kill a good mood faster than an arrow to the arse. "Does he know there's a grave with twelve hundred Brijnan villagers in it because you're a bleeding coward?"

"Shut it," Sirsha said, but she could think of nothing else. This was what she hated the most about R'zwana. Not what she said but how she made Sirsha feel, like a helpless child again, at the mercy of her vindictive big sister.

"Well"—R'zwana grinned at her nastily—"perhaps I'll get a chance to tell him about it. Seeing as we've decided to travel with you."

"R'zwana." J'yan appeared, hair still tousled from sleep. "Leave her be."

R'z grunted in irritation. "Still pining after her, I see," she said before disappearing back inside the cabin.

Sirsha and J'yan both looked after R'zwana before he turned back to Sirsha. "I'm not," J'yan said. "Pining after you."

Sirsha smiled. "I know that," she said. "I've seen you pine. Whatever happened to N'ral?"

"She and a daughter of the Songma Kin swore an oath." J'yan sighed theatrically. "My poor broken heart."

"Can't say I blame her. Who would want to be with an ugly goat like you?"

J'yan chuckled, a singular, hiccupping sound. It was the first time she'd heard him laugh in years. His smile was warm as he regarded Sirsha. "I missed you," he said quietly. "So much. My greatest regret is that I didn't stand up for you. It haunts me, Sirsha."

"What's done is done." Sirsha looked pointedly after her sister. "Unlike some people, I don't gnaw at old wounds. I'm going to make some biscuits. Saddle the horses?"

"Sirsha—"

"I don't want to talk about it," she said. "It was years ago now. I've left it in the past."

"But maybe that's not where it belongs," J'yan said. "You'll have to tell him eventually."

Sirsha walked away from him. "But not yet."

33
Aiz

Even as Aiz realized where Mother Div's spirit was, and that it must be a Durani who was keeping the cleric captive, the wall of sand roaring toward her and Ruh finally hit. It ripped at the wagons, pulled stakes from the ground, sent lanterns flying.

But Aiz did not care, because she knew from the way her blood tingled that Mother Div was close.

"Where is Tregan?" she called to Ruh.

"In the pen! Oh—" Ruh's eyes went wide at the man striding purposefully through the dust toward them. Elias.

Aiz grabbed the wind and shoved it at him, a wall that knocked him off his feet.

"Thank you, Ruh!" She took his shoulders, drawing his gaze even as he tried to see what had happened to his father. "Go to your ama's wagon! Get safe!"

The livestock pen wasn't far. As Aiz approached, Tribespeople were pulling the frightened horses from the pen and picketing them between the wagons to protect them from the storm. Everyone had their heads down. Faces covered.

No one looked at her. The stars were blocked by the dust. Aiz could barely see her hand in front of her face. If she was willing to ride without a saddle, she could get out of here and no one would be the wiser. The pen was on the southern edge of the encampment.

But where would she go? Where *was* Holy Div being held in that maze of spires and ravines and canyons?

Mother Div, she called out. *I know you are angry and weakened. Forgive me. But I am close. Guide me. Tell me where to go.*

Silence. And then a suggestion of a whisper. *North. Toward the tallest pinnacle.*

Aiz searched the remaining beasts for Tregan's brown coat. Someone—Tas, she thought—gestured at her, but Aiz ignored him and grabbed Tregan's bridle, leading her out of the pen.

Aiz swept the wind away from them. A lamp flared—one of the sentries trying to get her attention.

But they had to contend with the storm, and Aiz did not. She called her power to her, and whether it was because Mother Div was near, or she had finally learned the discipline to control it, the wind came, bending to her will like her own body. She cleared the dust from her and Tregan's faces, and opened a path through the storm.

I have more to give, Mother Div said. *Come, Aiz bet-Dafra. Find me.*

Ilar! Ilar! The wind called the name she'd chosen, and she remembered months ago when she'd fallen from the Aerie, hearing it just like that, screaming: *Aiz! Aiz!*

A small hand slipped into hers. Aiz's wind failed.

"Ilar! Why didn't you wait for me?"

"Ruh, go back to your family's wagon. It's not safe." The wind clawed at them, and Ruh's little body shook from the cold, but he didn't budge.

"I put a pillow in my bed. Sufiyan won't even notice! He never does. You're going to find her, aren't you? Mother Div. I'm going with you. You trusted me to help you hunt this story, Ilar. Trust me now."

"The wind—"

"You speak to the wind. I've seen you!"

Damn the child, but he was too observant. Aiz was gripped by urgency. Something huge flew past them—a tent or part of a wagon. Aiz couldn't tell.

"If you send me away, I'll follow! I want to meet her, Ilar. Mother Div— I feel— I feel like I've been waiting for her for a long time."

He held on to her though she tried to shake him off. He was surprisingly strong.

Tears streamed down Aiz's face, the wind whipping them away. The storm would pass. When it did, Elias would find her, and she doubted he'd be merciful enough to leave her alive this time. She had to leave.

"Fine!" she shouted over the wind. "But you must promise to do exactly as I say. No questions. No stories. Keep quiet and follow my lead. We've no idea what's out here and we must move carefully."

"I promise!"

Follow the wind, daughter of Kegar. Holy Div spoke in Aiz's mind, eager. Hopeful. *Let it bring you to me.*

Aiz pulled Ruh onto Tregan in front of her. They wound their way down an embankment, across an empty streambed, and through a broad swath of empty desert. The wind shoved Aiz forward, working in her favor, and she used only a little of her smithing to keep the way ahead clear of sand.

Far in the distance, a huge spire that reminded Aiz of home jutted like a broken finger into the sky.

Yes, Div whispered. *Come.*

As they approached the spire, Tregan shied back, whinnying nervously.

"It's okay, girl," Aiz whispered, rubbing the beast's neck. "Be brave for me."

Tregan continued reluctantly, and almost as soon as they reached the base of the spire, Ruh pointed to what looked at first like a shadow in the rock. When they got closer, it glowed an eldritch blue, like the belly of a cloud lit by a storm.

A hole in the desert that leads to the sky . . .

"It's a gate," Ruh whispered, which was when Aiz realized that she could *hear* his whisper.

The wind had stopped.

Aiz approached the gate warily, the *clip-clop* of Tregan's hooves suddenly too loud. As they neared it, a sliver of moon broke through the clouds long enough that Aiz made out a rocky trail winding into the dark.

Tregan picked her way forward for a quarter mile, until the rocks overhead narrowed and joined, transforming the trail into a tunnel. They should have been left in pitch darkness. But the walls glimmered, veined with a luminescent blue ore. The ceiling was carved with intricate symbols that Aiz couldn't quite make out. They seemed to writhe, as if in pain.

"Is that Sadhese, Ruh?"

The child looked up, the blue light reflecting off the silver of his irises. "I've never seen that language before. Ilar— This place doesn't feel right."

"I think— Ruh, I think a Durani has trapped Mother Div's spirit here," Aiz whispered. "We must free her. Like the heroes in your stories would."

The tunnel widened into a carved gate. It was decorated with images instead of runes, and Aiz flinched. Carved fire licked up the sides of the red stone columns, and screaming faces—of animals and humans— emerged from the flames, so real that she covered Ruh's eyes lest those tortured visages haunt his nightmares.

When they were safely past, Aiz began to shiver, a deep shuddering that had Ruh—apparently unaffected—turning in alarm.

Aiz felt as if they'd entered another world with less air, less life, less hope. A void that sank into her bones, hostile. She'd felt this way before: when she was fourteen and first learning to control her windsmithing. She'd lost control of a Sail and spiraled to the earth, the wind an enemy. Her ears popped from the pressure, her stomach was in her throat, and as the ground approached, she'd blacked out.

It was Cero who found her, his face stark white, tears streaming down his cheeks as he called her name, his throat raw.

"Onward, Ilar," Ruh whispered, bringing her back to the cave. "Look. Light."

Aiz dismounted, Tregan's lead in one hand and Ruh's fingers in the other. The child guided her forward, and Aiz became aware of her heartbeat, louder and louder with each step.

But it was not her heartbeat. As she entered a perfectly round chamber, its ceiling and far wall lost in shadow, the air completely still, Aiz realized the sound—the feeling—was coming from a hole in the center of the room.

The void.

Its pulsing felt oppressive. All-consuming. The stench hit Aiz next, the dust of crushed skulls, the seep of old blood. The floor was covered in the bones of animals and humans, some with scraps of flesh still attached.

"Ruh—" Aiz breathed. "Go. Back the way we came. Take Tregan." Whatever was in here, Aiz would battle it alone.

"Il-Ilar—" The child cowered behind her. "Look."

Deep in the shadows, something stirred.

A skeletal figure emerged out of the darkness, and Aiz was certain it was a specter of some sort. But no. She was flesh and bone—mostly bone—and she wasn't much older than Aiz.

"Hail, sister of shadow," the woman rasped, as if she was trying to remember how to speak. "Do you come to relieve me? I have waited long years, serving our master."

Sister of shadow? This, then, must be a Durani. A chaos storyteller. She thought Aiz was another of her order. When Aiz didn't answer, the girl took a step closer. "Why do you not speak?"

Ruh wept now, terrified. "Ilar, we're not safe—"

"Ah, sacrifices," the girl said. "Bring them closer, sister."

Aiz shook her head. "No." She drew her scim with a shaking hand. "Where is Mother Div? What is this place?"

The Durani looked around at the bone-strewn floor, the blood-brown walls. Her regard settled on the hole in the center of the room, and when she looked back at Aiz, her eyes were pure white.

"This is the home of the first story," she spoke, her voice deeper, guttural. "Elsewhere lives the story of joy and wisdom. But here lies desolation and misery, the only universal tongue, for pain needs no translation."

"Ilar." Ruh pulled at her desperately. "We need to leave!"

"Do you not wish to hear the story?" The girl smiled, a leering rictus. Ruh whimpered. "I thought children loved stories, and you"—she sniffed—"you are steeped with them." The girl lifted her hands to Aiz and stumbled forward as if to embrace her.

"Ah, sister, you have brought our master a great prize. A child of ancient magic."

Aiz grabbed Ruh then, throwing him onto Tregan's back, and slapped the mare hard on the rump, hoping to the Spires that the child would hang on.

Then she whirled to face the Durani. "You will release Mother Div." She lifted her scim. "Or I will destroy you."

The Durani curled her lip. "Who are—"

Aiz attacked, and though the Durani was nimble enough to skitter out of reach, she stumbled, and Aiz nicked her over her heart. It was a tiny wound—no more than a trickle of blood. But the Durani gasped as if Aiz had shoved a scim into her gut.

"No—" she whispered. "You fool!"

Aiz's blood quivered. A wave approached—no, it was here. The void pulled and yanked, compressing into a single point before exploding outward, knocking Aiz to her knees. Pain shot up her thigh, her bones snapping from the force of the blast.

The round chamber, lit before by the strange blue walls, fell dark. Aiz grasped her shattered leg, moaning, and tried to crawl away. The darkness seethed like a churning ocean, the shapes within it terrifying in their immensity.

Death closed in. Then it was upon her; pain burned through flesh, bone, and blood, and her vision went dark.

Aiz had spent her entire life avoiding death, and now she knew why. Death was pain. Death was blood. Death was as violent and vicious as living. Not a relief but an unending extension of the suffering during life.

How unjust, she thought, *that the unfairness of life should carry over.* She'd always thought that the veil between worlds meant that the worlds shifted. That the rules changed.

But death didn't claim her, not yet. A great hand reached out to draw her into a forever night, but an explosion of white blew the darkness away. Aiz awoke to a flicker of light, growing stronger. From the dome of shadow at the center of the cavern, a figure limned in blue approached Aiz.

A soft touch on Aiz's face. The tenderest voice.

Daughter. You found me.

The figure was hauntingly familiar, the likeness so similar to the contours of stone Aiz had stared at her whole life that it was as if Mother Div had stepped directly from a frozen, broken courtyard in Kegar into this desolate cave. Her skin was moon-pale, her hair brown, her eyes light. Like Aiz had always imagined.

"M-Mother Div?"

She nodded, and Aiz wept, because even though she'd told herself this day would come, she'd not really believed, deep down, that it would.

Aiz. Where is the book?

"Here—" Aiz scrabbled for her pack and pulled out the tome.

Read the first page.

The end of the Ninth Sacred Tale. Aiz knew it in her marrow. She opened the book reverently. She had done it. Aiz bet-Dafra had freed the savior of the Kegari. Not some highborn Hawk. Not one of the

Triarchs, who were Mother Div's own bloodline. A lowly Snipe. A forgotten orphan.

A daughter of the evening star.

She could see nothing of the chamber. Nothing of the Durani who had done this to Mother Div. Only darkness and Mother Div's glowing blue light.

Aiz turned to the first page. There was one paragraph. She read it by the light of Mother Div's luminescence.

"Gather, gather and listen well," Aiz read, "for my voice must not be forgotten. A storyteller came upon a shred of darkness so heavy it tore a void into the fabric of the earth. And instead—instead of turning her back to it, she listened to its tale."

The story ended. Aiz turned the page, frantic, but the book was now blank.

"Mother Div," Aiz said. "I swear, your story was here—"

The cleric eased the book from Aiz's hands.

"Fear not, daughter." Holy Div's voice took on a strange resonance, an echo that reverberated off the tight walls of the chamber until it was unbearable. "It lives in me now."

"Mother Div, please help me understand," Aiz begged, for whatever was happening was beyond her. "Was that the Ninth Sacred Tale? Was—was the Durani the storyteller?"

Mother Div merely smiled, her skin growing brighter and brighter until her features were no longer discernable.

Then, suddenly, many things happened at once.

The light in the chamber faded, transforming Mother Div into a gray shadow—one that shot toward the crumpled figure of the Durani, who rocked back and forth behind Aiz. The shadow tore the woman to bloody shreds, her body parts scattering across the chamber, a hellish harvest. Aiz gasped and tried to skitter backward. The pain in her leg was so bad she could barely crawl. Behind her, Mother Div held the

Durani's heart in her hand, throbbing and lit with an unholy glow.

"Ahhhh," Holy Div sighed, as if consuming a delectable meal. She dropped the heart, now an empty husk of a thing, and turned her burning gaze to Tregan, bucking in terror at the entrance to the chamber.

Tregan! The mare should have been long gone by now, with Ruh on her back. She scanned the chamber for the child. She couldn't tell if he'd escaped or been caught in the blast. She crawled toward her horse. But Mother Div was faster.

Tregan's eyes rolled back in her head in terror. Then Aiz's steadfast companion these many months became nothing but a bloody pulp, her great glistening heart clutched in Mother Div's glowing hand. Again, that sigh, obscene and consuming, and the heart's husk was cast to the floor.

"Human," Mother Div moaned. "Not animal. I need more."

She turned from Aiz, sniffing, her white eyes glowing brighter as they fixated on something—someone—beyond Tregan's scattered viscera.

Ruh. Covered in Tregan's blood. Frozen by dread as the shadow of Mother Div shot toward him.

"Ilar, help!"

Not Ruh. Not like this. Mother Div was consumed by bloodlust. Gobbling hearts, tearing that Durani apart. She was locked away too long. Corrupted, somehow.

Aiz dragged herself toward his voice, frantic to reach him. "No, no—" Aiz babbled, incoherent. "Run, Ruh—"

Div was faster. A clatter of bones. A shriek. Mother Div held something small and incandescent. Aiz knew then that sweet Ruh, who only knew villainy from his stories, was gone.

Because of Aiz. Because Aiz had involved him in the hunt for Mother Div's story, her spirit. Because Aiz hadn't had the strength to turn him away. Because Aiz was a damned fool.

The Kegari girl screamed. And screamed. She wanted to die herself.

She wanted to be consumed, to not feel this grief, this horror at her own actions. She'd sought out Mother Div. And she'd released her, not understanding that Mother Div was no longer a cleric, but something else entirely.

She crawled through Tregan's remains to Ruh, still whole and perfect but for his heart, shriveled and smoking in his chest.

"Oh—oh no—" Aiz clasped the body to her, voice rising in a shriek. "Ruh—"

Mother Div's voice surrounded Aiz. "Thank you, daughter of Kegar. For freeing me."

Aiz sobbed as she held Ruh's small body. "This isn't freedom," she screamed. "This is murder! You killed him. You—"

"I told you this would not be easy, child. I told you there would be sacrifices."

"But not Ruh," Aiz said. "You never said it would be him! And—and Tregan—"

"All things have a cost, Aiz bet-Dafra." Mother Div's voice hardened. "You agreed to pay it. My imprisonment was the work of the First Durani, a vicious, vengeful woman who used ill sorcery to trap me. She made it a condition of my freedom that to live, to survive in a body, to work magic, I require aid."

"Aid . . . ?" Aiz felt bile clawing up her throat again as she thought of Tregan and Ruh. "The—the hearts."

"It is a foul and ancient magic," Mother Div said, her voice dripping in malice. "But those I take are at peace. They are one with me in the moment that I take them. This child—he did not die in vain. He died that you might succeed."

"You will need more," Aiz said. "More hearts. What of—of animals, could you—"

"Animals are not enough," Mother Div said. "For power—true power—the sacrifices must be human, and pure of heart. You and I are linked. Chained to each other, as surely as Loha links you to a Sail when you fly. I have some freedom, but I am largely bound to your will. I cannot feed unless you allow me to."

Now, finally, Aiz understood what Div meant by *sacrifice* and her heart quailed at the horror of it. Everything about this was antithetical to what Div stood for. Yet it made a twisted sort of sense that this was what a Durani would do to Div's spirit.

"You ask me to trade lives."

"I ask you to think of the many instead of the few. Let me show you what you will receive in return. Perhaps you do not understand."

Mother Div knelt, and when Aiz cringed back, terrified, the cleric sighed and forced her hands to Aiz's face. Aiz was four again, helpless as her mother was dragged away by soldiers, somehow knowing she'd never see her again; she was six and freezing, the very idea of warmth forgotten; she was seven, and her stomach seemed to devour itself with hunger; she was eight, and Dafra cloister burned, and Tiral laughed, and all was aflame, and then—

—rain. Sun. Light illuminating the graves of Tiral and the Triarchs. A cloister rebuilt with pale yellow stone. The orphans unrecognizable with clean clothes and plump cheeks, like the children of the Tribal Lands. Fields of wheat and corn and rows of trees stretching to a horizon of blue hills. A distant waterfall feeding into a wide green river that wound through a breathtaking city. Aiz, beloved of her people, walking toward a glowing triangle of light—the Fount.

"Your homeland," Mother Div said. "Your future. If you choose it."

"I—I—" Aiz looked down at the body in her arms. She'd thought Ruh might one day meet Hani or Cero. She had thought her people and Ruh's could be allies.

"What future do you choose for your people, Aiz? Death? Or life?"

For a moment, Aiz's vision flashed black and yellow. She heard the gnash of teeth and the groan of beasts, a surging sea that hungered. But it was gone so quickly that she questioned whether she'd seen it at all.

She looked down at poor, broken Ruh. *This isn't fair*, she thought. *Why did he have to die? Why not Elias or Laia, or one of the useless others?*

But then Aiz heard Cero's hard voice in her head. *You were born knowing the world isn't fair. You work around it like always.*

With Mother Div's question echoing in her ears, Aiz laid Ruh down. She wiped her tears away. For months, she had plotted and planned for this moment. She'd known there would be sacrifices. *To step into the abyss and know Mother Div will catch you—this is faith.* Sister Noa had spoken those words months ago, quoting the Seventh Sacred Tale.

Aiz didn't have the luxury of mourning Ruh or wailing about the obliteration of her humanity. As before, this was a test. Aiz must plan and plot again. Kill Tiral and the Triarchs. Take over rulership of her people. Send emissaries to the Empress of the Martials and trade for Loha.

And then take her people home.

Aiz turned away from the carnage of the chamber, fixed the image of the Kegari homeland in her mind, and met Mother Div's waiting gaze.

"Life," Aiz said. "I want life. For myself. For the Kegari."

"Good." Mother Div nodded. "Then let us begin."

34
Quil

Sirsha was gone when Quil awoke. For a moment, he feared she'd left, desperate to escape any awkwardness with him and any bloodshed with her sister. But someone—Sirsha, he assumed—had left a still-hot biscuit atop his pack. He didn't think she'd leave him breakfast if she was planning to abscond.

He found her beside their saddled horses outside, finishing a cup of tea and flipping through his copy of *Recollections* by Rajin of Serra, frowning in disagreement at something he'd written.

Moments later, when Sirsha turned toward Quil, he lost his breath. Her dark hair was piled high on her head, and something about her expression, haughty and cold, but softening a touch when she looked at him, made his blood heat. He thought of last night, the warmth of her skin, the arch of her neck when she'd thrown her head back, the languor in her body when she sank into his arms, spent.

Everything felt sharper with her, stronger. He marveled at it. It'd been a long time since his body had felt anything but sorrow and exhaustion.

Sirsha's stern demeanor faltered at something on his face, and her brow furrowed.

Probably because you're leering at her.

He looked around, as if taking in the storm's damage, though he didn't give a fig. "R'zwana's gone?"

At that exact moment, the Raan-Ruku appeared at the edge of the forest like a freshly summoned demon.

"Finally finished primping, prince? Let's go."

Quil glanced at Sirsha's storm cloud face. "It might not be the worst idea," he said. "You mentioned that the killer was unlike anything you'd encountered before. R'zwana is useless, but maybe J'yan could help."

"J'yan's a battle Jaduna, prince," Sirsha said. "He'll help in fighting the thing, not tracking it. And I can't pinpoint it. Sometimes it's due east, sometimes south. Sometimes it disappears entirely. We could waste days riding up and down the Thafwan coast looking for that camp. Days we'll have to spend with *her*."

"We keep heading east." Quil drew on the reserve of calm that usually came to him when someone dear to him grew agitated. "Keep to the forests. The coast isn't far. But we are short on time. The longer we're out here, the more likely the Kegari are to spot us."

Sirsha glanced at him, head tilted. A slow smile spread across her face.

"Now that," she said, "is an excellent idea."

Four afternoons later, Quil and Sirsha were hidden in a clearing thickly bordered by trees and brush. R'zwana and J'yan had the horses a quarter mile away while Quil and Sirsha built up a fire.

The coast was miles away, and the Thafwan highlands had flattened into low hills and a patchwork of farmland. It was beautiful country, badly marred by burned-out barns and plumes of smoke that smudged the skyline.

The Thafwans, it seemed, had refused to host a Kegari war camp. And like in Jibaut, the Kegari appeared to have insisted.

Sirsha silently dropped a brace of rabbits on a stone next to the fire and prepared them for spitting. Quil glanced at her face, even more beautiful when she was intensely focused, as she had been the past few days. As they'd traveled, she'd stopped for long minutes, her hand to the ground, her head bent, listening to the whispers of the elements, so lost in them that he wanted to reach out and touch her shoulder to make sure she would come back.

But then, at night, she would find him. Usually after he finished his watch, sometimes before.

He always knew what she wanted, because he wanted the same with a surging desire that made his head spin. Last night, she'd led him away from the encampment, shoved him against a tree, and they'd kissed each other senseless. His hands had wandered, so had hers, and in the end, she'd bit his shoulder to keep from waking their companions, sending him over the edge.

Focus, Quil.

He fed the fire patiently as Sirsha set up a spit, and within an hour, they had two rabbits turning and wild onions baking in the fire's ashes.

The smell of roasting meat made Quil's mouth water. He wasn't the only one. The smoke curled thick and white into the sky above. A Sail that had been nothing but a stain on the horizon drew closer, circling them once before winging away.

"He'll be back," Quil said.

Sirsha nodded, brooding, until finally she glanced across the fire at Quil. "While we're waiting, there's something we should discuss. I've been thinking about it for the past few days." She turned the spit, and fat dripped into the fire, sending up a fresh plume of smoke. "Us. Our . . . trysts."

"Ah. Is that what we're calling them?"

Sirsha lifted her chin, which Quil noticed she did when she thought she was about to get resistance. "I thought we should lay some ground rules."

I'm more interested in the punishments for breaking them, actually. Quil had sense enough not to say it, but Sirsha read whatever passed across his face. Color rose in her cheeks. "Get your head out of the gutter," she said.

"Right, sorry."

He wasn't sorry. He didn't try to hide it. Sirsha looked away, still flushed. Her hand went to their coin.

"The design on our coin is growing too complex," she said. "You're a crown prince who must return to your people. I'm a tracker looking to get as far away from mine as possible. Let's not make this more complicated than it needs to be."

"Fine," Quil said, though it wasn't fine. Not at all. "What else?"

"No . . . romance, or poetry or flowers on bedrolls. No tokens of affection. No cuddling."

"What about when it's cold?" Quil couldn't help saying, and at the ire in her expression, he held up his hands. "Joking!"

"Nicknames are fine," she said. "They sell our Adah oath to R'zwana, at least. The occasional casual physical contact is acceptable. But nothing . . . sweet. No lingering touches or gentle pecks, or brushing my hair out of my face, or—"

Quil got up to kneel beside her. She fixed her dark gaze on him and opened her mouth to protest. Nothing came out.

He held her stare, tangling one hand in her dark hair and flicking up her shirt with the other so his palm was flush against her warm skin.

"So," he said quietly. "Nothing like this."

"I know what you're doing."

The flare of need in her eyes sent blood rushing to inconvenient places, and he pulled her closer slowly, until his lips were a hairsbreadth from hers.

"Do you?" he whispered. "Tell me, Sirsha, how am I supposed to know when you want me if you never touch me?"

"Assume I always want you," she murmured, and he couldn't help the curse that slipped from his mouth into hers as their lips met. She wrapped a leg around his waist and pulled him tight against her—

A whoosh overhead. Quil wrenched himself away. The Kegari Sail had returned. Too fast, the bastard. It circled again and then dropped onto a nearby stretch of flat land.

Quil brushed her hair back and kissed her lightly—in direct defiance of her orders. "I'll be close by."

He disappeared into the woods, heart still thundering, Sirsha's scent permeating his senses. *Sails. Kegari. Interrogation.* He made his way up to a copse of trees a dozen yards from Sirsha, stilling his body until he felt a part of the night sounds—cricket song and rustling leaves and the fire crackling. He'd need a clear shot at the Kegari if they gave her trouble. But that meant getting close while making sure they didn't see him.

Sirsha began to hum—rather hypnotically, Quil noted with a smile, unsurprised that there was yet another skill Sirsha Westering excelled at.

His neck prickled and he turned, scim at the ready—to find J'yan walking through the trees. He glanced up—a second Sail circled.

"I don't like this plan," J'yan whispered.

Quil turned back to the clearing. "Next time come up with a better one, then."

J'yan settled in beside Quil. They could just make out Sirsha's hair piled atop her head.

"She likes you," J'yan said. "More than she'll let on."

"Good to know, what with being her fiancé."

"You're no more her fiancé than I am." J'yan rolled his eyes. "Your secret is safe with me. Whatever you might think, I care about Sirsha. And I want to understand what lies between you. Why did you agree to speak the words of fidelity?" His voice was low and quiet. This was a man used to controlling his anger. Quil recognized a kindred spirit.

"Because R'zwana was going to kill her."

"An Adah oath is no small thing. Why save her?" J'yan leaned forward, and Quil realized then that it wasn't jealousy he was sensing from the man. It was fear. "Her other oath coin—to hunt this creature—is it you she made that ridiculous bargain with? You know what will happen if—"

Below, branches and twigs snapped. The Kegari pilot wasn't bothering to hide her approach. She emerged into the clearing, as heavily armed as the monsters who'd rained down the hells on Navium.

"Angh ot ma?"

Sirsha shook her head. "I speak Ankanese," she said.

The pilot nodded. "Greetings," she said to Sirsha. "May I join your fire?"

Sirsha nodded, and the woman folded her legs beneath her, holding her hands up to the flames.

"A lot of meat for one girl."

"My family will join me this evening," Sirsha said.

"A party, then." The Kegari woman smiled widely, revealing a mouth of rotting teeth. There was no joy in that smile—only a tired sort of bitterness. Something flashed in her hand—a whistle. She blew one long note.

In moments, another Sail appeared. And another. Until a small squadron of them spun down like circling crows.

Sirsha, to her credit, looked only mildly interested as eight more Kegari—all heavily armed—joined their compatriot in the clearing.

"We do love a party," the first woman said as the others gathered behind her. "Don't worry, girl. We'll make sure to leave a bit for your family."

One of the others chortled. Sirsha only smiled.

"From where do you travel?"

"Jaduna," Sirsha said. The Kegari exchanged glances. But instead of wariness, some other emotion passed between them. "I have a job in Farth."

"A Jaduna headed to the Thafwan capital," the woman said. "Fascinating. You know, we heard the most interesting story, up in Jibaut, didn't we?"

A few of the other Kegari rumbled their agreement.

"We heard there's a Jaduna traveling with—if you can believe it—a Martial prince. You wouldn't know anything about that?"

Sirsha shrugged. "You see any princes around here?"

"No," the Kegari woman said. "But that doesn't mean you don't know of any."

Two of the Kegari circled behind Sirsha, a big blond man and a dona'i, the latter pulling a whip from their belt. All the Kegari here were pilots, so they'd all be able to harness the wind—but Quil didn't know how strong they were. He drew his weapons, nodding to J'yan. Then he took a breath and let the thin, light throwing knives fly. The first took the blond down, the second sank into the gut of the dona'i. The third met a wall of wind, which would have knocked Quil back, but J'yan quelled it so Quil could get to Sirsha.

He wasn't far—a matter of seconds. But this was the risk, because in the time it took him and J'yan to get there, Sirsha had to stay alive.

Quil burst into the clearing, blades out, tearing through a Kegari woman coming at him, knocking away the arrows flying from the pilots who'd fled toward the woods. It was easy, infuriatingly easy. *These* were the great warriors who'd brought the Empire to its knees? Quil wished he could tell his aunt right now that without their Sails and bombs and their damned liquid metal, the Kegari were nothing.

Sirsha cried out in warning. "Quil!"

A heavy body slammed into his back, knocking the air out of him. He almost laughed, for he was eight when Elias had trained him to roll away from a blow, to move while he caught his breath. Quil was on his feet moments later, his fist flying into the face of the man who'd attacked him, knocking him to his knees. A moment later, Sirsha had buried a blade in the attacker's back.

The clearing was quieter now, the only sounds Sirsha's and Quil's heavy breaths, the pop of the fire, and the moans of the Kegari who lay on the ground dying.

A scream echoed from the woods—and was abruptly cut off.

R'zwana emerged a few seconds later, dragging a limp Kegari man by his hair, frowning in disgust. J'yan appeared from where he'd hidden with Quil, looking dispassionately at the bodies scattered around him.

"This one will talk." R'zwana tied up her prisoner. "J'yan, wake him up."

"That's it?" Quil said, and looked over R'zwana's shoulder, hoping he'd counted wrong. "You were supposed to grab two."

"If you wanted them alive," R'zwana snarled, "you shouldn't have killed so many, Martial."

J'yan knelt beside the man but shook his head. "I can't wake him. I'd need a Khind to heal him first," he said. "We'll have to wait for him to wake up on his own."

R'zwana took out a pair of brass beaters from the pack slung across her chest. "Stand aside."

"No." Quil turned his body so she couldn't get at the Kegari man. If they didn't get answers out of this pilot about the war camp and the Tel Ilessi, this entire operation would have been for nothing. Quil didn't have time to argue with her about interrogation methods.

His magic, quiet for so many weeks, stirred. *It's the only way*, it seemed to whisper.

"I need you to leave." He looked at the three of them. "All of you. Burn the Sails."

"You don't tell me what to do out here, Martial—"

"Go," Sirsha snapped at her sister. "Or I'm going on without you. You can't track. You won't be able to find us."

R'zwana looked at Sirsha with revulsion, but something else, too. Fear, perhaps. She took a branch from the fire and stalked off, J'yan and Sirsha following.

Quil settled himself in front of the unconscious pilot, considering. He could ponder every consequence of what he was about to do. Or he could just do it.

He lifted his hand to the man's forehead and let a trickle of magic flow through him, hoping Sirsha was too distracted to sense it. *Show me the camp.*

Quil had never made a request like this of his magic. But all Sirsha's talk of emotion and element had made him wonder in the past few weeks if he'd been asking the magic for memories without even realizing it.

Please, he added.

His magic flared, and images filled his head. The man walking out to a flat expanse of earth, the ocean crashing in the distance. Getting into the seat of a large Sail as crewmen loaded the weapons chutes.

The man pushed his arms through two sleeves, the fingers of his right hand dipping into a bowl with a hunk of hard white metal at its center.

As soon as he touched it, it turned to liquid, shooting along the pilot's skin and through the hollow reeds of the Sail, bringing it to life. The liquid seemed to bond with the man, becoming not just part of the Sail's structure but part of the pilot's.

An engine hummed, and the pilot was aloft, spiraling up, the ground dropping away. Quil caught a glance of coastline, a large inlet with a huge arch formation beyond the beach, and an estuary splayed to the south of it.

Now, Quil thought, *the Tel Ilessi.*

Abruptly, he was shoved out of the man's mind. He found himself back in the ravine, his blade loose in his hand. The Kegari man's eyes were open, bloodshot.

"Rue la ba Tel Ilessi!" The man thrust out his jaw, as if even the name of his leader gave him strength. "Kill me if you must, Martial," he growled in Ankanese. "Kill us all. But we will not betray our Tel Ilessi."

The pilot lunged forward. R'zwana had failed to tie him up properly, and Quil had been too enamored with his magic to check. He snatched the dagger at Quil's belt and plunged it into his own throat. Quil pressed his hands against the wound to stanch the bleeding. But it was useless. The man was dead—along with any chance of learning more about the Tel Ilessi.

35
Sirsha

From a rise in the prairie where the grasses hid them, Sirsha and the others looked down at the Kegari war camp, a sprawling mess of tents and fires, clotheslines and supply wagons. The sky-pigs had erected it in a shallow bowl of prairie about a half mile from the Thafwan coast. The top of the bowl was littered with boulders and scrub and rocks—which meant plenty of places to scout from with no one the wiser.

The only part of the camp that wasn't haphazard was the airfield on a swath of cleared land north of the camp, where hundreds of Sails lay in neat pools of canvas and reed, awaiting riders, and, Sirsha suspected, the liquid metal that gave them life.

It looked like any other military camp. Not a hint of anything supernatural.

But Sirsha felt the killer in the nausea that plagued her, the vaguely unpleasant stench in the air. The murderer lurked like a family secret somewhere in that muddy labyrinth, along with the Tel Ilessi. If Sirsha wanted to find her mark, she'd have to get closer.

Sirsha glanced at Quil crouched beside her, the fading light silhouetting him in gold. He said he'd persuaded the Kegari to tell him where the encampment was. But Sirsha suspected otherwise. She'd felt a twinge of—something—from Quil's direction during the interrogation. When she dug for it again, it was gone. And when she'd asked the elements for help, they'd shown her the monster's path instead, fixated on her mission.

"The moment you kill the Tel Ilessi, get out," she told Quil now. "Get to the horses and we'll meet you." She looked to J'yan and R'zwana, whispering to each other a few yards away. "J'yan should be able to keep us hidden all the way in."

"How long will the binding take?"

Sirsha shook her head. "I'm not going to bind her, Quil. I'm going to kill her. For Loli."

She'd decided it days ago, after yet another night when she dreamt of her friend, crawling like a wounded animal along the spongy ground of the Thafwan jungle, a cavity in her chest as she looked desperately for hearts to revive her own.

But it wasn't just Loli's death that made Sirsha want to finish this creature. It was the dead she'd seen in Navium, Jibaut, the Thafwan countryside. It was the way the creature targeted the young and strong. The way she seemed to relish the act of murder.

The wind blew Sirsha's hair into her face, and she shoved it back impatiently. She'd lost her hairpins at the cabin and had been tempted to cut off her hair a dozen times since.

"Perimeter guard is rubbish," Quil observed. The camp was gray in the near-dark, lamps and fires slowly flickering to life. "Too many entrances to count and only half of them are being watched."

"Are you complaining about our enemy's lax fortifications?"

Quil frowned. "It's odd that they were able to take the Empire when they don't know the basics of entrenching an army."

"They've conquered this land." Sirsha thought of the cratered Thafwan villages and scattered bodies they'd seen as they traversed the countryside. "They don't have a strict watch because they don't think they need one. Besides"—she nodded to a Sail spinning up into the clouds—"*that's* their perimeter watch."

"Either they really are the worst-run army in history, or this is a trap," Quil said, with such calm certainty that Sirsha almost looked behind her, expecting Kegari to be closing in.

"Does it change our plan?"

"We need more than one path out."

"Speak for yourself, prince. I've mapped out four. And"—she gave him an appraising look—"I'd wager half my money that you've mapped out double that. What has you so nervous?"

Quil's jaw was set as he surveyed the camp again before fixing his cat eyes on Sirsha. "I know you have to kill or capture that monster down there to satisfy the oath to Elias," he said. "But J'yan told me if someone else kills her, your blood oath dissolves. It's the payment you don't get."

Sirsha regarded him askance. "I need the payment, prince."

"You think you can do this alone," Quil said, and Sirsha didn't bother contradicting him because he'd give her sad eyes for lying. "Let R'zwana and J'yan help you."

"J'yan will get me in, and R'z—"

"I'm talking about the killing, Sirsh," Quil said. "Don't go in there alone because of the money. If Elias doesn't fulfill your payment, I will. I'll give you double. Triple. Whatever you want. Just—don't face her alone."

"Must be nice to have so much money that you can—"

He lifted a hand to her face with such tenderness that she fell silent. Her eyes stung because that was not at all how someone should look at you if your relationship was meaningless, and now their oath coin was burning, *damn* him—

"Please, Sirsha." Skies, she loved how he said her name. "Care about yourself as much as you care about those you love. As much as—as we care about you."

Behind them, R'zwana chuffed like a horse. "Are we going down there?" she asked. "Or shall we say goodbye for three hours?"

Quil shot her a glare and rose. Sirsha grabbed his hand, driven by a sudden fear that she wouldn't see him again. *You'll have to part eventually,* she reminded herself. *He's not for you. Nor you for him.* Her skin went cold at the thought.

She stopped herself from saying something she would regret. "Don't die, prince." Her voice sounded harsher than she'd meant it to.

His dimple flashed as he brought her wrist to his lips in a swift kiss that she wished didn't light her every nerve ending on fire. Then he was gone, disappearing through the grasses and into the maw of the enemy.

Sirsha turned to her sister, irritated that Quil had figured out her intention: to give R'z the slip and kill the monster alone.

But now, because she was a fool with a soft spot for broad-shouldered Martials with talented lips, Sirsha had to rethink her plan.

"Where is the killer?" R'zwana asked. "You haven't said, and I'm starting to suspect you don't want me to know."

"You're losing your magic," Sirsha said, because she needed something to hold over her sister. R'z turned on J'yan, practically frothing at the mouth.

"Don't growl at him," Sirsha said. "I figured it out on my own."

"Listen to her, R'z, for once in your life," J'yan said. "She's not the enemy."

"Ma doesn't know, or you wouldn't still be Raan-Ruku." Sirsha ignored the twinge of guilt she felt at the helplessness washing over R'z's face. "So, here's how it works from now on. I'll tell you what to do. You'll do it. And after we kill this murderer, *sister*, you'll never hunt me again. Understood?"

R'zwana gnashed her teeth, a deeply unpleasant sound. But then, thankfully, she nodded. J'yan sighed quietly, as relieved as Sirsha.

"I know you can't track," Sirsha said. "Can you bind?"

"It's only the tracking magic that's faded," R'zwana muttered. "I'm not— I'm still not as strong a binder as you."

"You're stronger together," J'yan said. "You always have been, much as that might annoy you." He turned to Sirsha. "What's the plan?"

They waited until full night to approach the camp from the west. As of yet, no alarm sounded—Quil hadn't reached the Tel Ilessi.

The narrow lanes were poorly lit, which made infiltration easier. But not easy, by any stretch. Soldiers patrolled, ate, cooked, trained, chatted, argued. They were everywhere, with scores of wind-wielding pilots among them. While Sirsha didn't doubt she could bind them easily, the camp was crowded enough that they'd have been discovered a dozen times over without J'yan hiding their passing.

As they penetrated deeper, Sirsha *felt* the killer. But her presence was subdued. Quiet. Sirsha saw a distortion in the earth ahead of her. *She awaits you*, the earth spoke. *Beware*. Sirsha kept moving east, the disparate strands of the trail coalescing, thick and viscous like an ooze in her mind, leading to the far side of the camp.

Behind her, R'zwana gasped.

Ahead, in the shadows of a low hill and past a row of supply wagons, a lone canvas tent hunched. No bigger than the rest. Yet it was set apart. Sirsha crouched amid a stack of crates, watching. There were no guards. No one entering or leaving. The Kegari passing the tent avoided even looking at it, giving it a wide berth.

Death. Pain. Unnatural. It churns, it eats, it is never satisfied. The earth whispered the words, as if frightened. A spike of terror lanced through Sirsha's body at the way the earth was damaged here, twisted. The natural magic that lay like a thin web over all things sagged brokenly, as if shredded by a rabid animal.

R'zwana stared at the tent like it was poison. "I can feel it."

"It's a trap," J'yan warned, and even he was affected, the freckles standing out starkly on his pale skin. "Remember that, and we can figure our way out of it."

Sirsha nodded. "Wait for my signal."

As she flitted through the camp, mud squelching beneath her boots, she touched Elias's oath coin and spoke to the elements. *Be with me.* They hummed back in response, a tremor only her bones could feel. Before her instinct told her to run as far and fast as possible from the tent, she walked through its flaps.

Within, it was bright and cheery, weirdly at odds with the oppressive feel of the place. There was a thin bedroll on a raised wooden cot. A finely carved Thafwan chair and table in one corner, and thick rugs on the floor instead of cold dirt. The brazier in the center of the tent crackled, the coals within blasting heat into the space. There was even a mirror in one corner.

For all its comforts, the tent was empty. Yet Sirsha could feel something oily and slick. Something watchful.

The tinkle of coins alerted her to the killer's presence, but Sirsha didn't turn, only looked up into the mirror to see her lurking. Sirsha's skin broke out in goose bumps. The creature had again taken the form of her mother, proud-faced and strong, fully coined. Every inch the Raani. Except for that hungry, too-wide gaze that did not belong on the face of any human.

Sirsha felt repulsed, like she needed to crawl out of her own skin. She wanted to murder the monster at that moment. Wrap magic around her so tight that she choked on it and died, as Loli Temba had died.

"S'rsha Inashi-fa." The killer bowed low. "I longed to look upon you again."

Hearing her full name in her mother's voice almost made Sirsha forget why she was here.

Bind her. She is a horror.

The elements brought her back to herself, and Sirsha turned to face the killer, not bothering to hide her disgust. "You knew I'd be coming and you didn't make me any tea? You've clearly never met my mother."

She plopped down on one of the seats and gestured to the other. "Join me?"

The monster cocked her head—something Sirsha's mother had never done in her life, and Sirsha wondered where she had learned that trick. From another human perhaps.

"Tell me your name," Sirsha said. "I'm sick of calling you *that infernal murderer*. It's tedious."

"You may call me Mother Div, Holy Cleric and Vessel of the Fount."

"I see that we have philosophical differences about the meaning of the word *holy*, so I'll call you Div. Or maybe Detestable Div, if I'm annoyed. Why are you stuck in here, then?" Sirsha leaned back, drawing on years of practiced nonchalance, even as she tried to get a read on the creature, to figure out how she would bind her. "I mean, it could be worse. I've been sleeping on rocks and twigs for the past two months because of you. But a creature of your . . . range should have better accommodations, no?"

"My range has been limited these past two weeks."

Skies, what a trick. Div really did sound exactly like the Raani. Gently, so gently that the creature couldn't possibly notice, Sirsha probed the earth.

The earth shriveled away. *Bind*, it said. *Bind her, child, or run.*

Sirsha swallowed, throat suddenly dry. "That must be unpleasant for a being such as yourself. Used to roaming the countryside, murdering whatever poor sap you happen across."

As Sirsha spoke, she reached for the binding magic she'd ignored for eight years. *Emotion exerted on an element.* In this case, the element was magic itself. She drew on it, casting it out like a lasso until it was a snug, glowing chain around Div's neck. Then, with a surge of satisfaction, Sirsha yanked. She allowed herself to smile, for she knew the strength of her own magic. It was firm and unyielding—a yoke Div couldn't break. Sirsha wouldn't need J'yan and R'zwana after all.

Div looked down, bemused.

"Tell me, child. Did you truly believe you could chain me?"

An odd sound, a popping in Sirsha's mind, as if she'd fallen from a great height. Sirsha's power stretched taut before streaming away from her. Something was yanking it free, devouring it.

Sirsha found her power linked to Div's for one brief, terrifying moment. It felt like staring into a void, into some empty grasping where the only emotion was hunger. A ravening need for *more*.

There should have been something else in that space. Something to balance it. But it was yawning and mindless and it gnawed at Div's insides, not because it was malevolent, but because it simply knew no other way to exist.

Div smiled and seemed to swell like a tick engorged on blood. She met Sirsha's gaze, and the Jaduna girl found that she was in the tent and not in the tent. Her feet were planted, but her mind was being drawn forward, into the now-white eyes of this creature that looked like her mother. Sirsha stared into the abyss, tipping down, called to the maw by a void within herself.

Some part of you broke that day your family cast you out, a voice crooned in Sirsha's mind. *The humanity drained out of you and left you a shell. You are tainted. You shall never love. Come, child. Come to one who will understand, for I, too, am empty.*

The voice was the Raani's and it sounded so reasonable, like Ma when she tried to persuade Sirsha to cooperate, to help the Kin track the Karjad when she didn't wish to.

But now, instead of digging in her heels, Sirsha listened. For she was older and wiser. She understood the loneliness of leaving her Kin, of trading one moment of weakness for years of forced solitude.

Sirsha stepped forward, reaching out to the Raani, when a hand grabbed her by her neck and yanked her back.

R'zwana. "Traitor!" she screamed. "You were to give us the signal. I knew we couldn't trust—"

J'yan pulled them both away from Div, lashing out at her with his battle magic. Div's simulacrum dissolved and she collapsed into a seething, snarling mass of tortured gray shadows. She created her own weather, an ill wind that whirled around the small tent like a tiny, vicious cyclone.

"Bind her!" R'zwana screamed over the wind. *"Bind her!"*

Sirsha threw her binding magic around Div again, but it disintegrated as if being gobbled up. "I—I can't—"

J'yan strained to hold Div in place, but Sirsha had felt the creature's power. She knew Div was toying with him.

"J'yan, stop! She's too strong. She *wants* you to use your magic! She feeds off it!"

"Go then, coward!" R'zwana shoved her. "Run, like you always do!"

R'zwana drew on her own limited ability to bind, but it wasn't enough. Her power had always been a droplet beside Sirsha's ocean.

Div took slow steps toward J'yan, a stalking animal. Sirsha grabbed his hand and pulled, but it was as if his feet were rooted to the earth.

"Let go, J'yan!" Sirsha screamed. "We need to run!"

"Hold it while I bind it, J'yan!" R'zwana gritted her teeth, her own magic like a tattered string of yarn around Div's swelling, writhing form. "Or we're all dead!"

"We can't, R'z!" J'yan dropped to his knees, magic fading. "Sirsha's right."

But by now, they were all pulled into the creature's strange, pulsating gravity, unable to back away.

Div's voice transformed into a menacing, earthy growl, and though she had no face, Sirsha could feel her smile. "Who first?"

R'zwana grabbed Sirsha and shoved her at Div. "Take her! She's more powerful!"

Sirsha had grown used to R'zwana's rejections. Her insults. But seeing her sister trying to feed her to a soul-devouring spirit fiend was a different sort of violence.

She had no time to grieve. Because Div ignored R'zwana and Sirsha, instead lunging for J'yan.

J'yan's gasp was swallowed by Div's hungry snarls. His body went limp and crumpled to the ground as Div hunched over him, his beating heart throbbing beneath her lips.

Sirsha opened her mouth to scream, but she couldn't even take in a breath. As J'yan's heart grayed to ash, a wretched cry tore from her chest.

R'zwana stared in horror. "No—you should have taken her," she said. "Why didn't you take her?"

As Div fed, R'zwana whirled on Sirsha, and the hatred in her gaze could have peeled the bark off a tree. Sirsha considered leaving her sister in the tent to die. But J'yan wouldn't want it, and she'd do this last thing for him. Her survival instinct took full hold, and she grabbed R'zwana's elbow in a vise grip and dragged her out of the tent.

"Get off me— Get—"

"Shut it!" Sirsha hissed. "You're going to get us bleeding killed!"

R'zwana looked around at the busy camp beyond the tent, dazed. Perhaps finally understanding the precariousness of their position, she fell quiet, following Sirsha as she ducked behind a hay wagon and then led them through the camp pell-mell, desperate to get away from that creature and its endless hunger. They avoided notice through sheer luck.

Sirsha stopped near the camp's perimeter, her hands on her thighs as she tried to catch her breath.

R'zwana finally spoke. "What—what was that thing?"

"I don't bleeding know!" Sirsha shoved her sister, her anger and grief at J'yan's death taking over. "I *told* you it was too strong! You didn't listen, you *awful*, pig-headed—"

"If you'd bound it when I said, J'yan would still—"

Sirsha reared back and punched her sister square in the face before she could finish her sentence. R'zwana staggered, dazed, and then collapsed. Sirsha resisted the urge to kick her, instead dragging her sister beneath a weapons cart and out of sight. She'd wake up soon enough and figure her own way out of the camp. Whether she survived or not—

Well, that was her problem. Sirsha looked back once toward Div's tent. "I'm sorry, J'yan," she sobbed. "I'm so sorry."

Then she ran.

36
Aiz

It was the sound Aiz hated the most. The savage snapping of a human body, followed by growls of Div's gluttonous feasting.

They'd left the cavern of horrors, Div holding Aiz like one would a sleeping child, flying as if she had a Sail. But there was no canvas above, no seat below, no Loha.

"How is this possible?" Aiz had gasped at the bite of wind in her face, shuddering so badly she feared Div would drop her.

"I am the spirit of Holy Div reborn, child. The greatest windsmither to live. I do not need a Sail to fly. Neither do you."

The Tribal Desert stretched beneath them, the brown earth gleaming like the furred back of an animal, the Jack trees glowing gold and pink as the sun rose.

"What do you mean," Aiz asked, "that I don't need a Sail?"

"You have my power at your disposal." Mother Div's dark hair streamed behind her like a flag. She offered Aiz a beatific smile.

Then she dropped her.

Aiz screamed as she fell, scrambling for the wind. She was going to die, and as Ruh's terrified face flashed through her memory, she realized she *deserved* to die—

A burst of power surged through her, like sunlight flushing her veins. She gasped, arresting her fall with such ease that she shot into the air a few feet before leveling. Mother Div drifted down beside her with the grace of a falling petal.

"That is just a taste," she said.

Over the next week, Mother Div healed her broken leg and taught her how to harness the wind, not just to fly, but to use as a weapon. Within days, Aiz's rudimentary control was magnified. She leveled trees. Tore a roof off a barn. Cracked the neck of a steer. She'd left everything in the cavern—her book, her pack, even her aaj. She needed none of it.

They moved quickly across the countryside at night, finding shelter during the day. The few times they ran into other travelers, Aiz interacted with them while Mother Div watched.

"My curse is not only that I must feed on the young and innocent," Div explained. "I am also unseen to all but you."

Aiz looked askance at Mother Div when she said this. She'd seen her feed, and it was clear Mother Div's prey saw *something* before they died.

But Aiz didn't ask for an explanation, for who knew what horrors Mother Div might speak of? Aiz's sleep was already plagued by nightmares. Mostly of Quil staggering through a sandstorm. *Ilar!* he called. *Ilo!* In the dream, he discovered her trail and followed her through the blue-veined canyon, past the strange runes and carvings and into the Durani's chamber.

Stop, she tried to scream. *Do not look.*

His steps quickened and he drew his scim. It fell from nerveless fingers as he entered the chamber. As he gasped in horror at the blood splattering the walls, Aiz's scim abandoned, her pack sticky with viscera.

She watched as he found Ruh.

Oh, Idaka, if you knew the still horror of a child dying from starvation, she thought, *or the terrible silence of a slum where every adult has been conscripted, you might understand why I allowed such a sacrifice.*

As he held Ruh's body, as he convulsed in grief, she longed to reach out to him. Hold him. She had used him, but she cared for him too. His grief rekindled her own, and she would always awaken with her face wet.

"Was it real?" she asked Mother Div the first night she had the dream.

The cleric nodded. "The last vestiges of the First Durani's magic," she said. "Haunting us still. Let me ease the dreams away, child. For I am a mindsmither and such a task is simple for me."

But Aiz shook her head. The dream reminded her of her sacrifice. It hurt. And she deserved the pain.

A week after leaving the chamber, Aiz waited at the beach on the southern edge of the Empire as, thankfully, Mother Div found sustenance far away.

Aiz felt a tug in her chest—Div's tether to her. It grew thinner the farther the cleric went, yet never wholly disappeared. When Aiz willed it, Mother Div would return. But she could offer Aiz no power unless she had fed.

It was a relief to have her gone. They couldn't read each other's thoughts, but each knew the other's will, the tenor of her feelings. It was suffocating.

Right now, for instance. A piercing hunger consumed Aiz, the kind that stank of death, the kind that she had grown up fearing. It was followed by a sudden fullness, as if she'd consumed a marvelous, nourishing meal. The feeling faded quickly, but it happened again and again. Until finally, Div was satiated and returned to Aiz. As she approached, Aiz looked away from the blood on her hem.

"I brought you a gift, daughter."

Something glimmered in Div's hand, and she opened it to reveal a block of Loha as big as a goose egg. It was more than Aiz had ever seen at once, even in the Aerie forges where the metal was alloyed. Enough to innervate a hundred Sails.

"You took this from an Empire soldier? A Mask?"

"From two." Div's face glowed with pride.

Aiz reached for her patience, finding what little remained to her. Div, she'd noticed, had a propensity for doing things by force. The product of being imprisoned for so long, perhaps.

"We will not steal the Loha," Aiz said. "We must still treat with the Empress of the Martials. If all her Masks are dead, and we come requesting the metal on their faces, she will not be inclined to hear our offer. Come. You have fed enough. We make for Kegar."

Div bowed her head, and though Aiz watched for resentment, she felt none.

"You must eat too, my daughter," the cleric said with a motherly attentiveness. "Let me bring you food, and then let us rest so you have the strength for the next leg of our journey."

They made their way south, Div traveling far for her sustenance. Aiz felt every death. Over time, the deaths grew more plentiful. Though not more necessary.

Div, Aiz realized quickly through their bond, was taking more than she needed.

Not long after leaving the Empire, they reached the border between Diyane and Kegar, marked by the snowy blue pinnacles of a massive mountain range. Dawn approached and they spiraled down to a forested clearing before the first rays of light broke the horizon. Mother Div brought Aiz bread and fruit she'd pilfered from somewhere, then waited eagerly for Aiz to set her free to feed.

After Div disappeared, Aiz set the food aside and focused on the cord between them. She waited for hunger, then the satiation. The third time it happened, she yanked on the cord with all her might.

Div appeared almost out of the air, crashing to the earth, kicking up a cloud of dust and pine needles. Her face and hands were covered in blood, and a ravenous frenzy appeared to have consumed her.

"That's enough." Aiz tried to steady the tremor in her voice. "No more. I know your strength. Three hearts are more than enough to get us across the mountains."

"I will not be strong enough for you!" Div warned as the bloodlust in her face faded. She wrung her hands. "What if you fall because I cannot keep you aloft?"

Aiz sensed no lie in the cleric's concern, and she softened her tone. "I think you don't realize how much you take, Mother Div. I blame the First Durani and what she did to you. She was truly a creature of spite, for these sacrifices are unnatural and counter to who you were in your first life. That's why you have me. I'll decide how much you need. And I say that you cannot feed in Kegar. The mother of our people cannot harm her children."

"How will we beat back your enemies? How will you defeat the false Tel Ilessi, Tiral?" Mother Div entreated.

"We'll find a way," Aiz said. "As you found a way to save our people once before. But not with you feasting on the blood of innocents. If you must take the young, take those who are near death or hungry."

Aiz shuddered, remembering her own bouts of starvation. She would have welcomed death, if only it would put an end to the gnawing in her belly. Maybe for some, Div would be a welcome release.

A few nights later, the lights of Kegar twinkled ahead of them. Aiz wept at the sight. The air smelled of Spire roses and fire pines. In the north, it was deep winter, but here in Kegar, summer crowned the mountains with the green and pink iceberry shrubs that awoke for only a few months.

"Why cry, child?" Mother Div said as they set down near a mountain creek north of the city. "Did you think you wouldn't see your home again? When I so diligently guided you?"

"Our home." Aiz wiped away her tears. Her desire to go to the cloister, to see if Noa and Olnas and Cero still lived, overwhelmed her.

"You miss your friends." Mother Div gathered wood for a fire.

Sometimes, it was like this between them. Aiz had but to think something and Mother Div would pick up on it. Aiz wondered if mothers and daughters were similar. Mother Div had three children herself, long ago. Perhaps she would see them in the faces of their descendants, the Triarchs.

"I tried to reach out to Cero before we reached Nur, when I still had the aaj," Aiz said. "But he's forgotten me, perhaps."

"Is he the kind to ignore you if you need him?"

Aiz didn't used to think so. But after weeks of silence, she wasn't sure.

"He didn't want me to return to Kegar," Aiz said as Mother Div lit a fire with a snap of her fingers. "But—but perhaps I could see him before I face Tiral. Talk over the plan with him."

"It was not Cero who survived the Tribal Lands," Mother Div reminded her. "Nor Cero who freed me. You do not need him, Aiz. Whatever you require, we will do together."

But Div's efforts cost her energy. And there was only one way to fill that deep well.

"You do not wish for me to take sacrifices from among the people." Div paced around the clearing. "But they should be glad to lay down their lives for their Holy Cleric, their Mother, for the Vessel of the Fount."

"It is one thing to take from among foreign populations, Div," Aiz said. "I mourn the innocent, but they are not my people. Their leaders have long known the Kegari are starving and done nothing to aid us. I *do* know our people. They have suffered enough."

Mother Div nodded, but Aiz caught a flash of a feral hunger in her eyes. It was gone in an instant, but Aiz marked it. She could not have Mother Div losing control amid the coming battle.

Aiz tightened her mental fist on Mother Div's leash. The cleric resisted, ever so briefly, before capitulating.

"It is for the best, Mother Div," she said. "Trust me. Now come. Sit. You can mindsmith, yes? Enter dreams? Let us see how far your skill reaches."

Four days later, Aiz was ready.

It was a bright, clear day. Still cold, for Kegar was never truly warm, not even on the first day of summer. But beautiful. A day of promise. A day of death.

Mother Div had brought Aiz much information since they'd arrived in Kegar. Dafra cloister was burned to cinders, its clergy scattered. But Olnas, Noa, and many of the other clerics and orphans had taken shelter in Dafra slum's abandoned houses.

Tiral's reign as Tel Ilessi was troubled. The late spring raids had gone badly. The villages of Bula banded against the Kegari, burning their own fields and choking the skies with smoke. Most of the Snipes were starving and even the Sparrows, generally better-off than their slum-dwelling peers, were going hungry. Tiral had purged Dafra slum, killing entire streets of people for defying his rule.

"The people are ready to cast out their false Tel Ilessi," Mother Div said as the day of the Summer Rites dawned. "More so now for the dreams I gave them of better days ahead."

Aiz smiled. It had been her idea for Mother Div to use her mindsmithing to scatter hope among the Snipes. Visions of the Return—and of Aiz leading them.

Aiz rose into the sky, Mother Div at her side, and surveyed the Kegari capital. Thousands would gather in the Aerie's airfield to hear High Cleric Dovan recite the Nine Sacred Tales, and to entreat Mother Div to bless her people in the warm months.

Aiz buzzed with anticipation—and resolve. Today, her people would be free from the false Tel Ilessi and the lies of the Triarchy. Today, they wouldn't just receive the blessing of Mother Div. They would behold Mother Div's power through Aiz herself.

She had chosen her clothing carefully—casting aside the embroidered linens and leathers of the Tribes for the ragged gray dress of a Snipe. She wanted the people to know she was one of them. That she had not forgotten them.

Aiz heard the crowd before she saw them, the hum of tens of thousands of voices coming from the sprawling fields around the Aerie. A wide, high dais draped in blue silk rose a dozen feet above the people. The

Triarchs—pale-faced Oona, curly-haired Ghaz, and gimlet-eyed Hiwa—listened from their thrones, faces impassive as High Cleric Dovan completed the Eighth Sacred Tale.

On a throne positioned above them, Tiral watched, the sun shining on his blond hair. His blue-clad pilots stood in neat rows to one side of the dais. Aiz tried and failed to spot Cero among them.

Tiral rose from the Tel Ilessi's throne to the speaker's lectern.

Aiz could kill him now. Knock him off the dais and use the wind to dash his brains against the earth below. Her body yearned to do it, so much that she'd half lifted her hands before remembering she must first accuse him of his crimes. She could not have him become a martyr.

"Are you with me, Mother Div?"

The cleric seemed to swell beside her. "Always, Aiz."

Aiz took careful aim and blasted the lectern to pieces. Tiral screamed and scrambled back, cowering, and Aiz landed on the dais, bringing a vicious wind with her, pinning him to the throne he'd stolen.

In the crowds, some cried out, some gasped. Clerics cloaked in gray knelt, praying to Mother Div. She was at Aiz's side, looking at the Triarchs with interest that bordered on hunger.

"They are powerful," Div breathed. "Such magic! But their minds are too cruel. They would not make good sacrifices."

"No," Aiz murmured, looking from Triarch to Triarch, remembering the last time she was here. Remembering how they treated her like offal.

Aiz raised her voice and called on the wind to carry it to her people.

"I am Aiz bet-Dafra, of Dafra slum," she said. "I am a child of Kegar and daughter of the evening star. You, Tiral bet-Hiwa, are a traitor to your people and your faith."

Tiral bared his teeth like a feral dog and tried to rise from the throne where he was so ungracefully pinned. But Aiz held him down, Div's power pouring into her.

"You have sacrificed countless children and clerics and Snipes to further your warmongering." Aiz's voice boomed across the silent crowd. "You have imprisoned innocents in the Tohr and killed them with your own hands. Most foully, you have claimed the mantle of the Holy Tel Ilessi. You have blasphemed against Mother Div and thus do I declare you apostate and transgressor. For this, you deserve death."

The Triarchs appeared stunned into silence. But Tiral?

Tiral laughed.

"Haven't you eaten enough dirt, Snipe?" He called up his own wind now and shoved against Aiz, grinning when she held firm. "Are you hungry for more?"

Aiz siphoned more power from Div, pushing against Tiral. But she'd forgotten his strength, and he anticipated her force, spinning to the side so Aiz staggered forward on the dais. He struck her from the back, knocking her to her knees, wrapping a tight noose of wind around her neck.

Aiz gritted her teeth and sent a missile of air straight into his forehead. Tiral's hold loosened and she lurched to her feet.

"Fight harder, Aiz!" Div's sweetness had soured to impatience so swiftly that she sounded like someone else entirely. "You cannot die, else I will be left with no anchor to this world, a lost spirit."

"More power!" Aiz screamed, for Tiral had compressed the air around Aiz into hot needles, and Aiz struggled to hold them back. Div complied, and Aiz repelled the attack with a shield like the one she'd used to save Quil weeks ago.

She struck out at Tiral with knives of air, hoping to end him quickly. He threw his own shield up, and Aiz fell back, her will flagging, her windsmithing sputtering. How was he able to resist Aiz, even with Div's power?

"I told you we needed more!" Div said, her implication clear. *More children. Kegari children.*

"The Triarchs!" Aiz gasped as Tiral flung his own throne at her. "Take them!"

"Their impurity will weaken me! Let me feed and I shall funnel such power into you that you can shred the skin from Tiral's bones."

"Not Kegari!" Aiz whimpered. "Not our children."

"We have no time, girl! Would you rather that they suffer under this tyrant?"

Aiz screamed her defiance and used the last of her strength to roll away from Tiral's attack, a blast of wind that nearly spun her off the dais. Her nails scraped against the wood as she scrabbled desperately to hold on.

"You cannot withstand another strike," Div said. "If you wish to win, Aiz, you must let me help you!"

Death was inches away. Seconds. If Aiz offered up the children of Kegar to Holy Div, she would be sacrificing her own people. And if she didn't, Tiral would remain Tel Ilessi, and Spires only knew what hells he would wreak upon them.

"He's coming, Aiz," Mother Div said. "Decide!"

37

Quil

Quil promised himself he wouldn't brood about Sirsha. She could take care of herself. She had for years.

The moment you kill the Tel Ilessi, get out. Quil's worry was that he wouldn't be able to kill the man. That the Tel Ilessi would use his magic to best Quil in battle.

He'd have to strike quickly, mercilessly. Before the bastard could call up his sorcery. First, though, Quil needed to find some sign of him—a glut of guards, a cluster of flags, a pile of skulls . . .

The war camp was sprawled across the base of a hidden coastal valley, and Quil circled it twice. He noted the smaller Sails landing and taking off from the airfield, as well as transport Sails massive enough to move large numbers of troops and weapons.

It was only on the airfields that the Kegari appeared organized. As Quil entered the camp, slinking from shadow to shadow, his low opinion of the enemy sank further. The place appeared to be divided into smaller camps based on class and internal division, as opposed to the needs of a large army.

The northern quadrant had waterproofed tents, cleared lanes, and soldiers in fine armor. The sprawling southern quadrants had threadbare tents with goats and dogs running between them. The soldiers wore clothes Martials wouldn't use for rags.

Quil's skin crawled from the sheer disorganization. He'd spent ages learning about army encampment protocol. Where to corral horses and livestock, where to dig latrines, where to put the infantry versus the cavalry. At one point Quil had rolled his eyes at Elias.

Won't I have generals to handle this?

Elias had chuckled and then made Quil and the other students spend two weeks putting up a "test" encampment—complete with latrine trenches they had to dig and use themselves. Quil cursed his teacher at the time—even as the rest of Elias's students cursed Quil.

But now Quil understood why Elias insisted on those lessons. The Martial army could destroy this entire camp with a dozen Masks and a few hundred legionnaires.

Quil moved deeper into the camp, filching a tattered Kegari cloak and blue armband. Up close, he'd fool no one. But from afar, he was just another tired soldier.

He scoured his surroundings for some sign of the Tel Ilessi and had nearly completed a third circuit of the camp when he spotted a flash of color in the finer sector nearest the airfield. A square pavilion with a flag flying outside it: a sun with four beams and a woman in the center. Well hidden. Well guarded. It backed to a low cliff face with heavy wagons on either side, as if to block anyone trying to sneak in.

The tent was well lit and within, a familiar, broad-shouldered shadow moved. A haughty voice drifted out.

The Tel Ilessi.

Quil's body went taut with anticipation. *Finally.* Now to get in. His best shot was the side backing to the cliff. Big tents always had a bit of give when up against uneven surfaces. The moon had disappeared behind a bank of clouds, and the torches at the front of the tent left the back in shadow. No one would see him if he timed it right.

Quil watched the patrols and just after one passed, he slipped from his hiding spot and past the large wagon.

The moment he reached the cliff, he realized that in the darkness, the tent only looked as if it backed to the boulder. In fact, the boulder formed one entire wall—the tent had been cut and secured to it. It was impossible to sneak in from the back.

Quil stifled a string of curses, frozen as the clouds cleared and the moon illuminated the camp—including the intruder loitering near the most well-guarded tent in the place.

"Ih! Va tu fi arda!"

For a second, Quil and the Kegari guard twenty feet away simply stared at each other, incredulous.

The prince recovered faster. *Suicide mission it is.* He drew his scim and ripped through the canvas.

Behind him, a warning cry went up. As he shoved into the tent, Quil sheathed his scim with one hand and drew his bow with the other. In the blink of an eye, three arrows hurtled toward the only person in the room, who sat at a desk facing away from him.

The arrows did not hit their mark.

They stopped midair, inches from the figure's back. Then they fell to the floor, and Quil felt that strange pressure in the air he'd experienced back in Jibaut. He tried to move but found he could barely breathe.

The Kegari leader stood. He had no blade. No weapons that Quil could see. It was clear he did not need them. When three soldiers rushed into the tent, the Tel Ilessi jerked up his hand.

"Ivashk."

The soldiers backed away without so much as a glance at each other, bowing their heads.

The Tel Ilessi stepped into the light, even as Quil fought against the invisible bonds holding him in place. The man's pale skin and sharp features were familiar to Quil from their encounter in Jibaut. As then, the Tel Ilessi was cold-eyed, but instead of disdain, his expression was amused.

"I'd heard you were determined," he said in perfect Ankanese. "Not witless. I'll release the wind. I trust you'll not draw your weapon. Sit down. We have much to discuss."

Quil didn't sit. He pretended to sit—and then he hurled a throwing knife from his sleeve straight into the Tel Ilessi's shoulder.

The man gasped as the blade sank into his skin, and he staggered back.

Quil closed the distance between them in an instant, short daggers in hand. He took advantage of the Tel Ilessi's surprise to sweep his legs out from under him. The bastard would have died then. Died with his throat slit open and his blood soaking the rugs in this accursed tent.

But the wind came for Quil, and this time it threw him against the hard boulder at the back of the tent. Pain tore through his spine, his vision doubled, and his knees nearly gave out. He caught himself on a table, trying to keep upright.

"Enough, Cero. Do not toy with him."

Quil froze, not because of the wind, but because of the voice. He looked up at the armored figure stepping through the front of the tent. Small-boned. Short brown hair. Pale skin and light eyes.

"Hello, Idaka."

"No—" His mind couldn't comprehend this, because the last time he'd seen her alive, she'd been speaking to Elias in the middle of a sandstorm. The last time he'd seen her at all, she'd been in pieces, scattered across a cavern in one of the most haunted places in the Empire. He'd found a book he'd seen her looking at sometimes—completely blank. The ring she was never without. Her pack.

And Ruh.

But now he understood what this *thing* standing in front of him was. Not the girl he'd threatened with a scim the first time he saw her, only to find he couldn't stop thinking about her. Not the girl he'd kissed beneath the desert stars. Not the first girl he'd ever loved, her eyes full of secrets he relished discovering. Not Ilo.

"You monster," Quil hissed. "Where's Sirsha?"

The creature stepped forward. Skies, she looked just like the real Ilar. The killer had done this to Sirsha when she took the form of her mother.

I knew it was the monster from the eyes. She didn't have my mother's eyes.

Quil stared, expecting to see a glimmer of malice. But the false Ilar's eyes were only tired and sad and achingly familiar. Quil's magic stirred. *Use me. Look inside her.*

"Where is Sirsha?" he demanded again, ignoring the pull of his power.

The false Ilar looked away. "The Jaduna you've been traveling with?"

Quil strained against the wind holding him, veins popping from his neck and arms as he pushed against it. "Damn you, where *is* she?"

"I don't have her, Idaka," false Ilar said. "She's probably with Mother Div. If she's as clever as Div thinks she is, she might even survive."

"Who the hells is Div?"

"Sit down, Idaka—"

"Stop calling me that!"

"Please. Quil. I have wanted to speak to you for so long. To—to explain." She turned to the tall man. "Why didn't you call me when he appeared?"

The man—Cero—shrugged and then winced as he pressed a cloth to his bloody wound. "I wanted to see what kind of man captured your heart."

The creature sighed and called out, "Tvho Ina!"

Two guards appeared at the entrance to the gate, but unlike with Cero, they bowed their heads in deference, and thumped their hearts thrice with their fists.

"*Rue la ba Tel Ilessi!*"

Quil stared at them—they were treating this simulacrum of Ilar as if she were the Tel Ilessi. When she gave them orders, they complied immediately, escorting Cero away.

Quil pushed experimentally against the wind; it held him as tightly as before.

"You knew me as Ilar," the creature said. "The only name I ever chose for myself. The name I was born with was Aiz bet-Dafra. And the name my people have given me is Tel Ilessi. I beg you, if you loved the girl I was, if you cared about me at all, listen to what I have to say."

Whatever this creature was, she believed herself, at least. The prince nodded once. Quil could pretend to listen—and strike when she least expected it.

"Weapons on the ground, please."

She eased the wind enough that he was able to unsheathe his scim and the dagger at his waist.

"The sleeves, too, Idaka." She said his name like the real Ilar, the slight accent on the first *a*, the half smile so familiar that Quil felt sick.

He dropped the blades in his sleeves. But not the one in his boot. She said nothing more and sat in a three-legged chair, gesturing for Quil to take the seat across from her.

Then monster Ilar began to tell a tale, her voice as resonant as when she traveled with the Tribes. She spoke of a failed attempt to assassinate a vicious commander. Wasting away in the prison her people called the Tohr; an escape, a ship, a seer. Arriving in the Tribal Lands. Asking Laia for help, saying she was Ankanese, when all the while she was something else. Learning of the First Durani, a storyteller full of lies, who had locked away the spirit of a Kegari cleric.

Quil would never have believed her, perhaps. Would have conjured a hundred excuses for why she couldn't be Ilar.

But then she described Ruh.

"I knew he was special from the first moment I met him," she said. "The way he told stories, the way the desert itself held its breath to listen. Oh, Quil, how I mourn him. But no—I'm jumping ahead of myself . . ."

The night deepened as she spoke, the smell of food and sweat and beast dissipated by a coastal wind. The camp sounds faded to a low hum. Quil's magic reared again.

Read her. Then you will know the truth. Get inside her mind. If she's not human, you will discern it.

Quil tried to resist. He feared what he would find. Yet he knew it was the only way to know if she really was Ilar, or if the monster had created an elaborate illusion. So, as the creature droned on, Quil spoke to his magic.

Show me, he said. *Show me what she is.*

His power flared and expanded, a flower opening to the sun. Then he was inside the false Ilar's memory as if he *was* her, his own consciousness in stasis as his magic carried him fully into her thoughts.

Tiral died quicker than Aiz wanted him to.

After Aiz released Div to feed—after the first flood of power rushed through her body, she wrapped the wind around Tiral's throat and squeezed. Tiral gasped and dropped to his knees as the entire airfield watched, silent. So many Snipes among them, starving and ragged and broken. *Not for much longer*, Aiz vowed in her mind. *Not while I breathe.*

Tiral grinned. "You used—the book—" he gasped. "Knew you would. It's why I didn't hunt you. Didn't need to."

Aiz's hold on the wind loosened.

"I was chosen," Aiz said. Tiral looked small this close to death. Aiz only ever feared him because she'd been a powerless child. Now she was a force even the mighty Tiral bet-Hiwa couldn't defeat. "Mother Div chose *me* instead of you. You dared to claim the mantle of the Tel Ilessi and Div *knew*."

Tiral wheezed, tears leaking down his face, and she thought

it was a death rattle until he grinned. "Spires, but you're a fool," he said. "I wish I could live, just to watch it eat you alive."

"Watch from the hells, apostate." Aiz remembered choking on the smoke of Tiral's fire long ago, wailing as the orphans' wing burned, listening to the cries of her friends—her family—fade. For years, she'd wanted this. To watch him hurt. Suffer.

But as she squeezed the life out of him, as he fell silent, she felt no satisfaction. Only a vague sense of emptiness. A hunger for something more.

Div's hand settled on her back, heavy and cold. Aiz sighed, thankful for the comfort.

Then she used the wind to rip Tiral's head clean from his body. The crowd gasped as she held it up, blood pouring from the stump.

"I am Aiz bet-Dafra," she roared with the same conviction with which she'd told the Nine Sacred Tales in the Tohr. "Daughter of the evening star, tale-spinner of the Tohr, and chosen of Mother Div. I am your Tel Ilessi."

She said the words because she knew they were true. Had she not healed herself from her fall at the Aerie, months ago? Had she not dreamt of Quil discovering the chamber, seen into his very mind? The skills might be rusty, perhaps, but—

"You will learn," Mother Div said. "I will teach you. Your people need a leader, Aiz. They need you."

The Kegari roared their approval; the flight squadrons looked on, uncertain of what to do now that their commander was dead. Aiz wondered what Quil would say if he could see her now. *My Ilo*. It felt like a different life when he said those words.

Am I still your Ilo, covered in blood, Quil?

One day, she would travel to the Empire, not as a fugitive but as an envoy of the Kegari. She and Quil could speak as equals about the sacrifices required to save one's people. If anyone could understand why she did what she did, it was a fellow leader.

Footsteps approached. The Triarchs. She threw Tiral's head at their feet as some in the crowd roared, "Kill them! Death to the Triarchs!"

Aiz was unsurprised when Triarch Hiwa, Tiral's father, stepped over the head, appearing only mildly perturbed.

"We thank you for freeing us from the farce that my son inflicted on us with the support"—he glared at High Cleric Dovan, on her knees and regarding Aiz with awe—"of these so-called clerics. You will be rewarded."

Div prowled behind Hiwa, hand on her nose as if to ward off a foul stench.

"He plans to kill you and the clerics," Div said. "Already he has made a pact with the others. End him, Aiz. Before his poison spreads."

A rush of power filled Aiz, cool and sweet. She did not use it. As awful as the Triarchs were, they understood the running of Kegar and its armies. After hearing Quil speak of all he had to learn, Aiz knew the Triarchs would be useful.

"Tiral manipulated the Nine Sacred Tales for his own gain," she told the Triarchs. "He burned the cloister, murdered Snipe children, and imprisoned and tortured our clerics." Aiz nodded to High Cleric Dovan, who bowed her head. "They supported him out of fear. That doesn't make them weak. It makes Tiral evil."

"Yes, yes," Triarch Oona said. "He was a fool and a cheat, but it was the clerics who—"

"You are no better!" Aiz's anger exploded. "You cast away Snipes and Sparrows alike as if we were nothing but dirt."

A roar of agreement from the crowd.

"You're supposed to lead us. Care for us. But you don't. It's the clerics who protect us. There are so many who would have nothing if not for the cloisters."

Aiz wrapped the wind around the necks of the Triarchs. They all reached for their own windsmithing immediately, but Aiz yanked it away.

"No more." Aiz's voice trembled. "I am the Tel Ilessi, and thus I declare that we are all children of the evening star. We are all beloved to Mother Div. No Kegari shall suffer more than another simply because of where they were born."

The Triarchs' silence was strategic. They would eventually plot against her. But she and Div could tackle that. If the Triarchs knelt, so would the rest of the highborns.

She transformed the wind into fists and turned them on the Triarchs' backs. Oona gasped, resisting; Hiwa paled. But then Triarch Ghaz dropped to his knees, bowing his curly head. The rest followed, and Aiz didn't have to exert her will upon the clerics or the pilots, on the people in the airfield, or those who, hearing that something momentous was occurring, now streamed from the streets of the city to watch.

By tens and hundreds and thousands, her people knelt.

A familiar and beloved voice spoke up from among the pilots. Cero stood, hand on his heart. He thumped his chest three times. "Tel Ilessi!" he shouted. "Tel Ilessi!"

A second voice rang from the crowd, its strength belying the frail body that carried it. Sister Noa. "Tel Ilessi! Tel Ilessi!"

Another voice took up the chant and another until it was a roar that shivered the dais.

"Tel Ilessi! Tel Ilessi! Tel Ilessi!"

Tears spilled down Aiz's cheeks as she looked out at their faces. She would not let them remain on this treacherous, lifeless spit of land. She would not let them starve here. They would find a way to their true home. Aiz would get them the Loha to do so.

They would need bigger Sails. Better ones. Cero was brilliant enough to engineer them. Aiz would reach a hand to the Empire for aid, and if they didn't reach back, she would force them to give her Loha with her newfound power.

Div had brought her people here a millennium ago. Now their Tel Ilessi would take them home.

"Gather the clerics," Aiz said to Dovan. "I would speak to them. And you—" She turned to the Triarchs. "Call up the leaders of the Hawk clans. I wish them to know the future I see. Are there any Ankanese in the city? Any seers?"

Triarch Ghaz was the quickest to nod. "Ambassador Danil and his retinue."

"Tell the ambassador that the true Tel Ilessi wishes to speak with Dolbra." Aiz thought of everything the woman had told her, the earnestness of her narrow face as she spoke. "We will need outside allies in this effort, and she has aided me once before. I believe she will again."

"Tel Ilessi?"

Noa's voice was so timid that Aiz almost didn't recognize it. But when she turned, her dear friend was making her slow way up the dais stairs, Olnas at her side.

Aiz enveloped them both in a hug, breathing in the familiar wet-wool scent of them.

"I didn't know if I'd ever see you again," she whispered. "I feared—"

"Our little Aiz, the Tel Ilessi!" Olnas wept freely, as if witnessing a miracle. "How, child? How did this—"

"Don't pester her with questions, love!" Noa batted Olnas away. "Let me look at you, my girl—"

Her wrinkled old face was full of affection when she took Aiz's cheeks in her hands. But her smile faded the longer she looked, and after a moment, she dropped her arms.

And took a step back.

"Aiz," she said quietly. "What has this cost you?"

In that moment, Aiz could have said a dozen things. She could have lied. She could have ignored Noa's question entirely. But she'd lied for months. Now, facing the woman who was like a mother to her, the truth was all she had.

"Too much, Sister," she said. "But it's too late to take it back now."

Cero appeared then, openly circumspect. He would have questions, Aiz knew. More than anyone else, he would prod her about the source of Mother Div's power. But she would deal with that later. Now she must think only of what was next for her people. Not questions Cero would have. Not the shadow of the little boy who helped her discover Mother Div. Not the Kegari children who'd died moments ago to feed Mother Div's need. Not Noa seeing something no one else saw, the rot at Aiz's core.

But even as Aiz tried to push away her disquiet, one word that Mother Div had uttered gnawed at her.

Your people need a leader.

Not *our*.

Your.

The images faded, and Quil returned to the war camp, to the Tel Ilessi pacing before him, still absorbed in whatever paltry excuses she was making for herself.

Strange that the whole world still existed outside this tent when everything he believed had been shattered. Quil felt apart from himself, as if watching from above, because the horror of being in his body and experiencing this betrayal was too staggering.

The memory told Quil all he needed to know. Ilar—or Aiz—was telling the truth. She was possessed by no demon other than her own ambition. She'd stood by as the creature she'd bound herself to—Mother Div—murdered Ruh and countless others. She'd bartered her humanity for power.

Ruh! Sweet, trusting Ruh who had tried to *help* Aiz. Quil's eyes went hot as he remembered Elias's broken sobs when Quil told him his son was gone. Laia's keening. Sufiyan's silence. All because of this . . . *thing* standing in front of him, feeling sorry for herself.

She might wear Ilar's skin, but she wasn't Ilar anymore. She'd never been Ilar. She'd never loved Quil, not truly. And it wasn't just her betrayal Quil reeled from. The Ankanese had been allied with Kegar all this time. Quil recognized the seer in Aiz's memory the moment she thought of the woman's face. Ambassador Ifalu—supposed friend to the Martials. Skies only knew how much damage she'd caused.

A crawling, full-body disgust gripped Quil. He'd been such a fool. Skies, everything he'd told her about Navium and Antium and Serra. About his aunt. About the drums and the Masks. Aunt Hel thought there was a spy among them. But it had been him. He hadn't even known it.

His chest twisted as he grieved again, not just for the girl who died in that terrible chamber, but for the boy he'd been, naive and starry-eyed enough to believe she was who she claimed to be. For Ruh, who had trusted them all, not knowing the fiend they'd allowed in their midst.

But now Quil knew. And he didn't have time for questions or stunned disbelief or even horror. That instinct bred into him from birth told him he'd have one chance to kill her. And it would only work if her guard was down.

So, Quil made himself look at the Tel Ilessi, listen—and wait.

38
Aiz

Standing in the war camp, surrounded by her army, the memory of Tiral's death seemed so long ago. Now Aiz observed Quil, weaponless and powerless, and her heart ached. He'd been kind to her. Loved her. If not for him, she would have known nothing of Loha or the Empire.

Aiz was not indifferent. Even now, she wished to touch him. To seek comfort in his arms.

Get what you need, Tel Ilessi, she told herself. *Forget the rest.*

"I have a holy mission to save my people, Quil." Aiz traced the *D* carved into her hand. "There are hundreds of thousands of Kegari, but there used to be millions. Long ago, we sent emissaries all over. When we offered our Sails to trade, we were told they were worthless, because only we could call the wind. When we offered our engines, the Mehbahnese took our secrets and gave us little in return. The only country that aided us is Ankana, but we cannot rely on their kindness forever.

"I'm not a fool. I know that raiding our neighbors will not sustain us. But if we go to our homeland across the sea, we can support ourselves. This is the heart of my holy task—we call it the Return."

"How *holy* can your task be if it requires the destruction of another land?"

"You haven't seen your people starve." Aiz craved understanding the way Div craved hearts. "You haven't watched children scream as their parents are conscripted, and then die in the gutter of cold and hunger."

"No." Quil met her gaze calmly. Too calmly. "But I have seen them begging for mercy while your army dropped bombs on them and cut them down."

"With good reason! For my people to return home, we need Loha to power our Sails. Enough to transport everyone. The Empire has it—the living metal your Masks wear on their faces. I tried to trade for it. I sent messages to the Empress through Ankana, but she refused to negotiate with us."

"There are other ways to make a life," Quil said. "Other places you could go."

Aiz was fascinated at how he battled his rage so that reason might prevail. Something about it made her sad—and disappointed. Even now, he sought calm. Control.

"Are you attempting to treat with me? We've scattered your population. Destroyed your cities. Aren't you angry?"

"My people are dying. Of course I'm angry. But anger won't help us reach an agreement—"

"If your aunt had traded with us, everything would be different. I offered to show your people how we manipulate the Loha—you hardly understand how to use it!" Aiz's blood boiled thinking about the patronizing tone of the Empress's letters. "She claimed to want a marriage alliance—offering you up like a lamb to the slaughter. All the while, she was spying on us and likely hiding your stores of Loha—"

"There *are* no stores of Loha," Quil said. "We only have the masks our soldiers wear. When one dies, the mask releases and is given to the next. There is no way to give it to you without murdering our own troops."

Aiz could feel the loathing rolling off Quil. She'd told him about Mother Div so he would understand. But it'd only made him hate her more.

"Is this Return you speak of worth the lives of Kegar's children?" Quil asked. "Is it worth their hearts?"

Aiz stilled. She hadn't told Quil of Div's price. "How did—"

"Answer the question, Tel Ilessi. Are your children's hearts worth the power that monster is feeding you?"

"I—I didn't mean for them to—"

"To die for your cause?" At her dismay, Quil shook his head in disgust. "When you sacrifice other people's children on the altar of your ambition, it's only a matter of time before you'll be willing to sacrifice your own. That's how evil works, Aiz."

"I had to bend the Triarchs and Hawks to my will!" Aiz burst out. "I had to ensure victory in our early battles with Bula and Armaana. We needed food, Quil. The deaths of a few to save the many is not a trade any should have to make. But I made it, and I will carry that burden if it means my people have a chance at a future. Do not think I take Ruh's sacrifice lightly—"

Quil's eyes went flat and despite herself, Aiz took a step back. "You keep his name out of your mouth," he growled. "Ruh was never yours to sacrifice."

Aiz's face burned in sudden shame. There was so much she wished yet to tell Quil. Her loneliness. The hunger within her, the emptiness. Since she'd killed Tiral, that hunger had gnawed at her as if a starving rat had been let loose in her gut. Sometimes, before Mother Div fed, Aiz was so consumed with the hunger that she wanted to tear apart whoever was closest to her to make the feeling stop.

But looking at Quil now, Aiz knew she'd find no empathy. She'd been foolish to seek it out in the first place. She stood tall; the only thing the Martials respected was strength.

"I offered your aunt a chance to save both our people. I'm offering you the same. Give us the Loha and we will leave the Empire."

"We don't mine it," Quil said, jaw rigid. "We don't know where it came from. I told you that in the desert, and unlike you, I wasn't lying with every sentence I spoke."

Aiz looked down at his arms, strong and corded with muscles. She thought of how she'd once forgotten her troubles in his larch leaf eyes. She remembered the hot days and cool nights and his mouth on hers.

She wondered if this woman, Sirsha, was his lover now. If she knew *how* he loved, with his whole body.

Aiz wished they could have met under other circumstances. Her, a cleric for a strong people seeking an alliance. Him, the wise prince, open to taking knowledge and offering it.

She shook the wish away. These were the thoughts of the girl she was. Not the Tel Ilessi she'd become.

"That metal came from somewhere," Aiz said. "You will tell me. Or you will sing your secrets to my interrogators and be grateful for the tongue to do it."

Quil looked away from her, as if the sight of her disgusted him. "It was better when I thought you dead."

Aiz sighed. He was a good man. Kind and giving. Worth loving. But naive and hopeful and weak because of it.

In that moment, he lunged at her.

She'd scrambled for the wind, and his knife—*where did he get the knife?*—was a breath from her throat when she managed to slam him back into the chair so hard it splintered.

Her mind twitched, and with a suddenness that never failed to leave her gasping, hunger took over, worse than before, violent and overpowering. She could not stand it—she would die from it—

Then fullness, rich and satisfying, so pleasurable that she bit her lip so she wouldn't make a sound.

Div had fed. And Quil was nothing against Aiz's power. She immobilized him as easily as a child crushing an ant, then whipped his blade away with a rope of wind. "I regret," she said, "that we couldn't come to an agreement. Cero."

In an instant, her friend entered the tent. His wound was dressed now, and she was relieved to see the color back in his face.

"Take him to the pens. Get the interrogators working on him. I want that Loha."

Cero inclined his head before bending to whisper to her. She turned to Quil.

"News that concerns you," she said. "The city of Serra has fallen. Their anti-Sail weaponry has been destroyed."

His aunt, Aiz didn't add, had given away her position. Kegari troops only waited for Aiz's word to strike.

Quil's body went rigid, the closest thing to fear that he'd show.

"I will not see you again, Quil." She moved toward him as frustration twisted his features. But no, not frustration alone. Sadness, too. Even knowing that it was Aiz who led the attack on his people, he mourned for her.

In response, she felt only a mild regret that someone she had once cared for could be so pathetic.

Aiz swept out of the tent as Mother Div oozed up from the encampment, glutted from her most recent meal.

Mother Div didn't speak. She knew Aiz's mind now and fed her a thick rope of power. Within seconds, Aiz's skin stung from the wind lash, and the Thafwan coast was far behind her. Serra had fallen. The Empress would soon be hers to question or interrogate as she wished. Quil knew her story, tying off the last piece of her old self. She should feel confident. Grounded.

But it wasn't enough. Aiz felt off still.

Hungry.

39
Sirsha

A selfish part of Sirsha wanted nothing more than to get the hells out of the Kegari encampment. *That* Sirsha was the one who'd survived being cast out by her Kin and the hardscrabble years that came after. *That* Sirsha would forget J'yan's smoking heart and R'zwana's betrayal. She would forget the creature whose mind she'd looked into; the vastness of it, the terror.

But she couldn't run, because something else had kindled in her heart beyond survival. Her Adah coin burned; her blood called to Quil. He was here, somewhere in this camp. Hopefully presiding over the dead carcass of the Tel Ilessi. Sirsha had to find him.

She forced herself to move deliberately. Thank the skies it was dark and the Kegari were lax with both patrols and fires. One wrong step and there would be two Jaduna bodies here tonight.

Sirsha shuddered, pushing J'yan's blank face and shredded chest from her mind. *Quil. Find Quil.*

She reached out with her magic, but the earth only showed her a path to Div. *Track, hunt, bind!* The wind shoved at her, trying to push her back the way she'd come.

"Do you want me to die?" she growled at the elements. "I can't bind her! You saw us try—I'll have to go about this another way, but right now, I must find Quil. Help me, please!"

The earth and wind only impelled her more frantically back toward Mother Div's tent.

She ceased using her magic and ran, searching for any sign of the Tel Ilessi. A flag, a Sail, a pack of stuffy guards. Arrogant leaders loved it when everyone knew their rank—it fed their ego. There must be *something* to indicate where the bastard was.

Quil, she thought. *Where's Quil?* A chant. A lifeline to keep another, far more terrifying question at bay:

What in the bleeding skies was that thing in the tent?

If it was a possessed spirit, it was the most powerful one Sirsha had ever encountered. But she'd hunted ghosts before, and her magic didn't warp the way it had with Div. Yet J'yan's eyes turned white before he died, a sure sign of contact with the spirit world. Sirsha's had too, the two times she'd gotten close to the creature. Not to mention the fact that it reeked of rotted earth.

Did it matter what it was? She couldn't kill it. She couldn't even bind the damned thing. She couldn't carry out this mission. Panic swept through her.

Hunt it, the elements whispered, insistent. Merciless. *You must hunt it.*

Unless Elias released her from her vow, the oath would slowly take control of her until it was all she could think about. Until she would throw herself at the monster—and die—rather than see the vow go unfulfilled.

Damn Elias and damn Div, too. Sirsha cursed the day she'd made that vow. She cursed herself for assuming Elias was another client with an easy job.

"Enough," she muttered. The vow was binding until Elias broke it. When she got to Ankana, she'd take the first ship to the Empire and find him. She'd make him break the oath. As one, the wind, earth, and even water hissed at the thought, pushing her back toward Div.

Skies, it was like having three bossy older sisters. Unlike R'z, the elements weren't trying to kill her—yet—so she ignored them, stepping behind a large mess tent as a knot of people passed.

Most were soldiers in worn gear, but one was different. Small and thin, with short brown hair that framed a pretty face. Sirsha stared at her from the shadows, feeling as if she should know her.

The earth cringed from the girl and the wind gave way to her, bending to her will with deep reluctance. Mother Div rose like a miasma from her tent and followed the girl at a distance. Instantly, Sirsha recognized the girl's spoor.

This was the Tel Ilessi.

Alive. And there was no sign of Quil. *Bleeding, burning skies.* If Quil had gotten himself killed, she'd drag his body to the Cloud Forest and demand a Songma, a spirit Jaduna, rustle up his ghost so she could shout at him.

The Tel Ilessi drew closer. Sirsha was no Deshma, like J'yan. She was a tracker with solid knife skills and a penchant for survival. That instinct kicked in now, and she eased into the shadows of the tent.

Power bulged malignantly from the woman—more power than Sirsha had ever felt. More than any one person should have.

The Tel Ilessi disappeared toward the airfield, Div oozing after, taking her misshapen darkness with her.

Hunt! the elements screamed.

Piss off, she hissed back. She couldn't bind that thing yet. And for now, the oath coin didn't control her. She wouldn't kill herself for it.

When Sirsha was certain the woman and her monstrous creature were gone, she stepped away from the tent—and straight into a blade of a human.

"Ah. The prince's little friend," the man said. She recognized his voice and the halo of power crackling around him. This was the fellow she *thought* was the Tel Ilessi. His nodded in satisfaction at the sight of her. "Just who I was looking for."

The man—someone called him Cero—pulled her to the east side of the camp. His guards, one bearded, one not, clapped her in manacles. They leered at her, grabbing handfuls of her body like the pigs they were. Sirsha attempted to shake them off, but they only laughed, and didn't stop until Cero barked an order at them.

She let her hate bubble up in her glare. She'd enjoy knifing them in the guts when she and Quil escaped.

Cero shooed the guards away as they approached a large, flag-festooned tent. Once inside, Sirsha's knees went weak in relief. Quil was within—chained, gagged, and surrounded by guards—but alive. Through their Adah coin, Sirsha felt joy flood him at the sight of her.

"Ivashk," Cero said to the soldiers, who promptly exited the tent, leaving him alone with Quil and Sirsha.

Apparently, this Kegari wasn't as smart as he was pretty.

Almost as soon as she thought it, the air around her tightened, holding her in place so she couldn't so much as twitch a pinkie.

Cero ungagged Quil. "Can't have you trying to escape. Not before you answer my questions, anyway."

"I thought you had interrogators for that." Quil rolled his shoulders, voice dangerously flat. "I was looking forward to running rings around them."

To Sirsha's surprise, Cero offered Quil a wry smile. "I was looking forward to hearing how badly they failed," he said. "Alas, no interrogators for you. Just me and the wind."

The air around them burned hotter—almost painful, but not quite. A warning.

Though not one Sirsha planned on heeding. Cero was powerful. But she could bind him. She began to gather her power.

"If this is about the Loha—" Quil said, but Cero shook his head.

"I know that if we want the Loha, we will have to destroy your Empire and assassinate the Masks one by one," Cero said. "Even that will not be enough, for the Tel Ilessi wishes us to return to our homeland across the sea." He didn't sound particularly happy about that fact. "I do hate war. I hate what it brings out in people. But there's something else I hate more. Witnessing the manipulation of my oldest friend."

Sirsha, focused almost entirely on her binding, paused in her efforts as Cero turned to her.

"This creature that calls itself Mother Div," he said. "You've tangled with it. Is it the Holy Cleric's spirit, or some other devilry?"

Sirsha couldn't have been more surprised if he'd pulled a lute from his bum and begun his questioning in verse.

"I'll tell you, pretty boy." Sirsha released her magic. Perhaps he could share something useful about Div. "But I need a bit more information than that."

"Aiz, our Tel Ilessi—your prince here knew her as Ilar—she stole a book more than a year ago," Cero said.

Sirsha's jaw dropped at the revelation. "Wait—the Tel Ilessi—and Ilar—and Aiz—"

"Are the same person, yes," Cero said. "Keep up. Aiz gave me the book to destroy at one point, but the damned thing wouldn't burn. I think it altered her mind. The—the things she's done—"

"The things you've let her get away with," Quil growled. "Is that what you meant?"

Cero's jaw stiffened. "Aiz said the book led her to free Mother Div, Kegar's holiest cleric," he went on quickly. "She says Div's spirit gives her power. But it feeds on children for that power. She has joined with this . . . thing. Whatever it is. You're a Jaduna. Can you free Aiz of the bond between them?"

"Yes." Sirsha didn't consider it a lie, exactly. More like an aspiration she hadn't yet made into a reality. "I'd need to get out of here. Speak to one of my contacts in Jibaut."

Cero huffed in frustration.

"You mean the bookseller? He read the book long before Aiz did, and is in thrall to this creature masquerading as Mother Div, like Aiz. There's an Ankanese seer who read it as well. When I asked them about it, neither could speak of it without going pale and sick."

You think you understand what you're dealing with, Kade had said. *But you don't.*

"Whoever wrote that book is evil. Whatever lives inside its pages *used* Aiz. It wants something. I need to know what the hells it wants. Because it isn't to help our people. All it has done is kill our young. Feed on us."

"I've heard of such magic," Sirsha said, though she had to scrape at the edges of her brain to remember. Some bleeding boring lesson that D'rudo had droned on about a decade ago. "My mother is the strongest living Inashi. She can bind it—whatever it is. But I'd need to get a message to her. Can't do that from inside a Kegari camp." She looked pointedly at her manacles.

Cero gave her a level stare. "If I wish to keep my heart in my chest," he said, "then I can't set you free. I can, however, leave the tent." He glanced at Quil, mockery creeping into his expression. "I assume for a mighty prince of the Martials, a few seconds will be enough."

Quil offered the barest nod. Cero stared at him a moment longer before turning and walking out. Two Kegari—the same ones who manacled Sirsha—entered the tent a second later, grinning. A woman joined the men, glanced between Sirsha and Quil, and commented. Whatever she said made the bearded guard chortle.

From across the tent, Quil watched, his expression murderous.

The beardless guard picked up Quil's scim from a pile of weapons beside the tent entrance and pretended to pick his teeth with it. Then he said something to Quil in Kegari that Sirsha was relatively sure amounted to "My sword is bigger than yours."

The beardless man wandered closer to Quil, spitting at him, his ridiculous grin growing wider when the globule landed on Quil's armor.

Quil smiled back.

Then his manacles clanked to the ground. He'd picked the lock—of course he had. He grabbed the beardless Kegari with one big hand and slammed the man's head so hard against the wooden post holding up the tent that the entire structure shook. The guard oozed to the ground.

The bearded guard was already out the door, screaming for help, while the woman called up the wind. Still bound, Sirsha lashed out with a binding, suppressing the hag's magic so quickly that she was still staring at her hands in mystification when Quil put a throwing knife through her gut.

The prince snatched up his scim and pushed something into Sirsha's hands as he strode past. Her hairpins.

"*That's* where they've been this whole time?"

"I grabbed them at the cabin," he said. "The morning after you admitted you've been lusting after me since the moment you saw me."

"I had *not* been lusting after you!"

"Your body said different, Jaduna."

The alarm went up, and a group of Kegari poured into the tent. Sirsha picked the locks on her manacles, only for a soldier to knock her to the dirt floor. She kicked him in the groin, stabbed him while he squealed, then rolled to her feet.

"I want them back!" Quil called as he fought off four Kegari at once. "The pins."

She could not *believe* they were having this conversation. She snatched up a knife and tore a rip in the eastern side of the tent. "Why are you obsessed with my pins?"

"I like how annoyed you look when you can't find them." He punched a Kegari coming at him, knocking him out cold. "It's sweet."

"*Sweet?*"

Quil didn't respond, as he was busy tearing through the newest wave of Kegari coming at him. Sirsha would have thought there were too many, but she'd seen him fight. She popped her head out into the dark, searching through the wagons and fires and shouting soldiers for an escape route along the slopes encircling the camp.

There—a path of rock and dirt that curved up the edge of the bowl thirty yards away. The earth rumbled, and a distant explosion sent a plume of dust into the sky. R'zwana, likely creating a distraction so she could escape. As most of the Kegari outside the tent turned toward the sound, Sirsha ran back to grab Quil's blood-slick hand and drag him from the fight.

A few of the Kegari shoved through the tear in the tent after them, shouting a warning to their fellows, but another explosion knocked them—and Quil—off their feet.

"Get *up*, Martial!" Sirsha roared, half dragging him. They could fade into the dark if they could just get out of sight.

"Where are your people?" he asked. "Did you—"

"We couldn't bind it," Sirsha said as they reached the hill and staggered up through the long coastal grasses. "And J'yan. He—he—"

Distantly, the ocean crashed against the rocks of the Thafwan coast. The first time Sirsha saw the sea, she was eight, J'yan was by her side, and they'd crashed into the waves for a whole day, delighted at a playmate that never tired of them.

Later, later, grieve him later. Right now, it was anger she needed—at R'zwana and Div and the bleeding Tel Ilessi. "J'yan's dead," Sirsha said. "I'll tell you the rest as we go—the horses are west of us. We should head north, cut across the airfield."

They half crawled, half climbed the path, silent and careful as stalking wolves. Slowly, any sign of pursuit began to fade—helped, no doubt by the explosions in the camp. For once, R'zwana had done something useful.

"All that for bleeding nothing," Sirsha panted as they finally reached the horses. "Div is unbound. The Tel Ilessi is alive—and she's . . . Ilar?"

"I'll explain everything." Quil took Sirsha's waist and swung her up onto the saddle. "But before I do, there's something you should know about me. Something I should have told you a while ago."

All his emotions bled through their oath coin—love, relief, fury, worry. And something else, too. *Magic!*

"You—you—" She *knew* she had felt something back when they'd ambushed the Kegari pilots! "*Magic*, prince? What in the hells? And you were accusing *me* of keeping secrets?"

He sighed and swung up onto his horse. "Shout at me later," he said. "For now, let's get the bleeding hells out of here."

40
Cero

Cero circled the cratered, smoking city of Serra thrice before landing. Even from the updrafts, the stench of death curdled the air.

He should have landed an hour before, but Aiz awaited him and Cero didn't relish telling her that the Martial crown prince had escaped.

Quil Farrar had been nothing like Cero expected. Aiz had described a soft, gentle boy, docile and naive as a pampered pup.

She'd never excelled at reading people. The Quil Farrar who tore through the side of the Tel Ilessi's tent with murder in his eyes was a man vibrating with wrath and starved for vengeance. Nothing gentle about him. The same went for his Jaduna companion.

Just as well. It would take a sharp blade and cunning mind to sunder Aiz from Mother Div.

It wasn't a thought Cero expected to have. Especially about the girl he'd loved since he understood what love was. But then, nothing in the past year had gone the way he'd thought it would.

The day Aiz returned to the capital, Cero's heart was riven in two: joy at seeing her, dismay that she'd returned to the wretchedness of Kegar. After the miracle of her victory over Tiral, Cero wondered if the stories she'd believed as a child had been true. Perhaps he was the fool for not having faith when everyone around him bled the Nine Sacred Tales.

But a few days after Tiral's death, Noa had come to Cero's quarters at the Aerie.

"There are four slaughtered children in Dafra slum," she'd whispered, as if terrified that the murderer, whoever it was, would kill her, too. "And something is wrong with Aiz . . ."

Soon, there were more dead children. Their deaths always corresponded with an especially spectacular display of Aiz's power. The windstorm she'd unleashed in Mehbahn. The highborn Hawk assassins she'd crushed a month after returning to Kegar.

For months, neither Cero nor Noa made the connection. And then, one day, they did.

It took them weeks to broach the subject with Aiz. They needn't have tiptoed around it.

Mother Div honors the children by choosing them as sacrifices, she'd said. *Do not diminish their martyrdom simply because you do not understand.*

What tripe. Those poor children didn't choose to die. Mother Div—or whatever it was that fed Aiz power—inflicted it on them.

As Cero landed at Serra's central airfield—a former market square—he pondered leaving for good. He had Loha. He spoke fluent Ankanese. His magic could take him wherever he wished to go.

Then he caught sight of Aiz approaching and his chest twisted at her small shoulders held so rigidly, like she was a puppet with strings forever taut. *That's why you don't go*, he thought irritably. *Because you're stupidly still hoping you can save her from whatever she's become.*

Could he save himself? Doubtful. He'd designed massive, troop-bearing aircraft for Aiz, created Loha weapons unlike anything the Kegari had used before, and streamlined the building of the Sails. He helped draw up an attack plan based on everything Aiz had learned from Quil. He hadn't dropped the bombs, but he might as well have.

He was as responsible as Aiz for every dead Martial. He was guilty. They all were, everyone who'd been too shocked or scared or cowardly to tell Aiz that her campaign of terror had to end.

"Triarch Ghaz's troops have the Empress's compound surrounded and a prison cell ready," Aiz said as she approached. He shelved any thoughts of telling her about Quil—she'd be in a better mood after the Empress's capture.

"Better be a lot of guards," Cero muttered. Helene Aquilla held off an army of Karkauns almost entirely alone. She wasn't Empress of the Martials for nothing.

"We don't need guards." Aiz straightened, and Cero wished to the Spires that her confidence had come to her because of anything other than the demon she'd linked herself to. "Mother Div is with us, and our cause is righteous. Remember why we are here, Cero. Not to cause suffering, but to save our people. To take them home. If the Empress had cooperated, none of this would have been necessary."

Surely someone who loves her people with such passion is redeemable. Almost the moment he thought it, Cero scoffed. "For the people" was a blood-soaked shield brandished by tyrants everywhere.

Aiz was no different.

Cero felt a chill. Mother Div must be near. She never showed herself around Cero, but the creature's fascination with him felt like the probing flicker of a serpent's tongue. He suppressed a shudder.

"Right," he said. "Let's get this over with."

Triarch Ghaz—who Cero trusted about as much as a broken compass—awaited them at the pilots' barracks. Within an hour, the three of them watched as the Triarch's troops surged into the Empress's compound.

Cero almost hoped the woman wouldn't be there. The more he'd learned about her, the more he'd come to respect someone who had lost everything and survived anyway.

Alas, Triarch Ghaz confirmed that the Empress was within. Aiz tore the roof off her compound, shredded the outer walls with her wind, and still, the Empress fought Triarch Ghaz's soldiers. Would have won, too, for she was cunning and preternaturally skilled at predicting her opponent's next move.

But she wasn't Aiz. The Tel Ilessi eventually pinned the woman to the floor with her wind, and the Triarch's soldiers clapped heavy iron manacles on her hands and feet, relieving her of her weapons.

Aiz gave a speech to the assembled soldiers—something stirring, no doubt. Cero didn't listen.

Instead, he watched the Empress—sagging between two guards, seemingly defeated. He almost missed the way her mouth quirked behind the mass of silver-blond hair in her face. Not quite a smile. It was too quick. But not far off.

Cero considered informing Aiz that this woman was far more dangerous than any of them were prepared for.

Perhaps if she still *had* been Aiz, he'd have told her. But as he watched her yank the Empress's head back and hiss something into her ear, Cero realized the girl he'd grown up with, the one he'd loved—she was gone. Not dead, perhaps. But in a deep, dark well, asleep. Cero did not know how to wake her.

But he knew of one person who might.

41
Aiz

Stone walls rose around Aiz, and she was reminded of the Tohr. Of all the places in the Empire, she hated the feel of this place the most. *Blackcliff*, it was called, built of stygian granite, along cliffs that dropped straight down into an unending stretch of desert.

Aiz hoped to find Loha here. To transfer thousands of Kegari over the seas, they needed a great deal of it. And this was, after all, where the Masks were trained.

But Blackcliff was stripped before it was abandoned. The Kegari didn't find so much as an arrowhead, let alone a cache of Loha.

Still, the place was useful—primarily because its dungeons were the most secure in the city.

"Holy Tel Ilessi." Aiz turned to find Triarch Ghaz making his way across the courtyard, flanked by soldiers from his clan. The moon painted his skin a wan, milky blue.

Ghaz knelt and thumped his heart thrice. He and the other Triarchs still chafed against her authority. She'd noticed small defiances, recently. Oona calling her Aiz instead of Tel Ilessi. Hiwa setting his clan up in a large villa without permission. Ghaz torturing captured Martials for information.

Though she let the last one go. It had, after all, netted her the Empress.

After Ghaz knelt long enough to know he'd displeased Aiz, she gestured him up.

"The Empress is ready for your interrogation," Ghaz said. "We have two guards stationed in the room, and four outside. And she's been . . . prepared. I believe she will talk."

Aiz's fingers twitched, and she considered calling Div to her. But the cleric was far away, seeking sustenance after assisting with an attack on a Tribal city this morning.

"I would ask you one thing, Tel Ilessi," Ghaz said as they walked through an arched stone hallway. "Many of our people have found the Empire's lands to be to our liking. Some speak of remaining here. Finding a new homeland amid the fertile fields north of this desert. I thought—"

Aiz shook her head. "The Empire is cowed because of our bombs. Already their generals plot a return. If we stay, we will face decades of insurgency. More importantly"—her voice grew strident—"we are not meant to remain here, Triarch Ghaz. The spirit of Mother Div speaks to me because I vowed to return us to our homeland. This is my holy mission, and I won't abandon it."

"Of course, Tel Ilessi. I only wished to inform you of the people's sentiments."

Aiz held his gaze for a few seconds so he could see her resolve. Then she squared her shoulders. "Take me to the prisoner."

Triarch Ghaz led her down a set of steps and into a dank hallway underground. They passed old, smoky pitch torches that barely lit the space around them, and crumbling stairwells. Spiders and rats skittered in the dark, and somewhere, water dripped.

Aiz pulled at the neck of her scaled armor, feeling stifled. They soon arrived at a low, narrow door. Within, chains clanked and shifted.

Aiz felt for Div—still far away. She shrugged off her unease. She did not need Div's aid. Nor did she want to listen to the cleric's lecturing. Div always had an opinion on how to do things, and of late, Aiz didn't usually agree.

"I will accompany you," Ghaz said. "In case she—"

"I caught her, Ghaz," Aiz said. "I'll meet her alone." She nodded to the guards, who opened the door for her.

Once inside, she found herself face-to-face with the Empress of the Martials.

Empress Helene Aquilla didn't have the look of a broken monarch, despite presiding over a broken empire. She'd been stripped of her armor and wore a torn shift, her scars clearly showing. She sat cross-legged with her manacled hands in her lap. Her hair looked freshly braided. If not for the bruises and cuts on her body and the wrath pulsing in her glare, Aiz wouldn't have known she'd survived a Kegari interrogation.

But that wasn't what stole the words from Aiz's lips. It was how much she looked like Quil.

When she'd captured the Empress, Aiz hadn't noticed the resemblance. But now she saw that, though Quil's hair fell in dark waves and Helene's was silvery blond, they both had the same high cheekbones and mouth, with a top lip fuller than the bottom. They even had the same sprinkling of freckles across their noses. Aiz could be looking at Quil's mother if she didn't know that his mother had died.

Even without that, all she had to do was meet the Empress's eyes to know this was Quil's kin; they looked at her with the same implacable hostility.

Get what you need, Aiz reminded herself. *Forget the rest.*

"I've been wanting to meet you for months," Aiz said. "Since Quil first told me about you in the desert."

The Empress said nothing.

Aiz kept well away from her. Being in a room with this woman felt like being trapped with a storm.

The Empress watched Aiz pace, face expressionless. Aiz searched her skin for the scars that marked where her mask had been before she'd torn it off. Quil had told Aiz that his aunt considered the scars a mark of strength.

"I don't expect you'll answer my questions. I will have to pry answers from you, I think. But like me, you are the leader of a nation. Like me, you had to fight to get there. Out of respect, I will ask before I take. Is it possible to remove the masks from your soldier's faces without killing them? As you removed your own twenty years ago?"

The Empress remained silent.

"We know that if we cut your Masks' heads off," Aiz said, "the metal releases. I have done this myself. But I would like the violence between our people to end. I'd like to take the metal without killing anyone."

The Empress blinked.

"I saw Quil," Aiz said. The Empress tried to retain her stoicism, but a twitch in her jaw gave her away. Triumph surged through Aiz's blood. "I spoke with him. I told him everything. And would you believe, he sat there and listened. Didn't even try to kill me, at first. He tried to treat with me. I wonder if that makes you ashamed?

"I told him that if we could get the Loha, we would leave," Aiz went on. "We don't want to stay here, Empress. This isn't our home."

The Empress looked more interested now. The hate had faded into cold calculation.

"I have a holy mission. To return my people to our homeland. We'd leave tomorrow—if only you told me where your Loha is. I don't want to hurt you anymore. I cared deeply for Quil—"

The Empress moved so fast that at first Aiz didn't understand what was happening. One moment, she was five feet from the woman. The next, Aiz was on her back, unable to speak because of the vise around her neck. The Empress's hand.

"That is the third time you have invoked the name of my nephew and heir." The Empress kept her voice low so the guards wouldn't hear her, but somehow that made her more terrifying.

"Three times too many," she said. "Quil listened to you because he loved you, once. Perhaps he thought that somewhere in here"—

she shook Aiz—"there might be a beating heart, or at the very least, a functioning brain. Someone who understood that we cannot mine Loha, and thus call off her sky-pigs so that fewer innocents died. He tried to treat with you because he loves his people. That doesn't make him weak. It makes him a better leader than you could hope to be."

Aiz couldn't breathe. White spots bloomed at the edges of her vision, and she clawed at the Empress's arm. She screamed for the wind in her mind, relishing the thought of tearing the Empress's head from her body in retaliation for this indignity.

But the wind did not come.

"You think because you spent a few months with my family that you know us," the Empress said. "You think we're soft because we have so much. But that only gives us more to fight for. Know this, *Tel Ilessi*. The only reason that you caught me is because I let you." The woman smiled, a knife's blade shining in the dark.

Now, finally, Aiz heard Helene's history in her voice. All that she'd lost and given and taken and sacrificed for her people.

And Aiz knew she had made a grave mistake in thinking the Empress was beaten.

"I wanted to meet you too, sky-rat." Helene twisted Aiz's head back to gaze upon her, hatred seeping from every pore. "I wanted to look into your face when the light died. Did you really think you could kill Ruhyan"—her voice cracked—"our beautiful Ruhyan, and his family wouldn't take their vengeance?"

Desperately Aiz reached for the link in her mind. *Div. Help.*

"You're nothing," the Empress said, and then fell silent, calm as she tightened her fist, looked into Aiz's eyes, and waited for her to die.

Div! Please!

She screamed it in her mind, and suddenly power flooded her, as if Div was right here instead of far away, feeding. Aiz's magic exploded out of her in an uncontrolled burst the likes of which she hadn't seen since before she was tossed in the Tohr. The walls of the dungeon shook, cracks spiderwebbing across them. The Empress flew back, skidding along the floor, but was on her feet almost instantly.

Aiz used another whip of wind to shove her away, but she needed more from Div. The door splintered open, and relief flooded Aiz. She expected her soldiers to sweep in, to tackle the Empress.

Instead, she saw bodies collapsed under rubble in the hallway. A huge, familiar figure entered, bloodied scims in each hand.

"You," Elias Veturius said.

Aiz threw all her power at the man, grim satisfaction filling her as she heard Elias's head hit the wall. She flitted past him, stumbling out the door and over the bodies, down the dark hallway.

She felt a sting—something hit her back. She clawed at it but couldn't feel it. She twisted the air behind her viciously, draining Div of everything she had, and bringing down the roof to block the Martials from coming after her.

By the time she reached the stairs and began crawling up them, she couldn't feel her legs anymore, and collapsed short of the top, breath wheezing out of her.

A figure crouched down next to her, glowing silver face chiding. "Next time, child," Div said, "call me before you enter a room with a Mask."

"I—I'm sorry," Aiz wheezed.

"No matter," Div said. "I'm here now. I will help you. Look at her. At the Empress. Invade her mind."

Aiz glanced back through the clouds of dust to see the Empress emerging from the rubble—escaping.

"Make an arrow of your intent," Mother Div said. "Pierce her with it. Seek the location of the Loha. It is there, inside her."

As in the desert, Aiz did not think, she simply acted. *Loha, Loha, show me the Loha.*

The Empress walked through an orchard. Rubble behind her. A house stood ahead, painted the drab colors of the desert, with palms shading it. Inside, it was bare. Abandoned. But in the center of the room, a rug, beneath the rug, a door, and inside—

Masks. More than twenty. Every last one a child.

42
Sufiyan

Ankana's capital, Burku, was a city of such awe-inspiring beauty that it was impossible for most people not to be moved by the vast arches and delicate columns, the floating bridges and geometric glass windows.

Sufiyan Veturius was unimpressed. Further, he was offended. A thousand miles north, multiple cities that were as beautiful had been reduced to rubble. And none of these rich sods knew or cared.

"We should check the Martial Embassy first," Arelia said. Sufiyan was gratified that she didn't seem much impressed by the city either. Though that might have been exhaustion. They'd ridden hard from Thafwa, and still, it had taken more than a week to reach Burku.

Sufiyan had been rubbish company. When Arelia brought up Quil, Sufiyan snapped at her. *I don't want to talk about a selfish, know-it-all princeling.*

Saying it had been satisfying. But now, after days of Arelia's silence, Sufiyan realized he had, perhaps, been a touch childish. He needed to make it up to her.

Perhaps he could ask her about aqueducts. Judging from the way she stared at Burku's, it would be a topic of great interest. And he liked listening to her talk. It was oddly soothing.

"Quil said Tas wouldn't be at the embassy," Sufiyan said. "He enjoys spending the Empress's money. We need to find the most expensive brothel in the city."

"The Bellflower," Arelia said, and at Sufiyan's raised eyebrows, she shrugged. "They have an underground fountain system that's a marvel of aquatic engineering," she said. "The Empress sent the engineering corps here to study it a year or so ago."

Despite his dislike of Burku and his general irritation at being sent off like a servant by Quil, Sufiyan found himself smiling. Arelia always managed to surprise him.

Two hours later, they approached the Bellflower. They'd cleaned up, boarded their horses, and now posed as a giddy married couple visiting the brothel on a lark. Arelia hooked her arm through Sufiyan's, and he found he was distracted by the way her fingers tightened on his wrist, the way her body pressed against his.

"Our dear friend Rano told us to ask for him by name." Sufiyan spoke down his nose to the doorman, using the fake name Quil had shared. The doorman, to Sufiyan's immense irritation, couldn't seem to lift his gaze above Arelia's bustline. "You *do* know Rano?"

"Fourth floor, northeast corner." The doorman collected their entry fee and, spotting Sufiyan's glower, averted his eyes. "The green room."

They entered to a high glass ceiling and long marbled hallways. A fountain sprawled across the central rotunda, jets of dancing water shooting from one corner of its pool to another, changing every few seconds. Sufiyan wanted to reach for the little sketch pad Quil had gotten him on his yearfall. He doodled in it here and there, but this was worth sitting down and studying for a day or two.

"The pressure system below the tiles is what allows those jets to shoot so high." Arelia's admiration was clear. "The sheer force of—" She caught herself, as she sometimes did. "Sorry."

"It's fine by me." Sufiyan glanced around, trying to figure out which way was northeast. "I wish I loved something that much. I used to, but—" He'd loved many things. Drawing. Medicine. Archery.

"You will again," Arelia said, squeezing his wrist so that he looked at her, surprised. "It will take time, is all."

Sufiyan didn't know what to say to that, so he grabbed Arelia's hand—something she didn't seem to mind—and pulled her ahead with the single-mindedness of an eager newlywed.

Laughter and other, more titillating sounds drifted out of the many rooms they passed, and Arelia craned her neck, trying to get a glimpse of whatever was going on within. Soon after leaving the fountain hall, they walked beneath a sculpture of two—or possibly three—people so closely entwined that it was difficult to figure out where one body began and another ended. Arelia stopped to stare, brow furrowed.

"Now, how would that even work—anatomically—considering that his leg is there, but hers is—"

"Now's not the time." Sufiyan's neck heated, which was ridiculous, as he was certain he had more carnal knowledge than Arelia. Yet here he was, lowering his gaze like a stuffy old grandfather. He cleared his throat. "Come back and get lessons if you're so interested."

"Hmm, I might."

He flushed at the image *that* conjured and focused on getting to the stairs.

They found Tas a few minutes later, surrounded by a bevy of half-clad companions, all laughing uproariously at something he'd said. Sufiyan wanted to shove them aside and hug the man who was like an older brother to him. He wanted to rejoice at the fact that, after so many weeks of hunting, Tas was exactly where Quil said he would be.

Except, of course, Tas was surrounded by prostitutes. And he was also spectacularly drunk.

"Bleeding hells," Sufiyan muttered. "Is he even going to recognize—"

"My dears!" Tas saw them and opened his arms. Arelia reddened, for when he stood up, he was wearing next to nothing. "You came! Oh, do excuse me, beauties." He leered at the two courtesans closest to him. "Friendship calls."

He staggered up, wrapping one arm around Sufiyan and the other around Arelia, smelling so strongly of wine that Sufiyan, who avoided alcohol, practically choked.

"About bleeding time," Tas hissed. Sufiyan got a good look at his friend's eyes—clear and bright. "Expected you weeks ago. Laugh, for skies' sake, there are watchers in these halls."

Arelia slapped Tas on the chest, giggling convincingly, and Tas swept them down a hallway and up a flight of stairs, talking about basking in the weather and devouring the food and delighting in the entertainment until finally, they entered another, simpler room. It had elegant pine furnishings and a large fireplace, but was thankfully empty of naked people.

As soon as the door shut, Tas dropped his arms and pulled on a robe, to Sufiyan's relief and Arelia's obvious disappointment.

"What the hells are you doing in a brothel?" Sufiyan asked. "I thought you were supposed to be spying. Not . . ." He waved his hand around suggestively.

"I *was* spying." Tas gave him a withering look. "I spent a month trying to get close to the harbormistress's favorite prostitute. He's a flighty one and usually only sees her. You two nearly ruined the whole thing." He took a closer look at Arelia.

"I don't think we've met," he said. "You're the engineer, right? I don't get to Navium much. Quil says you're brilliant. Didn't mention you were pretty." Tas grinned and Sufiyan struggled not to kick him.

"Probably because they're cousins," Sufiyan said icily. He'd forgotten how irritating Tas could be.

Arelia blushed and Tas laughed and held up his hands. "No need to look annoyed, little brother," he said. "I prefer lovers my own age. Now, where the hells is Quil? Sit, sit. Tell me everything."

Two hours, a meal, and a dozen arguments with Arelia later, Sufiyan had caught Tas up. The spy paced along a well-worn groove in the floor. Sufiyan wondered how much time he spent up here, doing Empress Helene's bidding.

"Your timing really couldn't have been worse," Tas finally said. "When you didn't show up a few weeks back, I assumed something went wrong and moved forward with a backup plan."

Sufiyan had known Tas his whole life. The man hadn't become a preeminent Empire spy by doing anything halfway.

"And you can't undo this plan," Sufiyan surmised. Tas shook his head and sat at his desk, pulling something from one of the drawers: a thin chain of glittering, purple-black metal.

It was oddly mesmerizing, and Sufiyan found he'd reached out to touch it without noticing. He flinched when his skin met the cold metal.

"It feels strange," Arelia said as she took the metal into her hand. "Dead."

"This metal is why I'm here," Tas said. "It's found only in Kegar and it suppresses magic."

Understanding and hope hit Sufiyan like lightning. "We need gobs of it," he said. "To bring the sky-pigs down. Tell me you have more."

"*I* don't have anything," Tas said. "The Ankanese are another matter. They deny the existence of the metal, but a source told me they're expecting a shipment soon. Didn't know when or where—"

"Thus, the wooing of the harbormistress's . . . friend," Arelia said. "Why not ask the High Seer for it? We have a treaty with Ankana. They're honor bound to aid us."

"That was supposed to be Quil's job," Tas said. "It was the entire reason the Empress sent him here. As a spy, I can't speak for the Empress. But the High Seer likes Quil. He was to ask for the metal and claim his intelligence sources confirmed its existence. He's a prince—they can't throw him out of the country for knowing things a monarch should know. I had it all worked out. But now—"

"Now you have to steal it," Sufiyan said.

"My source confirmed that the harbormistress is worked up about a shipment arriving in nine days. The dhow will bear a green flag—which means there's a seer on board. Boarding it would be an act of war. If it's traced back to the Empress—"

"There goes our treaty." Sufiyan sighed. Nothing came bleeding easy. "You can't blackmail the seer? Bribe them?"

"The Ankanese are irritatingly moral," Tas said. "Graft and blackmail carry life sentences, and I don't much like prison." He shuddered, an old memory flitting across his face. "Besides, they see the bleeding future. I don't know how to work around it."

"Their foresight is imprecise." Arelia looked out the window thoughtfully, and Sufiyan could practically hear the gears in her head turning. "It's good for large-scale threats, like wars. They're not like the jinn, who can see specifics. The seers are star-readers. They guess at the future. They might get hints of sabotage, but they won't know how, or when."

"Their guard will be down after the shipment's delivered," Sufiyan said. "Instead of stealing the ship—"

"Take the shipment." Tas pulled out a map of the Ankanese docks. "I considered that. But the shipment goes from the dhow to a barge and straight to the docks." He pointed to the map. "Then to the Vault of Seers. Once it's in, it's not coming out. The seers will have a full complement of troops escorting the metal. I've got a grouchy pirate captain who owes me a favor and you two. Even if we could take out a few hundred Ankanese soldiers, they'd chase us all the way back to the Empire."

Sufiyan examined the map of the harbor. It was far too shallow for larger dhows. Thus, the barges. Judging from the color of the ocean that he'd seen earlier, it had a sandy bottom.

"I have an idea." Sufiyan turned to Arelia. "It relates to what you said earlier—about aquatic engineering . . ."

Nine evenings later, just after sunset and with a storm soaking through his clothing and Arelia muttering beside him, Sufiyan was seriously questioning his sanity.

"This isn't going to work," Arelia said. "A hundred things could go wrong. A thousand."

"They won't," Sufiyan said, though Arelia was probably correct and Sufiyan fully expected to find himself in an Ankanese prison before the night was up.

"Ready, you two?"

Tas appeared behind them, unnaturally jaunty. He was in his element. *The madder the plan*, Sufiyan's ama used to say, *the happier he is*. The spy clapped one hand on each of their shoulders. "This is going to work," he said. "I feel it."

"What if it doesn't?" Arelia turned to Tas in a panic, rain dripping off her eyelashes. "The pulleys—I'm not sure how the storm will affect their function. I—I didn't expect these conditions—"

"Don't worry." Tas smiled. "Ankanese prisons aren't *that* bad. I hear there are windows. And not too many rats."

With that comforting pronouncement, he left, and Sufiyan found himself looking into Arelia's terrified face.

"It's going to be fine," he said.

"You don't know that!"

He took her fingers between his, mostly because she was shaking so hard that it was making *him* shake. And he needed steady hands tonight.

"But I know you. You're an incredible engineer. You were that student in the corps who annoyed everyone because you were so much smarter. Don't deny it," he said when she began protesting. "We both know it's true. You've thought this through, discussed it—" *Bleeding hells*, had she discussed it. He was seeing levers and pulleys and formulas in his dreams, she'd talked about it so much.

"Stick to the plan," he said. "I'll see you after. It will be perfect."

He squeezed her hands, and her shaking calmed, just a touch.

Ten minutes later, he was crouched amid a stack of abandoned pigeon crates on a high building overlooking the docks, his bow nocked and ready. From here, he could see everything: The long harbor and its boat slips and cranes. The unobtrusive barge at the far end of the dock, so decrepit that it looked on the verge of sinking. And the approaching Ankanese dhow, its green sails furled tight against the storm.

The sound of boots echoed through the empty streets—soldiers arriving with a wagon, tasked with escorting the shipment. Sufiyan ducked lower on the rooftop—there were more than three hundred troops down there. If they spotted him, he was done for.

Sailors poled a sturdy-looking barge out to the dhow, which rocked ponderously in the stormy seas. After an interminable amount of time, they loaded a large pallet on and rowed back.

The harbormistress herself oversaw the operation, guiding the barge into a dock, fitting a net around the pallet, and connecting it to a hook. The hook was attached to a crane via pulleys and a single rope.

A rope that was frayed. Too frayed to hold up such a heavy pallet, some might say.

The harbormistress bellowed for the crane operator to lift the pallet. It rose and swung over the barge, then over the water.

Sufiyan put his finger to the air. Tasted the windspeed, the direction.

Below, a fight spilled out of a nearby tavern; a group of rowdy pirates shouted obscenities and threw punches. The harbormistress, the soldiers, even the crane operator turned to look.

Which was when Sufiyan let his arrow fly. It sliced silently through the rope, and the pallet dropped into the ocean with an enormous splash. Cries of dismay rang out, accusations of a shoddy job by the harbormistress, the crane operator, the rope maker.

Sufiyan only heard the beginning of the chaos before he leaped to a nearby roof, and then down to the harbor streets. He pulled his cloak close, hurrying through the rain until he was a full two miles from the harbor and safely ensconced at a bustling tavern called the Pennybrush. As the dinner rush began, he booked a room with three bunks, ordered up dinner, and waited for Tas and Arelia.

After an hour, he felt his chest tighten in worry. After two, he paced, cursing to himself. By midnight, he struggled to draw breath. Tas should have been here shortly after Sufiyan. Arelia not long after that. He checked the window again and again. Nothing.

They'd been caught. Imprisoned. Killed. And he'd been lounging in this inn while the people he cared about suffered.

Just like Ruh. The thought made his body tremble, his vision blur. Ruh, his only little brother, who had amused and annoyed and enriched him in equal measure. Ruh, who had trusted him and tricked him, shoving a pillow under his blanket. Sufiyan hadn't even bothered to look carefully at his brother's bed the night he was murdered. He saw the lump, felt relief that the boy was asleep, and went back to playing cards with Tas.

Now he'd left Tas and Arelia behind. Quil and Sirsha had been gone for weeks. He'd never made up with his friend—and if he was dead—

As Sufiyan passed by the window, his blood turned to ice. Four cloaked figures approached the inn's front door. He couldn't see their faces, but through the rain he caught the glint of their armor, the shine of weapons. Footsteps pounded up the stairs.

Sufiyan drew his scim because he might be utterly useless at protecting his friends, but his parents would be broken if they lost their other son, too. The door slammed open and—

"Suf?" A familiar voice. Sufiyan stared for a long, confused moment before the figure lowered his hood.

Quil.

Sufiyan blinked, because if this was a hallucination, it was damned cruel. But his oldest friend was hugging him now, and Arelia was too. Tas closed the door and hissed at them all to keep quiet.

"The soldiers locked down the whole port," he said. "I thought they'd gotten you—"

"We only just escaped," Arelia said. "Had to hide out for hours. Then we noticed someone following us—"

"Me," Sirsha said wryly, though her voice was exhausted. "Tracking them—this one almost stuck a knife in me." She nodded to Tas.

Arelia kept talking, giddily relieved that their plan had worked. Her underwater pulleys seamlessly shifted the pallet of metal a dozen yards to a nearby dock, where Tas's pirates had loaded it onto their ship once the harbormistress left.

After a brief search, the harbormistress had dredged up the lost pallet—or something that looked a great deal like it. It was heaved out of the water and transported to the Vault of Seers.

"They'll figure it out soon," Tas said. "But the metal is long gone. We will be too. Burku's harbor is already locked down, but I have a shabka waiting at one of the coastal villages. It's a few days' ride north of here. We leave in the morning."

Sufiyan tried to take it all in, but he was struggling to understand that everything was all right. That his friends—his family—were safe.

"Breathe, Suf," Quil said in his quiet way. "We're here. We're all right."

"I'm sorry," Sufiyan said as the others talked. "Sorry I got angry at you, Quil. I—I won't again—"

Quil sighed then, and for the first time, Suf took in how awful he looked, his hair a mess, his eyes red-rimmed, his clothing, usually neat even after days on the road, askew.

"You'll get angry again, Suf," Quil said. "You'll have every right to. Especially after you hear what I have to say."

43
Sirsha

As Quil told his friends the story of what happened in the war camp—and of his own magic—Sirsha struggled to silence the voices in her mind.

The earth shifted, and a breeze scraped at the window of the room. Sirsha's ears filled with the roar of the sea. The three elements spoke as one.

Leave this place. Leave, and hunt Div.

Their voices had plagued her since she'd fled Thafwa, and grown more insistent the less she tried to think about Div. By the time she and Quil reached Burku, it was all she could do to ride in a straight line. Every part of her wanted to follow the pull of her vow out of the city.

A pull that would only grow stronger in the coming days, until it would supplant the need for food, water, sleep. Until it consumed her. She had weeks, at best.

She'd planned to head to Burku's docks. Get a ticket out of here, find Elias, and get him to release her from the vow. She'd pushed a blood oath before. It wasn't easy, but she could outlast it until she reached the Empire.

But a week on the road with Quil made it clear he was still planning on hunting the Tel Ilessi. And not just because of the carnage she'd unleashed on the Empire. That bitch had betrayed Quil and killed Sufiyan's little brother. For Quil it was personal. He wouldn't stop until she was dead.

Which created a problem for Sirsha.

Quil couldn't kill the Tel Ilessi while Mother Div lived. That creature fed the Tel Ilessi too much power. Div would kill Quil.

Unless Sirsha killed Div first.

"What do you mean you have *magic*?" Sufiyan practically shouted, and Sirsha grimaced at the sadness and shame she felt through Quil's oath coin. He'd nearly broken down when he'd told Sufiyan of the Tel Ilessi's true identity. To their credit, Quil's friends had shown wrath for that Kegari snake and empathy for Quil—Sirsha would have accepted nothing less. It wasn't Quil's fault his old lover was a lying hag.

The concealment of his magic, however, appeared to have struck a nerve.

A surge of tender exasperation swept through her. Of course, if anyone could suppress magic so even an Inashi couldn't sense it, it would be Quil. He wouldn't have wanted to burden anyone with the struggle of it. The magic also explained why he didn't have typical Martial suspicion of magic-users. Why it felt like he understood Sirsha. Had always understood her.

When he'd explained his magic, Sirsha classified him immediately. He was a Yaad. A type of magic-user so rare that Sirsha had never met one. Most had died out.

"If you do have magic," Arelia was saying, "then you should react to these—" She pulled a set of purple-black chains and manacles from her coveralls and Quil grimaced. Sirsha, barely paying attention to the conversation until that point, recoiled.

"Ikfa," she said. "You shouldn't have that!"

Tas, meanwhile, tried and failed to snatch them from Arelia. "Those were supposed to go to the Empire."

"They will, eventually," Arelia said. "But for now, we have them, and we can study them. Sirsha, I'd wondered if you'd be familiar with the metal, as a Jaduna—"

"We don't keep Ikfa," Sirsha said, pulling an ill-looking Quil away from the metal. Almost immediately, the color returned to his face. "We use magic to suppress magic. We only trust the jinn to be custodians of

Ikfa. When we find it, we give it to them. Don't tell me *that's* what you sent to the Empire—"

"We spoke of reactive forces before," Arelia said. "Is this Rajin's fifth law again? Does the metal—"

"It doesn't matter." Sirsha thanked the skies R'zwana wasn't here. Her sister's head would have exploded at the sight of so much of the hated metal. "Ikfa is dangerous to anyone with magic—"

Quil immediately perked up. "Then it will work on the Tel Ilessi," he said. "Do you think it'll work on Div?"

"I—I don't know." Sirsha hadn't considered such a thing because she'd never seen so much Ikfa at once. If it was found, it was usually no more than a thimble's worth. "I—"

Div. Hunt her. The elements possessed her. Took full control of her body. *Get up. Move. Hunt. Hunt. HUNT—*

Sirsha only realized she'd left the room when Quil grabbed her hand, pulling her from her trance.

"Sirsha." Quil had stopped her in the middle of the Pennybrush's narrow upper hall. What must he think of her, walking out in the middle of a conversation. "Are you all right?"

Sirsha didn't even consider hiding the truth. There didn't seem to be a point to doing so anymore.

"The vow I made to Elias," Sirsha said. "It's affecting my mind, Quil. I should have told you before—but I was too confident in myself. Too sure I'd catch the killer. An oath like this must be fulfilled. If it isn't, it will be the only thing I can think about—I'll be a danger to you—to everyone around me."

"I know," he said after a pause. "J'yan told me the night before he died. He thought the oath was to me—wanted me to break it." Quil looked off, face briefly murderous. "I'll have choice words for Elias the next time I see him."

"Get in line." Sirsha sighed and put a hand to her temple. "I need some air."

"Do you want company?"

Sirsha smiled, glancing over his shoulder. "Not as much as Arelia wants to know the precise internal mechanism you use to trigger your magic. Go on—I have a feeling you four have a lot to talk about. Tell her to keep that Ikfa away from you. I'll be back in a bit."

As Sirsha walked the streets of Ankana, her pack slung over her shoulder, she considered something Arelia had said of magic weeks ago. *Rajin's fifth law says that every action evokes an equal and opposite reaction.*

Sirsha learned the same concept as a child. After much pestering by Sirsha, her mother, the Raani, told her the story of the Nightbringer—the most skilled and wily of the jinn. A thousand years before, an enemy king imprisoned the jinn and stole their powers. The Nightbringer, the only one to escape the genocide, spent a millennium trying to free his people.

It was the indifference of Mauth, the Nightbringer's creator and the source of all magic, that set the jinn on his path, Sirsha's mother said. *And it was the love of Rehmat, his beloved wife, that released him from it. Sometimes, the only way to blunt the violence of twisted magic is to confront it with its opposite.*

Stars still scattered the dark sky, bright even with the streetlamps. In the north, it was late winter, but here in Ankana, it was a cool summer night, flowers and trees in bloom, the capital almost offensively beautiful.

It reminded Sirsha of the Cloud Forest. In a few months, it would be full spring there. The vines would be heavy with honeyflowers and the bees that loved them. The Raanis would bemoan the pollen staining every window of their homes in the Gandafur trees.

For Jaduna, spring and summer were the seasons of giving. Friends made daisy chains, lovers proposed, Adah oaths were celebrated. Sirsha was twenty now—an adult by Jaduna standards. This would have been the year she and J'yan had their full Adah ceremony, honoring the vow they'd made as children.

It would be weeks before R'zwana reached the Cloud Forest. Weeks before J'yan's Kin knew what happened to him. Sirsha hoped R'z told Ma about her fading magic. She hoped her sister made peace with what she'd lost.

Which might include Sirsha, if this vow—or Div—killed her.

I need more information, Sirsha told the elements. *Where can I find it?*

Hunt, the earth rumbled.

Hunt, the sea roared.

Read, the wind whispered.

The streets were empty, the stores shuttered. What the hells did the wind want her to read? A signpost?

Then she remembered she *did* have a book. *Recollections* by Rajin of Serra. She'd stolen it from Quil a few weeks ago.

Yes, the wind hissed, and Sirsha found a bench next to a lamppost and dug the battered little book out of her pack.

The old philosopher lived five centuries ago and did so love to drone on. But his insights were worth his verbosity, as long as you accepted that reading his work was like digging through horse dung for gold.

Even Jaduna instructors had a few of his books in their libraries. Most of them especially enjoyed his chapters on how the youth of his time were wastrels contributing to the destruction of society.

Sirsha had never read *Recollections*; as she flipped to a short section about Jaduna magical theory, she wished she had.

> *The Jaduna lasso their magic with emotion, using it to control an element. The emotion is most often desire—an exertion of willpower. They understand the third law—that magic cannot be destroyed, only contained or transformed.*

He waxed ecstatic for a bit about how the Jaduna eschewed the hoarding of power. Clearly, the old windbag never met R'zwana. Sirsha read on.

> *The Jaduna value the community over the individual. Humility above bluster. Service and giving above greed. Sacrifice above selfishness and magical gluttony.*

Sirsha shut the book, her mind snagging on Rajin's third law: *Magic cannot be destroyed, only contained or transformed.*

Sirsha hadn't been able to bind Div, let alone kill her. If Div couldn't be destroyed or contained, perhaps she could be transformed. Into a toadstool, perhaps. Or a particularly ugly tarantula.

Sometimes, the only way to blunt the violence of twisted magic is to confront it with its opposite.

She didn't know the source of Div's malignancy. But she'd learned enough about the types of magic extant in the world to take a guess.

All magic came from the same source. A force who was a legend whispered but unproven.

Mauth—*Death* in Old Rei. Mauth's presence was most strongly felt in the Waiting Place, where the humans and jinn unfortunate enough to be his servants passed traumatized ghosts from this world to a peaceful after, so they didn't wail everyone's ears off. Sufiyan's grandmother, the Bani al-Mauth, was one of these servants. Like the other ghost talkers, she cast the suffering and torment of the spirits into a seething dimension that abutted their own.

The Tribes called that miserable place the Sea of Suffering. Sirsha liked the Jaduna name better: Owa Khel—the Empty. A place of sallow yellow skies and haunted seas. She and J'yan told scary stories about it when they were kids, as D'rudo made them memorize entire texts on the subject.

A line from those texts came back to Sirsha: *And though the Sea of Suffering churns, ever restless, verily does Mauth preside, a bulwark against its hunger.*

Div wasn't hungry. She was *hunger*. A desire to consume that defied any sense of the ethical or moral. Pure selfishness.

Yes, the elements whispered.

"Indifference was counteracted with love," Sirsha muttered. "So, Div, with her greed, her hunger—"

Sacrifice above selfishness and magical gluttony.

Understanding was a knife twisting slowly inside her. Sirsha wanted to shout. Or perhaps slowly applaud the justice of the universe. Her actions had, after all, led to the deaths of more than a thousand innocent villagers. Intentional or not, she'd as good as killed them herself, and that sort of imbalance wouldn't be left unanswered.

Well, here it was. The answer. If Sirsha wanted to bind Div, she was going to have to sacrifice her own life to do so.

Now, the elements said as one, *you begin to understand.*

Bleeding hells. Would that she had been born a cat. Or a partridge. Something cute and fluffy that didn't have to think about things like magical laws and heartbreak.

When she returned to the inn, the dining room was empty—it was too early for the innkeeper, even. But Quil, hair still wet from the bath, leaned against the closed bar, lost in thought. He must be exhausted, but that resolve that formed his core, quiet and unshakable—she could feel it from here.

No more secrets. She needed to tell him that if they wanted Div to die, Sirsha would have to pay with her blood. He'd be a pest about it, of course, try every trick he knew to talk her out of it. But he deserved to know, not least because when she died, the oath coin would amplify his grief terribly.

Ah, the joys of Jaduna magic.

"Sirsha."

He turned to her, and the sound of her name on his lips echoed through her veins as if spoken by thunder instead of a man. Since she was a little girl, she'd always been S'rsha. That pause from deep in the throat, it was the highest honor of this world, for it meant she was a Jaduna, one of the first users of magic. Her line was long, her ancestors titans of their time. When she lost that pause—when she became *Seer-shah*, instead of S'rsha—it felt as if she'd been shoved out of her own body and into another one she cared nothing for.

But from Quil's mouth, her name felt beautiful again.

"Quil," she said. *Tell him. Tell him that you must die. That you need to say goodbye.*

But Sirsha knew he'd mull and dissect her words until he'd convinced himself there was a way out. For once, she didn't feel like a fight.

Sirsha grabbed his hand, wishing she could articulate the desire suffusing her, something more than *I need you and I wish I didn't*. They stumbled up the stairs, and any words still in Sirsha's head felt unnecessary when Quil closed the door and swept her up in his arms, lifting her effortlessly. She sighed as he backed her into the wall, kissing her as if some part of him knew they didn't have much time, as if he had to make up for everything he'd never get again.

She threaded her fingers through his hair and pulled away from his mouth to trace her lips along his jaw, his throat, smiling at the curse he uttered. He carried her to the bed, but she flipped him onto his back and caught a flash of dimple. Her heart leaped.

The lamps bathed them both in blue light, so she stripped him slowly, and almost didn't look at him, almost didn't appreciate his lean, muscled elegance, but then she made herself because, well, this was it for them, wasn't it?

"You're beautiful," she murmured. She straddled him, and pulled free her hairpins, letting her hair fall in a curtain around them. Her body craved him, craved the fullness she knew he would give her, but she fought against it and kissed him slow, the way she knew he liked.

He eased off her clothing, and slowly, so slowly, they joined, breaths shortening, his fingers almost painfully tight on her waist, golden eyes fixed on her, taking what she gave, giving all that he had in return.

"More," Sirsha gasped. "Closer."

He complied, and were these sounds coming from her, or someone else? He bit his full lip so he wouldn't give them away. These walls were thin, and it was quiet, and this was a family inn, for skies' sake, but he deserved to be able to shout when he was angry and gasp when he took his pleasure.

She leaned down and took his lips between hers so he could cry out into her, so they could cry out into each other, leaving their wanting and everything they couldn't say in each other's chests, in the chambers of their hearts.

After, when they lay next to each other, she turned to him to find him looking at her.

Their coin burned hot as she traced his face with one hand. Sirsha knew the pattern was blooming, and grief lanced through her, because if he was her Adah, her other half, then what would he do when she was gone? It would hurt—more than he could know. Not just the pain of love lost, but the sundering of a blood oath. She still felt the hole where J'yan's oath had been, years later.

But he wouldn't be alone. He had Sufiyan and Tas and Arelia. They would help him. He'd get through it.

"Sirsha." He caught her gaze and held her tight. "Your eyes look like you're saying goodbye. Come back. Be here with me."

She nodded, looking away so he wouldn't realize that she *was* saying goodbye. She just didn't have the strength to speak it aloud.

44
Quil

It was still dark when Quil left Sirsha sleeping. He kissed her forehead and slipped away, only to spot Tas sneaking out of the groom's quarters in the inn's courtyard.

Tas grinned. "I'll keep your secrets if you keep mine."

Quil chuckled. "Nice to see that some things don't change."

"All part of the job, little brother. That groom knows every guardsman in this district. If someone comes looking for us, we'll know. Where are you off to?"

"The High Seer," Quil said. "I'd like to have a few words with him about Ambassador Ifalu."

Tas nodded. "Tread carefully. The harbor's shut down and gate watches were doubled. They know someone stole the Ikfa."

A half hour later, Quil was face-to-face with the Eye of Ankana, one of the holiest men alive. But for all that High Seer Remi E'twa of Ankana painted himself as all-knowing, the look of surprise on his face when Quil entered his monkish quarters indicated an omnipotence that was more limited.

Maybe because Quil entered via one of the man's few windows, instead of through more diplomatic channels.

"Crown Prince Zacharias." Remi rose from a simple oak desk, where a pot of chamomile tea steeped. "It's a pleasure to see you again. I did not realize you were visiting Burku."

"Maybe you need better informants, High Seer Remi."

"Perhaps, crown prince." The High Seer smiled with genuine warmth, but Quil watched him warily as he pulled another mug from his cabinet. The prince took a risk being here. If the High Seer was part of the plot against the Martials, Quil could find himself imprisoned or killed. Ambassador Ifalu certainly had no qualms about murder.

The High Seer poured a mug of tea for Quil and offered it to him.

"May I express my sympathy at the suffering of your people," the High Seer said. "We were most saddened to learn—"

"Ambassador Ifalu has been feeding my people misinformation, High Seer." Quil didn't touch the tea, nor did he much feel like acknowledging the High Seer's sentiment. Better to get to the point. "She did this while pretending to be an ally and a representative of your people. Her treachery directly led to the deaths of thousands of Martials, Scholars, and Tribespeople, as well as the occupation of our homes by the Kegari."

"Ambassador Ifalu?" Remi's shock was sincere enough that Quil believed it. "Impossible. She is one of our most respected seers, crown prince. Forgive me, but you must be mistaken."

"I'm not," Quil said. The High Seer of Ankana didn't need to know about Quil's magic. "I know the ambassador as Ena Ifalu. Has she ever gone by another name? Dolbra, perhaps?"

Remi paled. "Dolbra was her daughter's name—she died at birth. Very few people knew that Ena named her. How did you come by this information?"

"Reliably." Quil considered the suspicion on the High Seer's face. He didn't believe Quil. But he hadn't thrown him out, either.

"High Seer, I have the utmost respect for you and your judgment. Last year, the Empress told me that you sought your replacement. Everyone expected you to name Ambassador Ifalu. Your councilors and advisers. Your people. The ambassador's family. Even Ena herself. But you haven't named her yet. Why?"

Remi took a sip of tea, but he held his cup so tight Quil thought the handle might shatter. "I'm not ready to step down yet."

"Your ability to read people is legendary," Quil said. "The reason you pushed for the Ankanese to open trade with the Empire was because you met the Empress. You saw who she was and who she could be. What do you see when you look at Ambassador Ifalu?"

The High Seer's teacup clattered as he placed it on its saucer.

"The ambassador has nothing to gain from allying herself with the Kegari," he said. "She would certainly not risk Ankana's relationship with the Empire. If we break our treaty with you, we also break it with the Mariners. The Tribespeople. You tell me, prince. Why would she risk such a thing?"

"Perhaps she doesn't care about the Empire or the Kegari." Quil had been mulling this over all night. "Perhaps she has another master. I have met the Kegari leader, High Seer. I have met the Tel Ilessi. Her power is immense, and dreadful. I wonder if she has allied herself with something unnatural, and if Ifalu has done the same. So again, I ask—when you look at Ifalu, what do you see?"

"Nothing," the High Seer murmured. "I see nothing. Her future is veiled. It has been for years, and though I have tried to see anything to do with her, I have failed."

"And you've told no one," Quil surmised. "Because doing so would indicate that your power was weakening, and you feared you'd be forced to step down."

"If she has betrayed your people—"

"It's not just my people," Quil said. "Yours, too. You had a shipment that was supposed to arrive in the Vault of Seers—"

"Yes," Remi said. "Mehbahnese ore engines, for our ships. I usually don't pay attention to such things, but it was stolen last night—"

"No," Quil said. "Not engines. Ikfa."

Remi recoiled as Sirsha had. "Impossible," he sputtered. "That substance is banned. And in any case, there's hardly enough of it in the world to—"

"There are mines full of it in Kegar." Quil shared what Tas had told him, for if the High Seer was in league with the Kegari, he already knew this information. "Ifalu had it shipped here. What, I wonder, would the Jaduna say to that? They are your allies too, are they not?"

Quil put his hands on the desk. "Look me in the eyes, High Seer Remi. Tell me if I lie about the ambassador's perfidy. If so, I will apologize and leave you. But after hearing what I told you, if you have even the slightest suspicion that Ifalu might have misled the Martials and betrayed her own people, I implore you to call her to you. Ferret out the truth. I'll take my leave while you do so. I will ask you for one thing, though."

Remi sighed. "You make many requests, prince."

"This one is fair. If I am right—if your ambassador is guilty as I say she is—then I need a favor."

Quil made it back to the Pennybrush a few hours later. The sun was well up and Tas, Arelia, Sirsha, and Sufiyan waited in the courtyard, packed and ready, their horses idling outside the stables.

"About bleeding time." Tas stood when Quil entered. "Don't know how the hells we're going to get out, they've closed nearly all the gates. What did the High—"

"Tas," Sirsha said, holding up a hand. "Listen."

Tas fell silent. Beyond the voices spilling from the inn's dining room, they all heard an unmistakable sound. Boots, marching in time, toward the inn.

"Did you lead the bleeding guards to us?" Tas stared at Quil, wide-eyed with incredulity. "Of all the amateur, basic—"

Before he could move on to more colorful language, soldiers poured into the courtyard. An officious-looking captain in finely tooled gold armor approached Quil without hesitation.

"Prince Zacharias of the Martial Empire," he said. "You are suspected of stealing a pallet of goods that belongs to the nation of Ankana. You will come with me to be questi—"

"We did it." Quil drew his sword and laid it down at the guards' feet, gesturing to the others "All of us. We're thieves. We confess."

45
Aiz

It took more than a week to find the children.

Not children, Aiz reminded herself as she and Cero—with whom she flew—approached Serra from the air. *They are killers. Masks.*

The little savages had, after all, booby-trapped the fields around the house they'd holed up in, deep in the Serran Mountain Range. Aiz had lost thirty soldiers before her troops even reached the dwelling, and another five inside. In the end, she'd been forced to blast the roof off with her wind and pin them one by one. Only then did the Kegari capture the Masks.

Now, under Triarch Ghaz's watchful eye, they awaited her at the pilots' barracks, gagged and heavily chained. Aiz was victorious. But she was also tired, her bones enervated from the use of so much power.

"What's taking so long?" Aiz called to Cero, who navigated their Sail through the mountains with painstaking care. She was still angry at him for losing Quil. After the Empress's escape, the news had been a terrible blow. Aiz had ordered Cero out of her sight, fearing her own anger. "We should have landed by now."

"Tel Ilessi," Cero said. "They're young. Children. Only fourteen."

"They're snakes, Cero. You saw how many of our soldiers they killed."

"Because we surrounded them. We gave them no choice."

Aiz bristled. Cero had pressed her, recently. Disdaining how Mother Div got her power. Questioning Aiz about the missing children in Kegar. Criticizing the treatment of captured prisoners.

"Those *children*," Aiz said, "are trained killing machines. We will remove their heads, and their masks, and feel no guilt in doing so."

Cero was silent the rest of the way to Serra. After a time, the city appeared below, a pocked, ruined shadow of its old self, the River Rei choked with debris. The signalers cleared them to land, and as they spiraled down to the makeshift airfield, the stench of smoke and refuse and blood choked Aiz's nostrils.

Guilt swept through her, bees beneath her skin. Ruh had loved this city. *The fountains are huge and there's an entire street of storytellers and another of kite makers, and another that sells silk in every color—*

Aiz wondered if Laia lived. If Elias and Kari and Zuriya lived. Then she realized she didn't care, really. Ruh was the only one she'd loved.

Something flickered at the edge of her vision. A flash of silver. A familiar giggle. Aiz turned as she dropped from the Sail, startled, seeking the child amid the ruins of Serra. For a second, she was certain Ruh was here.

"Tel Ilessi?"

Cero called to her, and she remembered. Ruh was dead.

"Come," she ordered Cero. "The Masks are at the barracks. It's not far."

"If you want to kill those children"—Cero stood rooted in the shadow of his Sail, fiddling with the straps on the pilot's chair—"go ahead. But I won't be a part of it."

As Sails took off and landed around them, Aiz examined her oldest friend. He was worn. He'd been by her side for months now, carrying out orders, listening to her talk about Mother Div, helping her plot the takeover of the Empire. He'd believed. But now he seemed tired. So many of her soldiers seemed tired. They needed a victory.

The Loha would give them that.

"Very well." She tried to sound reasonable. "I'll handle it myself. Why don't you take a few days away—"

"Before you murder those poor children"—Cero shoved his goggles on his head—"there's someone you need to speak to." Cero reached for Aiz's hand, tentatively, as if he thought she'd slap him away. "Don't be angry at me. You're not yourself, Aiz—"

"Tel Ilessi," she reminded him. The airfield was loud with the movement of aircraft, but that didn't mean that others couldn't hear. Respect must be maintained. "And I am more myself than I've ever been. I don't have time to—"

"Aiz, my love."

She turned to find the gnarled old figure of Sister Noa. She hadn't seen the sister in weeks—not since the war began. In Kegar, in the months of planning, Aiz grew more distant from Noa. For while High Cleric Dovan, Olnas, and the rest of the clergy looked at Aiz with apposite awe, Sister Noa only ever appeared chary. Even unfriendly at times.

"It's Tel Ilessi, Sister," Aiz said.

"Walk with me." Noa took Aiz's arm. The old woman was so frail, so small that Aiz let herself be tugged along.

Noa was silent as they reached the edge of the airfield, and began to pick their way through the quiet, rubble-strewn streets.

"So much death," Sister Noa said. "An apocalypse for these people. A genocide. I wonder if, a thousand years from now, they will think of us as their cataclysm."

"A thousand years from now, they will have all murdered each other," Aiz said, grimacing as she caught sight of a dog gnawing at something large and white in the ruins of a house. "They are a violent and warlike people, Sister Noa. In any case, it won't be any concern of ours. For we will be far away, across the sea. Home."

"Home, yes," Sister Noa murmured, slowing before what was once a large sculpture, surrounded by a fountain. The water was gray with ash now, shattered shards of clay poking out like scavenged bones. "*A fair gold and green land that was ours alone. It had at its heart a Fount of golden light, and that was the source of our magic.*" Noa smiled as she quoted the Nine Sacred Tales. "Do you know the stories of what caused the cataclysm, Aiz?"

"That isn't in the Nine Sacred Tales. Mother Div didn't mean for us to know."

"Or perhaps *Ten* Sacred Tales didn't have quite the same ring," Sister Noa said dryly. "But we do have records. Reliable ones, for Mother Div was nothing if not meticulous. The Fount, legend says, was poisoned. Tainted with evil magic. It didn't happen overnight. It was gradual, else Mother Div would not have had time to find a new homeland for her people."

Aiz tried to pull Noa from the broken fountain, but the old woman held firm.

"Our people turned on each other," Sister Noa said softly. "The tainted magic drove them mad, pitted parent against child, siblings against each other, leaders against their people. Tens of thousands died. The First City, the Home of the Fount was consumed. It was only people from the outer villages and districts whom Mother Div could save. *When humanity turns on its children*, she was rumored to say, *then you know we are lost.*"

Aiz felt a chill, thinking of what Quil had said to her at the war camp. *When you sacrifice other people's children on the altar of your ambition, it's only a matter of time before you'll be willing to sacrifice your own.*

Sister Noa turned to Aiz, and she flinched at the disappointment in the cleric's eyes.

"You are lost, Tel Ilessi. How many have died to satisfy this creature that feeds you power? And do not call her Mother Div. Our Holy Cleric would never sanction such violence. Not against the guilty, and certainly not against the innocent."

Sister Noa squeezed her hands with the same understanding she'd offered Aiz her whole life.

"Cast that thing from yourself, my girl. You can still lead us. You can still be our Tel Ilessi. But not like this."

Aiz's fury seethed low, like a carpet of fire ants. Something else surged beneath it: despair.

"Perhaps I am lost," she said. "Perhaps I did make sacrifices I didn't expect. And there—there is much that will haunt me. But if it is for my people, it is worth it. I can't turn back now, Sister, nor cast Mother Div from my mind. I will not."

"This cannot be who you are," Sister Noa pleaded. "Do you remember the question I used to ask you? What do you dream? Is it really this?" She gestured to the wreckage surrounding them. "Tell me, Aiz. Tell me what you dream."

Hunger gripped Aiz. Then satisfaction. Far away, Mother Div fed.

Aiz stared out at the destruction she'd wrought. "I dream of victory," she said. "And death."

Then she yanked her arm free from Noa and left to claim her Loha.

The young Masks knelt in the courtyard of the pilots' barracks, gagged, blindfolded, beaten. Aiz ordered their blindfolds removed. Their silver faces gleamed in the winter light.

Their hair and skin and genders ranged, but they all had the same worn, dark fatigues, the same set to their shoulders, the same defiance in their faces. As if they'd murder every Kegari they could get their hands on.

Ghaz, pacing before them, stopped when Aiz appeared and, at her order, removed the gag and blindfold of the first Mask.

The young woman looking back at her had red hair and brown eyes. Her lip curled as Aiz entered, and she spat on the courtyard's stones.

"If you're going to kill us and take our masks, get on with it," she said.

"So eager to die?"

"Eager for you to let me out of these chains so I can wrap them around your throat and watch you choke." The girl's voice was chillingly calm.

A sudden presence at her back had Aiz smiling, as did the cool rush of power filling her.

"Will you let this insolent pup speak to you so?" Div's righteous anger soothed Aiz's bruised ego. "Set your interrogators upon her. Perhaps she will know where there is more Loha."

"I'd rather take her mask, Mother Div."

The cleric considered. "Let me feed upon her," she said. "She is violent certainly, but young still, and pure."

Aiz was about to answer when a commotion on the edge of the airfield caught her attention. A Sail landed with all the grace of a wounded grouse, and a messenger stumbled from it, gasping for breath. Her hair was in disarray, her breath short with panic.

"Tel Ilessi!" She staggered toward Aiz. "An uprising in the southern part of the city. Nearly a full legion approaches. They—they just appeared. Out of nowhere! We're awaiting another arms shipment from Kegar. We don't have enough bombs to stop them. The—the Empress leads them."

"Why were we not told?" Aiz demanded. "Whose clan had watch duty?"

Ghaz had joined Aiz at the arrival of the messenger, and now he spoke. "Hiwa's."

She would kill the man herself. But now she required more power. A great deal more.

Mother Div sensed it, anticipated Aiz's need.

"A few hearts will not be enough to stop a Martial legion, daughter of Kegar," Mother Div warned. "I need more than that. If you are so deeply opposed to me taking more hearts, I can extract the power. But it requires . . . pain."

"I am ready." Aiz lifted her chin. Mother Div canted her head, teeth glinting.

"Not your pain, Aiz. Theirs." She nodded to the Masks. There was a devilish eagerness to Div. A surging excitement Aiz couldn't ignore.

"You mean to torture them."

"Yes. I would pull pain from these Masks," Div said, and at Aiz's look of disquiet, she held up a hand. "It is not something I will relish, child. That is why I have never mentioned it before."

"Tel Ilessi." Triarch Hiwa appeared from the rubble, accompanied by two dozen of his fighters. The panic on his face was embarrassing to witness. Aiz did not understand how this weaselly creature could be a descendant of Mother Div.

"There is a full Martial legion—"

"I am aware," Aiz said. "Tell Triarch Oona to lead her archers against them. Triarch Hiwa, you will lead the ground assault."

"I— But, Tel Ilessi," Hiwa spluttered. "We will be slaughtered."

"By the Martials or by my hand." Aiz brought her wind to bear, pressing on the Triarch's windpipe. "I'd say you'd have a better chance of surviving them."

She released him and he glared at her, gathering his wind. She knew he wouldn't dare to use it. He was too weak.

"Triarch Ghaz," Aiz said. "Take your men to fight alongside Hiwa's. Hold them off for as long as possible. I will be there soon."

"The Masks, Tel Ilessi. It is not safe—"

"I can hold them. Go."

Ghaz bowed and hurried away, taking his men. The red-headed Mask, seeing that there were no guards, grinned and began to rise. But Aiz forced her and her fellows down with fists of wind.

Div circled them. "Let me help, Tel Ilessi. You know your troops alone cannot destroy this legion. I can give you what you need. More."

You are lost, Tel Ilessi. Aiz regarded the young Masks. She thought of Ruh's shining silver eyes. What would he say if he saw her now?

An old emotion, fossilized in the sediment of Aiz's past self, threatened to break free. Anguish, keen as an eagle's talon. A sound emerged from her throat, the moan of a struck bird, the last shred of humanity clinging to Aiz's heart.

Yes, she was lost. Irredeemably so.

But Ruh died so Aiz could get this far. What use, if she gave up now?

Aiz considered Div. She'd let Div hunt and kill for months, and had managed to control her. In doing so, perhaps Aiz had limited herself by curtailing the power Div fed her. Perhaps Aiz had only begun to understand the well of strength Div had to offer.

"Yes," Div crooned. "Now you see."

Aiz nodded. "Do it," she said.

Moments later, the first Mask began to scream.

After, the Kegari soldiers who witnessed the shredding of the Martial legion would say that Mother Div herself descended from the sky and laid waste to the enemy when all seemed lost. Triarch Oona's red-clad archers had been overrun, the Triarch herself dying at the edge of Empress Helene's blade. Triarch Hiwa's troops turned and fled, though their leader had not been so lucky, an arrow slicing through his back as he bolted like a coward.

Only Triarch Ghaz's soldiers held firm. And when it seemed like they, too, would be destroyed, the Tel Ilessi appeared, glowing with fury. A shadow stood at her back, bearing the sunbeam crown.

The wind rose, vicious and unforgiving. It ripped the Martials to shreds. They turned tail, their Empress with them.

Aiz remembered little of it. She woke after, in the infirmary. The room was simple and white. A memory rose in her mind. Sister Noa beside the cloister's wide hearth, with Cero tucked under one arm and Aiz under the other.

Holy Cleric Div was most beloved to children, did you know? She hated the politics of ruling. Any chance she got, she would come to this cloister—this very one!—and play cat in the corner with children just like you.

Mother Div paced around Aiz now, her familiar features relaxing when she saw the girl awake.

"I thought it might be too much power for you," she said, coming to Aiz's side. "I thought I might have hurt you. I thought in saving your people, you might have destroyed yourself."

Your people.

Aiz remembered the power then. And how she'd gotten it. She remembered the screams of the children.

"You're not her, are you?" Aiz finally spoke the question she'd suppressed since Tiral's death. A question reawakened by her conversation with Noa. She did not look toward the creature that called itself Div.

"I am who you need me to be." The creature pulled its hair to one side and began to braid it.

"But you're not *her*." Aiz struggled to draw breath. "You don't know anything about my people. You don't care about us."

She thought of Tiral's last words. *I wish I could live, just to watch it eat you alive.*

"Tiral knew," Aiz said. "That's why he didn't hunt me. Did you— Did you talk to him, too—"

"Tiral is weak. Tiral is dead." The creature finished the braid and laid a light hand on Aiz's shoulder. "You are strong and so I helped you. I found that which you desired most—Loha."

"You found a reason to torture children."

"Because you needed aid." The creature squeezed Aiz's shoulder a touch too hard. "And you are wrong. I do care about your people. Because I care about you. Let that be enough."

It wasn't a request. It was a warning, and Aiz saw two paths before her. One in which she delved more deeply into exactly what she had awoken that cursed night in the Tribal Desert. And one in which she took what Div had to offer and gave her people a chance at life without pain and poverty and hunger clawing them to death from the inside.

Aiz swung her legs out of the bed and pulled on her boots. Her body throbbed, but Div—for that was who Aiz needed her to be—fed power into her steadily until the pain had faded.

A knock at the door. Cero.

"I'm fine." She stood. "Better than fine. We captured one of the generals, yes? Let us see if he knows—"

"You received a letter." Cero hardly spared her a glance, as if any wounds she had were no concern of his. He held up a scroll. "It came via one of our messengers in Ankana. From the High Seer himself." He handed it over, watching Aiz as she read it.

"A change of plans," she said. "We're going to Ankana."

PART IV
THE EMPTY

46
Quil

Ankanese prisons were, on the whole, not quite as awful as Martial ones. After the pompous soldier placed Quil and the others in a row of cells, the prince had seen only one rat. Tas even had a small window that looked out onto Burku's coast.

The questioning took hours—probably because Quil confessed to everything and the others denied the theft. But packs and weapons were confiscated, orders whispered, paperwork inked, and by late evening, the five of them were locked up behind iron bars. Sufiyan with Quil. Arelia with Sirsha across from him, and Tas beside them, alone. The other six cells were empty.

Just as Quil had requested.

Still, his friends weren't thrilled at the accommodations. After the guards left, Tas turned on Quil.

"I realize this *felt* like a good plan," Tas said through the cell bars, "but the Ankanese do not take theft lightly—"

"Ugh, there's an enormous spider in here," Sufiyan muttered from behind him.

"He must have a reason," Arelia called. "Why don't you explain, Quil?"

"He can't." Sirsha spoke up, and Quil smiled when he saw she'd discovered what he'd placed in her pocket—a hairpin. Her manacles dropped to the ground with a clank. "If you think about it, you'll figure out why. Though I'd suggest thinking about anything else. Div picked my mother's image from my mind. Who knows what else she can do?" She massaged her wrists and moved to Arelia. "Tas, check your pockets."

As Tas dealt with his own manacles, Quil unlocked Sufiyan's.

"I have a question for you," Sufiyan said, and at Quil's head shake, he spoke quickly. "Not about your plan. It's about after." He glanced up to make sure no one else was listening. "If—if we kill the Tel Ilessi and root out the Kegari, will you go back with me to where Ruh died? Will you tell me the truth about what happened to him?"

Quil went still. The cell roof was suddenly too low, the light too scarce. He'd spent the past year trying to forget that night, as the Bani al-Mauth had ordered him to. Now the images rose in his head. The blood. The violence. The eerie space in the center of the room that looked as if an otherworldly claw would emerge from it and snatch anyone who came near.

Dash that thought from your head, boy. You know better. You know the cost.

"Yes," Quil said. "I'll go there with you."

Somehow, Quil would convince the Bani al-Mauth to tell her only living grandson the truth: While Quil had been the first to arrive in the chamber, he hadn't been alone. The Bani al-Mauth had appeared moments after him and taken Ruh's broken body away.

Tell his family he's down there. The Bani al-Mauth pointed to a crevasse that had opened in the rock, too deep to be plumbed. *Tell them you saw his body fall. Don't say a word about me. Understood? The fate of our world depends on how well you tell that lie, boy.*

And so Quil had lied. First to Elias, who'd arrived minutes after the Bani al-Mauth left. Then to the rest of the Tribe. Later, when the Bani al-Mauth came to mourn Ruh's loss, Laia begged to speak to her child's ghost in the Waiting Place. *He must be there*, she'd screamed. *He must! You must know who did this to him!*

The Bani al-Mauth refused Laia's request with a chilling finality.

The boy is dead. Best accept it.

"Quil!" Sufiyan jostled him, nodding to Sirsha, whose face twisted in revulsion.

"They're approaching," Sirsha said. "Div and the Tel Ilessi. I can feel them."

By boat, the journey from Serra would take weeks. By air, and with Div's unnatural winds at her back, it had taken the Tel Ilessi only a day.

Quil went to the cot and pulled out two heavy sacks placed there at the order of the High Seer. The Ikfa, their packs, and weaponry were within. He tossed Sirsha her pack, Tas his scim, and Arelia her things, as well as the Ikfa manacles and one chain. He kept the other for himself.

His skin went clammy at its touch and his head spun. *You're fine.* This was no worse than the time Aunt Hel tossed him in the River Rei in the middle of a snowstorm.

"Reli, keep the manacles," he said. "Give Sirsha one of the chains."

"Quil." Sirsha paled. "I can't—"

"Just for a short while," Quil said. "To throw them off so they don't know you're here. Hide. Wait for the last possible moment. Let her think she's won. I'll buy you time. Sufiyan." Quil armed himself and handed Suf his bow and arrows. "You'll know what to do," he said. "When the time comes."

The air was thick with tension, but they did not have to wait long. Distantly, a gate clanged open, followed by one closer. Then the door at the end of their cellblock swung forward and High Seer Remi entered, trailed by the Tel Ilessi and Cero.

The latter looked up and met Quil's eyes. *I do hate war . . . but there's something else I hate more. Witnessing the manipulation of my oldest friend.*

Quil held his gaze. Cero tilted his head and twitched a nod, almost identical to the one Quil had given him in the encampment days earlier.

"As promised," Remi said—ostensibly to the Tel Ilessi, though Quil knew better.

"My thanks, High Seer Remi," she said. "I am grateful you see the way of things."

Remi bowed his head and backed through the cellblock door. It clanged behind him.

Quil moved to the bars of his enclosure, glaring out at the Tel Ilessi, letting frustration suffuse him, and keeping a small, careful sphere of calm hidden at his very core. Let her think him defeated. Let her crow over her victory.

The Tel Ilessi stalked closer, exultant.

"You thought you were so clev—" She stopped short and looked beyond Quil, to Sufiyan, whose arrows flew one after the other, so fast that the Tel Ilessi should have been lying in a pool of her own blood.

But she'd called up her wind almost immediately, warned, no doubt, by the monster she'd chained herself to. She knocked Sufiyan hard against the wall and he collapsed to the floor.

Quil slammed his cell door open as, across the hall, Tas did the same. The prince flung the Ikfa chains at the Tel Ilessi, thankful to be rid of them. The strength that surged through his blood at the chains' absence carried him toward the Tel Ilessi in three steps.

She screamed when the Ikfa hit her, her magic dying instantaneously. Quil drew his scim. He thought of her wretched defense for mass murder, of the children whose deaths she'd used to further her need for power. He swung his blade at the back of her neck without an iota of hesitation.

It stopped midair, clanging as if striking metal. The chains fell away from the Tel Ilessi, and Quil stared as a scim materialized. Then a hand. An arm. A body.

A face.

"Greetings, my son."

The man who stepped out of thin air was someone Quil had seen only once in his life, in a vision that still haunted him. Tall with broad shoulders, short hair, and yellow eyes. A face that was too harsh to be handsome, a voice that was too cruel to be a father's voice. And yet, Quil knew this man, would have known him even if he hadn't seen him in a vision.

Marcus Farrar. Quil's father.

47
Sirsha

Sirsha didn't recognize the form Div took. It was tall, broad, and hooded, and Quil staggered away from it like he'd seen a bleeding jinn, his back to the bars of one of the cells.

"You fight well, my boy," Div said in an oily voice, wielding a weapon as well as any Mask.

The eyes, Sirsha wanted to scream. *Look at the eyes!* But she couldn't draw Div's attention until she was certain she could bind her. The chains sapped Sirsha's strength—it was all she could do to remember she had magic.

"You're not him," Quil said. He'd recovered himself, and now matched Div's attack stroke for stroke. "He's dead."

"Of course he is." Div smiled, showing more teeth than possible for a human. "His spirit moved on. But his pain? His suffering and hate? I got all of it. Wouldn't it be better to know some parts of your father, boy, instead of nothing at all?"

Quil whipped his sword at Div, and she hissed when it cut into her. Then the creature chuckled as the wound healed. Tas attacked Div from the back, but the creature flicked him down the cellblock with a twitch of a finger.

The Tel Ilessi, having cast off the Ikfa, called up the wind and pinned Tas to the wall. She was so focused on the spy that she didn't notice Arelia until she'd barreled into her, knocking the Tel Ilessi on her back.

"Do you know what your father wished for you before your aunt murdered him, boy? *A brother at your back.* But your brothers aren't brothers, are they? You let one die. That one"—she nodded to Tas, dodging the Tel Ilessi's attacks—"only listens to you because you're his crown prince and he has no choice. The other is filled with seething hate—"

"Lies!" Sufiyan had staggered to his feet and now shot arrow after arrow into Aiz, each one bouncing off her air shield. "I'd describe my internal state as seething irritation at the most, you ugly demon spawn. Quil's not that bad most of the time—aaa—"

Cero, with two arrows in his chest, managed to stagger up and tackle Sufiyan. Of course—he might want his old friend free from Div, but he didn't want her to die in the process.

Sirsha growled as she lurked in the darkness of her cell. She ached to bind Div, to squeeze all the vitriol out of the monster and send it back to the oblivion it came from. Her friends were suffering—Tas bleeding badly from a head wound and scrambling for his sword. Arelia on her back, mouth open in a silent scream as the Tel Ilessi stole her breath. Cero and Sufiyan grappling on the floor, the latter kicking, clawing, and biting to get an upper hand.

Wait for the last possible moment.

"You are a creature of pain—born upon a wave of death—" Div's voice rose and her form changed as she took on the Tel Ilessi's face and form. Even as Div clashed her scim against Quil's, she leered at him, a twisted approximation of a lover. Sirsha cringed back, certain the creature would sense her. But she was wholly enthralled with Quil, who moved like quicksilver as he fended her off, his shoulders squared. "Mmm, I did not sense it before! You carry magic of your own, buried deep. Memory—but it's more than that, so much more. What's in that head of yours?"

"Put the scim down and find out, why don't you," Quil taunted with an uncharacteristic and distressing disregard for his life.

With Div so distracted, Sirsha called to the elements. *What is she?* she asked. *Show me.* The wind shrieked, the earth rumbled, and a vision of water filled her mind, a roiling ocean teeming with immense creatures, a flash of yellow sky.

Owa Khel—the Empty. The place that held the suffering and misery of millennia. Sirsha's suspicions were correct.

The monstrosity of such a thing wandering through the human world made Sirsha's skin shrink in terror. The Nightbringer had unleashed the Sea of Suffering in the Battle of Sher Jinaat, twenty years ago. Though it had been for only a moment, it had killed thousands and nearly consumed the world.

Div must have emerged when the wall between worlds was thin. Made a home in the Tribal Desert and lured people to her. Murdered them, fed on suffering, growing stronger and stronger until she found someone evil or desperate enough to free her.

How had she gotten into people's heads? *The book.* Though, if that was the case, Div would have needed an original anchor. Some twisted soul with whom she'd made contact when she arrived in the world. Sirsha thought of the story the Tel Ilessi told Quil. Of the First Durani, the monstrous storyteller who locked Div away.

Yes, the earth whispered to her. *The First Durani told a story that was not meant to be told. She became Div's anchor. Now, finally, you understand.*

Understanding wouldn't help Sirsha's friends. They were supposed to have killed the Tel Ilessi, but she was too strong. Arelia and Tas lay unmoving on the floor, and the Tel Ilessi whipped Sufiyan away from Cero, slamming Suf against the cellblock door. Only Quil stood unyielding, retorting to whatever horrors Div whispered at him, defiance carved into every muscle of his body. Fearless. Alone.

No longer.

Sirsha rushed forward, flinging the chains at the Tel Ilessi, pulling them tight. As they had before, they cut through the woman's magic like a hot knife through butter. She stumbled back, weak, and Sirsha swept up the manacles—fallen from Arelia's hands—and clapped them onto the Tel Ilessi's wrists.

The Tel Ilessi screamed. Sirsha had struggled to suppress a scream herself when she put those accursed chains on so Div wouldn't sense her. The pain would be crushing for someone of Aiz's power—and despite the repugnance of the Tel Ilessi's actions, Sirsha felt a twinge of sympathy for her.

Not enough to let her live. Sirsha tore a dagger from her belt, fully intending to stab the Tel Ilessi. But Sufiyan, free of the Tel Ilessi's magic, knocked Cero unconscious. The snarls coming from Sufiyan's throat as he surged toward the Tel Ilessi raised the hair on Sirsha's neck. She only just managed to get out of his way before Sufiyan stabbed the Tel Ilessi in the chest. "For Ruh—for Ruh—for Ruh—"

Aiz screamed for Div, but the monster ignored her, her attention fixed on Quil. He was hissing to Div now, luring the creature in, even as Div wrapped a tendril of magic around Quil, slowly pulling his life from him, savoring the way he fought her before she would inevitably tear out his heart.

Sometimes, the only way to blunt the violence of twisted magic is to confront it with its opposite.

Sirsha gathered her binding magic into a lasso and cast it about Div, yanking it mercilessly.

The creature hissed and threw it off, turning. Upon seeing who had interrupted her twisted rite, she smiled.

"Ah, the little witch." Div oozed into the form of Sirsha's mother, freezing Quil with a motion of her hand. "Come to save your lover? You'll have to do better than that."

Sirsha's magic scattered as the creature turned the enormity of its evil upon her.

"Kill me," Sirsha called to Div. "Not him."

The creature considered Sirsha with a broadening smirk, as if she couldn't believe her luck.

Yes, Sirsha thought to herself. *Closer.* The Jaduna buried her binding deep, the way she'd realized Quil did. There in her darkest heart, she let it build, for the timing was crucial. She must release it as Div attacked and hope that by powering her binding with a sacrifice—an emotion far stronger than mere desire—she would tear Div apart.

Div grabbed Sirsha and took a long, deep sniff at her throat.

Not yet, the elements whispered at Sirsha. *Hold the binding.*

Div laughed in delight and the sound fell like knives upon Sirsha's mind, for it was the cackle of a creature glutted on innocent souls. It was laughter underlaid with screams.

Sirsha sweated as she poured more of herself into the magic. As she thought: *Me, not Quil. Me, not Quil.*

Sirsha, the wind, earth, and sea spoke to her as one. *Is your sacrifice true? Do you offer yourself in place of the Martial prince?*

"Yes!" Sirsha screamed, even as she felt a terrible pain in her chest—Div reaching for her heart. "Obviously!"

Why?

Thinking the words was easier, of course. Love was pain. Love was hurt and betrayal. But it was also the reason she stood here, battling a creature of ancient and unrelenting hunger, instead of on a ship a few hundred miles away. Love was why for the first time since her family cast her out, Sirsha didn't feel alone.

"Because I love him, you cussed nags! Why else!"

Sirsha's magic swelled and flickered as if filled with lightning. For a moment, she saw Div's truest self, a seething mass of suffering. Sirsha felt a soul-deep relief that she was destroying such an abomination. That Div would no longer be allowed to exist in the world.

She poured her magic into the binding, triumphant as it built, and built, and built, until everything and everyone was swallowed by its light.

48
Quil

Because I love him, you cussed nags! Why else!

Quil heard Sirsha's outburst, saw her speaking to voices he couldn't hear. The coin at his throat burned white hot, but he couldn't *do* anything. He felt a sudden awareness of Sirsha, a glimpse of the inside of her. All the pain that she kept caged away, like a wild animal that she couldn't risk letting loose. But the love, too, infinite shades of it veined through her soul.

For a second, she was resplendent, garbed in her magic, her power finally unleashed. The light grew so brilliant that he had to look away, shielding his vision.

Then he felt an emptiness. A yawning chasm in the shape of the girl he realized he loved. Though the moon shone through the window of one of the jail cells, its light felt wan. The shadows of the cellblock contracted, slow and heavy as a lament.

Sirsha was gone.

Quil could move again, no longer held in place by Div. Sufiyan and Arelia limped toward him.

"What the bleeding hells happened?" Suf asked. His clothes were covered in blood. His hands shook, and he couldn't stop looking at the two prone bodies on the stone floor.

Cero and Aiz. Dead. He considered the former—so desperate to free his friend, desperate to protect her. And Aiz. *No, she's not Aiz. Nor is she Ilar. She is the Tel Ilessi. The beast who unleashed the hells on your people and her own.*

"We need to go." Tas lurched toward Quil, a gash on his head oozing an alarming amount of blood. "If the High Seer's soldiers find us down here with dead bodies, we'll be answering questions for days. We need to get back to the Empire. I'm assuming he told you a way out of here."

"He did, but we can't leave." Quil spun around the cellblock. "Not without Sirsha."

Arelia shook her head. "I don't know if her magic consumed her or if Div did, but I saw her disappear. One moment she was here, and the next..."

Quil reached for his oath coin. It was intricately carved now, a pattern so complex he could hardly follow it. It was also warm.

"She's alive," he said. "I know she is. We must find her—"

"We will." Tas pulled Quil away from the dead Kegari. "But not here."

Quil searched for Sirsha for days. He went to every market in Ankana. He went to the High Seer. But Remi E'twa was less worried about a missing Jaduna, and more concerned with the fact that Ambassador Ifalu, despite having been imprisoned, was nowhere to be found.

Just like Sirsha. No one had seen her. When he called out to her in his mind, he heard only a taunting silence.

"Maybe she used her magic to take the monster away," Arelia suggested at one point. "She bound it. We all saw it. Perhaps she took it to Elias."

But Quil knew that wasn't right. He could feel it in his bones, and with every day that passed, he grew more frantic. Sirsha wouldn't have just left. *Because I love him, you cussed nags!* Not the declaration of love that someone might dream of, and yet the words were precious to him.

Quil kept going back to the last night they had together. The sadness in Sirsha's eyes. As if she'd known her time was short.

No! Sirsha lived. He felt it in their coin and in his blood. Come what may, they would be reunited. He would love her if she let him, give over his body if she demanded it, be the home he knew she longed for. He would find her. He *needed* to find her.

But his people needed him too. And he could not abandon them to the predations of the Kegari.

Musa sent a wight detailing the near annihilation of a full legion. And though Sirsha had destroyed Div and Sufiyan had killed the Tel Ilessi, their demise was only the first step to expelling the Kegari from the Empire. So, after five days of searching, Quil asked Tas to find a ship. By the morning, he and his companions watched as Ankana's shores faded into the distance.

Quil still had hope even then. Sirsha would appear from belowdecks. Yawning, rolling her eyes. Telling him she'd found his frantic search highly entertaining.

But she didn't appear, and as the days passed and the miles vanished, Quil turned to the immense task before him: liberating the Empire from the Kegari, who had roosted all over his land like malignant tumors.

Quil ordered the ship to the Tribal Lands—to one of the smaller fishing villages that the Kegari hadn't yet noticed. Musa would meet them there. His recent message said the Ikfa had arrived, and the smiths were hard at work shaping it into weaponry.

Tas's pirate friends sailed swiftly, and neither Kegari nor any other marauder approached. Three weeks after departing Burku, as night fled from the approaching dawn, the captain shouted.

"Land ho!"

Quil was the only one of his group awake as the southern coast of the Tribal Lands materialized on the horizon. A bright spring sun illuminated bursts of wildflowers that stretched across the desert, their aroma cutting through the salty tang of the sea. Underlying it all was the scent of dust and creosote and Quil breathed deep. *Home.*

He pocketed the two silver hairpins he'd taken to fiddling with. The sun-white buildings of the sleepy fishing village came into view. The docks were empty. It was too late for the fishing boats, which were already out to sea, and too early for market. Quil's heart quailed as they approached the shoreline. As soon as he stepped back on land, it would mean he'd truly left Sirsha behind. The part of his journey that belonged to her would be over.

I will find her. The oath coin flared white hot, as if in agreement.

After the captain dropped the gangplank, Quil, heavily hooded, made his way off the ship, his gait rolling after weeks at sea. It wasn't until he'd reached the empty market at the end of the dock that a dark-garbed figure appeared from behind a cargo pulley.

There was something familiar about how she moved, and for a brief, overjoyed moment, Quil was sure Sirsha had found him.

But it took less than a second for him to realize this wasn't her. This woman was smaller, her stride shorter.

She approached Quil, and as he reached for his scim, she lowered her hood.

"Laia?"

The Kehanni nodded a greeting, opening her arms, and Quil hugged her, relieved that she was alive and unharmed. He turned back to the dhow to call out to Sufiyan, who he knew had been aching for his family. But Laia shook her head.

"I want more than anything to see my son, Quil," she said. "But I will wait. Walk with me. There is something I must tell you about the creature that murdered Ruh. The one you helped to hunt."

"You know about it?" Quil said as they turned onto a path that ran away from the village and toward the desert. "How—"

"I've known about it for a long while now, though it was only four weeks ago that I remembered I knew," Laia said, and Quil stiffened. When Sirsha had eradicated Div—when the creature's power had finally been broken.

Laia slowed as they reached the edge of the village, and stared out at a brilliant carpet of bone-white wildflowers.

"There are some stories that aren't meant to be shared, Quil," she said, gold eyes anguished. "There is one that should never have been told. Years ago, I hunted that story. I found it and listened and then released it upon the world. And in doing so, I planted the seeds of my own Ruh's death. Sit, child. Let me tell you of the First Durani. The first chaos storyteller. Me."

49
Aiz

To Aiz's surprise, death was kind. She did not hurt. She did not suffer. It was quiet and peaceful, and her body felt like a smile; like it had in those brief weeks with the Tribes, when she'd had clothes to warm her, food to fill her, and Quil to love her.

Her memories were strange. The Ankanese High Seer summoning her. Quil ambushing her.

Sufiyan stabbing her over and over again. *For Ruh—for Ruh—for Ruh—*

Aiz waited for Div's aid, but it never came, and she'd watched, oddly detached, as Sufiyan's knife sank into her chest. She thought she would be terrified to leave her people, angry at Sufiyan for taking her from them.

All she felt was relief. For the first time since she'd watched Mother Div rip Ruh's heart out, the horror-struck scream echoing in the back of her mind fell silent, awaiting death.

But death didn't come for her. Not yet.

Instead, pain. Blazing, nerve-crushing pain. She awoke to a flash of foggy night sky, the smell of blood, and an emptiness she couldn't understand or name. She blinked, trying to clear her vision as she took in the person next to her.

Cero.

She jerked fully awake. Cero's hand was draped on Aiz's waist. His face was deathly pale, and blood pooled around him on the stone floor of a prison.

Aiz scrambled to her knees and shook him, but he didn't move. Bloodsmithing. She needed to bloodsmith him back to life. She was the Tel Ilessi, for Spires' sake.

But she realized as she touched his warm skin that she must have already bloodsmithed him. For though he was unconscious, his chest moved. The arrows that had impaled him now littered the ground around them both.

She looked down at her own chest. She'd *felt* Sufiyan stab her. Over and over until she'd wondered how there was any flesh left to pierce. But though her shirt was shredded, her body was whole.

Aiz put her hands on Cero and willed him awake, wrapping the wind she could call around him in a warm blanket. The wind responded sluggishly.

She reached for Mother Div's magic, and when she didn't feel it, when all she encountered was her own paltry will, she groaned at the thought that Mother Div would again demand to feed.

And then, slowly, understanding dawned, and a terror that rolled through her like a fever. The emptiness within—she knew what it was.

Div was gone.

Aiz looked up at the bare cells around her. At the arrows and blood, and the stars through a window.

"Ai-Aiz—"

Cero's voice penetrated her horror.

"Cero." She pulled him to her. "Thank the Spires you're alive. I—saw you fall. I must have bloodsmithed you, though I don't remember—"

"Aiz, we must leave. It was High Seer Remi who betrayed us to them. We're not safe here. Do you have a way of getting in touch with the seer who is loyal to you?"

Dolbra, he meant. She didn't answer him. For the import of what had happened struck her as if the weight of the Spires had crashed down on her chest.

"Cero," she whispered. "Div is gone."

Cero's eyes grew bright—not with shock, but hope. "How—how do you know? Are you sure—"

But Aiz shook her head. She thought of Ruh, shrieking as he died. Of Mother Div's silken promises. She thought of the hunger that had gnawed at her for months, and the void within her now that it was gone. She remembered Sister Noa's warning. *You are lost.*

"A better question is, how will I rule? If I don't have Div, I'm not Tel Ilessi. Without her, I cannot take our people home. Without her, Cero, I am nothing."

50
Sirsha

The first thing Sirsha noticed when she regained consciousness was the roar of the ocean, so loud she wondered that it hadn't consumed her yet. Sand crumbled beneath her fingers, dry and cold. The sky gleamed like onyx. On the water, she saw no fishing boats. On the shore, no lights. No huts. Nothing to indicate that she was near civilization.

But that made sense. She was dead.

Her body felt peculiar. Light. She grasped at her necklace—only one coin remained, intricately patterned, laced with diamonds—Quil's coin. Elias's was gone.

She'd done it. She'd destroyed Div.

Relief flooded her and she whooped, the ocean swallowing the sound. For a moment at the end, she'd feared the binding wouldn't work. That Div would break free and claw out her heart. But the coin wouldn't have disappeared if Sirsha hadn't succeeded.

Though why Sirsha still cared about her oath if she was dead, she didn't know. Come to think of it, why would she have her coin with Quil if she was dead? The Raani always said the Adah oath transcended death. Perhaps this was what she meant.

A cool wave lapped at her feet, followed swiftly by one that slapped her in the face. She crawled up the beach, hacking up seawater.

"Not dead," she rasped, for she was certain that death wouldn't be quite so undignified. "Got it."

Somehow, she'd destroyed Mother Div without killing herself. A neat trick. She'd laugh at herself for her maudlin thoughts about self-sacrifice if she wasn't sopping wet and beginning to shiver. Where the skies *was* she?

She had sand in unfortunate places, so she shook off what she could, grumbling all the while. Then she dug her hand into her pack, still slung across her body. And still, thankfully, heavy with gold marks. Her wrist flashed—she still had Quil's bracelet.

"Quil?" she called out. "Sufiyan? Arelia?"

Only the waves responded with their endless roar. Perhaps she was near Burku. As she looked around, she spotted a rutted path that led away from the water. There might be a fishing village nearby, or a hut.

Her legs were unsteady, and it took long minutes for her to totter up the path. She spotted a strange glow—a fire? Her stomach rumbled. Hopefully it was a cookfire.

But the closer Sirsha got, the more uneasy she grew.

There didn't appear to be anyone around the fire. Yet a whole animal roasted on a spit over it. A fox, she realized as she got closer. Its mouth was open as if it had died shrieking.

"Qu-Quil?"

The glow of the fire weakened as if cowed. A figure silhouetted in dim blue light watched her. Sirsha's stomach clenched. She reached for her magic, not to protect herself, but to see. To feel what the hells was sitting in front of her. But even as she called on her power, she flinched back. Something about it felt tainted. Other.

"Greetings, S'rsha Inashi-fa." The figure stood, pushing back her hood—her face was Sirsha's, but of course it wasn't her at all. It was Div, and now Sirsha felt the link between them, a tie binding them as surely as if they'd been fused together in a forge. The moment she felt it, a vast hunger filled her. A ravenous need that had no end. She saw a roiling sea and yellow sky, the massive waves seething with shadows beneath the surface. Owa Khel. *The Empty.*

"I have been waiting for you to wake up, dear child," Div said. "Now that we are one, we are going to do such beautiful things together."

ACKNOWLEDGMENTS

Great thanks to you, reader, for coming with me on another adventure. I would not get to do any of this if not for you.

My love and gratitude to:

My family for their patience and support. Special thanks to Kashi, the best dragon caretaker; the boys for being my reason; Amer for emergency draft-reading and general radness; my parents and in-laws for the duas; and Tala for a quarter century of true sisterhood and cheerleading, baybays and all.

Alexandra, as ever, for your belief and love; Nicola for calls, sanity checks, laughter, and saying, "Hey, you probably shouldn't send that email"; Lauren for helping me muddle my way through this one, and for all the memes and hissing; Renée for a decade of awesomeness and for spot-on writing and life advice; Haina for keeping it real; Abby for your generous spirit; and Adam for your Adam-ness.

My brown crew of rad—Heelah, Lilly, Anum, Uzma, Isra, Saira, Nyla, Sana. And to my many other wonderful friends, whose kindness and love I am so fortunate to have.

Ruta, my singular editor, who supports my evil plot ideas and whose enthusiasm, sharp eye, and humor are such a gift.

Casey—for everything.

The fabulous Penguin team: I am so lucky that my work has had such a loving home with you for a decade. With my whole heart, thank you to every single one of you who has worked on my books and been part of this journey.

My foreign rights team and international publishers, who put my work into the hands of readers across the globe with excitement and dedication.

Cathy—for believing in me even when I'm wailing and howling.

Deonna, for laughing at my dumb jokes and helping me to stay sane (and organized).

Micaela Alcaino, for your kindness and for loving my books enough to create extraordinary covers for them.

And last, Al Haqq, who shines the light of truth, even in the darkest places.

Who is Laia of Serra?
And how did she and Elias Veturius meet?

Turn the page to read the first chapter
of the book that first brought this vast,
magical world to life.

I: Laia

My big brother reaches home in the dark hours before dawn, when even ghosts take their rest. He smells of steel and coal and forge. He smells of the enemy.

He folds his scarecrow body through the window, bare feet silent on the rushes. A hot desert wind blows in after him, rustling the limp curtains. His sketchbook falls to the floor, and he nudges it under his bunk with a quick foot, as if it's a snake.

Where have you been, Darin? In my head, I have the courage to ask the question, and Darin trusts me enough to answer. *Why do you keep disappearing? Why, when Pop and Nan need you? When I need you?*

Every night for almost two years, I've wanted to ask. Every night, I've lacked the courage. I have one sibling left. I don't want him to shut me out like he has everyone else.

But tonight's different. I know what's in his sketchbook. I know what it means.

"You shouldn't be awake." Darin's whisper jolts me from my thoughts. He has a cat's sense for traps—he got it from our mother. I sit up on the bunk as he lights the lamp. No use pretending to be asleep.

"It's past curfew, and three patrols have gone by. I was worried."

"I can avoid the soldiers, Laia. Lots of practice." He rests his chin on my bunk and smiles Mother's sweet, crooked smile. A familiar look—the one he gives me if I wake from a nightmare or we run out of grain. *Everything will be fine*, the look says.

He picks up the book on my bed. "*Gather in the Night*," he reads the title. "Spooky. What's it about?"

"I just started it. It's about a jinn—" I stop. Clever. Very clever. He likes hearing stories as much as I like telling them. "Forget that. Where were you? Pop had a dozen patients this morning."

And I filled in for you because he can't do so much alone. Which left Nan to bottle the trader's jams by herself. Except she didn't finish. Now the trader won't pay us, and we'll starve this winter, and why in the skies don't you care?

I say these things in my head. The smile's already dropped off Darin's face.

"I'm not cut out for healing," he says. "Pop knows that."

I want to back down, but I think of Pop's slumped shoulders this morning. I think of the sketchbook.

"Pop and Nan depend on you. At least talk to them. It's been months."

I wait for him to tell me that I don't understand. That I should leave him be. But he just shakes his head, drops down into his bunk, and closes his eyes like he can't be bothered to reply.

"I saw your drawings." The words tumble out in a rush, and Darin's up in an instant, his face stony. "I wasn't spying," I say. "One of the pages was loose. I found it when I changed the rushes this morning."

"Did you tell Nan and Pop? Did they see?"

"No, but—"

"Laia, listen." Ten hells, I don't want to hear this. I don't want to hear his excuses. "What you saw is dangerous," he says. "You can't tell anyone about it. Not ever. It's not just my life at risk. There are others—"

"Are you working for the Empire, Darin? Are you working for the Martials?"

He is silent. I think I see the answer in his eyes, and I feel ill. My brother is a traitor to his own people? My brother is siding with the Empire?

If he hoarded grain, or sold books, or taught children to read, I'd understand. I'd be proud of him for doing the things I'm not brave enough to do.

The Empire raids, jails, and kills for such "crimes," but teaching a six-year-old her letters isn't evil—not in the minds of my people, the Scholar people.

But what Darin has done is sick. It's a betrayal.

"The Empire killed our parents," I whisper. "Our sister."

I want to shout at him, but I choke on the words. The Martials conquered Scholar lands five hundred years ago, and since then, they've done nothing but oppress and enslave us. Once, the Scholar Empire was home to the finest universities and libraries in the world. Now, most of our people can't tell a school from an armory.

"How could you side with the Martials? How, Darin?"

"It's not what you think, Laia. I'll explain everything, but—"

He pauses suddenly, his hand jerking up to silence me when I ask for the promised explanation. He cocks his head toward the window.

Through the thin walls, I hear Pop's snores, Nan shifting in her sleep, a mourning dove's croon. Familiar sounds. Home sounds.

Darin hears something else. The blood drains from his face, and dread flashes in his eyes. "Laia," he says. "Raid."

"But if you work for the Empire—" *Then why are the soldiers raiding us?*

"I'm not working for them." He sounds calm. Calmer than I feel. "Hide the sketchbook. That's what they want. That's what they're here for."

Then he's out the door, and I'm alone. My bare legs move like cold molasses, my hands like wooden blocks. *Hurry, Laia!*

Usually, the Empire raids in the heat of the day. The soldiers want Scholar mothers and children to watch. They want fathers and brothers to see another man's family enslaved. As bad as those raids are, the night raids are worse. The night raids are for when the Empire doesn't want witnesses.

I wonder if this is real. If it's a nightmare. *It's real, Laia. Move.*

I drop the sketchbook out the window into a hedge. It's a poor hiding place, but I have no time. Nan hobbles into my room. Her hands, so steady when she stirs vats of jam or braids my hair, flutter like frantic birds, desperate for me to move faster.

She pulls me into the hallway. Darin stands with Pop at the back door. My grandfather's white hair is scattered as a haystack and his clothes are wrinkled, but there's no sleep in the deep grooves of his face. He murmurs something to my brother, then hands him Nan's largest kitchen knife. I don't know why he bothers. Against the Serric steel of a Martial blade, the knife will only shatter.

"You and Darin leave through the backyard," Nan says, her eyes darting from window to window. "They haven't surrounded the house yet."

No. No. No. "Nan," I breathe her name, stumbling when she pushes me toward Pop.

"Hide in the east end of the Quarter—" Her sentence ends in a choke, her eyes on the front window. Through the ragged curtains, I catch a flash of a liquid silver face. My stomach clenches.

"A Mask," Nan says. "They've brought a Mask. Go, Laia. Before he gets inside."

"What about you? What about Pop?"

"We'll hold them off." Pop shoves me gently out the door. "Keep your secrets close, love. Listen to Darin. He'll take care of you. Go."

Darin's lean shadow falls over me, and he grabs my hand as the door closes behind us. He slouches to blend into the warm night, moving silently across the loose sand of the backyard with a confidence I wish I felt. Although I am seventeen and old enough to control my fear, I grip his hand like it's the only solid thing in this world.

I'm not working for them, Darin said. Then whom is he working for?

Somehow, he got close enough to the forges of Serra to draw, in detail, the creation process of the Empire's most precious asset: the unbreakable, curved scims that can cut through three men at once.

Half a millennium ago, the Scholars crumbled beneath the Martial invasion because our blades broke against their superior steel. Since then, we have learned nothing of steelcraft. The Martials hoard their secrets the way a miser hoards gold. Anyone caught near our city's forges without good reason—Scholar or Martial—risks execution.

If Darin isn't with the Empire, how did he get near Serra's forges? How did the Martials find out about his sketchbook?

On the other side of the house, a fist pounds on the front door. Boots shuffle, steel clinks. I look around wildly, expecting to see the silver armor and red capes of Empire legionnaires, but the backyard is still. The fresh night air does nothing to stop the sweat rolling down my neck. Distantly, I hear the thud of drums from Blackcliff, the Mask training school. The sound sharpens my fear into a hard point stabbing at my center. The Empire doesn't send those silver-faced monsters on just any raid.

The pounding on the door sounds again.

"In the name of the Empire," an irritated voice says, "I demand you open this door."

As one, Darin and I freeze.

"Doesn't sound like a Mask," Darin whispers. Masks speak softly with words that cut through you like a scim. In the time it would take a legionnaire to knock and issue an order, a Mask would already be in the house, weapons slicing through anyone in his way.

Darin meets my eyes, and I know we're both thinking the same thing. If the Mask isn't with the rest of the soldiers at the front door, then where is he?

"Don't be afraid, Laia," Darin says. "I won't let anything happen to you."

I want to believe him, but my fear is a tide tugging at my ankles, pulling me under. I think of the couple that lived next door: raided, imprisoned, and sold into slavery three weeks ago. *Book smugglers*, the Martials said. Five days after that, one of Pop's oldest patients, a ninety-three-year-old man who could barely walk, was executed in his own home, his throat slit from ear to ear. *Resistance collaborator.*

What will the soldiers do to Nan and Pop? Jail them? Enslave them?

Kill them?

We reach the back gate. Darin stands on his toes to unhook the latch when a scrape in the alley beyond stops him short. A breeze sighs past, sending a cloud of dust into the air.

Darin pushes me behind him. His knuckles are white around the knife handle as the gate swings open with a moan. A finger of terror draws a trail up my spine. I peer over my brother's shoulder into the alley.

There is nothing out there but the quiet shifting of sand. Nothing but the occasional gust of wind and the shuttered windows of our sleeping neighbors.

I sigh in relief and step around Darin.

That's when the Mask emerges from the darkness and walks through the gate.

READ ALL FOUR BOOKS OF THE EMBER QUARTET, AVAILABLE WHEREVER BOOKS ARE SOLD.

PRAISE FOR THE *NEW YORK TIMES* BESTSELLING SERIES

"One of the best YA series of the last decade." —**BUZZFEED**

"A captivating, heart-pounding fantasy." —**US WEEKLY**

"This series is an epic hero's journey, with love, adventure, and magic woven throughout. Recommended for every young adult collection."
—*SLJ*

"Excellent." —**KIRKUS REVIEWS**

"*An Ember in the Ashes* glows, burns, and smolders—as beautiful and radiant as it is searing." —**THE HUFFINGTON POST**